Bestiarium Cryptozoologicum

Bestiarium Cryptozoologicum

Mystery Animals and Unknown Species in Classic Science Fiction and Fantasy

CHAD ARMENT, EDITOR

COACHWHIP PUBLICATIONS
Landisville, Pennsylvania

Bestiarium Cryptozoologicum
Copyright © 2010 Coachwhip Publications

ISBN 1-61646-009-1
ISBN-13 978-1-61646-009-9

Cover: Mammoth © Aloysius Patrimonio

CoachwhipBooks.com

CONTENTS

The Jheen (1893)   7

In the Avu Observatory (1894)   17

Æpyornis Island (1894)   25

The Fiend of the Cooperage (1897)   37

The Brazilian Cat (1898)   50

The Killing of the Mammoth (1899)   71

The Spell of the Bird (1900)   88

A Relic of the Pliocene (1901)   99

The Monarch of St. Elias (1901)   110

The Great White Serpent of the Maiorli (1902)   118

Alfred Jenkins and the Didi (1903)   130

The Gregosaur of Black Lake (1905)   143

The Death-Trap (1908)   149

Last of the Race (1910)   164

The Air Serpent (1911)   173

The Terror of Blue John Gap (1912)   184

The Horror of the Heights (1913)   202

The Humming Bats (1914)   219

The Devil's Fish (1914)   231

An Alaskan Monster (1915)   239

The Last Egg of the Great Auk (1920)   249

The Shame Of Gold (1922)   264

An Undiscovered "Isle in the Far Sea" (1926)   278

The Jheen

CHARLES L. HILDRETH

*The All Merciful has turned their feet
backward as a warning to men*

The country between Bandalore and Kamus is, without exception, the most utterly forlorn, wretched, and desolate region in all western India. The road—if a mere jungle track, more frequently trodden by wild animals than man, may be so styled—wanders hither and thither in an aimless fashion, as if it were out for a stroll, rather than on government business; now exploring a swamp where the thick, black mud welters up to your horse's knees with a foul, fever suggesting smell; again toiling straight up a steep hill, evidently for the purpose of doing reverence to a heap of stones marking the tomb of some local saint; or leading you miles out of your way to an old well, whose filthy contents would have sickened Dives himself.

At long intervals you come upon a miserable village squatted in the jungle, your nose having warned you of its proximity some time before it manifests itself to your vision. At still wider intervals, you find the station bungalows—for the most part tumbledown affairs with lounging doors, windows curtained with half a generation of cobwebs and dust, roofs whose sins of admission are most flagrant during the wet season, and floors—made of brick when they are not merely trodden earth—forming preserves well stocked with every species of small deer, for whose sustenance bountiful nature has provided the cuticle of man.

7

After a long day's ride over such a road as I have described, even a station bungalow presents a certain charm. The musty grass mattress is a shade better than the bare ground, albeit one's bedfellows make a night of it at a revel where one is not a feaster but is feasted upon. The burned chops of a centenarian goat serve at least to fill the void after an early breakfast of *chupatties* and *dal*—leaden cakes and muddy beans.

Such, at all events, that damp, chill September night, was the opinion of Julian and myself, two young engineers in government employ, forerunners of the Hyderabad and Bhwaulpoor Railway. Our party consisted of three persons besides ourselves—two native servants and a guide from Kotree. The *khansaman*, or keeper of the bungalow, welcomed us with a smile as broad as a dog's in hot weather, and with assurance of the instant preparation of a banquet fit for Lucullus; which, at the end of an hour, materialized in the shape of a detestable curry.

After we had devoured what was placed before us with the appetite of youth and the philosophy of seasoned travellers, Julian and I dragged a couple of stools out upon the veranda, and, resting our backs against the wall, found solace for the ills of life in tobacco. Too weary to talk, we smoked in silence. I had closed my eyes, and with the soft rustle of the palms and the fitful, far off moaning of a jackal becoming entangled with the fringes of an incipient dream, I was fast nodding into complete slumber, when a sudden movement on the part of my companion aroused me.

"What is that?" he ejaculated. "Didn't you hear it?"

"No," said I, "I heard nothing. What was it like?"

"It was—hark! There it is again!"

Such a sound I had never heard before. It was certainly not human; and in all my experience with the animal life of India, my ears had never been saluted with the like. I cannot describe it. I cannot compare it with any other thing. If I say it was shrill and far reaching, yet inexpressibly sweet and mournful; echoing through the dusky aisles of the forest, as if from some hidden glade miles away, yet clear and distinct as the notes of a flute close at hand; a sound that stirred the heart and sent cold thrills creeping

over the skin, as does some sudden, exquisite change in music;
awakening vague, melancholy longings for something lost or something unattainable—saying all this, I still have utterly failed to convey the impression made upon me by that mysterious cry.

Looking at Julian, I saw, by the glimmer of the candle from
within, that there was a strange, rapt expression on his face.

"What can it be? What *can* it be?" he muttered, as if half to
himself.

"I don't know," I replied, struggling to speak calmly, and to
shake off the unholy spell upon me. "Some sort of night bird, I
imagine."

"Bird!" he repeated irritably. "Such sounds as those never came
from the throat of a fowl."

"This region is a kind of *terra incognita*," I responded. "How
do we know what strange creatures, bird, beast, or reptile, inhabit
these unexplored woods and jungles?"

"No," he said doggedly, "neither bird, beast, nor reptile. If the
soul of a woman lost by some great sin of passion possessed a voice
after death—"

I laughed. "'The woman wailing for her demon lover,' as
Coleridge says? Well, my dear fellow, I'm afraid you'll have to
accept the unromantic owl with his tenor note, or even the jovial
jackal."

"Hush! listen!"

A third time came that weird cry, if possible yet more sad, more
sweet, more yearning, more utterly heart enthralling in its nameless, tempting tenderness. In spite of myself, I sprang to my feet
with an impulse to go somewhere, do something, I knew not what.

Julian glanced at me somberly. "You feel it, too," he said quietly. "My better sense tells me that you must be right, and that it
is, in fact, some kind of bird or animal. But why should it affect us
as it does? It seems to be calling to me, beseeching me " he put his
hand to his head, and spoke in a slow, dreamy way. "It is like a
voice out of the past, bringing back my early boyhood, and faces
and emotions long since forgotten." He broke off and laughed
harshly. "I never suspected myself of a poetic talent, yet here I am

in the heart of an Indian jungle, going into lyrics over an owl, or—what did you say?—a jackal."

He laughed again, and, leaning back against the wall, crossed his hands over his knees and drew upon his pipe till his face glowed ruddily in the light from the bowl.

For a considerable space neither of us spoke. I was in a most perplexing frame of mind. I was listening eagerly, hoping to hear the cry again, yet, at the same time, in some irritating fashion, dreading to hear it. However, it was not repeated; and presently, with a curt "Good night," Julian arose, knocked the ashes out of his pipe, and went into our sleeping chamber. For half an hour longer I remained upon the veranda, smoking, and reasoning myself out of the unnatural and absurd agitation which had fallen upon me. *Item*—a good story to tell on Julian when we rejoined our mess.

Pulling off my shoes, coat, and vest with as little noise as possible, I lay down upon my mattress and drew the blanket over my shoulders. For a long time I lay staring, wide awake. Julian was asleep, but was very restless; groaning and turning from side to side, as if disturbed by bad dreams. Finally I fell into a troubled slumber, starting awake again and again, with that wild, melancholy cry ringing in my ears, to hear only the deep breathing of my comrade and the low swish of the palms beside the bungalow.

The clatter of pots and pans and the smell of boiling coffee awoke me early on the following morning. Poor Julian called me to his bedside with a husky request for water, and I saw instantly by his leaden ringed eyes and purple features that he had a touch of jungle fever. There was no going on for that day, and after administering a stiff dose of quinine, I sat myself down with some old engineering reports we happened to have with us, and possessed my soul in patience. Towards evening the fit passed over and Julian was able to sit up and drink a cup of the decoction which the *khansaman* called tea.

After supper, leaving my companion dozing on his mattress, to escape the stifling atmosphere of the bungalow, I took my stool upon the veranda and lit a pipe. It was one of the dull, oppressive

evenings, hot as an oven, yet with an unwholesome chill—a para-
dox only to be experienced in India. A pale, yellowish fog hung
over the trees, trailing in wisps along the dank turf, shutting out
the stars, and penetrating the lungs with an acrid, suffocating
sensation. The effect upon my spirits was intolerably depressing,
and I was on the point of going inside again, when Julian appeared
with stool and pipe. He looked sallow and weak, but declared himself better.

During the day, by mutual consent, as it seemed, we had both
avoided reference to our experience of the previous evening. Yet
neither of us had forgotten it; our very avoidance of the subject
proved that. And now, as we sat smoking and talking, I knew that
Julian, like myself, was nervously wondering if those mysterious
sounds would be repeated. For my part, I was heartily ashamed of
my own folly. To work one's self into such a state over the screech
of a night bird! It was pitiable! It was preposterous! If a lunacy
commission had haled me before it at that moment, I doubt if I
should have found the courage to make a defense.

However, as eight o'clock passed, then nine, and it began to
draw toward ten, without event, my common sense reassumed the
ascendant. I had knocked out my pipe, and was proposing that we
should retire, when Julian suddenly put out his hand and checked
me. His quicker ear had caught a sound which had escaped mine.

Ah! Low, tremulous, thrilling as the heart broken sigh of a
mourning woman, it rose, wavered, sank, and died away in the
depths of the forest. Hand clutching hand, and eye gazing into eye
with wild questioning, we stood and listened. Again it came, louder,
clearer, more beseeching, more tempting; falling softly into silence
with a long, delicious moan that shook the soul and sent the blood
burning along the veins and beating in the temples. The unholy
sweetness of that cadence—for, even then, I felt that there was
something wicked, diabolic, unnatural in it—I shall never forget.
Julian trembled and panted.

"Take me in," he gasped, gripping me convulsively. "Take me
where I can't hear that, or I shall yield to it—I shall rush out there
where it is, and be lost!"

I did not fully comprehend the cause of his words, for I was too confused and excited myself; but I was filled with a sense of peril, peril to us both; from what, in what way, I did not stop to think. I hurried him into the bungalow, shut the door and windows, lighted a candle with shaking fingers, and then sat down before him. Our eyes met, and we burst into a fit of laughter, loud, long and hysterical.

"Well, for a prize pair of fools!" I ejaculated, when I could speak.

He became suddenly grave, and looked at me haggardly. "What is it?" he said in a whisper. "Are we both mad?"

"Fever," I responded; "developed in you; incipient in me. That's what it is: fever."

He made no reply. Now that the excitement had worn off, he seemed very weak and scarcely able to stand. I helped him off with his shoes and outer clothing, and covered him up with his blanket. I sat beside him for a while in silence, until, by his regular breathing, I judged he was asleep; then I, too, retired to my mattress. I was still so confounded and distraught that I was unable to think connectedly, and it was this, doubtless, that enabled me to get asleep in a very few moments.

An hour later I started up, wide awake with the idea that some one had called me in a loud voice. I was oppressed with an ugly sensation of being alone. I listened for Julian's breathing, but everything was deadly silent in the room. For a moment I lay quiet, with an icy chill running over me; then I arose and groped over to his mattress. I put out my hand and touched his pillow. His head was not there. He was not in bed.

Terrified as I should not have been under ordinary circumstances, I blundered about in the dark till I found and lighted the candle. Then I saw that the blanket had been cast off the mattress and that Julian's shoes, clothing, and cap were gone. Hurrying on my own garments, I went upon the veranda. Julian was nowhere in sight. I called to him, first in a low tone, then louder, until, in my fright, my voice rose to a shout that must have startled the inhabitants of the jungle half a mile around. It elicited no response from Julian, but brought the servants and the old *khansaman* upon the veranda, rubbing their eyes and inquiring what was the matter.

I was hurriedly explaining the cause of my alarm, when faintly and afar off, miles away, it seemed, once again arose that weird cry. The effect upon the old *khansaman* was instantaneous. With a groan of abject fear he seized me by the arm and attempted to drag me into the bungalow.

"The Jheen! The Jheen!" he cried in alarm.

"What is the 'Jheen'?" I asked, resisting his frantic efforts. "Answer me, can't you?"

"The unholy one! The destroyer of men, body and soul! Oh, sahib, I beseech you! I implore you, come inside and shut your ears, or you are lost!"

"You old fool!' I shouted, shaking his withered frame to and fro in my alarm and impatience. "If you do not give me a rational answer I will throttle you."

But as he went on staring, moaning, and babbling, I followed him into his kitchen, where there was a light, and pushing him into a seat, said sternly, "Now tell me in a few words what you mean. Be quick about it, for my friend is out there somewhere."

"Then he is lost," replied the old man solemnly. "He has been tempted into the jungle by the Jheen, and will never be seen again."

"But what is the Jheen?" I cried, stamping in rage.

"The spirit of a woman," he said in a whisper; "a beautiful woman who has died in sin. They haunt old and solitary places, luring unwary travelers with their sweet voices, to devour them. You may always know them by their feet, which are turned backward."

I had heard something of the kind before, but no one in India pays attention to the thousand and one hobgoblin stories of the natives. Now I was simply irritated at having wasted time in listening to the old fool's twaddle. There was nothing in the shape of a lantern about the place, and I was compelled to do the best I could with a candle. Putting my revolver in my pocket, I ordered the servants to accompany me. This they flatly refused to do, and giving them a hearty kick apiece, I went out on my search for Julian alone.

I had not gone a dozen steps when my candle was extinguished by the wind. I thrust it aside and stumbled on, shouting and fixing my revolver as I went, and pausing every few yards to listen. There was no reply, and no sign to guide me in my hunt. Finally, after shouting myself hoarse, firing off all my cartridges, and bruising myself with several heavy falls, I gave it up in despair and returned to the bungalow.

I shall never forget the four long, anxious hours I spent, trying to extract something sensible from the moaning, whimpering natives, starting at every sound, hoping it might be the footstep of my returning friend. But he came not, and with the first gleam of dawn I darted out to renew my search. The old *khansaman* now declared himself willing to accompany me. "Jheens," he said, confidently, "work their evil spells only in the darkness."

A short distance from the bungalow we came upon the print of an English shoe, which I knew to be Julian's, in the wet soil. The track led us directly into the jungle for a quarter of a mile, until we came to an old, disused well beneath a grove of bhopal trees. The *khansaman*, who was a little in advance, suddenly stopped short and uttered a terrified exclamation. He was gazing with starting eyes at something on the ground before him. I hurried to his side and saw that he was pointing to the print of a small naked foot— evidently a woman's—clearly outlined in the mud. Near it were the impressions of both of Julian's shoes, close together, as if he had come to a halt.

Following up the tracks, I saw that they led at right angles, deeper into the forest, the small naked feet beside the shoes.

"Why, he must have met some woman here," I exclaimed, looking at the old man in amazement. "Who could she have been?"

"The Jheen," he replied quaveringly. "Oh, poor young sahib! We shall never see him again."

"Nonsense!" I replied, angrily; though despite my better sense the *khansaman's* solemn manner sent a chill to my heart. "He has come across some pretty native girl—"

"Do living girls walk backward?" asked the old man, with still deeper solemnity.

I had not examined the female tracks closely hitherto, but now I stooped down and studied them. Certainly there was something strange about these footprints. The toes seemed to have impressed themselves most deeply, while the heels dragged after in an unaccountable fashion. Moreover, the heels pointed away from each other at a wide angle, while the great toes nearly touched. No, certainly, I had never seen any woman walk as this woman must have walked.

"What in heaven's name does it mean?" l asked, still staring at the mysterious tracks.

"The footprints of a Jheen," replied the old man doggedly, "the unholy one whose voice we heard last night, the evil spirit in the guise of a beautiful woman whose feet are turned backward. Sahib, we may as well return. Your friend is lost;" and the old *khansaman* mournfully shook his grizzled locks.

I paid no heed to him, but with my head in a whirl, I continued to follow the tracks through the jungle till we came to an open space, in the center of which was a deep, black looking pool, perhaps ten yards in diameter. The footprints led straight toward this pool.

Arriving at the brink I paused aghast, for here were visible evidences of a desperate struggle; the ground was trodden, and the rank vegetation crushed and ground to a pulp. In the midst of the trodden space a white object caught my attention. It was a linen cuff torn out at the button holes and spotted with blood. It was Julian's; I knew the cuff button, which was still in place.

While, horror stricken, I was examining the cuff, the old man brought me Julian's cloth traveling cap, which he had found among the reeds by the pool. Upon the crown was a dark splash which was not water. Besides the cuff and the cap, an hour's search revealed no other traces of my missing friend. No footprints led away from the pool. There was no further sign of his mysterious companion, nor of any other living creature.

In a state of mind which I cannot even now recall without a shudder, I returned to the bungalow, and, getting together a body of natives from a neighboring village, scoured the country for miles around. I also had the pool dragged. After three days' unavailing search. I was reluctantly compelled to give up my attempt, and to continue my sorrowful journey toward Kamus alone.

If you ask me to offer a solution of my poor friend's mysterious disappearance, I can say that he may have wandered away in a paroxysm of fever, and fallen into the pool; but remember that I had the pool carefully dragged. He may have been seized by some wild animal; though we found no trace of any such animal. Finally, he may have been lured away by a native woman, acting as decoy for assassins. How then account for the fact that there were no tracks leading away from the pool?

For myself, when I think of the woman's footprints, and the old *khansaman's* tale of the Jheens whose feet are turned backward, and most of all, when I recall that weird cry we heard—well, I do not know what to say.

In the Avu Observatory
H. G. WELLS

The observatory at Avu, in Borneo, stands on the spur of the mountain. To the north rises the old crater, black against the unfathomable blue of the sky. From the little circular building, with its mushroom dome, the slopes plunge steeply downward into the black mysteries of the tropical forest beneath. The little house in which the observer and his assistant live is about fifty yards from the observatory, and beyond this are the huts of their native attendants.

Thaddy, the chief observer, was down with a slight fever. His assistant, Woodhouse, paused for a moment in silent contemplation of the tropical night before commencing his solitary vigil. The night was very silent. Now and then voices and laughter came from the native huts, or the cry of some strange animal was heard from the midst of the mystery of the forest. Nocturnal insects appeared in ghostly fashion out of the darkness, and fluttered round his light. He thought, perhaps, of all the possibilities of discovery that still lay in the black tangle beneath him; for to the naturalist the virgin forests of Borneo are still a wonderland, full of strange questions and half-suspected discoveries. Woodhouse carried a small lantern in his hand, and its yellow glow contrasted vividly with the infinite series of tints between lavender-blue and black in which the landscape was painted. His hands and face were smeared with ointment against the attacks of the mosquitoes.

Even in these days of celestial photography, work done in a purely temporary erection, and with only the most primitive appliances in addition to the telescope, still involves a very large amount of cramped and motionless watching. He sighed as he thought of the physical fatigues before him, stretched himself, and entered the observatory.

The reader is probably familiar with the structure of an ordinary astronomical observatory. The building is usually cylindrical in shape, with a very light hemispherical roof capable of being turned round from the interior. The telescope is supported upon a stone pillar in the centre, and a clockwork arrangement compensates for the earth's rotation, and allows a star once found to be continuously observed. Besides this, there is a compact tracery of wheels and screws about its point of support, by which the astronomer adjusts it. There is, of course, a slit in the movable roof which follows the eye of the telescope in its survey of the heavens. The observer sits or lies on a sloping wooden arrangement, which he can wheel to any part of the observatory as the position of the telescope may require. Within it is advisable to have things as dark as possible, in order to enhance the brilliance of the stars observed.

The lantern flared as Woodhouse entered his circular den, and the general darkness fled into black shadows behind the big machine, from which it presently seemed to creep back over the whole place again as the light waned. The slit was a profound transparent blue, in which six stars shone with tropical brilliance, and their light lay a pallid gleam, along the black tube of the instrument. Woodhouse shifted the roof, and then proceeding to the telescope, turned first one wheel and then another, the great cylinder slowly swinging into a new position. Then he glanced through the finder, the little companion telescope, moved the roof a little more, made some further adjustments, and set the clockwork in motion. He took off his jacket, for the night was very hot, and pushed into position the uncomfortable seat to which he was condemned for the next four hours. Then with a sigh he resigned himself to his watch upon the mysteries of space.

There was no sound now in the observatory, and the lantern waned steadily. Outside there was the occasional cry of some animal in alarm or pain, or calling to its mate, and the intermittent sounds of the Malay and Dyak servants. Presently one of the men began a queer chanting song, in which the others joined at intervals. After this it would seem that they turned in for the night, for no further sound came from their direction, and the whispering stillness became more and more profound.

The clockwork ticked steadily. The shrill hum of a mosquito explored the place and grew shriller in indignation at Woodhouse's ointment. Then the lantern went out and all the observatory was black.

Woodhouse shifted his position presently, when the slow movement of the telescope had carried it beyond the limits of his comfort.

He was watching a little group of stars in the Milky Way, in one of which his chief had seen or fancied a remarkable colour variability. It was not a part of the regular work for which the establishment existed, and for that reason perhaps Woodhouse was deeply interested. He must have forgotten things terrestrial. All his attention was concentrated upon the great blue circle of the telescope field—a circle powdered, so it seemed, with an innumerable multitude of stars, and all luminous against the blackness of its setting. As he watched he seemed to himself to become incorporeal, as if he too were floating in the ether of space. Infinitely remote was the faint red spot he was observing.

Suddenly the stars were blotted out. A flash of blackness passed, and they were visible again.

"Queer," said Woodhouse. "Must have been a bird."

The thing happened again, and immediately after the great tube shivered as though it had been struck. Then the dome of the observatory resounded with a series of thundering blows. The stars seemed to sweep aside as the telescope swung round and away from the slit in the roof.

"Great Scott!" cried Woodhouse. "What 's this?"

Some huge, vague, black shape, with a flapping something like a wing, seemed to be struggling in the aperture of the roof. In another moment the slit was clear again, and the luminous haze of the Milky Way shone warm and bright.

The interior of the roof was perfectly black, and only a scraping sound marked the whereabouts of the unknown creature.

Woodhouse had scrambled from the seat to his feet. He was trembling violently and in a perspiration with the suddenness of the occurrence. Was the thing, whatever it was, inside or out? It was big, whatever else it might be. Something shot across the skylight, and the telescope swayed. He started violently and put his arm up. It was in the observatory, then, with him. It was clinging to the roof, apparently. What the devil was it? Could it see him?

He stood for perhaps a minute in a state of stupefaction. The beast, whatever it was, clawed at the interior of the dome, and then something flapped almost into his face, and he saw the momentary gleam of starlight on a skin like oiled leather. His water-bottle was knocked off his little table with a smash.

The sense of some strange bird-creature hovering a few yards from his face in the darkness was indescribably unpleasant to Woodhouse. As his thought returned he concluded that it must be some night-bird or large bat. At any risk he would see what it was, and pulling a match from his pocket, he tried to strike it on the telescope seat. There was a smoking streak of phosphorescent light, the match flared for a moment, and he saw a vast wing sweeping towards him, a gleam of grey-brown fur, and then he was struck in the face and the match knocked out of his hand. The blow was aimed at his temple, and a claw tore sideways down to his check. He reeled and fell, and he heard the extinguished lantern smash. Another blow followed as he fell. He was partly stunned, he felt his own warm blood stream out upon his face. Instinctively he felt his eyes had been struck at, and, turning over on his face to protect them, tried to crawl under the protection of the telescope.

He was struck again upon the back, and he heard his jacket rip, and then the thing hit the roof of the observatory. He edged as far as he could between the wooden seat and the eyepiece of the instrument, and turned his body round so that it was chiefly his feet that were exposed.

With these he could at least kick. He was still in a mystified state. The strange beast banged about in the darkness, and presently clung to the telescope, making it sway and the gear rattle.

Once it flapped near him, and he kicked out madly and felt a soft body with his feet. He was horribly scared now. It must be a big thing to swing the telescope like that. He saw for a moment the outline of a head black against the starlight, with sharply-pointed upstanding ears and a crest between them. It seemed to him to be as big as a mastiff's. Then he began to bawl out as loudly as he could for help.

At that the thing came down upon him again. As it did so his hand touched something beside him on the floor. He kicked out, and the next moment his ankle was gripped and held by a row of keen teeth. He yelled again, and tried to free his leg by kicking with the other. Then he realised he had the broken water-bottle at his hand, and, snatching it, he struggled into a sitting posture, and feeling in the darkness towards his foot, gripped a velvety ear, like the ear of a big cat. He had seized the water-bottle by its neck and brought it down with a shivering crash upon the head of the strange beast. He repeated the blow, and then stabbed and jobbed with the jagged end of it, in the darkness, where he judged the face might be.

The small teeth relaxed their hold, and at once Woodhouse pulled his leg free and kicked hard. He felt the sickening feel of fur and bone giving under his boot. There was a tearing bite at his arm, and he struck over it at the face, as he judged, and hit damp fur.

There was a pause; then he heard the sound of claws and the dragging of a heavy body away from him over the observatory floor. Then there was silence, broken only by his own sobbing breathing, and a sound like licking. Everything was black except the parallelogram of the blue skylight with the luminous dust of stars, against which the end of the telescope now appeared in silhouette. He waited, as it seemed, an interminable time.

Was the thing coming on again? He felt in his trouser-pocket for some matches, and found one remaining. He tried to strike this, but the floor was wet, and it spat and went out. He cursed. He could not see where the door was situated. In his struggle he had quite lost his bearings. The strange beast, disturbed by the splutter of the match, began to move again. "Time!" called Woodhouse, with a sudden gleam of mirth, but the thing was not coming at him again. He must have hurt it, he thought, with the broken bottle. He felt a dull pain in his ankle. Probably he was bleeding there. He wondered if it would support him if he tried to stand up. The night outside was very still. There was no sound of any one moving. The sleepy fools had not heard those wings battering upon the dome, nor his shouts. It was no good wasting strength in shouting. The monster flapped its wings and startled him into a defensive attitude. He hit his elbow against the seat, and it fell over with a crash. He cursed this, and then he cursed the darkness.

Suddenly the oblong patch of starlight seemed to sway to and fro. Was he going to faint? It would never do to faint. He clenched his fists and set his teeth to hold himself together. Where had the door got to? It occurred to him he could get his bearings by the stars visible through the skylight. The patch of stars he saw was in Sagittarius and south-eastward; the door was north—or was it north by west? He tried to think. If he could get the door open he might retreat. It might be the thing was wounded. The suspense was beastly. "Look here!" he said, "if you don't come on, I shall come at you."

Then the thing began clambering up the side of the observatory, and he saw its black outline gradually blot out the skylight. Was it in retreat? He forgot about the door, and watched as the dome shifted and creaked. Somehow he did not feel very frightened or excited now. He felt a curious sinking sensation inside him. The sharply-defined patch of light, with the black form moving across it, seemed to be growing smaller and smaller. That was curious. He began to feel very thirsty, and yet he did not feel inclined to get anything to drink. He seemed to be sliding down a long funnel.

He felt a burning sensation in his throat, and then he perceived it was broad daylight, and that one of the Dyak servants was looking at him with a curious expression. Then there was the top of Thaddy's face upside down. Funny fellow Thaddy, to go about like that! Then he grasped the situation better, and perceived that his head was on Thaddy's knee, and Thaddy was giving him brandy. And then he saw the eyepiece of the telescope with a lot of red smears on it. He began to remember.

"You've made this observatory in a pretty mess," said Thaddy.

The Dyak boy was beating up an egg in brandy. Woodhouse took this and sat up. He felt a sharp twinge of pain. His ankle was tied up, so were his arm and the side of his face. The smashed glass, red-stained, lay about the floor, the telescope seat was overturned, and by the opposite wall was a dark pool. The door was open, and he saw the grey summit of the mountain against a brilliant background of blue sky.

"Pah!" said Woodhouse. "Who 's been killing calves here? Take me out of it."

Then he remembered the Thing, and the fight he had had with it.

"What *was* it?" he said to Thaddy— "the Thing I fought with—"

"*You* know that best," said Thaddy. "But, anyhow, don't worry yourself now about it. Have some more to drink."

Thaddy, however, was curious enough, and it was a hard struggle between duty and inclination to keep Woodhouse quiet until he was decently put away in bed, and had slept upon the copious dose of meat-extract Thaddy considered advisable. They then talked it over together.

"It was," said Woodhouse, "more like a big bat than anything else in the world. It had sharp, short ears, and soft fur, and its wings were leathery. Its teeth were little, but devilish sharp, and its jaw could not have been very strong or else it would have bitten through my ankle."

"It has pretty nearly," said Thaddy.

"It seemed to me to hit out with its claws pretty freely. That is about as much as I know about the beast. Our conversation was intimate, so to speak, and yet not confidential."

"The Dyak chaps talk about a Big Colugo, a Klang-utang—whatever that may be. It does not often attack man, but I suppose you made it nervous. They say there is a Big Colugo and a Little Colugo, and a something else that sounds like gobble. They all fly about at night. For my own part I know there are flying foxes and flying lemurs about here; but they are none of them very big beasts."

"There are more things in heaven and earth," said Wood-house,—and Thaddy groaned at the quotation,— "and more particularly in the forests of Borneo, than are dreamt of in our philosophies. On the whole, if the Borneo fauna is going to disgorge any more of its novelties upon me, I should prefer that it did so when I was not occupied in the observatory at night and alone."

Æpyornis Island

H. G. Wells

The man with the scarred face leant over the table and looked at my bundle.

"Orchids?" he asked.

"A few," I said.

"Cypripediums?" he said.

"Chiefly," said I.

"Anything new?—I thought not. *I* did these islands twenty-five—twenty-seven years ago. If you find anything new here—well, it's brand new. I didn't leave much."

"I'm not a collector," said I.

"I was young then," he went on. "Lord! how I used to fly round." He seemed to take my measure. "I was in the East Indies two years, and in Brazil seven. Then I went to Madagascar."

"I know a few explorers by name," I said anticipating a yarn. "Who did you collect for?"

"Dawsons. I wonder if you've heard the name of Butcher ever?"

"Butcher—Butcher?" The name seemed vaguely present in my memory; then I recalled *Butcher v. Dawson*. "Why!" said I, "you are the man who sued them for four years' salary—got cast away on a desert island—"

"Your servant," said the man with the scar, bowing. "Funny case, wasn't it? Here was me, making a little fortune on that island, doing nothing for it neither, and them quite unable to give me notice. It often used to amuse me thinking over it while I was there. I did calculations of it—big—all over the blessed atoll in ornamental figuring."

25

"How did it happen?" said I. "I don't rightly remember the case."

"Well—you've heard of the Æpyornis?"

"Rather. Andrews was telling me of a new species he was working on only a month or so ago. Just before I sailed. They've got a thigh bone, it seems, nearly a yard long. Monster the thing must have been!"

"I believe you," said the man with the scar. "It was a monster. Sinbad's roc was just a legend of 'em. But when did they find these bones?"

"Three or four years ago—'91 I fancy. Why?"

"Why?—Because *I* found 'em—Lord!— it's nearly twenty years ago. If Dawsons hadn't been silly about that salary they might have made a perfect ring in 'em.—*I* couldn't help the infernal boat going adrift."

He paused. "I suppose it's the same place. A kind of swamp about ninety miles north of Antananarivo. Do you happen to know? You have to go to it along the coast by boats. You don't happen to remember, perhaps?"

"I don't. I fancy Andrews said something about a swamp."

"It must be the same. It's on the east coast. And somehow there's something in the water that keeps things from decaying. Like creosote it smells. It reminded me of Trinidad. Did they get any more eggs? Some of the eggs I found were a foot and a half long. The swamp goes circling round, you know, and cuts off this bit. It's mostly salt, too. Well— What a time I had of it! I found the things quite by accident. We went for eggs, me and two native chaps, in one of those rum canoes all tied together, and found the bones at the same time. We had a tent and provisions for four days, and we pitched on one of the firmer places. To think of it brings that odd tarry smell back even now. It's funny work. You go probing into the mud with iron rods, you know, Usually the egg gets smashed. I wonder how long it is since these Æpyornises really lived. The missionaries say the natives have legends about when they were alive, but I never heard any such stories myself.[1] But certainly those eggs we got were as fresh as if they had been new-laid. Fresh! Carrying them down to the boat one of my nigger chaps dropped one on a rock and it smashed. How I lammed into the beggar! But sweet it was as if it was new-laid, not even smelly, and its mother dead these four hundred years perhaps. Said a centipede had bit him. However, I'm getting off the straight with the story. It had taken us all day to dig into the slush and get these eggs out unbroken, and we were all covered with beastly black mud, and naturally I was cross. So far as I knew they were the only eggs that had ever been got out not even cracked. I went afterwards to see the ones they have at the Natural History Museum in London: all of them were cracked and just stuck together like a mosaic, and bits missing. Mine were perfect, and I meant to blow them when I got back. Naturally I was annoyed at the silly devil dropping three hours' work just on account of a centipede. I hit him about rather."

The man with the scar took out a clay pipe. I placed my pouch before him. He filled up absent-mindedly.

"How about the others? Did you get those home? I don't remember—"

"That's the queer part of the story. I had three others. Perfectly fresh eggs. Well, we put 'em in the boat, and then I went up to the tent to make some coffee, leaving my two heathens down by the beach—the one fooling about with his sting and the other helping him. It never occurred to me that the beggars would take advantage of the peculiar position I was in to pick a quarrel. But I suppose the centipede poison and the kicking I'd given him had upset the one—he was always a cantankerous sort—and he persuaded the other.

"I remember I was sitting and smoking and boiling up the water over a spirit-lamp business I used to take on these expeditions. Incidentally I was admiring the swamp under the sunset. All black and blood red it was, in streaks—a beautiful sight. And up beyond, the land rose grey and hazy to the hills, and the sky behind them red, like a furnace mouth. And fifty yards behind the back of me was these blessed heathen—quite regardless of the tranquil air of things—plotting to cut off with the boat and leave me all alone with three days' provisions and a canvas tent, and nothing to drink whatsoever, beyond a little keg of water. I heard a kind of yelp behind me, and there they were in this canoe affair—it wasn't properly a boat—and perhaps twenty yards from land. I realised what was up in a moment. My gun was in the tent, and besides I had no bullets—only duck shot. They knew that. But I had a little revolver in my pocket and I pulled that out as I ran down to the beach.

"'Come back!' says I, flourishing it.

"They jabbered something at me, and the man that broke the egg jeered. I aimed at the other—because he was unwounded and had the paddle, and I missed. They laughed. However, I wasn't beat. I knew I had to keep cool, and I tried him again and made him jump with the whang of it. The third time I got his head, and over he went, and the paddle with him. It was a precious lucky shot for a revolver. I reckon it was fifty yards. He went right under. I don't know if he was shot, or simply stunned and drowned. Then I began to shout to the other chap to come back, but he huddled up in the canoe and refused to answer. So I fired out my revolver at him and never got near him.

"I felt a precious fool, I can tell you. There I was on this rotten, black beach, flat swamp all behind me, and the flat sea, cold after the sunset, and just this black canoe drifting steadily out to sea. I tell you I damned Dawsons and Jamrachs and Museums and all the rest of it just to rights. I bawled to this nigger to come back, until my voice went up into a scream.

"There was nothing for it but to swim after him and take my luck with the sharks. So I opened my clasp-knife and put it in my mouth and took off my clothes and waded in. As soon as I was in the water I lost sight of the canoe, but I aimed, as I judged, to head it off. I hoped the man in it was too bad to navigate it, and that it would keep on drifting in the same direction. Presently it came up over the horizon again to the south-westward about. The afterglow of sunset was well over now and the dim of night creeping up. The stars were coming through the blue. I swam like a champion, though my legs and arms were soon aching.

"However, I came up to him by the time the stars were fairly out. As it got darker I began to see all manner of glowing things in the water— phosphorescence, you know. At times it made me giddy. I hardly knew which was stars and which was phosphorescence, and whether I was swimming on my head or my heels. The canoe was as black as sin, and the ripple under the bows like liquid fire. I was naturally chary of clambering up into it. I was anxious to see what he was up to first. He seemed to be lying cuddled up in a lump in the bows, and the stern was all out of water. The thing kept turning round slowly as it drifted—kind of waltzing, don't you know. I went to the stern and pulled it down, expecting him to wake up. Then I began to clamber in with my knife in my hand, and ready for a rush. But he never stirred. So there I sat in the stern of the little canoe, drifting away over the calm phosphorescent sea, and with all the host of the stars above me, waiting for something to happen.

"After a long time I called him by name, but he never answered. I was too tired to take any risks by going along to him. So we sat there. I fancy I dozed once or twice. When the dawn came I saw he was as dead as a doornail and all puffed up and purple. My three eggs and the bones were lying in the middle of the canoe, and the keg of water and some coffee and biscuits wrapped in a Cape 'Argus' by his feet, and a tin of methylated spirit underneath him. There was no paddle; nor in fact anything except the spirit tin that one could use as one, so I settled to drift until I was picked up. I held an inquest on him, brought in a verdict against some snake, scorpion or centipede unknown, and sent him overboard.

"After that I had a drink of water and a few biscuits, and took a look round. I suppose a man low down as I was don't see very far; leastways, Madagascar was clean out of sight, and any trace of land at all. I saw a sail going south-westward—looked like a schooner, but her hull never came up. Presently the sun got high in the sky and began to beat down upon me. Lord!—it pretty near made my brains boil. I tried dipping my head in the sea, but after a while my eye fell on the Cape 'Argus,' and I lay down flat in the canoe and spread this over me. Wonderful things these newspapers. I never read one through thoroughly before, but it's odd what you get up to when you're alone, as I was. I suppose I read that blessed old Cape 'Argus' twenty times. The pitch in the canoe simply reeked with the heat and rose up into big blisters.

"I drifted ten days," said the man with the scar. "It's a little thing in the telling, isn't it? Every day was like the last. Except in the morning and the evening I never kept a look-out even—the blaze was so infernal. I didn't see a sail after the first three days, and those I saw took no notice of me. About the sixth night a ship went by scarcely half a mile away from me, with all its lights ablaze and its ports open, looking like a big firefly. There was music aboard. I stood up and shouted and screamed at it. The second day I broached one of the Æpyornis eggs, scraped the shell away at the end bit by bit, and tried it, and I was glad to find it was good enough to eat. A bit flavoury—not bad, I mean, but with something of the taste of a duck's egg. There was a kind of circular patch about six inches across on one side of the yolk, and with streaks of blood and a white mark like a ladder in it that I thought queer, but I didn't understand what this meant at the time, and I wasn't inclined to be particular. The egg lasted me three days, with biscuits and a drink of water. I chewed coffee berries too—invigorating stuff. The second egg I opened about the eighth day. And it scared me."

The man with the scar paused. "Yes," he said— "developing.

"I daresay you find it hard to believe. *I* did, with the thing before me. There the egg had been, sunk in that cold black mud, perhaps three hundred years. But there was no mistaking it. There was the—what is it?—embryo, with its big head and curved back and its heart beating under its throat, and the yolk shrivelled up and great membranes spreading inside of the shell and all over the yolk. Here was I hatching out the eggs of the biggest of all extinct birds, in a little canoe in the midst of the Indian Ocean. If old Dawson had known that! It was worth four years' salary. What do *you* think?

"However, I had to eat that precious thing up, every bit of it, before I sighted the reef, and some of the mouthfuls were beastly unpleasant. I left the third one alone. I held it up to the light, but the shell was too thick for me to get any notion of what might be happening inside; and though I fancied I heard blood pulsing, it might have been the rustle in my own ears, like what you listen to in a seashell.

"Then came the atoll. Came out of the sunrise, as it were, suddenly, close up to me. I drifted straight towards it until I was about half a mile from shore—not more, and then the current took a turn, and I had to paddle as hard as I could with my hands and bits of the Æpyornis shell to make the place. However, I got there. It was just a common atoll about four miles round, with a few trees growing and a spring in one place and the lagoon full of parrot fish. I took the egg ashore and put it in a good place well above the tide lines and in the sun, to give it all the chance I could, and pulled the canoe up safe, and loafed about prospecting. It's rum how dull an atoll is. When I was a kid I thought nothing could be finer or more adventurous than the Robinson Crusoe business, but that place was as monotonous as a book of sermons. I went round finding eatable things and generally thinking; but I tell you I was bored to death before the first day was out. It shows my luck—the very day I landed the weather changed. A thunderstorm went by to the north and flicked its wing over the island, and in the night there came a drencher and a howling wind slap over us. It wouldn't have taken much, you know, to upset that canoe.

"I was sleeping under the canoe, and the egg was luckily among the sand higher up the beach, and the first thing I remember was a sound like a hundred pebbles hitting the boat at once and a rush of water over my body. I'd been dreaming of Antananarivo, and I sat up and holloaed to Intoshi to ask her what the devil was up, and clawed out at the chair where the matches used to be. Then I remembered where I was. There were phosphorescent waves rolling up as if they meant to eat me, and all the rest of the night as black as pitch. The air was simply yelling. The clouds seemed down on your head almost, and the rain fell as if heaven was sinking and they were baling out the waters above the firmament. One great roller came writhing at me, like a fiery serpent, and I bolted.

Then I thought of the canoe, and ran down to it as the water went hissing back again, but the thing had gone. I wondered about the egg then, and felt my way to it. It was all right and well out of reach of the maddest waves, so I sat down beside it and cuddled it for company. Lord! What a night that was!

"The storm was over before the morning. There wasn't a rag of cloud left in the sky when the dawn came, and all along the beach there were bits of plank scattered—which was the disarticulated skeleton, so to speak, of my canoe. However, that gave me something to do, for, taking advantage of two of the trees being together, I rigged up a kind of storm shelter with these vestiges. And that day the egg hatched.

"Hatched, sir, when my head was pillowed on it and I was asleep. I heard a whack and felt a jar and sat up, and there was the end of the egg pecked out and a rum little brown head looking out at me. 'Lord!' I said, 'you're welcome,' and with a little difficulty he came out.

"He was a nice friendly little chap, at first, about the size of a small hen—very much like most other young birds, only bigger. His plumage was a dirty brown to begin with, with a sort of grey scab that fell off it very soon, and scarcely feathers—a kind of downy hair. I can hardly express how pleased I was to see him. I tell you, Robinson Crusoe don't make near enough of his loneliness. But here was interesting company. He looked at me and winked his eye from the front backwards like a hen, and gave a chirp and began to peck about at once, as though being hatched three hundred years too late was just nothing. 'Glad to see you, Man Friday!' says I, for I had naturally settled he was to be called Man Friday if ever he was hatched, as soon as ever I found the egg in the canoe had developed. I was a bit anxious about his feed, so I gave him a lump of raw parrot fish at once. He took it and opened his beak for more. I was glad of that, for, under the circumstances, if he'd been fanciful, I should have had to eat him after all.

"You'd be surprised what an interesting bird that Æpyornis chick was. He followed me about from the very beginning. He used to stand by me and watch while I fished in the lagoon and go shares in anything I caught. And he was sensible, too. There were nasty green warty things, like pickled gherkins, used to lie about on the beach, and he tried one of these and it upset him. He never even looked at any of them again.

"And he grew. You could almost see him grow. And as I was never much of a society man, his quiet, friendly ways suited me to a T. For nearly two years we were as happy as we could be on that island. I had no business worries, for I knew my salary was mounting up at Dawsons'. We would see a sail now and then, but nothing ever came near us. I amused myself too by decorating the island with designs worked in sea-urchins and fancy shells of various kinds. I put ÆPYORNIS ISLAND all round the place very nearly, in big letters, like what you see done with coloured stones at railway stations in the old country. And I used to lie watching the blessed bird stalking round and growing, growing, and think how I could make a living out of him by showing him about if ever I got taken off. After his first moult he began to get handsome, with a crest and a blue wattle, and a lot of green feathers at the behind of him. And then I used to puzzle whether Dawsons had any right to claim him or not. Stormy weather and in the rainy season we lay snug under the shelter I had made out of the old canoe, and I used to tell him lies about my friends at home. It was a kind of idyll, you might say. If only I had had some tobacco it would have been simply just like Heaven.

"It was about the end of the second year our little Paradise went wrong. Friday was then about fourteen feet high to the bill of him, with a big broad head like the end of a pickaxe, and two huge brown eyes with yellow rims set together like a man's—not out of sight of each other like a hen's. His plumage was fine—none of the half mourning style of your ostrich—more like a cassowary as far as colour and texture go. And then it was he began to cock his comb at me and give himself airs and show signs of a nasty temper.

"At last came a time when my fishing had been rather unlucky and he began to hang about me in a queer, meditative way. I thought he might have been eating sea-cucumbers or something, but it was really just discontent on his part. I was hungry too, and when at last I landed a fish I wanted it for myself. Tempers were short that morning on both sides. He pecked at it and grabbed it, and I gave him a whack on the head to make him leave go. And at that he went for me. Lord!

"He gave me this in the face." The man indicated his scar. "Then he kicked me. It was like a cart horse. I got up, and seeing he hadn't finished I started off full tilt with my arms doubled up over my face. But he ran on those gawky legs of his faster than a race horse, and kept landing out at me with sledge-hammer kicks, and bringing his pickaxe down on the back of my head. I made for the lagoon, and went in up to my neck. He stopped at the water, for he hated getting his feet wet, and began to make a shindy, something like a peacock's, only hoarser. He started strutting up and down the beach. I'll admit I felt small to see this blessed fossil lording it there. And my head and face were all bleeding, and—well, my body just one jelly of bruises.

"I decided to swim across the lagoon and leave him alone for a bit, until the affair blew over. I shinned up the tallest palm-tree and sat there thinking of it all. I don't suppose I ever felt so hurt by anything before or since. It was the brutal ingratitude of the creature. I'd been more than a brother to him. I'd hatched him. Educated him. A great, gawky, out-of-date bird! And me a human being—heir of the ages and all that.

"I thought after a time he'd begin to see things in that light himself, and feel a little sorry for his behaviour. I thought if I was to catch some nice little bits of fish, perhaps, and go to him presently in a casual kind of way, and offer them to him, he might do the sensible thing. It took me some time to learn how unforgiving and cantankerous an extinct bird can be. Malice!

"I won't tell you all the little devices I tried to get that bird round again. I simply can't. It makes my cheek burn with shame even now to think of the snubs and buffets I had from this infernal curiosity. I tried violence. I chucked lumps of coral at him from a safe distance, but he only swallowed them. I shied my open knife at him and almost lost it, though it was too big for him to swallow. I tried starving him out and struck fishing, but he took to picking

along the beach at low water after worms, and rubbed along on
that. Half my time I spent up to my neck in the lagoon, and the
rest up the palm-trees. One of them was scarcely high enough, and
when he caught me up it he had a regular Bank Holiday with the
calves of my legs. It got unbearable. I don't know if you have ever
tried sleeping up a palm-tree. It gave me the most horrible night-
mares. Think of the shame of it too! Here was this extinct animal
mooning about my island like a sulky duke, and me not allowed to
rest the sole of my foot on the place. I used to cry with weariness
and vexation. I told him straight that I didn't mean to be chased
about a desert island by any damned anachronisms. I told him to
go and peck a navigator of his own age. But he only snapped his
beak at me. Great ugly bird—all legs and neck!

"I shouldn't like to say how long that went on altogether. I'd
have killed him sooner if I'd known how. However, I hit on a way
of settling him at last. It's a South American dodge. I joined all my
fishing lines together with stems of seaweed and things, and made
a stoutish string, perhaps twelve yards in length or more, and I
fastened two lumps of coral rock to the ends of this. It took me
some time to do, because every now and then I had to go into the
lagoon or up a tree as the fancy took me. This I whirled rapidly
round my head and then let it go at him. The first time I missed,
but the next time the string caught his legs beautifully and wrapped
round them again and again. Over he went. I threw it standing
waist-deep in the lagoon, and as soon as he went down I was out of
the water and sawing at his neck with my knife—

"I don't like to think of that even now. I felt like a murderer
while I did it, though my anger was hot against him. When I stood
over him and saw him bleeding on the white sand and his beautiful great legs and neck writhing in his last agony—Pah!

"With that tragedy, Loneliness came upon me like a curse.
Good Lord! you can't imagine how I missed that bird. I sat by his
corpse and sorrowed over him, and shivered as I looked round the
desolate, silent reef. I thought of what a jolly little bird he had been
when he was hatched, and of a thousand pleasant tricks he had
played before he went wrong. I thought if I'd only wounded him I

might have nursed him round into a better understanding. If I'd had any means of digging into the coral rock I'd have buried him. I felt exactly as if he was human. As it was I couldn't think of eating him, so I put him in the lagoon and the little fishes picked him clean. Then one day a chap cruising about in a yacht had a fancy to see if my atoll still existed.

"He didn't come a moment too soon, for I was about sick enough of the desolation of it, and only hesitating whether I should walk out into the sea and finish up the business that way, or fall back on the green things.

"I sold the bones to a man named Winslow—a dealer near the British Museum, and he says he sold them to old Havers. It seems Havers didn't understand they were extra large, and it was only after his death they attracted attention. They called 'em Æpyornis— what was it?"

"*Æpyornis vastus*," said I. "It's funny, the very thing was mentioned to me by a friend of mine. When they found an Æpyornis with a thigh a yard long they thought they had reached the top of the scale and called him *Æpyornis maximus*. Then some one turned up another thigh bone four feet six or more, and that they called *Æpyornis Titan*. Then your *vastus* was found after old Havers died, in his collection, and then a *vastissimus* turned up."

"Winslow was telling me as much," said the man with the scar. "If they get any more Æpyornises, he reckons some scientific swell will go and burst a blood-vessel. But it was a queer thing to happen to a man; wasn't it—altogether?"

[1] No European is known to have seen a live Æpyornis, with the doubtful exception of MacAndrew, who visited Madagascar in 1745. *H. G. W.*

The Fiend of the Cooperage

Arthur Conan Doyle

It was no easy matter to bring the *Gamecock* up to the island, for the river had swept down so much silt that the banks extended for many miles out into the Atlantic. The coast was hardly to be seen when the first white curl of the breakers warned us of our danger, and from there onwards we made our way very carefully under mainsail and jib, keeping the broken water well to the left, as is indicated on the chart. More than once her bottom touched the sand (we were drawing something under six feet at the time), but we had always way enough and luck enough to carry us through. Finally the water shoaled, very rapidly, but they had sent a canoe from the factory, and the Krooboy pilot brought us within two hundred yards of the island. Here we dropped our anchor, for the gestures of the negro indicated that we could not hope to get any farther. The blue of the sea had changed to the brown of the river, and, even under the shelter of the island, the current was singing and swirling round our bows. The stream appeared to be in spate, for it was over the roots of the palm trees, and everywhere upon its muddy greasy surface we could see logs of wood and debris of all sorts which had been carried down by the flood.

When I had assured myself that we swung securely at our moorings, I thought it best to begin watering at once, for the place looked as if it reeked with fever. The heavy river, the muddy, shining banks, the bright poisonous green of the jungle, the moist steam in the air, they were all so many danger signals to one who could read them. I sent the longboat off, therefore, with two large hogsheads, which should be sufficient to last us until we made St. Paul de Loanda. For my own part I took the dinghy and rowed for the island, for I could see the Union Jack fluttering above the palms to mark the position of Armitage and Wilson's trading station.

When I had cleared the grove, I could see the place, a long, low, whitewashed building, with a deep veranda in front, and an immense pile of palm-oil barrels heaped upon either flank of it. A row of surf boats and canoes lay along the beach, and a single small jetty projected into the river. Two men in white suits with red cummerbunds round their waists were waiting upon the end of it to receive me. One was a large portly fellow with a greyish beard. The other was slender and tall, with a pale pinched face, which was half-concealed by a great mushroom-shaped hat.

"Very glad to see you," said the latter, cordially. "I am Walker, the agent of Armitage and Wilson. Let me introduce Dr. Severall of the same company. It is not often we see a private yacht in these parts."

"She's the *Gamecock*," I explained. "I'm owner and captain— Meldrum is the name."

"Exploring?" he asked.

"I'm a lepidopterist—a butterfly-catcher. I've been doing the west coast from Senegal downwards."

"Good sport?" asked the Doctor, turning a slow yellow-shot eye upon me.

"I have forty cases full. We came in here to water, and also to see what you have in my line."

These introductions and explanations had filled up the time whilst my two Krooboys were making the dinghy fast. Then I walked down the jetty with one of my new acquaintances upon either side, each plying me with questions, for they had seen no white man for months.

"What do we do?" said the Doctor, when I had begun asking questions in my turn. "Our business keeps us pretty busy, and in our leisure time we talk politics."

"Yes, by the special mercy of Providence Severall is a rank Radical, and I am a good stiff Unionist, and we talk Home Rule for two solid hours every evening."

"And drink quinine cocktails," said the Doctor. "We're both pretty well salted now, but our normal temperature was about 103 last year. I shouldn't, as an impartial adviser, recommend you to stay here very long unless you are collecting bacilli as well as butterflies. The mouth of the Ogowai River will never develop into a health resort."

There is nothing finer than the way in which these outlying pickets of civilization distil a grim humour out of their desolate situation, and turn not only a bold, but a laughing face upon the chances which their lives may bring. Everywhere from Sierra Leone downwards I had found the same reeking swamps, the same isolated fever-racked communities, and the same bad jokes. There is something approaching to the divine in that power of man to rise above his conditions and to use his mind for the purpose of mocking at the memories of his body.

"Dinner will be ready in about half an hour, Captain Meldrum," said the Doctor. "Walker has gone in to see about it; he's the housekeeper this week. Meanwhile, if you like, we'll stroll round and I'll show you the sights of the island."

The sun had already sunk beneath the line of palm trees, and the great arch of the heaven above our head was like the inside of a huge shell, shimmering with dainty pinks and delicate iridescence. No one who has not lived in a land where the weight and heat of a napkin become intolerable upon the knees can imagine the blessed relief which the coolness of evening brings along with it. In this sweeter and purer air the Doctor and I walked round the little island, he pointing out the stores, and explaining the routine of his work.

"There's a certain romance about the place," said he, in answer to some remark of mine about the dullness of their lives. "We are living here just upon the edge of the great unknown. Up there," he continued, pointing to the north-east, "Du Chaillu penetrated, and found the home of the gorilla. That is the Gaboon country—the land of the great apes. In this direction," pointing to the south-east, "no one has been very far. The land which is drained by this river is practically unknown to Europeans. Every log which is carried past us by the current has come from an undiscovered country. I've often wished that I was a better botanist when I have seen the singular orchids and curious-looking plants which have been cast up on the eastern end of the island."

The place which the Doctor indicated was a sloping brown beach, freely littered with the flotsam of the stream. At each end was a curved point, like a little natural breakwater, so that a small shallow bay was left between. This was full of floating vegetation, with a single huge splintered tree lying stranded in the middle of it, the current rippling against its high black side.

"These are all from up country," said the Doctor. "They get caught in our little bay, and then when some extra freshet comes they are washed out again and carried out to sea."

"What is the tree?" I asked.

"Oh, some kind of teak, I should imagine, but pretty rotten by the look of it. We get all sorts of big hardwood trees floating past here, to say nothing of the palms. Just come in here, will you?"

He led the way into a long building with an immense quantity of barrel staves and iron hoops littered about in it.

"This is our cooperage," said he. "We have the staves sent out in bundles, and we put them together ourselves. Now, you don't see anything particularly sinister about this building, do you?"

I looked round at the high corrugated iron roof, the white wooden walls, and the earthen floor. In one corner lay a mattress and a blanket.

"I see nothing very alarming," said I.

"And yet there's something out of the common, too", he remarked. "You see that bed? Well, I intend to sleep there tonight. I don't want to buck, but I think it's a bit of a test for nerve."

"Why?"

"Oh, there have been some funny goings on. You were talking about the monotony of our lives, but I assure you that they are sometimes quite as exciting as we wish them to be. You'd better come back to the house now, for after sundown we begin to get the fever-fog up from the marshes. There, you can see it coming across the river."

I looked and saw long tentacles of white vapour writhing out from among the thick green underwood and crawling at us over the broad swirling surface of the brown river. At the same time the air turned suddenly dank and cold.

"There's the dinner gong," said the Doctor. "If this matter interests you I'll tell you about it afterwards."

It did interest me very much, for there was something earnest and subdued in his manner as he stood in the empty cooperage, which appealed very forcibly to my imagination. He was a big, bluff, hearty man, this Doctor, and yet I had detected a curious expression in his eyes as he glanced about him—an expression which I would not describe as one of fear, but rather that of a man who is alert and on his guard.

"By the way," said I, as we returned to the house, "you have shown me the huts of a good many of your native assistants, but I have not seen any of the natives themselves."

"They sleep in the hulk over yonder," the Doctor answered, pointing over to one of the banks.

"Indeed. I should not have thought in that case they would need the huts."

"Oh, they used the huts until quite recently. We've put them on the hulk until they recover their confidence a little. They were all half mad with fright, so we let them go, and nobody sleeps on the island except Walker and myself."

"What frightened them?" I asked.

"Well, that brings us back to the same story. I suppose Walker has no objection to your hearing all about it. I don't know why we should make any secret about it, though it is certainly a pretty bad business."

He made no further allusion to it during the excellent dinner which had been prepared in my honour. It appeared that no sooner had the little white topsail of the *Gamecock* shown round Cape Lopez than these kind fellows had begun to prepare their famous pepper-pot—which is the pungent stew peculiar to the West Coast—and to boil their yams and sweet potatoes. We sat down to as good a native dinner as one could wish, served by a smart Sierra Leone waiting boy. I was just remarking to myself that he at least had not shared in the general flight, when, having laid the dessert and wine upon the table, he raised his hand to his turban.

"Anything else I do, Massa Walker?" he asked.

"No, I think that is all right, Moussa," my host answered. "I am not feeling very well tonight, though, and I should much prefer if you would stay on the island."

I saw a struggle between his fears and his duty upon the swarthy face of the African. His skin had turned of that livid purplish tint which stands for pallor in a negro, and his eyes looked furtively about him.

"No, no, Massa Walker," he cried, at last, "you better come to the hulk with me, sah. Look after you much better in the hulk, sah!"

"That won't do, Moussa. White men don't run away from the posts where they are placed."

Again I saw the passionate struggle in the negro's face, and again his fears prevailed.

"No use, Massa Walker, sah!" he cried. "S'elp me, I can't do it. If it was yesterday or if it was tomorrow, but this is the third night, sah, an' it's more than I can face."

Walker shrugged his shoulders.

"Off with you then!" said he. "When the mail-boat comes you can get back to Sierra Leone, for I'll have no servant who deserts me when I need him most. I suppose this is all mystery to you, or has the Doctor told you, Captain Meldrum?"

"I showed Captain Meldrum the cooperage, but I did not tell him anything," said Dr. Severall. "You're looking bad, Walker," he added, glancing at his companion. "You have a strong touch coming on you."

"Yes, I've had the shivers all day, and now my head is like a cannon-ball. I took ten grains of quinine, and my ears are singing like a kettle. But I want to sleep with you in the cooperage tonight."

"No, no, my dear chap. I won't hear of such a thing. You must get to bed at once, and I am sure Meldrum will excuse you. I shall sleep in the cooperage, and I promise you that I'll be round with your medicine before breakfast."

It was evident that Walker had been struck by one of those sudden and violent attacks of remittent fever which are the curse of the West Coast. His sallow cheeks were flushed and his eyes shining with fever, and suddenly as he sat there he began to croon out a song in the high-pitched voice of delirium.

"Come, come, we must get you to bed, old chap," said the Doctor, and with my aid he led his friend into his bedroom. There we undressed him and presently, after taking a strong sedative, he settled down into a deep slumber.

"He's right for the night," said the Doctor, as we sat down and filled our glasses once more. "Sometimes it is my turn and sometimes his, but, fortunately, we have never been down together. I should have been sorry to be out of it tonight, for I have a little mystery to unravel. I told you that I intended to sleep in the cooperage."

"Yes, you said so."

"When I said sleep I meant watch, for there will be no sleep for me. We've had such a scare here that no native will stay after sundown, and I mean to find out tonight what the cause of it all may be. It has always been the custom for a native watchman to sleep in the cooperage, to prevent the barrel hoops being stolen. Well, six days ago the fellow who slept there disappeared, and we have never seen a trace of him since. It was certainly singular, for no canoe had been taken, and these waters are too full of crocodiles for any man to swim to shore. What became of the fellow, or how he could have left the island is a complete mystery. Walker and I were merely surprised, but the blacks were badly scared and queer Voodoo tales began to get about amongst them. But the real stampede broke out three nights ago, when the new watchman in the cooperage also disappeared."

"What became of him?" I asked.

"Well, we not only don't know, but we can't even give a guess which would fit the facts. The niggers swear there is a fiend in the cooperage who claims a man every third night. They wouldn't stay in the island—nothing could persuade them. Even Moussa, who is a faithful boy enough, would, as you have seen, leave his master in a fever rather than remain for the night. If we are to continue to run this place we must reassure our niggers, and I don't know any better way of doing it than by putting in a night there myself. This is the third night, you see, so I suppose the thing is due, whatever it may be."

"Have you no clue?" I asked. "Was there no mark of violence, no bloodstain, no footprints, nothing to give a hint as to what kind of danger you may have to meet?"

"Absolutely nothing. The man was gone and that was all. Last time it was old Ali, who has been wharf-tender here since the place was started. He was always as steady as a rock, and nothing but foul play would take him from his work."

"Well," said I, "I really don't think that this is a one-man job. Your friend is full of laudanum, and come what might he can be of no assistance to you. You must let me stay and put in a night with you at the cooperage."

"Well, now, that's very good of you, Meldrum," said he heartily, shaking my hand across the table. "It's not a thing that I should have ventured to propose, for it is asking a good deal of a casual visitor, but if you really mean it "

"Certainly I mean it. If you will excuse me a moment, I will hail the *Gamecock* and let them know that they need not expect me."

As we came back from the other end of the little jetty we were both struck by the appearance of the night. A huge blue-black pile of clouds had built itself up upon the landward side, and the wind came from it in little hot pants, which beat upon our faces like the draught from a blast furnace. Under the jetty the river was swirling and hissing, tossing like white spurts of spray over the planking.

"Confound it!" said Dr. Severall. "We are likely to have a flood on the top of all our troubles. That rise in the river means heavy rain up-country, and when it once begins you never know how far it will go. We've had the island nearly covered before now. Well, we'll just go and see that Walker is comfortable, and then if you like we'll settle down in our quarters."

The sick man was sunk in a profound slumber, and we left him with some crushed limes in a glass beside him in case he should

awake with the thirst of fever upon him. Then we made our way
through the unnatural gloom thrown by that menacing cloud. The
river had risen so high that the little bay which I have described at
the end of the island had become almost obliterated through the
submerging of its flanking peninsula. The great raft of driftwood,
with the huge black tree in the middle, was swaying up and down
in the swollen current.

"That's one good thing a flood will do for us," said the Doctor.
"It carries away all the vegetable stuff which is brought down on
to the east end of the island. It came down with the freshet the
other day, and here it will stay until a flood sweeps it out into the
main stream. Well, here's our room, and here are some books and
here is my tobacco pouch, and we must try and put in the night as
best we may."

By the light of our single lantern the great lonely room looked
very gaunt and dreary. Save for the piles of staves and heaps of
hoops there was absolutely nothing in it, with the exception of the
mattress for the Doctor, which had been laid in the corner. We
made a couple of seats and a table out of the staves, and settled
down together for a long vigil. Severall had brought a revolver for
me and was himself armed with a double-barrelled shotgun. We
loaded our weapons and laid them cocked within reach of our
hands. The little circle of light and the black shadows arching over
us were so melancholy that he went off to the house, and returned
with two candles. One side of the cooperage was pierced, however,
by several open windows, and it was only by screening our lights
behind staves that we could prevent them from being extinguished.

The Doctor, who appeared to be a man of iron nerves, had
settled down to a book, but I observed that every now and then he
laid it upon his knee, and took an earnest look all round him. For
my part, although I tried once or twice to read, I found it impossible to concentrate my thoughts upon the book. They would always wander back to this great empty silent room, and to the
sinister mystery which overshadowed it. I racked my brains for
some possible theory which would explain the disappearance of
these two men. There was the black fact that they were gone, and

not the least tittle of evidence as to why or whither. And here we were waiting in the same place—waiting without an idea as to what we were waiting for. I was right in saying that it was not a one-man job. It was trying enough as it was, but no force upon earth would have kept me there without a comrade.

What an endless, tedious night it was! Outside we heard the lapping and gurgling of the great river, and the soughing of the rising wind. Within, save for our breathing, the turning of the Doctor's pages, and the high, shrill ping of an occasional mosquito, there was a heavy silence. Once my heart sprang into my mouth as Severall's book suddenly fell to the ground and he sprang to his feet with his eyes on one of the windows.

"Did you see anything, Meldrum?"

"No, did you?"

"Well, I had a vague sense of movement outside that window." He caught up his gun and approached it. "No, there's nothing to be seen, and yet I could have sworn that something passed slowly across it."

"A palm leaf, perhaps," said I, for the wind was growing stronger every instant.

"Very likely," said he, and settled down to his book again, but his eyes were for ever darting little suspicious glances up at the window. I watched it also, but all was quiet outside.

And then suddenly our thoughts were turned into a new direction by the bursting of the storm. A blinding flash was followed by a clap which shook the building. Again and again came the vivid white glare with thunder at the same instant, like the flash and roar of a monstrous piece of artillery. And then down came the tropical rain, crashing and rattling on the corrugated iron roofing of the cooperage. The big hollow room boomed like a drum. From the darkness arose a strange mixture of noises, a gurgling, splashing, tinkling, bubbling, washing, dripping—every liquid sound that nature can produce from the thrashing and swishing of the rain to the deep steady boom of the river. Hour after hour the uproar grew louder and more sustained.

"My word," said Severall, "we are going to have the father of all the floods this time. Well, here's the dawn coming at last and that is a blessing. We've about exploded the third night superstition, anyhow."

A grey light was stealing through the room, and there was the day upon us in an instant. The rain had eased off, but the coffee-coloured river was roaring past like a waterfall. Its power made me fear for the anchor of the *Gamecock*.

"I must get aboard," said I. "If she drags she'll never be able to beat up the river again."

"The island is as good as a breakwater," the Doctor answered. "I can give you a cup of coffee if you will come up to the house."

I was chilled and miserable, so the suggestion was a welcome one. We left the ill-omened cooperage with its mystery still unsolved, and we splashed our way up to the house.

"There's the spirit lamp," said Severall. "If you would just put a light to it, I will see how Walker feels this morning."

He left me, but was back in an instant with a dreadful face.

"He's gone!" he cried hoarsely.

The words sent a thrill of horror through me. I stood with the lamp in my hand, glaring at him.

"Yes, he's gone!" he repeated. "Come and look!"

I followed him without a word, and the first thing that I saw as I entered the bedroom was Walker himself lying huddled on his bed in the grey flannel sleeping suit in which I had helped to dress him on the night before.

"Not dead, surely!" I gasped.

The Doctor was terribly agitated. His hands were shaking like leaves in the wind.

"He's been dead some hours."

"Was it fever?"

"Fever? Look at his foot!"

I glanced down and a cry of horror burst from my lips. One foot was not merely dislocated, but was turned completely round in a most grotesque contortion.

"Good God!" I cried. "What can have done this?"

Severall had laid his hand upon the dead man's chest.

"Feel here," he whispered.

I placed my hand at the same spot. There was no resistance. The body was absolutely soft and limp. It was like pressing a saw-dust doll.

"The breast-bone is gone," said Severall in the same awed whisper. "He's broken to bits. Thank God that he had the laudanum. You can see by his face that he died in his sleep."

"But who can have done this?"

"I've had about as much as I can stand," said the Doctor, wiping his forehead. "I don't know that I'm a greater coward than my neighbours, but this gets beyond me. If you're going out to the *Gamecock*—"

"Come on!" said I, and off we started. If we did not run it was because each of us wished to keep up the last shadow of his self-respect before the other. It was dangerous in a light canoe on that swollen river, but we never paused to give the matter a thought. He bailing and I paddling we kept her above water, and gained the deck of the yacht. There, with two hundred yards of water between us and this cursed island we felt that we were our own men once more.

"We'll go back in an hour or so," said he. "But we need have a little time to steady ourselves. I wouldn't have had the niggers see me as I was just now for a year's salary."

"I've told the steward to prepare breakfast. Then we shall go back," said I. "But in God's name, Dr. Severall, what do you make of it all?"

"It beats me—beats me clean. I've heard of Voodoo devilry, and I've laughed at it with the others. But that poor old Walker, a decent, God-fearing, nineteenth-century, Primrose-League Englishman should go under like this without a whole bone in his body—it's given me a shake, I won't deny it. But look there, Meldrum, is that hand of yours mad or drunk, or what is it?"

Old Patterson, the oldest man of my crew, and as steady as the Pyramids, had been stationed in the bows with a boat-hook to fend off the drifting logs which came sweeping down with the current. Now he stood with crooked knees, glaring out in front of him, and one forefinger stabbing furiously at the air.

"Look at it!" he yelled. "Look at it!"

And at the same instant we saw it.

A huge black tree-trunk was coming down the river, its broad glistening back just lapped by the water. And in front of it—about three feet in front—arching upwards like the figure-head of a ship, there hung a dreadful face, swaying slowly from side to side. It was flattened, malignant, as large as a small beer-barrel, of a faded fungoid colour, but the neck which supported it was mottled with a dull yellow and black. As it flew past the *Gamecock* in the swirl of the waters I saw two immense coils roll up out of some great hollow in the tree, and the villainous head rose suddenly to the height of eight or ten feet, looking with dull, skin-covered eyes at the yacht. An instant later the tree had shot past us and was plunging with its horrible passenger towards the Atlantic.

"What was it?" I cried.

"It is our fiend of the cooperage," said Dr. Severall, and he had become in an instant the same bluff, self-confident man that he had been before. "Yes, that is the devil who has been haunting our island. It is the great python of the Gaboon."

I thought of the stories which I had heard all down the coast of the monstrous constrictors of the interior, of their periodical appetite, and of the murderous effects of their deadly squeeze. Then it all took shape in my mind. There had been a freshet the week before. It had brought down this huge hollow tree with its hideous occupant. Who knows from what far distant tropical forest it may have come! It had been stranded on the little east bay of the island. The cooperage had been the nearest house. Twice with the return of its appetite it had carried off the watchman. Last night it had doubtless come again, when Severall had thought he saw something move at the window, but our lights had driven it away. It had writhed onwards and had slain poor Walker in his sleep.

"Why did it not carry him off?" I asked.

"The thunder and lightning must have scared the brute away. There's your steward, Meldrum. The sooner we have breakfast and get back to the island the better, or some of those niggers might think that we had been frightened."

The Brazilian Cat

ARTHUR CONAN DOYLE

It is hard luck on a young fellow to have expensive tastes, great expectations, aristocratic connections, but no actual money in his pocket, and no profession by which he may earn any. The fact was that my father, a good, sanguine, easy-going man, had such confidence in the wealth and benevolence of his bachelor elder brother, Lord Southerton, that he took it for granted that I, his only son, would never be called upon to earn a living for myself. He imagined that if there were not a vacancy for me on the great Southerton Estates, at least there would be found some post in that diplomatic service which still remains the special preserve of our privileged classes. He died too early to realize how false his calculations had been. Neither my uncle nor the State took the slightest notice of me, or showed any interest in my career. An occasional brace of pheasants, or basket of hares, was all that ever reached me to remind me that I was heir to Otwell House and one of the richest estates in the country. In the meantime, I found myself a bachelor and man about town, living in a suite of apartments in Grosvenor Mansions, with no occupation save that of pigeon-shooting and polo-playing at Hurlingham. Month by month I realized that it was more and more difficult to get the brokers to renew my bills, or to cash any further post-obits upon an unentailed property. Ruin lay right across my path, and every day I saw it clearer, nearer, and more absolutely unavoidable.

What made me feel my own poverty the more was that, apart from the great wealth of Lord Southerton, all my other relations were fairly well-to-do. The nearest of these was Everard King, my father's nephew and my own first cousin, who had spent an adventurous life in Brazil, and had now returned to this country to settle down on his fortune. We never knew how he made his money, but he appeared to have plenty of it, for he bought the estate of Greylands, near Clipton-on-the-Marsh, in Suffolk. For the first year of his residence in England he took no more notice of me than my miserly uncle; but at last one summer morning, to my very great relief and joy, I received a letter asking me to come down that very day and spend a short visit at Greylands Court. I was expecting a rather long visit to Bankruptcy Court at the time, and this interruption seemed almost providential. If I could only get on terms with this unknown relative of mine, I might pull through yet. For the family credit he could not let me go entirely to the wall. I ordered my valet to pack my valise, and I set off the same evening for Clipton-on-the-Marsh.

After changing at Ipswich, a little local train deposited me at a small, deserted station lying amidst a rolling grassy country, with a sluggish and winding river curving in and out amidst the valleys, between high, silted banks, which showed that we were within reach of the tide. No carriage was awaiting me (I found afterwards that my telegram had been delayed), so I hired a dogcart at the local inn. The driver, an excellent fellow, was full of my relative's praises, and I learned from him that Mr. Everard King was already a name to conjure with in that part of the county. He had entertained the school-children, he had thrown his grounds open to visitors, he had subscribed to charities—in short, his benevolence had been so universal that my driver could only account for it on the supposition that he had parliamentary ambitions.

My attention was drawn away from my driver's panegyric by the appearance of a very beautiful bird which settled on a telegraph-post beside the road. At first I thought that it was a jay, but it was larger, with a brighter plumage. The driver accounted for its presence at once by saying that it belonged to the very man whom we were about to visit. It seems that the acclimatization of foreign creatures was one of his hobbies, and that he had brought with him from Brazil a number of birds and beasts which he was endeavouring to rear in England. When once we had passed the gates of Greylands Park we had ample evidence of this taste of his. Some small spotted deer, a curious wild pig known, I believe, as a peccary, a gorgeously feathered oriole, some sort of armadillo, and a singular lumbering in-toed beast like a very fat badger, were among the creatures which I observed as we drove along the winding avenue.

Mr. Everard King, my unknown cousin, was standing in person upon the steps of his house, for he had seen us in the distance, and guessed that it was I. His appearance was very homely and benevolent, short and stout, forty-five years old, perhaps, with a round, good-humoured face, burned brown with the tropical sun, and shot with a thousand wrinkles. He wore white linen clothes, in true planter style, with a cigar between his lips, and a large Panama hat upon the back of his head. It was such a figure as one associates with a verandahed bungalow, and it looked curiously out of place in front of this broad, stone English mansion, with its solid wings and its Palladio pillars before the doorway.

"My dear!" he cried, glancing over his shoulder; "my dear, here is our guest! Welcome, welcome to Greylands! I am delighted to make your acquaintance, Cousin Marshall, and I take it as a great compliment that you should honour this sleepy little country place with your presence."

Nothing could be more hearty than his manner, and he set me at my ease in an instant. But it needed all his cordiality to atone for the frigidity and even rudeness of his wife, a tall, haggard woman, who came forward at his summons. She was, I believe, of Brazilian extraction, though she spoke excellent English, and I excused her manners on the score of her ignorance of our customs. She did not attempt to conceal, however, either then or afterwards, that I was no very welcome visitor at Greylands Court. Her actual words were, as a rule, courteous, but she was the possessor of a pair of particularly expressive dark eyes, and I read in them very clearly from the first that she heartily wished me back in London once more.

However, my debts were too pressing and my designs upon my wealthy relative were too vital for me to allow them to be upset by the ill-temper of his wife, so I disregarded her coldness and reciprocated the extreme cordiality of his welcome. No pains had been spared by him to make me comfortable. My room was a charming one. He implored me to tell him anything which could add to my happiness. It was on the tip of my tongue to inform him that a blank cheque would materially help towards that end, but I felt that it might be premature in the present state of our acquaintance. The dinner was excellent, and as we sat together afterwards over his Havanas and coffee, which later he told me was specially prepared upon his own plantation, it seemed to me that all my driver's eulogies were justified, and that I had never met a more large-hearted and hospitable man.

But, in spite of his cheery good nature, he was a man with a strong will and a fiery temper of his own. Of this I had an example upon the following morning. The curious aversion which Mrs. Everard King had conceived towards me was so strong, that her manner at breakfast was almost offensive. But her meaning became unmistakable when her husband had quitted the room.

"The best train in the day is at twelve-fifteen," said she.

"But I was not thinking of going today," I answered, frankly—perhaps even defiantly, for I was determined not to be driven out by this woman.

"Oh, if it rests with you—" said she, and stopped with a most insolent expression in her eyes.

"I am sure," I answered, "that Mr. Everard King would tell me if I were outstaying my welcome."

"What's this? What's this?" said a voice, and there he was in the room. He had overheard my last words, and a glance at our faces had told him the rest. In an instant his chubby, cheery face set into an expression of absolute ferocity.

"Might I trouble you to walk outside, Marshall?" said he. (I may mention that my own name is Marshall King.)

He closed the door behind me, and then, for an instant, I heard him talking in a low voice of concentrated passion to his wife. This gross breach of hospitality had evidently hit upon his tenderest point. I am no eavesdropper, so I walked out on to the lawn. Presently I heard a hurried step behind me, and there was the lady, her face pale with excitement, and her eyes red with tears.

"My husband has asked me to apologize to you, Mr. Marshall King," said she, standing with downcast eyes before me.

"Please do not say another word, Mrs. King."

Her dark eyes suddenly blazed out at me.

"You fool!" she hissed, with frantic vehemence, and turning on her heel swept back to the house.

The insult was so outrageous, so insufferable, that I could only stand staring after her in bewilderment. I was still there when my host joined me. He was his cheery, chubby self once more.

"I hope that my wife has apologized for her foolish remarks," said he.

"Oh, yes—yes, certainly!"

He put his hand through my arm and walked with me up and down the lawn.

"You must not take it seriously," said he. "It would grieve me inexpressibly if you curtailed your visit by one hour. The fact is—there is no reason why there should be any concealment between relatives—that my poor dear wife is incredibly jealous. She hates that anyone—male or female—should for an instant come between us. Her ideal is a desert island and an eternal *tête-à-tête*. That gives you the clue to her actions, which are, I confess, upon this particular point, not very far removed from mania. Tell me that you will think no more of it."

"No, no; certainly not."

"Then light this cigar and come round with me and see my little menagerie."

The whole afternoon was occupied by this inspection, which included all the birds, beasts, and even reptiles which he had imported. Some were free, some in cages, a few actually in the house. He spoke with enthusiasm of his successes and his failures, his births and his deaths, and he would cry out in his delight, like a schoolboy, when, as we walked, some gaudy bird would flutter up from the grass, or some curious beast slink into the cover. Finally he led me down a corridor which extended from one wing of the house. At the end of this there was a heavy door with a sliding shutter in it, and beside it there projected from the wall an iron handle attached to a wheel and a drum. A line of stout bars extended across the passage.

"I am about to show you the jewel of my collection," said he. "There is only one other specimen in Europe, now that the Rotterdam cub is dead. It is a Brazilian cat."

"But how does that differ from any other cat?"

"You will soon see that," said he, laughing. "Will you kindly draw that shutter and look through?"

I did so, and found that I was gazing into a large, empty room, with stone flags, and small, barred windows upon the farther wall. In the centre of this room, lying in the middle of a golden patch of sunlight, there was stretched a huge creature, as large as a tiger, but as black and sleek as ebony. It was simply a very enormous and very well-kept black cat, and it cuddled up and basked in that yellow pool of light exactly as a cat would do. It was so graceful, so sinewy, and so gently and smoothly diabolical, that I could not take my eyes from the opening.

"Isn't he splendid?" said my host, enthusiastically.

"Glorious! I never saw such a noble creature."

"Some people call it a black puma, but really it is not a puma at all. That fellow is nearly eleven feet from tail to tip. Four years ago he was a little ball of back fluff, with two yellow eyes staring out of it. He was sold me as a new-born cub up in the wild country at the head-waters of the Rio Negro. They speared his mother to death after she had killed a dozen of them."

"They are ferocious, then?"

"The most absolutely treacherous and bloodthirsty creatures upon earth. You talk about a Brazilian cat to an up-country Indian, and see him get the jumps. They prefer humans to game. This fellow has never tasted living blood yet, but when he does he will be a terror. At present he won't stand anyone but me in his den. Even Baldwin, the groom, dare not go near him. As to me, I am his mother and father in one."

As he spoke he suddenly, to my astonishment, opened the door and slipped in, closing it instantly behind him. At the sound of his voice the huge, lithe creature rose, yawned and rubbed its round, black head affectionately against his side, while he patted and fondled it.

"Now, Tommy, into your cage!" said he.

The monstrous cat walked over to one side of the room and coiled itself up under a grating. Everard King came out, and taking the iron handle which I have mentioned, he began to turn it. As he did so the line of bars in the corridor began to pass through a slot in the wall and closed up the front of this grating, so as to make an effective cage. When it was in position he opened the door once more and invited me into the room, which was heavy with the pungent, musty smell peculiar to the great carnivora.

"That's how we work it," said he. "We give him the run of the room for exercise, and then at night we put him in his cage. You can let him out by turning the handle from the passage, or you can, as you have seen, coop him up in the same way. No, no, you should not do that!"

I had put my hand between the bars to pat the glossy, heaving flank. He pulled it back, with a serious face.

"I assure you that he is not safe. Don't imagine that because I can take liberties with him anyone else can. He is very exclusive in his friends—aren't you, Tommy? Ah, he hears his lunch coming to him! Don't you, boy?"

A step sounded in the stone-flagged passage, and the creature had sprung to his feet, and was pacing up and down the narrow cage, his yellow eyes gleaming, and his scarlet tongue rippling and quivering over the white line of his jagged teeth. A groom entered with a coarse joint upon a tray, and thrust it through the bars to him. He pounced lightly upon it, carried it off to the corner, and there, holding it between his paws, tore and wrenched at it, raising his bloody muzzle every now and then to look at us. It was a malignant and yet fascinating sight.

"You can't wonder that I am fond of him, can you?" said my host, as we left the room, "especially when you consider that I have had the rearing of him. It was no joke bringing him over from the centre of South America; but here he is safe and sound—and, as I have said, far the most perfect specimen in Europe. The people at the Zoo are dying to have him, but I really can't part with him. Now, I think that I have inflicted my hobby upon you long enough, so we cannot do better than follow Tommy's example, and go to our lunch."

My South American relative was so engrossed by his grounds and their curious occupants, that I hardly gave him credit at first for having any interests outside them. That he had some, and pressing ones, was soon borne in upon me by the number of telegrams which he received. They arrived at all hours, and were always opened by him with the utmost eagerness and anxiety upon his face. Sometimes I imagined that it must be the Turf, and sometimes the Stock Exchange, but certainly he had some very urgent business going forwards which was not transacted upon the Downs of Suffolk. During the six days of my visit he had never fewer than three or four telegrams a day, and sometimes as many as seven or eight.

I had occupied these six days so well, that by the end of them I had succeeded in getting upon the most cordial terms with my cousin. Every night we had sat up late in the billiard-room, he telling me the most extraordinary stories of his adventures in America—stories so desperate and reckless, that I could hardly associate them with the brown little, chubby man before me. In return, I ventured upon some of my own reminiscences of London life, which interested him so much, that he vowed he would come up to Grosvenor Mansions and stay with me. He was anxious to see the faster side of city life, and certainly, though I say it, he could not have chosen a more competent guide. It was not until the last day of my visit that I ventured to approach that which was on my mind. I told him frankly about my pecuniary difficulties and my impending ruin, and I asked his advice—though I hoped for something more solid. He listened attentively, puffing hard at his cigar.

"But surely," said he, "you are the heir of our relative, Lord Southerton?"

"I have every reason to believe so, but he would never make me any allowance."

"No, no, I have heard of his miserly ways. My poor Marshall, your position has been a very hard one. By the way, have you heard any news of Lord Southerton's health lately?"

"He has always been in a critical condition ever since my childhood."

"Exactly—a creaking hinge, if ever there was one. Your inheritance may be a long way off. Dear me, how awkwardly situated you are!"

"I had some hopes, sir, that you, knowing all the facts, might be inclined to advance—"

"Don't say another word, my dear boy," he cried, with the utmost cordiality; "we shall talk it over tonight, and I give you my word that whatever is in my power shall be done."

I was not sorry that my visit was drawing to a close, for it is unpleasant to feel that there is one person in the house who eagerly desires your departure. Mrs. King's sallow face and forbidding eyes had become more and more hateful to me. She was no longer actively rude—her fear of her husband prevented her—but she pushed her insane jealousy to the extent of ignoring me, never addressing me, and in every way making my stay at Greylands as uncomfortable as she could. So offensive was her manner during that last day, that I should certainly have left had it not been for that interview with my host in the evening which would, I hoped, retrieve my broken fortunes.

It was very late when it occurred, for my relative, who had been receiving even more telegrams than usual during the day, went off to his study after dinner, and only emerged when the household had retired to bed. I heard him go round locking the doors, as custom was of a night, and finally he joined me in the billiard-room. His stout figure was wrapped in a dressing-gown, and he wore a pair of red Turkish slippers without any heels. Settling down into an arm-chair, he brewed himself a glass of grog, in which I could not help noticing that the whisky considerably predominated over the water.

"My word!" said he, "what a night!"

It was, indeed. The wind was howling and screaming round the house, and the latticed windows rattled and shook as if they were coming in. The glow of the yellow lamps and the flavour of our cigars seemed the brighter and more fragrant for the contrast.

"Now, my boy," said my host, "we have the house and the night to ourselves. Let me have an idea of how your affairs stand, and I will see what can be done to set them in order. I wish to hear every detail."

Thus encouraged, I entered into a long exposition, in which all my tradesmen and creditors from my landlord to my valet, figured in turn. I had notes in my pocket-book, and I marshalled my facts, and gave, I flatter myself, a very businesslike statement of my own unbusinesslike ways and lamentable position. I was depressed, however, to notice that my companion's eyes were vacant and his attention elsewhere. When he did occasionally throw out a remark it was so entirely perfunctory and pointless, that I was sure he had not in the least followed my remarks. Every now and then he roused himself and put on some show of interest, asking me to repeat or to explain more fully, but it was always to sink once more into the same brown study. At last he rose and threw the end of his cigar into the grate.

"I'll tell you what, my boy," said he. "I never had a head for figures, so you will excuse me. You must jot it all down upon paper, and let me have a note of the amount. I'll understand it when I see it in black and white."

The proposal was encouraging. I promised to do so.

"And now it's time we were in bed. By Jove, there's one o'clock striking in the hall."

The tingling of the chiming clock broke through the deep roar of the gale. The wind was sweeping past with the rush of a great river.

"I must see my cat before I go to bed," said my host. "A high wind excites him. Will you come?"

"Certainly," said I.

"Then tread softly and don't speak, for everyone is asleep."

We passed quietly down the lamp-lit Persian-rugged hall, and through the door at the farther end. All was dark in the stone corridor, but a stable lantern hung on a hook, and my host took it down and lit it. There was no grating visible in the passage, so I knew that the beast was in its cage.

"Come in!" said my relative, and opened the door.

A deep growling as we entered showed that the storm had really excited the creature. In the flickering light of the lantern, we saw it, a huge black mass coiled in the corner of its den and throwing a squat, uncouth shadow upon the whitewashed wall. Its tail switched angrily among the straw.

"Poor Tommy is not in the best of tempers," said Everard King, holding up the lantern and looking in at him. "What a black devil he looks, doesn't he? I must give him a little supper to put him in a better humour. Would you mind holding the lantern for a moment?"

I took it from his hand and he stepped to the door.

"His larder is just outside here," said he. "You will excuse me for an instant won't you?" He passed out, and the door shut with a sharp metallic click behind him.

That hard crisp sound made my heart stand still. A sudden wave of terror passed over me. A vague perception of some monstrous treachery turned me cold. I sprang to the door, but there was no handle upon the inner side.

"Here!" I cried. "Let me out!"

"All right! Don't make a row!" said my host from the passage. "You've got the light all right."

"Yes, but I don't care about being locked in alone like this."

"Don't you?" I heard his hearty, chuckling laugh. "You won't be alone long."

"Let me out, sir!" I repeated angrily. "I tell you I don't allow practical jokes of this sort."

"Practical is the word," said he, with another hateful chuckle. And then suddenly I heard, amidst the roar of the storm, the creak and whine of the winch-handle turning and the rattle of the grating as it passed through the slot. Great God, he was letting loose the Brazilian cat!

In the light of the lantern I saw the bars sliding slowly before me. Already there was an opening a foot wide at the farther end. With a scream I seized the last bar with my hands and pulled with the strength of a madman. I *was* a madman with rage and horror. For a minute or more I held the thing motionless. I knew that he was straining with all his force upon the handle, and that the leverage was sure to overcome me. I gave inch by inch, my feet sliding along the stones, and all the time I begged and prayed this inhuman monster to save me from this horrible death. I conjured him by his kinship. I reminded him that I was his guest; I begged to know what harm I had ever done him. His only answers were the tugs and jerks upon the handle, each of which, in spite of all my struggles, pulled another bar through the opening. Clinging and clutching, I was dragged across the whole front of the cage, until at last, with aching wrists and lacerated fingers, I gave up the hopeless struggle. The grating clanged back as I released it, and an instant later I heard the shuffle of the Turkish slippers in the passage, and the slam of the distant door. Then everything was silent.

The creature had never moved during this time. He lay still in the corner, and his tail had ceased switching. This apparition of a man adhering to his bars and dragged screaming across him had apparently filled him with amazement. I saw his great eyes staring steadily at me. I had dropped the lantern when I seized the bars, but it still burned upon the floor, and I made a movement to grasp it, with some idea that its light might protect me. But the instant I moved, the beast gave a deep and menacing growl. I stopped and stood still, quivering with fear in every limb. The cat (if one may call so fearful a creature by so homely a name) was not more than ten feet from me. The eyes glimmered like two disks of phosphorus in the darkness. They appalled and yet fascinated me. I could not take my own eyes from them. Nature plays strange tricks with us at such moments of intensity, and those glimmering lights waxed and waned with a steady rise and fall. Sometimes they seemed to be tiny points of extreme brilliancy—little electric sparks in the black obscurity—then they would widen and widen until all that corner of the room was filled with their shifting and sinister light. And then suddenly they went out altogether.

The beast had closed its eyes. I do not know whether there may be any truth in the old idea of the dominance of the human gaze, or whether the huge cat was simply drowsy, but the fact remains that, far from showing any symptom of attacking me, it simply rested its sleek, black head upon its huge forepaws and seemed to sleep. I stood, fearing to move lest I should rouse it into malignant life once more. But at least I was able to think clearly now that the baleful eyes were off me. Here I was shut up for the night with the ferocious beast. My own instincts, to say nothing of the words of the plausible villain who laid this trap for me, warned me that the animal was as savage as its master. How could I stave it off until morning? The door was hopeless, and so were the narrow, barred windows. There was no shelter anywhere in the bare, stone- flagged room. To cry for assistance was absurd. I knew that this den was an outhouse, and that the corridor which connected it with the house was at least a hundred feet long. Besides, with the gale thundering outside, my cries were not likely to be heard. I had only my own courage and my own wits to trust to.

And then, with a fresh wave of horror, my eyes fell upon the lantern. The candle had burned low, and was already beginning to gutter. In ten minutes it would be out. I had only ten minutes then in which to do something, for I felt that if I were once left in the dark with that fearful beast I should be incapable of action. The very thought of it paralysed me. I cast my despairing eyes round this chamber of death, and they rested upon one spot which seemed to promise I will not say safety, but less immediate and imminent danger than the open floor.

I have said that the cage had a top as well as a front, and this top was left standing when the front was wound through the slot in the wall. It consisted of bars at a few inches' interval, with stout wire netting between, and it rested upon a strong stanchion at each end. It stood now as a great barred canopy over the crouching figure in the corner. The space between this iron shelf and the roof may have been from two or three feet. If I could only get up there, squeezed in between bars and ceiling, I should have only one vulnerable side. I should be safe from below, from behind, and from each side. Only on the open face of it could I be attacked. There, it is true, I had no protection whatever; but at least, I should be out of the brute's path when he began to pace about his den. He would have to come out of his way to reach me. It was now or never, for if once the light were out it would be impossible. With a gulp in my throat I sprang up, seized the iron edge of the top, and swung myself panting on to it. I writhed in face downwards, and found myself looking straight into the terrible eyes and yawning jaws of the cat. Its fetid breath came up into my face like the steam from some foul pot.

It appeared, however, to be rather curious than angry. With a sleek ripple of its long, black back it rose, stretched itself, and then rearing itself on its hind legs, with one forepaw against the wall, it raised the other, and drew its claws across the wire meshes beneath me. One sharp, white hook tore through my trousers—for I may mention that I was still in evening dress—and dug a furrow in my knee. It was not meant as an attack, but rather as an experiment, for upon my giving a sharp cry of pain he dropped down again, and springing lightly into the room, he began walking swiftly round it, looking up every now and again in my direction. For my part I shuffled backwards until I lay with my back against the wall, screwing myself into the smallest space possible. The farther I got the more difficult it was for him to attack me.

He seemed more excited now that he had begun to move about, and he ran swiftly and noiselessly round and round the den, passing continually underneath the iron couch upon which I lay. It was wonderful to see so great a bulk passing like a shadow, with hardly the softest thudding of velvety pads. The candle was burning low—so low that I could hardly see the creature. And then, with a last flare and splutter it went out altogether. I was alone with the cat in the dark!

It helps one to face a danger when one knows that one has done all that possibly can be done. There is nothing for it then but to quietly await the result. In this case, there was no chance of safety anywhere except the precise spot where I was. I stretched myself out, therefore, and lay silently, almost breathlessly, hoping that the beast might forget my presence if I did nothing to remind him. I reckoned that it must already be two o'clock. At four it would be full dawn. I had not more than two hours to wait for daylight.

Outside, the storm was still raging, and the rain lashed continually against the little windows. Inside, the poisonous and fetid air was overpowering. I could neither hear nor see the cat. I tried to think about other things—but only one had power enough to draw my mind from my terrible position. That was the contemplation of my cousin's villainy, his unparalleled hypocrisy, his malignant hatred of me. Beneath that cheerful face there lurked the spirit of a mediaeval assassin. And as I thought of it I saw more clearly how cunningly the thing had been arranged. He had apparently gone to bed with the others. No doubt he had his witness to prove it. Then, unknown to them, he had slipped down, had lured me into his den and abandoned me. His story would be so simple. He had left me to finish my cigar in the billiard-room. I had gone down on my own account to have a last look at the cat. I had entered the room without observing that the cage was opened, and I had been caught. How could such a crime be brought home to him? Suspicion, perhaps—but proof, never!

How slowly those dreadful two hours went by! Once I heard a low, rasping sound, which I took to be the creature licking its own fur. Several times those greenish eyes gleamed at me through the darkness, but never in a fixed stare, and my hopes grew stronger that my presence had been forgotten or ignored. At last the least faint glimmer of light came through the windows—I first dimly saw them as two grey squares upon the black wall, then grey turned to white, and I could see my terrible companion once more. And he, alas, could see me!

It was evident to me at once that he was in a much more dangerous and aggressive mood than when I had seen him last. The cold of the morning had irritated him, and he was hungry as well. With a continual growl he paced swiftly up and down the side of the room which was farthest from my refuge, his whiskers bristling angrily, and his tail switching and lashing. As he turned at the corners his savage eyes always looked upwards at me with a dreadful menace. I knew then that he meant to kill me. Yet I found myself even at that moment admiring the sinuous grace of the devilish thing, its long, undulating, rippling movements, the gloss of its beautiful flanks, the vivid, palpitating scarlet of the glistening tongue which hung from the jet-black muzzle. And all the time that deep, threatening growl was rising and rising in an unbroken crescendo. I knew that the crisis was at hand.

It was a miserable hour to meet such a death—so cold, so comfortless, shivering in my light dress clothes upon this gridiron of torment upon which I was stretched. I tried to brace myself to it, to raise my soul above it, and at the same time, with the lucidity which comes to a perfectly desperate man, I cast round for some possible means of escape. One thing was clear to me. If that front of the cage was only back in its position once more, I could find a sure refuge behind it. Could I possibly pull it back? I hardly dared to move for fear of bringing the creature upon me. Slowly, very slowly, I put my hand forward until it grasped the edge of the front, the final bar which protruded through the wall. To my surprise it came quite easily to my jerk. Of course the difficulty of drawing it out arose from the fact that I was clinging to it. I pulled again, and three inches of it came through. It ran apparently on wheels. I pulled again . . . and then the cat sprang!

It was so quick, so sudden, that I never saw it happen. I simply heard the savage snarl, and in an instant afterwards the blazing yellow eyes, the flattened black head with its red tongue and flashing teeth, were within reach of me. The impact of the creature shook the bars upon which I lay, until I thought (as far as I could think of anything at such a moment) that they were coming down. The cat swayed there for an instant, the head and front paws quite close to me, the hind paws clawing to find a grip upon the edge of the grating. I heard the claws rasping as they clung to the wire-netting, and the breath of the beast made me sick. But its bound had been miscalculated. It could not retain its position. Slowly, grinning with rage, and scratching madly at the bars, it swung backwards and dropped heavily upon the floor. With a growl it instantly faced round to me and crouched for another spring.

I knew that the next few moments would decide my fate. The creature had learned by experience. It would not miscalculate again. I must act promptly, fearlessly, if I were to have a chance for life. In an instant I had formed my plan. Pulling off my dress-coat, I threw it down over the head of the beast. At the same moment I dropped over the edge, seized the end of the front grating, and pulled it frantically out of the wall.

It came more easily than I could have expected. I rushed across the room, bearing it with me; but, as I rushed, the accident of my position put me upon the outer side. Had it been the other way, I might have come off scathless. As it was, there was a moment's pause as I stopped it and tried to pass in through the opening which I had left. That moment was enough to give time to the creature to toss off the coat with which I had blinded him and to spring upon me. I hurled myself through the gap and pulled the rails to behind me, but he seized my leg before I could entirely withdraw it. One stroke of that huge paw tore off my calf as a shaving of wood curls off before a plane. The next moment, bleeding and fainting, I was lying among the foul straw with a line of friendly bars between me and the creature which ramped so frantically against them.

Too wounded to move, and too faint to be conscious of fear, I could only lie, more dead than alive, and watch it. It pressed its broad, black chest against the bars and angled for me with its crooked paws as I have seen a kitten do before a mouse-trap. It ripped my clothes, but, stretch as it would, it could not quite reach me. I have heard of the curious numbing effect produced by wounds from the great carnivora, and now I was destined to experience it, for I had lost all sense of personality, and was as interested in the cat's failure or success as if it were some game which I was watching. And then gradually my mind drifted away into strange vague dreams, always with that black face and red tongue coming back into them, and so I lost myself in the nirvana of delirium, the blessed relief of those who are too sorely tried.

Tracing the course of events afterwards, I conclude that I must have been insensible for about two hours. What roused me to consciousness once more was that sharp metallic click which had been the precursor of my terrible experience. It was the shooting back of the spring lock. Then, before my senses were clear enough to entirely apprehend what they saw, I was aware of the round, benevolent face of my cousin peering in through the open door. What he saw evidently amazed him. There was the cat crouching on the floor. I was stretched upon my back in my shirt-sleeves within the cage, my trousers torn to ribbons and a great pool of blood all round me. I can see his amazed face now, with the morning sunlight upon it. He peered at me, and peered again. Then he closed the door behind him, and advanced to the cage to see if I were really dead.

I cannot undertake to say what happened. I was not in a fit state to witness or to chronicle such events. I can only say that I was suddenly conscious that his face was away from me—that he was looking towards the animal.

"Good old Tommy!" he cried. "Good old Tommy!"

Then he came near the bars, with his back still towards me.

"Down, you stupid beast!" he roared. "Down, sir! Don't you know your master?"

Suddenly even in my bemuddled brain a remembrance came of those words of his when he had said that the taste of blood would turn the cat into a fiend. My blood had done it, but he was to pay the price.

"Get away!" he screamed. "Get away, you devil! Baldwin! Baldwin! Oh, my God!"

And then I heard him fall, and rise, and fall again, with a sound like the ripping of sacking. His screams grew fainter until they were lost in the worrying snarl. And then, after I thought that he was dead, I saw, as in a nightmare, a blinded, tattered, blood-soaked figure running wildly round the room—and that was the last glimpse which I had of him before I fainted once again.

I was many months in my recovery—in fact, I cannot say that I have ever recovered, for to the end of my days I shall carry a stick as a sign of my night with the Brazilian cat. Baldwin, the groom, and the other servants could not tell what had occurred, when, drawn by the death-cries of their master, they found me behind the bars, and his remains—or what they afterwards discovered to be his remains—in the clutch of the creature which he had reared. They stalled him off with hot irons, and afterwards shot him through the loophole of the door before they could finally extricate me. I was carried to my bedroom, and there, under the roof of my would-be murderer, I remained between life and death for several weeks. They had sent for a surgeon from Clipton and a nurse from London, and in a month I was able to be carried to the station, and so conveyed back once more to Grosvenor Mansions.

I have one remembrance of that illness, which might have been part of the ever-changing panorama conjured up by a delirious brain were it not so definitely fixed in my memory. One night, when the nurse was absent, the door of my chamber opened, and a tall woman in blackest mourning slipped into the room. She came across to me, and as she bent her sallow face I saw by the faint gleam of the night-light that it was the Brazilian woman whom my cousin had married. She stared intently into my face, and her expression was more kindly than I had ever seen it.

"Are you conscious?" she asked.

I feebly nodded—for I was still very weak.

"Well; then, I only wished to say to you that you have yourself to blame. Did I not do all I could for you? From the beginning I tried to drive you from the house. By every means, short of betraying my husband, I tried to save you from him. I knew that he had a reason for bringing you here. I knew that he would never let you get away again. No one knew him as I knew him, who had suffered from him so often. I did not dare to tell you all this. He would have killed me. But I did my best for you. As things have turned out, you have been the best friend that I have ever had. You have set me free, and I fancied that nothing but death would do that. I am sorry if you are hurt, but I cannot reproach myself. I told you that you were a fool—and a fool you have been." She crept out of the room, the bitter, singular woman, and I was never destined to see her again. With what remained from her husband's property she went back to her native land, and I have heard that she afterwards took the veil at Pernambuco.

It was not until I had been back in London for some time that the doctors pronounced me to be well enough to do business. It was not a very welcome permission to me, for I feared that it would be the signal for an inrush of creditors; but it was Summers, my lawyer, who first took advantage of it.

"I am very glad to see that your lordship is so much better," said he. "I have been waiting a long time to offer my congratulations."

"What do you mean, Summers? This is no time for joking."

"I mean what I say," he answered. "You have been Lord Southerton for the last six weeks, but we feared that it would retard your recovery if you were to learn it."

Lord Southerton! One of the richest peers in England! I could not believe my ears. And then suddenly I thought of the time which had elapsed, and how it coincided with my injuries.

"Then Lord Southerton must have died about the same time that I was hurt?"

"His death occurred upon that very day." Summers looked hard at me as I spoke, and I am convinced—for he was a very shrewd fellow—that he had guessed the true state of the case. He paused for a moment as if awaiting a confidence from me, but I could not see what was to be gained by exposing such a family scandal.

"Yes, a very curious coincidence," he continued, with the same knowing look. "Of course, you are aware that your cousin Everard King was the next heir to the estates. Now, if it had been you instead of him who had been torn to pieces by this tiger, or whatever it was, then of course he would have been Lord Southerton at the present moment."

"No doubt," said I.

"And he took such an interest in it," said Summers. "I happen to know that the late Lord Southerton's valet was in his pay, and that he used to have telegrams from him every few hours to tell him how he was getting on. That would be about the time when you were down there. Was it not strange that he should wish to be so well informed, since he knew that he was not the direct heir?"

"Very strange," said I. "And now, Summers, if you will bring me my bills and a new cheque-book, we will begin to get things into order."

The Killing of the Mammoth

H. TUKEMAN

Mr. Conradi's sudden death is still fresh in the public mind, and a letter that I have before me from that generous, but eccentric, millionaire will explain my position, and the *raison d'être* of the following pages, in the fewest words. The letter was evidently dictated from his death-bed.

> To H. Tukeman, Esq.,
>   Wadington Hall, Kent.
> *Dear Sir*: In the event of my death, I release you fully from your promise of secrecy in regard to the killing of the mammoth, and I express the hope that you will make public the facts relating to the same. I have always refused to make any statement as to how or where I obtained this specimen, allowing the public to draw whatever inference it pleased but now that its existence is fully known to the scientific world I see that I have done you some injustice, merely to gratify a whim of my own. The price I paid you included this gratification—as set forth in our contract—but I am satisfied to go down to posterity as the donor to my country of the most remarkable specimen of fauna in the world.
>   Thanking you for your faithful adherence to the spirit and letter of our contract, I am,
>   Yours faithfully,
>   Horace P. Conradi.

It was I then, Henry Tukeman, who secured the specimen of the "Conradi Mammoth," as it has been called, now in the Smithsonian museum, Washington, U. S. A., pictures of which monopolized the papers and magazines in the summer of last year, and over which the scientists of both continents are still quarreling. Mr. Conradi's offer to me was of such magnitude (at least three times what I could have expected to get from any other source) that I, a poor man, found myself unable to refuse it. Many people will, undoubtedly, call me unpatriotic in thus allowing a foreign country to obtain this wonderful specimen, and to this charge I can only reply that the re-purchase of Wadington Hall, with its noble deer park and broad acres, has been the dream of my life. For, till my father broke the entail and sold the estate, it had been handed down from father to son since the time of William the First, as the date and the Latin inscription over the old stable doorway testify.

In 1890, I journeyed, by way of St. Michaels and the Yukon River, to Alaska. The Klondike had not then been discovered, and the Alaska Commercial Company's steamer failing to get further than Fort Yukon, owing to the lateness of the season, it was at this point I found myself when winter set in. A small tribe of Indians live at Fort Yukon. A clerk at the trading-post, a private trader, and a missionary and his wife were the only whites there in 1890, except when a rare visitor called from Circle City, a mining camp eighty miles up the Yukon River. The fort, however, had its traditions, and I listened later to many an interesting yarn from the old tribesmen, who told in broken *patois* of the doings of the "Company" fifty years ago, when the Hudson Bay Company represented civilization from this far northwestern limit of their fur trade on the Pacific Slope, and from the Arctic Circle, to the Atlantic coast of stormy Labrador.

The Hudson Bay Company abandoned Fort Yukon many years ago, but the statement that I was a "Hudson Bay man" (an unpaid account was my mental justification), and the fact that I had had some years' experience with northern Indians, enabled me soon to become intimate with the tribe, though at the expense of losing the society of the white residents of the fort.

After I had decided to winter at Fort Yukon, I occupied a roomy, vacant cabin. One night I had opened some old "Graphics" for the benefit of "Joe"—otherwise "Na-thu-joyi-a"—an ancient head-man in the tribe. I was explaining the habits of the various animals portrayed in a series of African hunting scenes. Turning the page, we came to the picture of an elephant, whereupon old Joe became very excited, and finally explained to me, with some reluctance, that he had seen one of these animals "up there," indicating the north with his hand. Nor could any denial of mine that any such animals existed on this continent shake him. To humor the old fellow, I asked him to tell me the tale, which he did after much persuasion; and I repeat it here, though for my readers' sake I omit the broken *patois*.

"Once, many summers ago, me an' Soon-thai, we go up the Porcupine River—Soon-thai is my son; he is dead; now. By an' by we leave the river, an' go up a little river many days, to the mountain. But the mountain is too steep an' very high, an' we cannot climb up it. We go back a little way, an' we shoot a moose at the mouth of a little gully. Soon-thai, he goes off, an' he finds the gully ends in a little cliff, an' he climbs up it, an' finds a cave. He is brave, Soon-thai—he goes in the cave, an' at the end is a small hole, an' Soon-thai looks through it, an' sees an easy way to climb up the mountain. There is a creek in the gully, which runs in the ground near the cave, but the water is bad.

"I go back, an' I blaze a big tree at the canoe, like this" —crossing his fingers— "where the gully is, for it is hard to see from the river. By an' by we take some meat, an' we go through the cave, an' it is full of big bones, bigger than my body, an' I am afraid; but we go through the little hole into the sunlight, an' I have courage, an' we climb to the top of the mountain.

"Beyond we see a big valley, an' lakes an' trees there, an' far away, on the other side of the valley, we see the mountains, an' beyond them, very far off, high mountains, with the snow on them which never goes away.

"Soon-thai is brave, plenty brave, an' he says, 'We shoot plenty beaver in the valley, eh?' I say, 'No, that is the devil's country,' an' I tell him it is the country called in Indian Tee-Kai-Koa (the devil's footprint). Then Soon-thai, he is a little afraid, but by an' by he says, 'Come, my father, we will not stay long; in two days we will shoot plenty beaver, an' then we will run back.'

"So we go down the mountain, an' we find lakes with plenty of beaver an' ducks an' geese, an' it is the month of the first salmon, an' the geese cannot fly, so we get plenty; but we see no moose or caribou sign in the valley. By an' by, after two days, we make a raft, an' cross a long lake, like a river, an' next day we see Tee-Kai-Koa!"

The old man paused, and stiffened in his seat; I sat silent and motionless, waiting.

"At sunrise we go in the woods to hunt. By an' by Soon-thai comes to me—he is a little way off on one side—an' he whispers, 'Look!' An' I come where he says, an' I see that sign, an' my knees are weak, an' shake. The ground is not hard there, an' I see a sign like this"—he drew a circle on the door— "an' deep in the ground as this"—he placed a finger on his arm, half-way from the finger-tip to the elbow. "An' I can lay my gun in the footmark, except for this much"—he indicated a finger length. "But Soon-thai, he is brave; he says, 'I will see this devil, an' if he is no bigger than a very big bear, I will shoot him from a tree, perhaps.' But I—I am afraid, yet I follow Soon-thai as if I slept. Oh, he was brave, my son—very brave!

"Presently we hear a splashing in a lake which is beyond some willows; an' there are no trees there; but we creep in very softly, an' we come to the reeds, an' wade through them to the edge, up to our knees in the water. He is there, the Tee-Kai-Koa, standing on the other side of the little lake."

The old man rose, and pointed before him. A strange glitter was in his eye, and the beads of perspiration stood out on his forehead. I could not doubt for a moment that he was describing what he had really seen. "He is throwing water over himself with his long nose, an' his two teeth stand out before his head for ten gun-lengths, turned up, an' shining like a swan's wing in the sunlight.

His hair is black an' long, an' hangs down his sides like driftweed from the tree branches after the floods, an' this cabin beside him would be as a two-weeks bear cub beside its mother. We do not speak, Soon-thai an' I, but we look, an' look; an' the water he throws over his back runs in little rivers down his sides. Presently he lies down in the water, an' the waves come through the reeds up to our armpits, so great is the splash. Then he gets up an' shakes himself, an' all is a mist like a rain storm round him.

"Suddenly Soon-thai throws up his gun, an' before I can stop him, he fires—*boom!*—at Tee-Kai-Koa. Ah, the noise! It is a cry like a thousand thousand geese, only shriller an' louder, an' it fills the valley till it reaches to the mountains, an' all the world seems to have nothing in it but that angry cry. As the gunsmoke rises above the reeds, Tee-Kai-Koa sees it, an' begins to run through the water towards it, an' the noise of his splashing is as of all the wild fowl in the world rising from a calm lake at sunset.

"We turn an' run, Soon-thai an' I. We run through the reeds to the willows, an' to the timber. But once I turn, an' I can see plainly a streak of red blood on the long nose of Tee-Kai-Koa, as he throws it in the air an' fills the valley with his cry. The smoke of the gun has blown across the little lake between us, an' he turns to it, an' stops, an' whistles like a steamboat when the white steam is escaping.

"We run through the trees away from our camp, for it is towards it Tee-Kai-Koa has gone, chasing the smoke, an' after we have run a long distance, we rest an' listen. But again we hear the great cry of Tee-Kai-Koa as he seeks us, an' we have new strength in our legs to run on an' on, till the sun has gone down an' come up again to where it stood when Soon-thai fired his gun. We have no axe, nothing but our guns; but the fear of that which is behind us makes us strong to travel on without sleep or food."

The old Indian sat down and wiped his hand over his forehead, and for fully ten minutes no word was spoken,—he perhaps thinking of his dead son, I racking my brains to remember what my school edition of Cuvier said about mammoths, for I had confirmed a wild idea that had flashed through my brain when the elephant's picture was first noticed. Presently the old man rose, and stepped to the door of the cabin. I made a motion to him to stay, but he shook his head. "I am old an' tired," he said simply; "an' to talk of Soon-thai, my son, makes me weak like a woman. Do not seek Tee-Kai-Koa, white man, lest you have no tale to tell us as I have told you." And he stepped out into the clear, frosty night, leaving me to wonder how he had divined my thoughts so accurately.

Later I got Joe's account of his return from the land of Tee-Kai-Koa. He had crossed the first range of mountains on the side of the valley opposite that on which he had entered it, and found on the further side of the mountains high, precipitous cliffs, which he had the greatest difficulty in descending. Making a boat out of a moose-skin, he had gone "many days" down a stream which flowed into the Chandelar, a river entering the Yukon about one hundred miles below the mouth of the Porcupine. While in the valley they had seen the huge footprints of the mammoth, but never more than those of one animal, and always of the same size, so that it seemed as if this prehistoric giant must be the last of his race alive there.

In the tribe of Indians wintering at Fort Yukon was an active, intelligent young fellow named Paul, who spoke English well, and was always in demand during the summer months as pilot on the steamers of the A. C. Company. Paul had a strain of white blood in his veins, derived, doubtless, from some hardy Scotchman of the old company, and I found, after becoming intimate with him, that he had as much curiosity as I had about Tee-Kai-Koa and a profound contempt for the superstition of its being a "devil."

When I told Paul of some elephant-shooting experiences of mine in Africa in the '70's, he proposed, in the most matter-of-fact way, that we should go off together during the coming summer, and bag the mammoth, if he really was there. He was doubly eager when I told him of the vast fortune awaiting any man who could get this absolutely unique specimen of supposedly extinct fauna to the hands of taxidermists in civilization. I had nothing heavier than a couple of Lee-Metfords, a weapon which I had never tried, even as an elephant rifle, and which seemed to be still less suitable as a mammoth slayer. But I had plenty of solid nickel bullets, and I was satisfied these would penetrate the hide or massive skull. It was therefore merely a question of quantity.

By spring we had all our plans completed for the journey, and I had a rough idea formulated as to how I should hunt the mammoth, and (what was equally difficult) preserve, when we had killed him, his vast hide and bones. Paul and I both swore secrecy: he because he did not wish the tribe to know, I for commercial reasons; and giving out that I had had a letter from the Hudson Bay Company calling me to the Mackenzie River district, we bid good-by to Fort Yukon on a fine morning early in July, and prepared to pole our way up the Porcupine River in a long, narrow poling-boat which we had built for the purpose.

I shook old Joe cordially by the hand, and promised to avoid the "devil's footprint" country, though I think the old fellow had a vague suspicion of what I had in mind, roused by my many questions throughout the winter. A round of presents to the Indians (not forgetting an extra one for Joe's pretty daughter) made my departure more easy, for I had become excellent friends with the tribe, and they were genuinely sorry to lose me. I held out no likelihood of returning for several summers, while Paul had stated that he would stay with me till I went "outside" once more to the "Grand Pays" and civilization. He had no kith or kin to worry about, and the handsome scamp's attentions to the girls were too impartial to call for any particular and individual congratulation.

On the nineteenth day after leaving Fort Yukon, we arrived at the mouth of the "little river" described by Joe, easily identified by a high, sandy bank on the right hand. The high water in the Porcupine had delayed us, and after the second day on the "little river" we were unable, even with the utmost exertion, to make more than six or seven miles a day. Sometimes twice or thrice a day we would unload, to drag our boat over shallows or around log-jams, and on one occasion we had to portage everything a mile overland to avoid a canon. We had cut our outfit down to the simplest necessaries, but I had secured from the steamer 500 feet of stout rope, three double-blocks and tackle, augers, a whipsaw, and a few other tools; and these, with our cooking utensils, winter clothing, and a few supplies, necessitated many weary journeys on the portages. And then the mosquitoes! I have had some experience of them, but I have never seen them so bad as they were on the upper reaches of the river during the month of July.

On August 2d—my birthday, I recollected—we came to the blazed tree. There we cached our stuff, pushing on to look out our route and have a peep at the "devil's country." The blaze was deeply cut, and showed plainly, though it was evidently many years old. The dug-out canoe had been washed away by a freshet. The gully was apparently nothing but a depression in the mountain-side, and it terminated in an abrupt declivity. This cliff extended, as far as we could see, to the head of the river. Soon-thai's object in climbing it had probably been to inspect some massive bones which projected from a ledge about fifty feet up. Above this rose an unscalable ascent of rocks and earth. Climbing to the ledge, we found the cave, or tunnel, as it more properly was. It was about 200 feet long, and wide enough for three men to walk abreast. The entire length was literally paved with gigantic mammoth bones, which made even the matter-of-fact Paul exclaim. I experimented on a skull, and also on a piece of spinal vertebræ, and was glad to find that the solid bullet of the .303 drilled through them with ease.

The end of the tunnel was blocked by a recent fall of rock and rubbish, which it took us some hours to remove. Had we not known there was an exit, we should have turned back, believing this to be a cave. Having effected a passage through, we found the "gully" to be in reality a considerable creek, which had evidently been blocked by a rock slide or an eruption. The water sank into the ground near the exit from the tunnel. I did not notice where the creek joined the river we had just left. Three hours' easy climbing took us to the summit of the divide from the tunnel.

I shall not easily forget the first view we had of the Tee-Kai-Koa River and Valley, as they will now be named on the maps. The sun was low in the sky when we won the summit of the divide, and a high range of snow-clad mountains to the northeast stood out so distinctly that they seemed to be but a few miles away. They were very rugged and precipitous, and dark patches of perpendicular cliffs assumed fantastic shapes against the intensely white background. As I knew the Noyukuk River must rise in these ranges, I estimated the distance to be about 200 miles. Below us extended a valley fifty miles wide, bounded by a range of low mountains which hardly ran above the timber line. This valley ran southward for about seventy miles, when the mountains on either side contracted sharply. I was at once satisfied that Joe's "long lake" was in reality a sluggish river, and I had no doubt I should find a deep cañon where the valley ended. Looking north, the valley showed no sign of narrowing, but turned to the northeast behind the opposite mountain range. From one end of it to the other, as far as eye could see, shining patches of water showed here and there, and the pine trees appeared to be larger than I should have expected to find them in these latitudes. The descent to the valley was on an easy incline.

I will not detail the weary work of the portage from the "little river." We had to use our blocks and tackle to land our stuff at the tunnel entrance. We had difficulty in obtaining water in our camp on the creek, the creek water being undrinkable from the presence in it of copper ore. And there were delays and troubles without number. Finally, however, we had everything at the summit, and a few days later, on the banks of the Tee-Kai-Koa River. As to Paul, I have never met his equal in any of my travels. He was strong, active, untiring, cheerful, and full of a native ingenuity which overcame obstacles as soon as they appeared, while his courage, and his quiet and absolute confidence in our ultimate success, acted as a nerve tonic to me when I found myself speculating whether we had too heavy an undertaking on hand.

We rafted across the Tee-Kai-Koa, the current being hardly perceptible, and camped on a small island about one hundred yards from the main bank. My plan of campaign was based largely on an assumption which, on reflection, I am bound to admit had very little foundation. Joe had told me how the mammoth had run after the gun smoke, and assuming the huge beast to be fearless—what living thing could inspire it with fear? I speculated—I decided to make a fire within and beneath a pile of green logs, the largest I could find, and then from the biggest adjacent tree to open fire with our Lee-Metfords, trusting to the brute's blindly attacking the log pile and fire, under the impression that this was the source of danger. But from the moment of reaching the mammoth's country, we were extremely careful to build no campfires, unless the smoke blew back across the river, and only allowed ourselves the smallest fires by which to cook our meals. We found some large pieces of cottonwood bark, which helped us, since after being thoroughly dried in the sun this bark will burn to a white heat, and is almost smokeless. Paul kept the camp amply supplied with young ducks and geese; shooting them with a bow and arrow from a moose-skin canoe, the raw hide for which we had brought with us. He used an arrow with a large barbed head sharpened to a knife-like edge; fired from a hide in the reeds, it would skim into an unwary brood, often cutting the throats of two or three at a flight.

The first day that we explored back from the river we found enormous footprints of the mammoth, but they were not fresh. The track was nearly circular, and even on hard ground the indentations were made to stay, while in the softer soil around the lakes they were frequently three or four feet deep. Though lichen was abundant in the valley, I saw no caribou sign, nor, indeed, signs of any other game whatever.

On August the 29th, we had our first sight of the mammoth. There he stood in a little clearing, the great beast that only one other living man had seen, tearing up great masses of lichenous moss and feeding as an elephant feeds. His lifelike presentation—an enduring testimony to the wonderful patience and skill of American taxidermists—which now occupies the new wing of the Smithsonian museum, has been so fully pictured in the magazines and newspapers of every country in the civilized world—has not his picture been hung on the line in the Royal Academy this year?—that it is idle for me to describe him closely, and I need only speak of the feeling of awe inspired by the sight of this stupendous beast, quietly feeding in oblivion of the two pigmies who were planning his destruction. His long, thick hair, hanging down beneath his belly like a fringe, had the effect of shortening considerably the appearance of his legs. The points of the immense tusks looked as if they could hardly belong to their owner, being, as all the world knows, thirty-one feet, nine inches away from the bases. The portion between the points and the bases was hidden from our sight by the scrub and long tufts of grass.

Paul must have watched him very coolly, for on comparing notes in camp (we had slipped quietly back without disturbing the monster), I found that he had observed details, such as the smallness of the eye and the absence of any tail, which had escaped my notice. The shortness of the trunk, as compared with an elephant's, was what struck me the most.

About twenty-five miles below our first camp we had found a clump of spruce trees larger than any we had seen in the valley, and here we set to work. At one side of the two largest trees, and across a small dry watercourse, we built a solid erection of five rounds of logs, and placed within this a mass of dry and rotten wood, leaving one small hole where we could crawl in and light it. On top of the "house" we felled the nearest large trees, and others we felled and drew up by the aid of our block and tackle, stacking them up in such a manner as to leave a slight air-space, but pinning them very solidly together with green birch. When the structure was completed, it looked like a huge drift-pile of green logs. We put ladder pegs up to the branches (about sixty feet up) of the two highest standing trees, and selecting suitable places, built seats, and took up rope, with which we could lash ourselves in if necessary. By the end of September we had everything prepared, and we had but to prove the truth of my supposition, namely, that smoke would attract our quarry.

We had from time to time reconnoitered, and found that the mammoth was slowly working towards us. At first I thought it remarkable that we should have found him so near the place where the Indians had seen him years before; but the rapid lichenous growth in the vicinity probably made it a favorite spot, and the lonely giant had it all to himself. On October the 11th, the wind was favorable for our experiment, and having gone over the details carefully, we proceeded to make a preliminary trial, on the failure or success of which hung the fate of our large venture.

The mammoth had now worked up to within three miles of the wood-pile. Having first located him, we laid pieces of dry rotten wood about 300 yards apart through the trees, and directly in line. Having done this for about a mile and a half, and selected a large tree into which we drove ladder pegs, we crept back, and were lucky enough to find the mammoth standing on the far side of a small lake. We lighted the first piece of rotten wood, and then ran back to the tree at our best speed, igniting the other pieces on our way, and a final one near our tree, into which we hastily climbed to watch the result of our experiment.

We were scarcely ensconced among the branches when a cry resounded over the valley which made the chills run down my back. I have heard the scream of an angry bull elephant, the roar of an African lion, and the savage, half-human cry of the great gorilla; but none of these compare with the awe-inspiring cry of a mammoth. Perhaps the Indian's description of "a thousand thousand geese" approaches it most nearly, for there were two distinct pitches; but the very immensity of the volume of sound as the brute approached us confused any comparison I tried to make. For five, perhaps ten, minutes we waited, strung up to the highest pitch of excitement. Then suddenly the huge form loomed up through the trees, and seeing our smoking fire, he rushed at the burning logs with a cry which shook the very branches on which we sat, and with his ponderous foot trampled them into the ground. Though the tree was fully seventy-five feet away from him, it trembled noticeably, and I was glad that I had placed our log-pile twice that distance away, with the dry watercourse to still further isolate us from the vibration. My chance conjecture had evidently hit the mark: the mammoth, with the instinct born when volcanoes were active and fire was the only foe to be dreaded by these mighty beasts, had hastened to stamp out the threatened conflagration.

Having satisfied himself that the fire was out, Tee-Kai-Koa proceeded to smell the ground. Our scent evidently troubled him somewhat, for he frequently blew with a sound not unlike escaping steam. After a while he turned away, and struck into the woods at right angles to the course we had to make to our camp. We climbed down the tree, and hastened off, well satisfied as to the result of our plan.

By the 16th, everything was ready, and before daylight we placed our rifles and cartridges in our stations in the trees. We then started out, and by 10 A.M. had located our quarry, about three miles away. He seemed to be restless, and kept sniffing the air. A very quiet breeze was blowing in the tree tops. We fired an armful of dry wood, and started back as fast as we could run; but the moment the smoke rose, that terrible cry came booming down the valley behind us, and we felt the earth vibrate as the mammoth charged down in our direction. High up in the branches of a stout tree we had felt comparatively safe; but it was a very different matter on the ground, and we knew it was a veritable race for life as we tore through the woods, touching off the prepared fires with a match as we passed.

At last we came to the log-pile, and in a few seconds a thin wreath of smoke announced that the battle would soon begin. We hastened to our respective stations, and awaited developments. We were not kept in suspense long. Rushing forth from the forest, and charging up to the wood-pile with an ear-splitting cry, the king of the primeval forests stood beneath us in all his pride of strength. He was evidently puzzled for a moment by the huge log-pile confronting him, through which the smoke was now rolling in a thick volume. But with the crack of our rifles came the most appalling scream of rage I have ever heard, and the vast brute, apparently unaffected by our shots, attacked the wood-pile with incredible fury. Charging his enormous tusks beneath it, he gave a mighty heave, and for a second lifted the whole mass of green logs—remember they were pinned together, and stood at least twenty-five feet high—clear off the ground. Finding this more than even his colossal strength could compass, he seized a top timber, a solid green log twenty-five feet long and over a foot in diameter, and threw it clear behind him.

Meanwhile our rifles had not been idle, and I had already got through my second magazine-full, generally aiming behind the ear. So loud was the noise, scream following scream till the hills rang with the sound, that I could not hear the report of my rifle; but the barrel, hot in my hand, told me that the wicked little bullets were speeding on their mission. I glanced at Paul, and saw him aiming and firing with a coolness that I envied, for the din in my ears confused and worried me, and the sweat was running down my face as I fired again and again at the massive target.

The mammoth seemed to have no idea that his assailants were above him, but blindly attacked the burning wood-pile, seizing the logs and hurling them this way and that, till I saw it was only a matter of minutes until the whole edifice should be scattered far and wide. One log, smaller than the rest, came hurling through the air into my refuge, and crashed through the branches over-head. Another struck the tree about half-way up, splintering the bark, and nearly shaking me off my seat.

But the end was drawing near, for the great brute was bleeding profusely from the mouth and ears, and staggered uncertainly back and forth. A feeling of pity and shame crept over me as I watched the failing strength of this mighty prehistoric monarch whom I had outwitted and despoiled of a thousand peaceful years of harmless existence. It was as though I were robbing nature, and old Mother Earth herself of a child born to her younger days, in the dawn of Time.

Suddenly the noise ceased, the mammoth seeming to realize that the danger came from the trees behind him rather than from the now demolished wood-pile. Our rifles cracked again, this time to a square forehead shot. But the huge animal stumbled uncertainly forward, crossed the dry ditch, and turned towards Paul's tree, as if to tear it down. I saw Paul seize the piece of rope and quickly lash it round him, when the mammoth, stumbling half-way past the tree, suddenly swayed from side to side, pitched forward on his knees, and slowly, very slowly, subsided. As he rolled gently on his side, the tree, torn from its roots by the weight, fell forward, and for one horrible moment I thought that Paul and the tree would be dashed to the ground. But at an angle of forty-five degrees the tree swayed and stopped, upheld by the weight lying on its long roots, and Paul walked down the trunk, and climbed on to the body of the mammoth, waving and cheering to me.

When I joined him and stood beside our quarry, I could hardly realize that we had killed so enormous an animal with such comparative ease and with the diminutive weapons that we held in our hands. Now that the excitement was over, I found that I had become deaf from the noise, nor did I recover my hearing for some days.

The deed was done, and we now had to justify it by saving the skin, bones, and every portion capable of preservation. This proved a tremendous task. The skin we cut into sections, using our block and tackle, attached to a tree, to pull it back. We skinned one side completely in this way; then took out the ribs, and removed the immense entrails, by the same means. The weather was our salvation, being cool and frosty at night; for though we worked like beavers, it took us ten days to get all the hide removed, scraped, and carefully rolled, and the several pieces tagged to identify their positions. The tusks were the most difficult things for us to handle, for with the portion of skull attached to them their weight was enormous. By the middle of December, the bones were all removed from the body, and carefully cleaned and numbered. When once we had the hide safely away, we were able to light a large fire and roast a lot of the meat. This greatly helped in cleaning the bones. I took careful measurements of the lungs, heart, and all the perishable portions. We worked steadily till nearly the end of January, not leaving the camp at all. The meat was not unpalatable, but terribly tough. We buried the best portions in the ever-frozen ground, and were thus able to preserve it perfectly.

It is unnecessary to detail how we spent the rest of the dark winter days, until they lengthened sufficiently for us to explore the valley at its lower end, about thirty miles from our camp. As I had expected, it terminated in a narrow and extremely deep cañon, where the river went rushing over the rocks, and I saw at once that no boat could possibly ascend it. We found this gloomy gorge to be about three and a half miles long. We could see the stars overhead when the sun was shining, so high and straight were its walls; and with the noise of the water beneath the ice, in this gloom, it was one of the weirdest places I have ever been in. At the foot of the cañon the valley widened as suddenly as at the head, and I saw that the river was navigable.

Our only chance of getting our prize out of the valley was to sleigh it over the ice through the canon; so we hurried back, and proceeded with all possible despatch to this rather formidable task. Fortunately, the months of March and April were remarkably fine, and as the sleigh trail improved with usage, and the sun began to make its power felt, we were able to increase our loads. We moved everything to the head of the cañon, and then made two trips a day to the foot, camping below. Finally we built a solid cache of heavy green logs in a safe place, and having shut everything securely in it, we built a small boat, and waited for the opening of the river.

The rest of my story is told in a few words. We journeyed down the Tee-Kai-Koa River to the Chandelar, and thence to the Yukon and St. Michaels, and proceeded by the first steamer to San Francisco. There I met Mr. Conradi—quite by accident—and finding him deeply interested in zoology, I disclosed the secret of the prize we had left on the banks of the Tee-Kai-Koa. I had kept the matter secret because I wished to find out for myself from the various authorities in America and Europe something as to the value of the mammoth. My design was, if possible, to get the British Museum authorities to purchase it. Mr. Conradi's offer astounded me—it was in millions of dollars—and after a week's thought I closed with him.

Paul absolutely refused to accept more than a quarter share, arguing, not without reason, that even this portion was more than he knew what to do with or could possibly spend. Civilization had few attractions for him; he soon tired of 'Frisco, and used to long impatiently for the wilds. He and I went north that summer, and wintered on the Tee-Kai-Koa River near our cache. In the spring, we conveyed the mammoth to a certain place on the Yukon River, where we met Mr. Conradi, and everything was packed in specially prepared cases. At the mouth of the river we were met by Mr. Conradi's steam yacht, which had wintered in North Sound, and at once sailed for San Francisco.

I do not know what it cost him to keep the crew silent; but judging from the wildness of the conjectures made by the newspapers in dealing with the matter, and from the fact that it never got published that the specimen was taken aboard at the mouth of the Yukon, the sum paid for secrecy was certainly sufficient, and must have been considerable. I believe that the most generally accepted theory heretofore has been that Mr. Conradi found the carcass frozen in an iceberg in the Arctic Ocean. The various dimensions of the mammoth, both of the skeleton and the mounted specimen, are too well known to need tabulating here. The measurements, exactly as taken by me, were handed to the Smithsonian authorities by Mr. Conradi for publication, and accepted without question as his own.

The Spell of the Bird

Frank Aubrey

"Fascination? Does anyone believe in fascination? Yes, *I* do, and I don't mind who hears me say it or who laughs at it. If you had had the experience I once went through, you would believe in it too!"

The speaker was one of a group at the Kaieteur Hotel, Georgetown, British Guiana. He was a tall, powerful-looking man, with a shrewd, intellectual face and a grave, reserved manner. He had been sitting silent and almost unnoticed in a corner while a long and, at times, animated discussion had been going on around him concerning forest life in the interior of our South American colony. His name was Creldon—George Creldon—and he was, as I afterwards heard, one of the best known and most respected of the planters in Demerara. He was looked upon, too, as an authority upon wild sports and forest travel, having formerly spent much of his time in hunting or prospecting trips in the interior.

To those who know Georgetown, it will be unnecessary to say that we were all indulging in the drink *par excellence* of the country, commonly called a "swizzle."

When the first feelings of surprise caused by Creldon's unexpected declaration had passed away, and the pronounced comments to which it gave rise had quieted down, we soon found ourselves ordering a further "swizzle" each as a fit and becoming preparation to listening to his story. It was as follows—

"When certain persons," Creldon began, looking round at some of us with a severe air of correction, "declare so confidently that this or that 'cannot' be true, they would do well to remember that our knowledge of the great forests of Guiana and Brazil is in reality very limited indeed. There are vast tracts which are absolutely unexplored; have never, so far as we know, been traversed by either Indians or white men. And since the more shy of the animal creation ever shun or forsake those parts where man is to be met with, however seldom, therefore it is fair to assume that we do not yet know all the creatures that may exist in those impenetrable recesses.

"Mr. W. H. Hudson, a naturalist, who has lived for many years in South America, has lately in his book, 'The Naturalist in La Plata,' startled and indeed astonished the zoological world by making known many strange things that' were before altogether unknown and unsuspected. He declares, among other matters, that he has just once seen, and then lost, creatures entirely new to naturalists; and this alone should teach us that the Indians may not always be wrong in their beliefs, or in the tales they tell of strange and wonderful animals or reptiles that still lurk in the forest depths. I am not, of course, maintaining that all their wild tales and fantastic beliefs are true; I only suggest that here and there, there may be a better foundation for them than many, perhaps, would think. I have myself seen strange creatures that are entirely unknown to zoologists, but they got away before I could shoot or catch them. What, however, I am about to relate is by far the strangest, the most extraordinary adventure that ever occurred to me. I can only tell it as it happened; and I do not suggest any explanation beyond reminding you that there are in nature already many known instances of creatures—the very ones most likely, one would think, to keep apart—combining or working together for mutual profit or protection. There are the birds that hop in and out of the open mouths of the crocodiles and pick their teeth and jaws clean for them, the great reptiles never taking advantage of the trustfulness of their feathered friends. Then there are the 'pilot-fish' that accompany the shark; and in Guiana we have several very curious, almost incredible, examples. Thus we know that, as a rule, birds feed freely on ants and wasps among other insects; yet in Guiana are frequently to be found settlements or colonies in which mocking-birds, ants, and wasps and wild bees are banded together for mutual protection. The birds leave the insects alone, and, in return, the latter protect the nests of the birds during their absence; and woe betide any unlucky tiger-cat or monkey that ventures near the nests after the young ones or the eggs. The wasps and bees will attack it as ferociously as if it had tried to rob their own nests; and the ants will attack snakes in the same way. Even plants and ants form protective alliances, as in the case of some of the 'vetches,' which encourage ants of one kind to live on them in order that they may fight off the 'leaf-cutting' ants, which destroy so many other plants and trees in the forests of South America. These are facts that have been noted and vouched for by such well-known authorities as Sir Robert Schomburgk, Mr. Bates, Mr. Barrington Brown, Mr. W. H. Hudson, and others.

"Now, amongst the Indians, in some places, is a deep-seated belief in the existence of a monstrous serpent of unusually terrifying aspect but of a sluggish nature, which is always accompanied by one or a pair of birds equally rare but of strikingly beautiful plumage. This serpent is called in some parts 'Kragi,' in others 'Krao'; and in others, again, there is no particular name for it, and it is ranked as a kind of 'Camoodi,' which is the Indian term for the great boa-constrictor of Guiana. The bird is called the Kalon, or sometimes the Krao-Kalon, and is declared to entice victims into the neighbourhood of the serpent, so that the latter may seize them with very little trouble or exertion; the bird being afterwards rewarded by being allowed to pick out the strangled creature's eyes and other tit-bits before the dead body is swallowed by the reptile.

"So much by way of preliminary explanation. Now to my story—

"While at Rio one time—it was in my 'restless' days, when I wandered about pretty well all over South America—I became acquainted with a young fellow to whom I took a great fancy; we quickly, in fact, became firm friends. He was an Englishman named Geoffrey Bingham, a fine, handsome, courageous chap as you need wish to meet with. He had hunted big game in Africa and India, and knew his way about a bit, I can tell you, for all he was not then twenty-five years of age. He had well-to-do parents in England, who allowed him enough to either live at home comfortably or wander about as pleased his fancy. He told me he was going up-country to join a man he knew who had discovered an ancient gold-mine, from which he was taking out a fair amount of dust, though he was only working it in a quiet way with a few friendly Indians; and after some talk and some persuasion on his part I agreed to accompany him. There were no grand expectations of great wealth held out as likely to be our reward; nor, on the other hand, was any premium asked for the privilege of joining in.

"'It's just this way,' Hingham said. 'Old Soltram—that's the old boy who found the mine—doesn't want the thing talked about, and a lot of tag-rag and bobtail brought about his ears; at the same time it's pretty lonely out there, and he is not at all averse to one or two fellows of the right sort coming to help on the give-and-take principle. That is, if you work for the dust yourself, you must pay your own Indians and hand over to Soltram a percentage on what you find; or, if you don't care to bother about that sort of work, you can go out hunting for us and keep the larder supplied, and we will pay *you* a percentage on what *we* get.'

"He further told me that Soltram hadn't much faith in the mine proving a good one for long. He believed it had been about worked out when he found it, and that he had only pitched by chance on a drift that had been missed by the ancient workers; and this might come to an end at any moment. So I agreed to go, rather for the mere sake of the hunting and adventure than with any idea of making money.

"When all our arrangements were completed we started in canoes up the river routes, then across pampas and forest till we got into the corner, as it were, where Venezuela, Brazil, and British Guiana all meet. And we came to a halt in that wild and little-known region of mountain and primeval forest which forms part of the borderland that has been in dispute for a hundred years past between Great Britain and Venezuela. A terribly wild district it is, full, however, of savage grandeur, being situated only a few degrees from the equator, where nature is to be seen both at her best and her worst. Here are to be found the highest waterfalls, and, in some respects, the most wonderful mountains and table-lands in the world, and all sorts of climates, from that of the temperate zone on the table-lands to the seething swamps of equatorial South America in the valleys. And here, too, is to be seen the most wonderful vegetation of the whole continent; some tracts being absolutely carpeted with begonias, orchids, gloxinias, and other plants and flowers so rare and—in England—so costly, that to secure them would be enough to turn the head—and make the fortune—of any collector who should be the first to come among them.

"Here, in this strange, little-known region, we found Soltram established, with his primitive gold-extracting plant, his Indians, his dogs, and—his daughter! Yes, extraordinary as it seemed, he had actually a daughter living with him, and a very charming young girl I found her too. At first I thought that this must have been the real attraction that had brought Bingham so far afield; but I soon found it was not so. He and Ledra Soltram, as presently became apparent, were good friends, and nothing more. Indeed, he made a confidant of me about this time, and confessed that he had a sweetheart awaiting him in England, to whom he intended to return when this adventure—which was to be the last of his wanderings—came to an end.

"Thus the field was left entirely open for me, and I fell over head and ears in love before I had been there a week. Nor was I without encouragement from the young lady herself, and ere long I began to bless my luck that had thus led me to her side. At first I elected to do the hunting and keep the larder supplied, since this gave me many opportunities of being alone with Ledra, while the others were away at the mine. Soltram had built a very substantial log hut about a quarter of a mile from his mine, in a clearing at the edge of a thick, almost impenetrable belt of forest. Round about was quite a small settlement, his Indians having erected huts for themselves and begun to cultivate patches of open ground. From the huts a pathway had been cut through the dense wood to the base of a cliff, where was a cavern with a small stream of water flowing out of it, and this was the mouth of the old mine. Inside were many galleries running this way and that, some, one above the other, with steps or wooden ladders to connect them. Soltram himself was a rather fine-looking old boy with white hair and beard, not a bad sort, but, as I soon discovered, of a greedy, avaricious disposition. Notwithstanding his name, I judged him to be of Scotch descent, and this I afterwards found to be a correct guess. Who he was and how he came to be there does not matter here: it would make my story too long were I to go into all such details. Suffice it that he had somehow found his way there, dragging his daughter about with him, and had happened on an old mine, from which he was now getting out a few pounds' worth of gold a week clear of expenses. But the yield was not so good as it had been, and it seemed quite on the cards that at any moment it might come to a dead stop.

"At first, I say, I elected to do the hunting and fresh-meat-providing for the establishment; but after a time the gold-seeking fever seized upon me as well as the others. Honestly, I do not think this would have been the case if I had not been so madly in love with Ledra. I saw enough, however, of Soltram's temperament to understand that he had high ideas concerning his daughter—especially if he himself should become rich—and to feel certain he would never, in such a case, give his consent to her marrying one so moderately well off as myself. Hence, if I wished to find favour in his eyes, it behoved me to hie me each day to the mine, there to work hard for my share of whatever was going. Then, if the venture *should* turn out well, and Soltram become wealthy, I also might be not far behind. Besides, there was always the chance that I might, individually, stumble upon some very rich find that might cause Soltram to regard me as a desirable son-in-law straight away. So I came to an arrangement, engaged a gang of Indians on my own account, and set to work, other Indians being told off to form daily hunting parties to supply the necessary fresh meat. Only once or so a week, Bingham and I would accompany these hunting parties, partly for a change, and partly to keep our hands in. Thus some months passed, during which we got a good deal of gold from the old mine, and I had grown quite used to the life. I had, indeed, every reason to be well satisfied, for I was making money and making love at the same time. Then, however, came a sudden and tragical end to our enterprise.

"One day, about noon, we—*i.e.*, Soltram, Bingham, and myself—had come to the mouth of the mine from the distant workings to have our midday meal, as was our custom. This was brought for us from the huts by Indians, and Ledra would often come with them and chat with us while we ate, going back with the Indians—who on such occasions were chiefly women, girls, and boys—so soon as we had finished and returned to our work.

On this particular morning, when we got out in the open air, we found Ledra there, but not her attendants. She had, in fact, run on in front and outstripped them. For this she was reproved by her father; but while he was scolding her she uttered an exclamation and darted from his side. A clearing of considerable extent had been made round the mouth of the mine, and this was littered about with heaps of debris, logs of timber, and so on. I then saw that Ledra was chasing a bird of wonderfully beautiful plumage. It was, in some respects, like the Bird of Paradise, but in brilliancy of colouring it surpassed any bird I had ever seen. It seemed quite tame, and frequently almost allowed its pursuer to come up to it; when, however, with a coquettish little flutter, it would evade capture with remarkable agility, and affect to hide among the logs or behind some heap of rubbish.

"Thinking that Ledra would like me to shoot it in order to se-cure the skin if she were unable to catch the bird, I turned back into the mine for my gun. I had left a double-barrelled piece loaded with shot in one barrel and ball in the other in the first gallery over the entrance. The end of this gallery was open, but fenced round with a sort of barred bay window on the outside, and shut off by a partition and door on the inside, forming an apartment where we could lock up our spare tools and other stores. The ob-ject of barring the window was, of course, that no one should be able to get in by climbing up the rock when the gates which pro-tected the main entrance were closed and padlocked.

"Just as I had taken up the gun I heard an outcry, and paused for a moment to look out through the bars to see what was going on below. The Indians had arrived with our meal, but had evidently taken alarm at something and were fleeing in terror, each one having incontinently thrown down whatever he or she was carrying. Much surprised, I looked anxiously for Ledra, and saw that she was standing still in the middle of the open space, while her father had gone after the bird, which had now perched itself on one of the lower boughs of a tree at the edge of the clearing. Meantime, the Indians had every one disappeared, with shouts which I could not then distinguish, but which I afterwards knew to be 'Krao-Kalon' and 'Kragi.' Suddenly the bird began to sing, and it had the most charming, thrilling note I ever heard in my life. Indeed, it was not like the song of a bird at all; it resembled nothing so much as the music given out by an Æolian harp when the wind sweeps across its strings. The effect was inexpressibly sweet; yet mingled with it was a weird, wild note that somehow repelled while it charmed. And as the notes swelled out fuller and louder, I could not but stand still and listen in a very ecstasy of pleasure and delight; which, however, began soon to change to a cold horror, as I realised, all at once, that *I could not move!*"

Here the narrator paused, and passed his hand across his eyes as though to shut out some horrible sight. His manner was so earnest that it visibly impressed us all; and no one spoke. After a brief space he resumed—

"I cannot describe to you the astonishment, the alarm, with which I realised what I have just told you—namely, that I was unable to move. I was overrun by a mixture of feelings in which surprise, perplexity, horror, incredulity, and wonder were all jumbled up together. Yet were my senses almost abnormally acute; I remember, as I looked helplessly out, how I saw the brilliant sunshine pouring down and lighting up portions of the scene, in glaring contrast to the deep, gloomy shadows that lay among the trees of the forest beyond. I remember Soltram, as he stood with his back to me, just under the bough on which the bird had perched. So near was he to the creature that, with a long stick, he could have knocked it over. Yet he stood still and never moved even his head. I saw Ledra out in the sunlight, her broad hat swaying slightly, her

hands clasped together, standing like one turned to stone; and just
below me I saw Bingham, who had stepped out and then stopped;
and he, too, was as motionless as the others.

"And still that infernal bird sang on. Happing his wings, his
silver-and-gold plumage sparkling and flashing in the sun. And
slowly there rose up in my mind a presentiment, a foreboding of
some horror yet to come, and I watched and waited for—I knew
not what.

"All the time there was in my mind a feeling as of resentment
against these other three that they stood thus and did nothing. Why
did not Bingham or Soltram move, or do or say something? I
wondered to myself, thinking that I was the only one who felt the
spell, and vaguely angry that these others did not move or offer to
come to my assistance. I tell you it is an awful thing to have all
your physical faculties numbed like that, and yet to be able to see
and hear all that goes on before you!"

Again the speaker paused and wetted his lips from the glass
before him. No one spoke, and he resumed—

"I know it must sound strange—incredible—to you who have
never passed through such an experience, yet to me, at the time, it
was actual enough. Even now I cannot bear to recall what I went
through, but, having begun it, I must go on with it, I suppose.

"The bird sang on, and the unnatural quiet that seemed to have
fallen upon all the world beside continued until I heard a slight
rustling. It came from near Soltram, and looking across, I saw,
slowly rising through the bushes, the most hideous head it has ever
been my lot to look upon. That it belonged to some member of
the serpent tribe was soon evident; but in grisly repulsiveness it
exceeded even what a magnified rattlesnake might be supposed to
be like; and there are not many things in the world more horrible,
I imagine, than the expression, if one may so term it, that lurks in
the head and jaws of a rattlesnake. The creature that now slowly
came into view, however, exceeded in gruesome hideousness anything that I ever imagined. Like the rattlesnake, its mouth seemed
to be formed in the likeness of a set sneer of the most sinister
malignancy; but the eyes were much larger in proportion and had

a baleful glare in their yellowish-green depths that sent cold shivers through you as you met and endured their fixed, cold gaze. A
hood, somewhat after the shape of that of the cobra, two horns,
and a kind of crest on the neck at the back of the head completed
the terrible picture. And still, while it rose slowly, menacingly
beside him, Soltram, who seemed to be looking straight at it, never
moved; and still that bird-fiend sang on and flapped its wings, and
appeared to be revelling in the very height of enjoyment."

Again the speaker paused, but still there was silence in the
group around him, and he once more resumed—

"Slowly, and with a sickening deliberation, which fold only too
clearly how absolutely certain he felt of his prey, that terrible beast
drew nearer and nearer to Soltram, swaying slightly to and fro,
and protruding its forked tongue, which darted in and out of its
now open jaws. I remember wondering vaguely why Soltram did
not run away, not comprehending that he was in the same condition as myself. At last the monster gave a quick leap, and fixed its
fangs in the throat of its victim, and immediately coil after coil
wound round Soltram's body, till I could hear, even where I was,
the fearful sound of cracking bones....

"Presently the creature slowly relaxed its folds, and, after lying inert for a short space, fixed its leering eyes upon Ledra, and
began to creep towards her. I madly strove to burst the bonds that
seemed to hold me as if in a vice, but still I could neither move nor
cry out. The sweat poured off my face; I am sure my eyes must
have appeared, could anyone have seen them, to be bursting out
of my head with horror. Yet still I could not move, could not even
cry out; still Bingham was motionless, too; and still the bird sang
on, and still the monster—which I could now see was a serpent of
gigantic size, with a frightful, scaly shape—crept slowly nearer, ever
nearer, towards the one I loved beyond all else in the world.

"Then poor Ledra gave one long, agonised shriek, and fell fainting on the ground; and at that the fiendish bird stopped singing.
Whether the cry startled it, or whether it thought it now time to
claim its own perquisites, I cannot say. But it flew down, and going up to the dead man—who was lying on his back—hopped on to

his face. But the awful spell was broken; the blood was again rushing through my veins, and I felt myself nerved with a savage, desperate revenge. I raised the piece I held in my hand, cocked it, and aiming carefully, sent a bullet crashing through the head of the great snake, which at once began to writhe and twist about in horrid contortions. Then I turned the barrel loaded with shot on the bird—or, rather, tried to; but the hateful creature had already disappeared, frightened, I suppose, by the sound of the shot; and, in fact, I never saw it again. I then rushed down and out into the clearing, and there with the undischarged barrel blew the head off the still struggling monster; and Bingham now coming to my assistance, we carried the unconscious girl inside, and we laved her face with water from the cool stream that ran through the cavern.

"I won't tell you of the anxious time we had of it with the stricken daughter; but she was well nursed and tended by the Indian women, and slowly came back to the world and to health if not to good spirits. Then she begged so piteously to be taken away from the place that had for her such unendurable associations that I gave up all thought of anything except how best and quickest to get her down to the coast. And as Bingham did not care to stay by himself, we gave up the mine to the Indians and soon started off together to get back through Venezuela. Eventually we arrived without mishap at Georgetown, where I placed my charge for a while in the care of my mother. A few months later we were married and settled down on my father's estate here, where we have lived ever since. But though it is now many years since it happened, neither I nor my wife will ever forget the 'bad quarter of an hour' we passed through while looking on at the grim tragedy enacted before our eyes, chained down as we were and rendered physically helpless by that diabolical bird and the weird spell of its strange song."

A Relic of the Pliocene

JACK LONDON

I wash my hands of him at the start. I cannot father his tales, nor will I be responsible for them. I make these preliminary reservations, observe, as a guard upon my own integrity. I posses a certain definite position in a small way, also a wife; and for the good name of the community that honors my existence with its approval, and for the sake of her posterity and mine, I cannot take the chances I once did, nor foster probabilities with the careless improvidence of youth. So, I repeat, I wash my hands of him, this Nimrod, this mighty hunter, this homely, blue-eyed, freckle-faced Thomas Stevens.

Having been honest to myself, and to whatever prospective olive branches my wife may be pleased to tender me, I can now afford to be generous. I shall not criticize the tales told me by Thomas Stevens, and, further, I shall withhold my judgment. If it be asked why, I can only add that judgment I have none. Long have I pondered, weighed, and balanced, but never have my conclusions been twice the same—forsooth! because Thomas Stevens is a greater man than I. If he have told truths, well and good; if untruths, still well and good. For who can prove? or who disprove? I eliminate myself from the proposition, while those of little faith may do as I have done-go find the said Thomas Stevens, and discuss to his face the various matters which, if fortune serve, I shall relate. As to where he may be found? The directions are simple: anywhere between 53 north latitude and the Pole, on the one hand; and, on the other, the likeliest hunting grounds that lie between the east coast of Siberia and farthermost Labrador. That he is there, somewhere, within that clearly defined territory, I pledge the word of an honorable man whose expectations entail straight speaking and right living.

Thomas Stevens may have toyed prodigiously with truth, but when we first met (it were well to mark this point), he wandered into my camp when I thought myself a thousand miles beyond the outermost post of civilization. At the sight of his human face, the first in weary months, I could have sprung forward and folded him in my arms (and I am not by any means a demonstrative man); but to him his visit seemed the most casual thing under the sun. He just strolled into the light of my camp, passed the time of day after the custom of men on beaten trails, threw my snowshoes the one way and a couple of dogs the other, and so made room for himself by the fire. Said he'd just dropped in to borrow a pinch of soda and to see if I had any decent tobacco. He plucked forth an ancient pipe, loaded it with painstaking care, and, without as much as by your leave, whacked half the tobacco of my pouch into his. Yes, the stuff was fairly good. He sighed with the contentment of the just, and literally absorbed the smoke from the crisping yellow flakes, and it did my smoker's heart good to behold him.

Hunter? Trapper? Prospector? He shrugged his shoulders No; just sort of knocking round a bit. Had come up from the Great Slave some time since, and was thinking of traipsing over into the Yukon country. The Factor of Koshim had spoken about the discoveries on the Klondike, and he was of a mind to run over for a peep. I noticed that he spoke of the Klondike in the archaic vernacular, calling it the Reindeer River—a conceited custom that the Old Timers employ against the *che-cha-quas* and all tenderfeet in general. But he did it so naively and as such a matter of course, that there was no sting, and I forgave him. He also had it in view, he said, before he crossed the divide into the Yukon, to make a little run up Fort o' Good Hope way.

Now Fort o' Good Hope is a far journey to the north, over and beyond the Circle, in a place where the feet of few men have trod; and when a nondescript ragamuffin comes in out of the night, from nowhere in particular, to sit by one's fire and discourse on such in terms of "traipsing" and "a little run," it is fair time to rouse up and shake off the dream. Wherefore I looked about me; saw the fly, and, underneath, the pine boughs spread for the sleeping furs; saw the grub sacks, the camera, the frosty breaths of the dogs circling on the edge of the light; and, above, a great streamer of the aurora bridging the zenith from southeast to northwest. I shivered. There is a magic in the Northland night, that steals in on one like fevers from malarial marshes. You are clutched and downed before you are aware. Then I looked to the snowshoes, lying prone and crossed where he had flung them. Also I had an eye to my tobacco pouch. Half, at least, of its goodly store had vamoosed. That settled it. Fancy had not tricked me after all.

Crazed with suffering, I thought, looking steadfastly at the man—one of those wild stampeders, strayed far from his bearings and wandering like a lost soul through great vastnesses and unknown deeps. Oh, well, let his moods slip on, until, mayhap, he gathers his tangled wits together. Who knows?—the mere sound of a fellow-creature's voice may bring all straight again.

So I led him on in talk, and soon I marvelled, for he talked of game and the ways thereof. He had killed the Siberian wolf of westernmost Alaska, and the chamois in the secret Rockies. He averred he knew the haunts where the last buffalo still roamed; that he had hung on the flanks of the caribou when they ran by the hundred thousand, and slept in the Great Barrens on the muskox's winter trail.

And I shifted my judgment accordingly (the first revision, but by no account the last), and deemed him a monumental effigy of truth. Why it was I know not, but the spirit moved me to repeat a tale told to me by a man who had dwelt in the land too long to know better. It was of the great bear that hugs the steep slopes of St. Elias, never descending to the levels of the gentler inclines. Now God so constituted this creature for its hillside habitat that the legs of one side are all of a foot longer than those of the other. This is mighty convenient, as will be readily admitted. So I hunted this rare beast in my own name, told it in the first person, present tense, painted the requisite locale, gave it the necessary garnishings and touches of verisimilitude, and looked to see the man stunned by the recital.

Not he. Had he doubted, I could have forgiven him. Had he objected, denying the dangers of such a hunt by virtue of the animal's inability to turn about and go the other way—had he done this, I say, I could have taken him by the hand for the true sportsman that he was. Not he. He sniffed, looked on me, and sniffed again; then gave my tobacco due praise, thrust one foot into my lap, and bade me examine the gear. It was a *mucluc* of the Innuit pattern, sewed together with sinew threads, and devoid of beads or furbelows. But it was the skin itself that was remarkable. In that it was all of half an inch thick, it reminded me of walrus-hide; but there the resemblance ceased, for no walrus ever bore so marvellous a growth of hair. On the side and ankles this hair was well-nigh worn away, what of friction with underbrush and snow; but around the top and down the more sheltered back it was coarse, dirty black, and very thick. I parted it with difficulty and looked beneath for the fine fur that is common with northern animals, but found it in this case to be absent. This, however, was compensated for by the length. Indeed, the tufts that had survived wear and tear measured all of seven or eight inches.

I looked up into the man's face, and he pulled his foot down and asked, "Find hide like that on your St. Elias bear?"

I shook my head. "Nor on any other creature of land or sea," I answered candidly. The thickness of it, and the length of the hair, puzzled me.

"That," he said, and said without the slightest hint of impressiveness, "that came from a mammoth."

"Nonsense!" I exclaimed, for I could not forbear the protest of my unbelief. "The mammoth, my dear sir, long ago vanished from the earth. We know it once existed by the fossil remains that we have unearthed, and by a frozen carcass that the Siberian sun saw fit to melt from out the bosom of a glacier; but we also know that no living specimen exists. Our explorers—"

At this word he broke in impatiently. "Your explorers? Pish! A weakly breed. Let us hear no more of them. But tell me, O man, what you may know of the mammoth and his ways."

Beyond contradiction, this was leading to a yarn; so I baited my hook by ransacking my memory for whatever data I possessed on the subject in hand. To begin with, I emphasized that the animal was prehistoric, and marshalled all my facts in support of this. I mentioned the Siberian sand bars that abounded with ancient mammoth bones; spoke of the large quantities of fossil ivory purchased from the Innuits by the Alaska Commercial Company; and acknowledged having myself mined six and eight-foot tusks from the pay gravel of the Klondike creeks. "All fossils," I concluded, "found in the midst of debris deposited through countless ages."

"I remember when I was a kid," Thomas Stevens sniffed (he had a most confounded way of sniffing), "that I saw a petrified watermelon. Hence, though mistaken persons sometimes delude themselves into thinking that they are really raising or eating them, there are no such things as extant watermelons."

"But the question of food," I objected, ignoring his point, which was puerile and without bearing. "The soil must bring forth vegetable life in lavish abundance to support so monstrous creations. Nowhere in the North is the soil so prolific. Ergo, the mammoth cannot exist."

"I pardon your ignorance concerning many matters of this Northland, for you are a young man and have travelled little; but, at the same time, I am inclined to agree with you on one thing. The mammoth no longer exists. How do I know? I killed the last one with my own right arm."

Thus spake Nimrod, the Mighty Hunter. I threw a stick of firewood at the dogs and bade them quit their unholy howling, and waited. Undoubtedly this liar of singular felicity would open his mouth and requite me for my St. Elias bear.

"It was this way ' he at last began, after the appropriate silence had intervened. "I was in camp one day—"

"Where?" I interrupted.

He waved his hand vaguely in the direction of the northeast, where stretched a terra incognita into which vastness few men have strayed and fewer emerged. "I was in camp one day with Klooch. Klooch was as handsome a little *kamooks* as ever whined betwixt the traces or shoved nose into a camp kettle. Her father was a full-blood Malemute from Russian Pastilik on Bering Sea, and I bred her, and with understanding, out of a clean legged bitch of the Hudson Bay stock. I tell you, O man, she was a corker combination. And now, on this day I have in mind, she was brought to pup through a pure wild wolf of the woods—gray, and long of limb, with big lungs and no end of staying powers. Say! Was there ever the like? It was a new breed of dog I had started, and I could look forward to big things.

"As I have said, she was brought neatly to pup, and safely delivered. I was squatting on my hams over the litter—seven sturdy, blind little beggars—when from behind came a bray of trumpets and crash of brass. There was a rush, like the wind-squall that kicks the heels of the rain, and I was midway to my feet when knocked flat on my face. At the same instant I heard Klooch sigh, very much as a man does when you've planted your fist in his belly. You can stake your sack I lay quiet, but I twisted my head around and saw a huge bulk swaying above me. Then the blue sky flashed into view and I got to my feet. A hairy mountain of flesh was just disappearing in the underbrush on the edge of the open. I caught a rear end glimpse, with a stiff tail, as big in girth as my body, standing out straight behind. The next second only a tremendous hole remained in the thicket, though I could still hear the sounds as of a tornado dying quickly away, underbrush ripping and tearing, and trees snapping and crashing.

"I cast about for my rifle. It had been lying on the ground with the muzzle against a log; but now the stock was smashed, the barrel out of line, and the working-gear in a thousand bits. Then I looked for the slut, and—and what do you suppose?"

I shook my head.

"May my soul burn in a thousand hells if there was anything left of her! Klooch, the seven sturdy, blind little beggars—one, all gone. Where she had stretched was a slimy, bloody depression in the soft earth, all of a yard in diameter, and around the edges a few scattered hairs."

I measured three feet on the snow, threw about it a circle, and glanced at Nimrod.

"The beast was thirty long and twenty high," he answered, "and its tusks scaled over six times three feet. I couldn't believe, myself, at the time, for all that it had just happened. But if my senses had played me, there was the broken gun and the hole in the brush. And there was—or, rather, there was not—Klooch and the pups. O man, it makes me hot all over now when I think of it. Klooch! Another Eve! The mother of a new race! And a rampaging, ranting, old bull mammoth, like a second flood, wiping them, root and branch, off the face of the earth! Do you wonder that the blood-soaked earth cried out to high God? Or that I grabbed the hand-axe and took the trail?"

"The hand-axe?" I exclaimed, startled out of myself by the picture. "The hand-axe, and a big bull mammoth, thirty feet long, twenty feet—"

Nimrod joined me in my merriment, chuckling gleefully. "Wouldn't it kill you?" he cried. "Wasn't it a beaver's dream? Many's the time I've laughed about it since, but at the time it was no laughing matter, I was that danged mad, what of the gun and Klooch. Think of it, O man! A brand-new, unclassified, uncopyrighted breed, and wiped out before ever it opened its eyes or took out its intention papers! Well, so be it. Life's full of disappointments, and rightly so. Meat is best after a famine, and a bed soft after a hard trail.

"As I was saying, I took out after the beast with the hand-axe, and hung to its heels down the valley; but when he circled back toward the head, I was left winded at the lower end. Speaking of grub, I might as well stop long enough to explain a couple of points. Up thereabouts, in the midst of the mountains, is an almighty curious formation. There is no end of little valleys, each like the other much as peas in a pod, and all neatly tucked away with straight, rocky walls rising on all sides. And at the lower ends are always small openings where the drainage or glaciers must have broken out. The only way in is through these mouths, and they are all small, and some smaller than others. As to grub—you've slushed around on the rain-soaked islands of the Alaskan coast down Sitka way, most likely, seeing as you're a traveller. And you know how stuff grows there—big, and juicy, and jungly. Well, that's the way it was with those valleys. Thick, rich soil, with ferns and grasses and such things in patches higher than your head. Rain three days out of four during the summer months; and food in them for a thousand mammoths, to say nothing of small game for man.

"But to get back. Down at the lower end of the valley I got winded and gave over. I began to speculate, for when my wind left me my dander got hotter and hotter, and I knew I'd never know peace of mind till I dined on roasted mammoth-foot. And I knew, also, that that stood for *skookum mamook puka-puk*—excuse Chinook, I mean there was a big fight coming. Now the mouth of my valley was very narrow, and the walls steep. High up on one side was one of those big pivot rocks, or balancing rocks, as some call them, weighing all of a couple of hundred tons. Just the thing. I hit back for camp, keeping an eye open so the bull couldn't slip past, and got my ammunition. It wasn't worth anything with the rifle smashed; so I opened the shells, planted the powder under the rock, and touched it off with slow fuse. Wasn't much of a charge, but the old boulder tilted up lazily and dropped down into place, with just space enough to let the creek drain nicely. Now I had him."

"But how did you have him?" I queried. "Who ever heard of a man killing a mammoth with a hand-axe? And, for that matter, with anything else?"

"O man, have I not told you I was mad?" Nimrod replied, with a slight manifestation of sensitiveness. "Mad clean through, what of Klooch and the gun? Also, was I not a hunter? And was this not new and most unusual game? A hand-axe? Pish! I did not need it. Listen, and you shall hear of a hunt, such as might have happened in the youth of the world when caveman rounded up the kill with hand-axe of stone. Such would have served me as well. Now is it not a fact that man can outwalk the dog or horse? That he can wear them out with the intelligence of his endurance?"

I nodded.

"Well?"

The light broke in on me, and I bade him continue.

"My valley was perhaps five miles around. The mouth was closed. There was no way to get out. A timid beast was that bull mammoth, and I had him at my mercy. I got on his heels again, hollered like a fiend, pelted him with cobbles, and raced him around the valley three times before I knocked off for supper. Don't you see? A race-course! A man and a mammoth! A hippodrome, with sun, moon, and stars to referee!

"It took me two months to do it, but I did it. And that's no beaver dream. Round and round I ran him, me travelling on the inner circle, eating jerked meat and salmon berries on the run, and snatching winks of sleep between. Of course, he'd get desperate at times and turn. Then I'd head for soft ground where the creek spread out, and lay anathema upon him and his ancestry, and dare him to come on. But he was too wise to bog in a mud puddle. Once he pinned me in against the walls, and I crawled back into a deep crevice and waited. Whenever he felt for me with his trunk, I'd belt him with the hand-axe till he pulled out, shrieking fit to split my ear drums, he was that mad. He knew he had me and didn't have me, and it near drove him wild. But he was no man's fool. He knew he was safe as long as I stayed in the crevice, and he made up his mind to keep me there. And he was dead right, only he hadn't figured on the commissary. There was neither grub nor water around that spot, so on the face of it he couldn't keep up the siege. He'd stand before the opening for hours, keeping an eye on me and flapping mosquitoes away with his big blanket ears. Then the thirst would come on him and he'd ramp round and roar till the earth shook, calling me every name he could lay tongue to. This was to frighten me, of course; and when he thought I was sufficiently impressed, he'd back away softly and try to make a sneak for the creek. Sometimes I'd let him get almost there—only a couple of hundred yards away it was—when out I'd pop and back he'd come, lumbering along like the old landslide he was. After I'd done this a few times, and he'd figured it out, he changed his tactics. Grasped the time element, you see. Without a word of warning, away he'd go, tearing for the water like mad, scheming to get there and back before I ran away. Finally, after cursing me most horribly, he raised the siege and deliberately stalked off to the water hole.

"That was the only time he penned me,—three days of it,—but after that the hippodrome never stopped. Round, and round, and round, like a six days' go-as-I-please, for he never pleased. My clothes went to rags and tatters, but I never stopped to mend, till at last I ran naked as a son of earth, with nothing but the old hand-axe in one hand and a cobble in the other. In fact, I never stopped, save for peeps of sleep in the crannies and ledges of the cliffs. As for the bull, he got perceptibly thinner and thinner—must have lost several tons at least—and as nervous as a schoolmarm on the wrong side of matrimony. When I'd come up with him and yell, or lam him with a rock at long range, he'd jump like a skittish colt and tremble all over. Then he'd pull out on the run, tail and trunk waving stiff, head over one shoulder and wicked eyes blazing, and the way he'd swear at me was something dreadful. A most immoral beast he was, a murderer, and a blasphemer.

"But toward the end he quit all this, and fell to whimpering and crying like a baby. His spirit broke and he became a quivering jelly-mountain of misery. He'd get attacks of palpitation of the heart, and stagger around like a drunken man, and fall down and bark his shins. And then he'd cry, but always on the run. O man, the gods themselves would have wept with him, and you yourself or any other man. It was pitiful, and there was so much of it, but I only hardened my heart and hit up the pace. At last I wore him clean out, and he lay down, broken-winded, broken-hearted, hungry, and thirsty. When I found he wouldn't budge, I hamstrung him, and spent the better part of the day wading into him with the hand-axe, he a sniffing and sobbing till I worked in far enough to shut him off. Thirty feet long he was, and twenty high, and a man could sling a hammock between his tusks and sleep comfortably.

Barring the fact that I had run most of the juices out of him, he was fair eating, and his four feet, alone, roasted whole, would have lasted a man a twelvemonth. I spent the winter there myself."

"And where is this valley?" I asked.

He waved his hand in the direction of the northeast, and said: "Your tobacco is very good. I carry a fair share of it in my pouch, but I shall carry the recollection of it until I die. In token of my appreciation, and in return for the moccasins on your own feet, I will present to you these *muclucs*. They commemorate Klooch and the seven blind little beggars. They are also souvenirs of an unparalleled event in history, namely, the destruction of the oldest breed of animal on earth, and the youngest. And their chief virtue lies in that they will never wear out."

Having effected the exchange, he knocked the ashes from his pipe, gripped my hand good night, and wandered off through the snow. Concerning this tale, for which I have already disclaimed responsibility, I would recommend those of little faith to make a visit to the Smithsonian Institute. If they bring the requisite credentials and do not come in vacation time, they will undoubtedly gain an audience with Professor Dolvidson. The *muclucs* are in his possession, and he will verify, not the manner in which they were obtained, but the material of which they are composed. When he states that they are made from the skin of the mammoth, the scientific world accepts his verdict. What more would you have?

The Monarch of St. Elias

FRANK LILLIE POLLOCK

It is not often remembered by most people that there were about three hundred miners in the Yukon territory for years previous to the big finds, laboriously panning out gold at the rate of about four dollars a day. They are now quite unable to account for their missing the present rich mines, and the fact that they had been missing them for years made these veterans somewhat suspicious of the rush in '96; for, like a prophet, a gold boom is often least honored in its own country. Now some of them are thinking regretfully of millions just overlooked. I know, for I was one of them.

There were three of us in '94—Lowden from Seattle, Eustache the French-Canadian, and myself. We were not exactly in the Klondike region that season, but in the southwestern portion—the Mount St. Elias district. We had prospected all that section in July and August, and finding the richest signs on an unnamed creek between the head of the Chittyna River and Lake Kluahne, we built a dug-out cabin and applied ourselves to "burning out" our claim. Snow flew in October, but we kept it out of the diggings, and exhumed large quantities of dirt from the "pay streak," in readiness for the spring wash-up. We were not too abundantly supplied with provisions, and as our stock diminished we became more dependent upon what game we could shoot in the hills. This method of provisioning took time, and we disliked it on that account, for hunting weather is mining weather; but it was on these expeditions that we heard of the "Monarch of St. Elias."

The Indians told us of it, and nobody knew exactly what it was. Their accounts seemed to indicate a sort of bear, but of a weird and novel species. They described the animal as of gigantic size and terrible ferocity, exceeding in these particulars even the northern grizzly.

More than that, it was able to climb trees with facility, and did not sleep through the winter, but continued its awful career regardless of season. Few of them had ever seen the beast, and those few had not stayed to examine its peculiarities. Their fear of it was extreme, and not a savage of them would hunt in the region which it had taken for its own.

We white men did not devote much consideration to these legends, being miners and not hunters. We believed the animal, if not merely a superstition of the aborigines, to be some old grizzly of unusual size, and temper sharpened by age. As to his tree-climbing and other strange abilities, we took them for pure fiction. One detail which made us regard the whole thing as mythical was the firm asseverations of the Indians that the animal had *always* inhabited the Mount St. Elias—ever since the coming of their race.

We had intended going out for supplies to the trading-post of the Alaska Company, eighty miles south, at New Year's, but a blizzard intervened. On the day after Christmas a terrific snowstorm set in from the west, and for nearly a week there was no going outside the cabin. In fact, the cabin itself was so completely buried that when we at last got out it showed merely as a smoking snowdrift—a sort of arctic volcano.

On January 9 the weather was fine and clear, but cold—so cold! We had a little tin thermometer at the cabin, and the mercury stayed in the bulb all day long—which was not so long, after all, for the sun did not rise until half-past ten, and disappeared again at half-past two. But the question of food was an increasingly serious one. We were short already, and in Alaska a man simply cannot *live* without plenty of fat meat, sugar, and hot tea. I was the only one who knew the way to the trading-post, so they gave me an allowance of the scanty "grub," and bundled me off upon my snowshoes several hours before daybreak on the morning of the 10th.

The snowshoeing was good, though somewhat soft, and I expected to be back within eight days. It was quite dark in the creek bottom when I started, but away to the south Mount St. Elias held up a perfect white cone, touched at the peak with a crimson flush, like a finger-tip. Toward this gigantic landmark. I went all through the protracted morning twilight, at the long snowshoe trot of the voyageur. I traveled light. The narrow toboggan I dragged behind me held merely my rifle, ax, sleeping outfit, camp-kettle, and a few pounds of provisions.

By degrees the ruddy tinge crept down the snowy cone, and at its appointed time the sun came up, cold and white, in the southeast. It described its brief arc behind the mountain's shoulder, and sank out of sight again in about five hours, when St. Elias again colored brilliantly, fading gradually till he at last stood up clearly white in the early moonlight. It was long after dark when I camped in a sheltered gorge, and it was long before dawn when I set out again. I crossed the western spur of the mountain and, as there is no temptation to dawdle with the mercury at -30°, I arrived on the third day at the company's little settlement.

I remained there about thirty hours, and bought bacon, flour, sugar, and beans, giving raw gold-dust in payment. It snowed heavily on the second day, so that when I set out on the return journey I found the traveling very heavy, snowshoes and toboggan sinking deep into the fleecy covering. It was about 7 A.M. when I started, for daylight is too small a subject for consideration at that season, and there was a moon.

I quickly foresaw that I would be able to return by no means as rapidly as I had come. Perhaps the difficulties of the road made me careless as to my direction. At any rate, after about eight hours of hard tugging and tramping uphill, I suddenly came out upon the face of a precipice, upon which the trail shelved away into nothingness. I looked about me. The place was perfectly unfamiliar to me.

Above, the mountain sloped gently up a fir-grown slope; but, beneath, the cliff dropped sheer to a depth that made me dizzy to think of. I retreated a few rods, and tried to think where I had missed my way. But I was tired enough to sleep without taking off my snowshoes, and I presently decided to camp where I was till dawn, and then to retrace my steps.

I was close under the central peak of Mount St. Elias. The great cone seemed to hang threateningly right over my head; I had to look almost straight up to see the summit. A perpendicular face of rock offered an excellent wind-break, and I camped in a clump of spruces that grew against it. Half a dozen of these I cut down, transformed the trunks and limbs into fire-wood and the twigs into a mattress, and lighted a blaze close against the cliff-side.

The bitterly cold east wind did not reach me in my shelter, but from time to time a great cloud of dry snow would be blown from some heights above and come sifting in a powdery shower through the tree-tops. It was long after sunset, but a semi-moon shone brilliantly, if now and then, through driving cloud-rack, and lighted the somber wilderness. It was going to be a bitterly cold night, and after supper I laid in a stock of fire-wood, heaped on a dozen logs, and proceeded to *dress* for bed. An extra pair of caribou-skin socks I put on, three extra pairs of moccasins, a woolen cap under my fur one, and two pairs of gloves, and, thus fortified, I wrapped myself in three pairs of blankets, and crawled into my sleeping-bag, which I buttoned up over my head.

I was awakened sharply by a nervous sensation—that nightmare feeling of peril that becomes an instinct with frontiersmen accustomed to sleep in danger. The bag was close around my head and I could see nothing; but I felt cold. I had an impression that the fire had become low; then I heard a faint underground rumble, and I unfastened the flap of the bag and looked out.

The fire had burned very low, and had sunk almost out of sight in a hollow of its own making. The heat had laid bare a portion of the neighboring rock wall, and for the first time I observed what appeared to be the upper end of a large crack or crevice in the rock. It seemed about three feet wide, and the lower part was still concealed by the snow, and from this opening came again the deadened rumble I had heard.

Vague ideas of an earthquake entered my drowsy mind, but I had no time given me for speculation. A huge dark mass seemed to project itself from the cave. There was a snarl, a powerful wild-beast odor, and the faint light gave me a horrible glimpse of cavernous jaws, gleaming tusks, and a wrinkled, hairy face, about three feet from my own.

With a startled shout, I executed a wild roll and somersault backward, sleeping-bag and all, into the deep snow behind me. I went completely out of sight, I suppose, into the fluffy drifts, and continued to wallow, panic-stricken, to get as far as possible from that frightful apparition.

After several moments of frenzied endeavor to efface myself, I became conscious that I was not pursued, and paused to look cautiously back. My visitant still stood in the camp, gazing fixedly in my direction. But what was it? In the twilight it loomed as big as an ox—a long, thin-flanked, tailless body, with almost the shape of a panther, and the attitude of a bear. I could not clearly make out its color, which was probably a dark gray or brown.

Up to this moment I had not thought of the mysterious beast of the Indians, but at sight of this gigantic unknown creature I recalled the savage stories with a thrill of superstitious horror. Its appearance had been so sudden that my nerves were badly shaken. I endeavored to collect myself, and lay breathing heavily, with my eyes fixed upon the strange animal, that stood still, swinging its head with a sinuous and yet bear-like movement.

I was so involved in the drifts that I suppose I was almost invisible, and after a few curious snorts the beast turned away and walked slowly around my camp. In this promenade it came upon something which it investigated with loud sniffs, and which I afterward ascertained to have been the flour-sack. In a moment more I heard the strong cloth go *r-r-r-p*. Next it lighted upon the sugar-bag, and I immediately heard a piggish sound of feeding.

This action of the beast affected me with an amazing sense of relief; it was so very natural, so very bearish. The gloom and impressiveness of the surroundings, and the dramatic effect and mystery of the animal's appearance, had strangely worked upon me; but this awe began to be replaced by the hunter's instinct; besides, I was enraged at the destruction of our priceless supplies.

But presently both these emotions were blotted out by the intense cold. I cannot even attempt to convey to a southerner how cold it was. The air seemed fairly to crackle with the frost. The wind had gone down; so had the moon; and the silence in that ghastly desert was like death itself, and death I knew it would be if I remained long motionless in that temperature without a fire.

But my fire was in the possession of the adversary, and so were my matches, and, worst of all, my rifle. In spite of my numerous wrappings, I began to shiver, partly with cold and partly with excitement, as I tried to think of some plan for circumventing the beast, which was still guzzling its—or rather our—sweets.

If I could only get the brute away from the camp long enough for me to get my Winchester and put on my snowshoes, I would have it at a disadvantage in the deep snow. But at present I had little doubt that it could move with much more facility than I could. Thus I felt a natural reluctance to attract its attention, and at the same time I had no idea that it would return to its cave. I did not wish it to do this, in fact, for I became determined to solve the mystery while I had the opportunity, since I had no doubt that this creature was the Indians' legendary terror.

Several minutes passed while I considered the situation and grew numb. Finally I disengaged myself from sleeping-bag and blankets, and waded up close to the edge of the trampled camp-space. The animal ceased its operations at my approach, and bristled up, standing tensely on guard and snarling viciously. In desperate resolution, I packed a large snowball as well as I could from the dry snow, and threw it at the animal. The snow hit the animal on the ear.

With a savage roar it rushed at me. The moment it left the camp it plunged over its back, and I floundered aside from its charge. In the instant thus gained I struggled into the camp, and had time to seize the gun and to draw it from its buckskin cover before the beast turned. The plunge into the light snow seemed to bewilder it for a second. It wheeled, however, and made at me, coming through the drifts like a snow-plow; and as it came I shot full at its breast.

There was a long streak of dazzling flame, and a crashing report that mingled with a coughing roar. Through the smoke I hazily perceived the brute still plunging toward me, blood streaming down its chest and shoulders, and its little wicked eyes fairly blazing in the gloom. I fired again as it came on, and leaped aside to avoid the rush. It went blindly past me for a few feet, and then dropped, bleeding profusely, upon the snow.

It lay quite still for a few moments, and I approached the possible corpse with considerable circumspection. At a range of ten feet I fired again, aiming at the fatal spot at the base of the ear; but my hand shook as I pulled.

The shot acted like magic. At the report, the animal sprang bodily into the air, horrible with extended claws and wide, gory jaws. Blood and snow flew in every direction. Without knowing how it happened, I found myself plunging into the snow again with huge strides, frantically wrenching at the lever of my rifle, which had for a moment jammed. But when I looked back the foe had not followed. It had started, as if dazed, in the opposite direction, and was plowing through the snow, leaving a trail as if a team of horses had passed.

I hastened to put on my snowshoes and follow; but in the few moments thus lost the beast gained several rods, and was already out of sight in the gloom. I had some idea of what was going to happen, and shuffled over the snow at a run. When I had the animal in view again, it was near the precipice, and still charging blindly forward. I fired twice without stopping it or making it turn, and in another instant over it went. I heard a dull thump as its body struck some projecting crag, and then there was silence. I might listen long before I would hear the sound of its fall from the bottom of that deep abyss.

The mystery had eluded me to the last. But I investigated the hole from which it proceeded, and found it the mouth of a cavern, running down for some distance among the rocks. It had been masked by the drifts before my fire had melted them away. Whether the animal was hibernating there or was merely snowed up by the great storm, I cannot guess. According to the Indians' story, the latter would be most probable.

I picked up the correct trail without difficulty on the morrow, with the firm resolve to return as soon as possible, seek out some means of access to the bottom of the chasm, and search for the body of my strange antagonist. But ill fortune again intervened, for I arrived at our cabin in the midst of a blinding snow-storm which effectually obliterated my old trail, and I could form no definite notion of the course I had taken when I went astray.

Neither can I offer any reasonable theory as to the nature of the beast I slew. Of course, it is not impossible that there are actually new species in the unexplored Alaskan wilderness, but this is a somewhat desperate hypothesis.* Eustache argued that it might have been a "cinnamon" bear strayed up from the south and grown thin with the increased rigor of the struggle for existence. At any rate, we never encountered another specimen, though we observed that the death of the beast had not put an end to the Indians' fears. According to them, it continued to rule savagely over its icy St. Elias domain.

---

* The recent Harriman expedition to Alaska reports the discovery of a species of bear as big as an ox. Possibly the Monarch of St. Elias was one of these "Kodiak bears."

The Great White Serpent of the Malorli

Alexander Ricketts

The wedding ceremony was over, and Harding had congratulated the bride and groom in the calm, conventional manner.
As he turned to go, he stood for a long moment in the doorway,
gazing back on them with an inscrutable look. Then he went out
into the night. All that night he tramped the streets with restless
energy, but the morning found him leaning upon the rail of a liner,
staring blankly at the shores of the bay as they glided by, and if
any one had been rash enough to tell him that when he next saw
them a wife would be standing at his side, he would have revelled
in throwing his informant overboard. And that was the last his
friends saw of him for years.

Forgetting is a hard job for a man like Harding, but even he
found, as time went by, that the memory of the girl he loved did
not sting him so often or sharply, and the restless desire for
change—any change, so long as it was a change—which had driven
him hither and thither all over Europe and most of Asia, and
plunged him recklessly into any adventure which suggested itself,
did not lash him on so relentlessly. Instead, there came a time when
any action became an effort, a time when all he sought was quies-
cence of mind and body. He was not gloomy or misanthropic. He
had never been either; but the fierce fires of his longing for her
who had given herself to another were at last under his control,
and he felt the reaction from the turmoil as a strong man does
after strenuous conflict.

In this mood he turned his steps to North Africa. On a prior visit fate had put it in his way to do a favor to the sheik of one of the desert tribes, and he now recalled the frank invitation to be his guest for as long as he would. With considerable difficulty Harding located the sheik, and at considerable danger joined him. The tribesmen do not forget, and his welcome was undoubted. The life contented him. The dignified courtesy of the men, never intruding but always cordially ready to companion him, the slow, infrequent speech, the long, thoughtful silences, all soothed his distracted spirit, and in aimless roving, either with the sheik's tribe or with others akin to it, he passed many years in the Desert.

The weird tales of the story-tellers, told in the flickering light of the camp-fire while the steady stars shone above them with the strong, full light of the desert nights, and all around stretched the vast reaches of barren sand, fascinated him. Particularly one—it was hardly a story, simply a collection of rumors and guesses woven into a narrative—about the Great White Serpent of the Malorli interested him. It was to the effect that somewhere in the forest on the further side of the Great Desert dwelt a tribe of serpent worshippers. The object of their adoration was a monstrous snake, pure white, and of prehistoric size. This god was fed upon human sacrifices, but refused all not white like itself. The worshippers being negroes of quite phenomenal blackness were therefore compelled to kidnap the sacrifices where they might. Diligent inquiry convinced Harding that the tale had this much foundation: There was not a tribe among the desert rovers that had not for many, many years mysteriously lost a member. Sometimes it was a man, sometimes, a woman, but the lost was always youthful and always gone without a trace except that the following morning in the midst of the camp would be found a rudely carved ivory snake. Pursuit was invariably futile.

Again Harding's mood changed. He began to long for something different. What it should be he didn't care. Civilization did not attract him, but the aimless life he was living no longer satisfied him. Then it was that this fascinating story fastened upon his imagination, and he resolved to investigate it.

Upon making his determination known, the old sheik tried to dissuade him. Then he offered to accompany Harding, himself and his young men. This Harding refused, saying, with a smile. "No, no, Sheik Ilderim; one man can go in a quest like this where two cannot. I go alone, and if I stay, there are few to mourn me."

"Then may Allah be with you, my son," replied Sheik Ilderim, stroking his beard sadly, but too courteous to offer further opposition to his guest. "If go you will, we will take you to the farthest oasis; there you shall take the two fleetest camels, for perchance if you fail to reach the forest on the first you can return on the second, and there, if you return not for ten years, you will always find some of us awaiting to welcome or succor you, and may Allah guide your camel. Allah is Allah!"

A month later amid the lamentations of the tribe Harding set out from the oasis. He travelled light, for he knew that speed was of the utmost importance. He carried a rifle, revolver and knife, but he knew that if strategy would not gain the goal he sought force could not. His precious store of parched grain and dried dates, with a water-skin, were loaded on the led-camel, the other—they were both the pick of the herd—bore himself. He travelled by night, shielding himself as best he could from the insupportable rays of the sun in the daytime, and urging his camels to their best speed. Still, when at length the one he rode sank down dying, he could see nothing in all the world but the waste of desolate sand measuring away in all directions inimitably.

But he had no thought of turning back. Lightening himself of the rifle, he mounted the spare camel, with no weapons but his revolver, a handful of extra cartridges and his knife, and pushed on. Another night's travel, and another, and in the middle of the third his second camel fell beneath him with a gasp almost human.

Slowly Harding scanned the horizon. Nothing but barren sand met his questioning gaze. Throwing away his revolver and cartridges, hesitating a moment over his knife, but deciding to retain that, he stuffed a handful of dates into his pocket, drained the last drops of water and pushed out on foot into the desert. On and on he plodded, his mind set only on never giving up until he had reached the farthest point possible to human endurance.

The sun came up and found him doggedly stumbling on. Suddenly he stopped, shaded his eyes with his hands for a minute, and gave a hoarse cry of wonder. There, bearing directly down upon him was a group of perhaps a dozen camels, but they were of a size and strength and speed such as he had never seen, and leading them rode three repulsive negroes, black as glistening coal.

The next moment he was surrounded, and with lightning-like swiftness bound and laid in a covered litter slung between two of the camels. Then the whole party, turning directly back, bore him swiftly away, retracing its tracks; but in all of it, to his utter amazement, he was handled with the gentlest care.

A long day's journey brought them to the edge of a vast forest. There he was transferred to another party of negroes more repulsive, if that were possible, than his captors, and at once a march was begun into the forest. Up to this time not a word had been spoken, but now he was surprised to find his guards quite ready to talk with him. Their speech was a sort of mongrel Arabic which he had little difficulty in comprehending, and they eagerly assured him that no harm was intended him, but upon the object of his capture they maintained a stolid silence. And all their actions bore out their assurances. Indeed, he was not only treated kindly, but with a deference and consideration which caused him the most gruesome anticipations.

For five days they marched steadily, deeper and deeper into the forest. On the sixth they reached a little village on the edge of a small lake, and the whole populace gave itself up immediately to feasting and rejoicing over their arrival. As the villagers thronged around him, Harding became quite uncomfortable over his prominence in the holiday, especially when the maidens openly admired his complexion and figure, and more so as the haunting suspicion never left him that it was due entirely to his being destined as the next sacrifice to the Great White Serpent, if that storied reptile really existed. With a steadily sinking heart he reflected that he could only await developments, escape being clearly impossible, although he was allowed to go unbound.

A day and a night they rested in the village. The next, after elaborate and evidently ceremonial bathing in the lake, the party donned white robes, putting one also on Harding, and set forth along a well-used road leading from the village. An hour's walk brought them to a mighty river. Both its banks for a long distance up and down were crowded with waiting negroes, maintaining a solemn silence, but what instantly riveted Harding's attention was a small island directly in the centre of the stream. It was covered, until in many places the water lapped the walls, with a circular stone structure some fifty feet high, and pierced here and there by gateways with pointed arches.

The arrival of the party was greeted with loud acclaim by the multitudes thronging the banks of the river, and as they marched through to a barge awaiting them, the cries of joy and welcome sounded like a death knell in Harding's ears, for he grimly suspected that he himself had little occasion to feel joyous.

They were met at the largest gateway of the stone structure by a number of men robed in white also, and conducted into a lofty and spacious hall. Harding's eyes rapidly swept the room in hopes some way of escape might appear, but as they scanned the lower end of it he felt his knees tremble beneath him, and the hand of fear upon his throat. The next second, however, he recovered himself, and, outwardly calm, gazed upon the most horrible sight he had ever had to face.

It was no mere story-teller's myth. There, coiled fold upon fold, was an enormous snake. It was a glistening, phosphorescent white, except where its heavy-lidded eyes shone like lifeless rubies, and it seemed to Harding that all the hall was filled with a dull and sickly radiance shimmering from its coils. He could not guess what its length might be, but at the thickest its body was certainly as big around as a barrel.

Around and around in a great circle in front of it swung the priests, their white robes swinging and swaying with their motions, chanting as they danced a dirge-like melody that sent the chills creeping up and down Harding's spine and stiffened the hairs upon the' back of his neck. Faster and faster they circled, now contracting their ring, now expanding it, weaving and whirling, swaying and swinging, until Harding grew dizzy watching them. Then, with a thunderous triumphant shout, they stopped, forming the two sides of a lane straight from Harding to the serpent.

And then he rubbed his eyes in sheer bewilderment, forgetting his awful peril. For, from amongst the folds of the coiled serpent, lightly sprang a maiden so radiant in her pure loveliness that his heart stood still as she slowly and bashfully advanced up the lane between the silent priests, and stood blushing before him, but with her glorious eyes fixed confidently upon his, and her hands outstretched trustingly for his in a mute appeal. She was irresistible. Harding gathered her hands firmly in his, and hardly knowing what he was doing, drew her closer and closer to him until his lips reverently touched her forehead.

At this the priests burst into joyous acclaim, and from their midst came the oldest, who laid his hands upon their heads, saying, "Man and wife ye now are."

Then, turning to the assembled priests, he cried, "Behold, O Slaves of the Serpent, behold ye the Children of the Serpent! Let all worship and care for them as ye would the seed of the Great White Serpent shall not die."

They were then taken to the roof of the building and shown to the crowds outside with the same words, and from that multitude instantly rose shout after shout of joy and thanksgiving. From there they were conducted to another part of the building, separated from the Hall of the Serpent by heavy wooden doors, and left alone.

Harding looked long upon the wife he had so unexpectedly married, and drew a long breath.

"We-ell," he said. "Well, this being food for a snake isn't so awful after all. Come here, little one."

With a glad little cry, the girl, who had been standing before him demurely waiting his pleasure, sprang to his side and clasped her hands upon his arm.

"You are content?" she asked, anxiously exploring his eyes.

"Content?" laughed Harding, putting his arms fondly around her. "More than that. I never expected to be so happy in my life. But what does it all mean? I thought I was to be fed to his Royal Snakeship as a particularly dainty tidbit."

Then Haidee, his wife, told him of the cult of the Serpent. The Great White Serpent was old, so old that no one knew when its worship had begun. Within the memory of the oldest priest, and of his father, and of his father before him, it had always lived in the temple; it on one side, and those known as its Children on the other, cared for and waited on by its Slaves, the negroes. Six times in the year was it fed with a pure white bullock without spot or blemish. Then for days it lay torpid and motionless, and none dared intrude upon it. At other times it came and went up or down the river, a stream from which swept across the end of the Hall of the Serpent through doors made for that purpose, as it chose, but always it returned for the feeding. But, at intervals, it was fed upon human sacrifices. Harding shuddered, and drew Haidee closer to him, questioning her eagerly.

Yes, the Children of the Serpent were the sacrifices. If it were not so, the Slaves of the Serpent would perish miserably from the earth. When a child came to the Children of the Serpent it was taken from them, and carefully reared by a woman selected from all those who were Slaves of the Serpent. Then, when it was seen that it would live, was the time of the sacrifice, and both parents, instead of the bullock, were sacrificed to the Serpent. And when the child had grown to a marriageable age, the Desert Men were sent out on their strong and swift camels to find a mate for it, for they must both be white, nor did they ever fail to bring one, even as he himself had been brought. So the line of the Children of the Serpent never died, nor did the Great White Serpent ever lack its human sacrifices.

But if there was no child? No, Haidee did not know what then. It had never happened. Probably the Children of the Serpent would be sacrificed just the same, and the Desert Men would be sent out for both a man and a woman. She did not know, and why seek trouble? There was always a child.

During the days that followed, in all his happiness in Haidee, Harding's mind was ever busy planning their escape. He would not accept the dreadful fate which overhung them, with Haidee's fatalism, as inevitable, and it was a continual spur to his ingenuity, but without success. He learned that the priests who had crowded the Hall of the Serpent on the day of his arrival were also the chiefs of the villages scattered throughout the forest, and from their number he could easily see that for him and Haidee to traverse it without being discovered was an impossibility. Escape by land was out of the question.

But there was the river at their very door. If only they could float down that undiscovered it must take them to the sea, and whatever their fate then it must be less horrible than the one awaiting them. He had plenty of time and materials to construct a raft, for no one ever ventured to come to the temple unless they signalled for them to bring food, except upon the days of worship. But the fishermen on the river, and the women and children always on its banks made such a scheme impossible in the daytime, and a quiet investigation showed Harding that, no matter how free they seemed to be, a close guard was kept upon every exit from the temple at night. Almost he lost hope.

One of his pleasures during all this time was in weaning his wife away from her superstitious worship of the Serpent. Brought up to reverence it as a god, as she of course had been, it was long before his patient teaching of higher and better things prevailed, nor could she ever look upon it with the utter abhorrence which filled his soul at the bare thought of it. Still, she did come, helped doubtless by her great love for him, to think of it as a mere reptile. Nor did she shudder any longer at the sacrilege when Harding, in his moments of despair, declared that before they should become its victims he would kill it, and endure whatever punishment the infuriated savages might inflict.

Twice had Harding been forced to witness the sacrifice of the white bullock to the Great White Serpent. Each time the sight of the slimy folds slowly crushing the living, screaming animal into a shapeless mass of broken bones and quivering flesh, the careful moistening of it with fetid saliva, and the deliberate deglutition of it had filled him with such sickening disgust and loathing that he could hardly stagger, faint and nauseated, from the horrid scene.

After the third time he covered his quivering face with shaking hands, and sank down weak and nerveless upon a skin at his wife's side. Quickly she caught his head to her bosom, and sought to soothe him by every endearment known to a loving woman.

"Oh, Haidee, Haidee," he cried, shivering with loathing even in her arms, "it—it actually screamed while being swallowed. It did. It did. It was alive yet. I heard it. Oh, my God!"

Little by little he regained command over his unstrung nerves, and ashamed of his outbreak, began fiercely planning the death of the great snake.

"I'll slash its head off to-morrow with that heavy knife I cut the rushes for your basket-making with," he declared, pacing excitedly back and forth. "I'll kill the beastly worm, and skin it, and make—" he stopped suddenly, and stood motionless for a few moments lost in thought. Then he continued, more excitedly, "Why didn't I think of this before? It'll work. I know it'll work. That infernal snake can go wherever it pleases. And its hide is waterproof, of course. Haidee, my dearest, how long will it take you to weave two great baskets—so big?"

He held his hands wide apart.

"What is it, beloved? Tell me all," asked Haidee, alarmed by the wild excitement in his face.

With rapid words Harding explained the plan that had flashed upon him, developing it as he spoke. He would kill the snake, and carefully skin it. Then he would place the basket-work inside the skin, and draw that up around it. It would make a canoe which he was sure would hold them, and the girth of the snake was so large that they could draw the skin clear over the top of the basket-work, and lie inside until they were safe from observation. The head he could hold above water by running a pole up the neck, and a couple of poles spliced together would hold the tail out behind. The basket-work would give enough roundness to the body to deceive anybody, especially in the water, and as the snake swam up or down the river at pleasure no one would think anything strange at seeing it or would dare investigate too closely. It would certainly be a couple of days before they would be missed, perhaps longer, and by that time he hoped to be beyond pursuit. In any event, no more horrible fate could be theirs than the one to which they were doomed.

Haidee caught his enthusiasm, and at once set to work. They really, upon sober second thought, had plenty of time, for the snake never was seen for at least two weeks after it had gorged a bullock, during which time it lay torpid in its hall digesting its meal, and until the end of that time it would excite suspicion at once if it were seen in the river.

The day at last dawned, however, when the Great White Serpent would again be stirring. Haidee's basket-work, made as nearly waterproof as possible, was ready, and the knife had been sharpened to a razor-edge upon a smooth stone Harding had found on the bank of the river. Grasping it firmly, he gave his wife a long embrace, and swinging open the door, stepped resolutely within the Hall of the Serpent.

There it lay, stretched at its enormous length, inert and motionless still from its gorge, the Great White Serpent of the Malorli. Softly but swiftly Harding dashed towards its head. As he approached, it opened its eyes lazily and fixed them full upon him with a sinister stare. There was something so evil, so malignant, so cruel and devilish in their pallid depths that for an instant they halted him as an icy hand seemed to clutch his heart. The next, he had taken the last stride, and surely and mightily struck the blow. The keen, heavy knife bit clear through the backbone, right at the base of the skull. There was a mighty heave of the huge body, and Harding leaped across it just in time to avoid being enveloped in the fatal embrace of its horrid folds. Writhing and twisting, coiling and uncoiling, now lashing out with tremendous force, next contracting into fearful knots, the enormous reptile thrashed wildly about the hall. A dozen times Harding missed an awful death by the least fraction of an inch before he gained the door his wife bravely held open for him. Breathless and panting they watched the earth-shaking death throes of the monster.

At last, with a mighty quiver from head to tail, it lay still in death. With a shout of triumph Harding sprang to its side, and slipped the point of his knife under the thick skin where his blow had laid it open. Rip, rip, rip, and he had it slit clear to the tail, still faintly moving. He worked with feverish energy, Haidee valiantly helping, for now they had little time to spare, and he found that before their strength was equal to drawing the skin from under he had to cut the body into lengths. They hardly took time to breathe. The sweat streamed from them. A dozen times their strength seemed exhausted. But, as night fell, the basket-work was in place, the thick skin drawn up around it and sewn up, except for a slit big enough to admit them, and made as waterproof at the seam as possible with melted beeswax, the pole holding the head above water propped securely in place, the other spliced one extended the tail, and, as he held this oddest of vessels buoyantly floating upon the stream running across the end of the Hall, and noted its naturalness, Harding at last felt with an exultant thrill that escape was a possibility.

Haidee was already inside with a small store of provisions. Harding stepped lightly in and stretched himself upon the bottom, after one keen look around to see that all was right so far. He drew the skin together above them, and the current swept them out upon the broad bosom of the river. For good or ill their strange voyage had begun.

And it went better than even Harding in his most sanguine moments had dared hope. For three nights and two days they drifted with the current, without accident or molestation, and shortly after dawn of the third day he was suddenly awakened from the light doze he had permitted himself by the sound of rifle shots and the noise of bullets zipping into the water at his side. With his heart in his mouth he peered cautiously out. There, hardly a hundred yards away, came steaming up a little launch with a man, a white man, standing in the bow, blazing hopefully away at what he mistook for a snake.

With a joyous shout Harding sprang to his feet. "Hold on! Hold on there!" he shouted, waving his arms with reckless disregard of an upset. "Do you want to start international complications by shooting us?"

"Ah, beg pardon I'm sure," replied the sportsman, dropping his rifle in surprise. "I didn't know it was your private yacht, you know. But what the devil—oh, beg pardon, a lady, too."

Explanations were soon made. The stranger was an English sportsman exploring the river in his launch, but at once he turned back and carried them to the nearest port where steamships touched. The snake's skin probably adorns his home at this minute, as Harding, with great generosity, never wanting to set eyes on it again, presented him with it.

A few weeks later Harding and Haidee stood upon the deck of a vessel watching the shores of Africa fade into the distance.

"And now to get word of my safety to good old Sheik Ilderim," he murmured, looking fondly into her eyes, "and then home, my dearest."

And Haidee answered, the love-light shining back at him happily, "Where your home is, O beloved, there is mine."

Alfred Jenkins and the Didi

ANONYMOUS

Alfred Jenkins they called him on the Victoria Regina, though the name suited his personality about as well as a pair of plaid trousers and a billycock hat would have suited his red-skinned young person, which bore no clothing save a calico 'lap' or apron. He belonged to one of the sparse native tribes of British Guiana, being an Ackawoise Indian from the borders of that debatable land, west of the Cuyuni River, which some years ago seemed likely to make trouble between Britain and Venezuela.

When I came across him he was down at the coast on the Victoria Regina sugar plantation, and had been steadily working there for four consecutive years. As the passionate attachment of the Guiana Indian to his native forests rarely allows him to stay at the coast for any serviceable length of time, Alfred Jenkins's long spell of plantation-work was something quite phenomenal. My friend Byngham, the manager of the Victoria Regina, suggested as a possible explanation that the Ackawoise had probably killed some Indian back in his own country, and hoped by working down at the coast to escape the blood atonement which the relatives of the dead man would be certain to exact; but, at the same time, Byngham stultified his own suggestion by saying that he didn't believe Alfred Jenkins could harm a fly.

Certainly the dusky face that looked out of its frame of long black hair was a strong support to Byngham's belief. Its prevailing expression was a somewhat melancholic but altogether amiable reserve; though that was not the expression his face chanced to wear the first time I saw him. He was standing listlessly by the *magass-logé* (the refuse canes from which the juice has been expressed), staring into space with a look of such tragically intense longing and despair on his face that it caught and held my attention until he, becoming aware of my presence, turned sharply round and began gathering up a heap of *magass* to take to the furnace for fuel. That curiously pathetic look which I had surprised on the Indian's face somehow made me take an interest in him; and having, as the guest of a bachelor planter, more time on my hands than I knew what to do with, I gave some of it to cultivating the acquaintance of Alfred Jenkins with fair words and gifts of tobacco.

Alfred Jenkins could talk English—negro English—remarkably well for an Indian; but for some time he responded to my conversational advances with a discouraging though courteous reticence. Then one day, as I talked to him of the great forests of the interior, I suddenly knew, though he spoke no word, that his heart, for the first time, had turned to me as a man and a brother. I myself had hunted among the great tree-columns in the green-domed, dimly lighted vastnesses of these forests, and had eaten *labba* flesh and drank bush-water; and these facts put that into my speech which reached his heart. Afterwards he readily communicated his simple impressions of the world as he had known it.

One afternoon I took it into my head to go a-fishing with hook and line in the sea, and Alfred Jenkins rowed me out a mile or so beyond the *courida*-lined shore in a boat that Byngham kept inside the *koker* of the Victoria Regina trench. As we waited patiently for the fish to bite, I suddenly bethought myself to ask Alfred Jenkins what had been amiss with him that day I first saw him standing by the *magass-logé*.

"You looked, indeed, as if you wanted something very badly that you had no chance of getting," I said.

"Oah, sah, me felt bery much bad dat time," he said simply. "Carry *magass* to furnace no good. Work in cane-fields no good. What dey give eat da heah no good. Notting no good da heah. Only forest him good all ober. Me sick—sick for de smell ob de much big forest! But me neber see him no moah. Neber make de *labba* jump out ob his hole an' see him take de water! Neber go watch for de *abouyahs* under de saouari tree! Neber, neber no moah!"

His "neber, neber no moah" sounded almost as mournful as the tones of a passing bell.

"But what keeps you from going back to your own place if you want to?" I asked bluntly.

A look of ghastly fear passed like a spasm over his face. My words had evidently conjured up before his eyes some vision of no ordinary dread. This made me curious to know what possible terror the forest could hold for him strong enough to overcome his passionate craving for the life that is the only life worth living to the Guiana Indian. So, after a little coaxing, I prevailed on him to tell me his story. I give it here, pretty nearly in his own words, but done into readable English.

"It began in the beginning with my brother. He had not gone hunting for some days, for a little son had just been born to him, and he could not leave his *benab* (Indian hut) till the child's spirit grew strong enough to take no harm as it went with him, unseen, through the forest. There was only cassava to eat, and he was glad when the time came for him to go hunting again; but all that day he could kill nothing. He started no *labbas* when he poked a stick into their burrows among the tangled tree-woods; he went on the tracks of the tapir and the deer, but he did not see either tapir or deer; he watched the feeding-grounds of the peccaries and the cavies, but none came to feed. He came home and was very sad, for he saw that his luck in the chase was gone.

"Then, that he might bring his luck back again, he rubbed into his blood the juice of two different *beenas* (plants with acrid juices with which the Indians inoculate themselves to get luck in the chase)—the *beena* that makes a man good at killing peccaries, and the *beena* that makes him good at killing *labbas*. But he could not have rubbed in enough juice, for when he went hunting next day it was the same as the day before: he killed no peccary, and no *labba*, and no beast of any kind; and he went to the creek, but the fish would not let him catch them. His heart was very sore, and he remembered that his wife could only give him cassava-cakes for supper.

"As he turned to leave the creek he saw something move on the ground behind some leaves and tangled lianas. Sure that it would be something good to eat, he shot an arrow amongst the leaves quick as a flash of lightning. A very strange cry came from behind the leaves, like the cry of a piccaninny; just one cry, but it told my brother that his arrow had not missed. He was glad, because he thought his luck was coming back to him; and he put in his hand among the leaves and pulled out the thing he had shot. He looked, and thought it was a baby-monkey. He looked again, and saw it was not a baby-monkey. He looked again, and wondered much, for it looked like his own little piccaninny, which he had last seen asleep in the little hammock slung round his wife's neck as she set out for the cassava-ground that morning; but the skin of the little thing he held in his hands was covered with a thin red down which felt soft and silky, like the stuff that fills the pod of the silk cotton-tree. Then a very great fear was my brother's, for it came into his mind that the creature he held in his hands was a little Didi picca-ninny.

"Not many Indians have seen Didi; but all fear them. They are less than human, and they are more than human: the hairy wild-men of the forest. It is not good for the Indian to meet the Didi, for the Didi are very strong and fierce and cunning, and they do not love the Indian. It is well there are not many Didi, and that they do not let themselves be seen very often nowadays.

"When my brother saw that the dead thing in his hands was a baby Didi he threw it away from him, and turned to flee, in much fear. As he turned, a full-grown she-Didi, panting with making much haste, rushed forward and picked up the dead little one from the ground, with a great cry which made my brother run very fast. Another cry—this time not sorrowful but angry—made him look back, and he saw the Didi coming after him, with her piccaninny clasped tight in her long, hairy arms. He ran very fast, and he got to the clearing where his *benab* stood before the Didi could reach him. She did not follow him beyond the edge of the clearing. She stayed there, and in the darkness of the night she wailed with loud, strange, sad cries for her piccaninny that was dead; and sometimes she screamed fierce words. No man knows the Didi tongue; but my brother *felt* the meaning of the words she screamed, and he trembled, and his wife trembled, so that their hammocks swung against each other.

"When the morning came my brother was not any more afraid. The cries had stopped, and he was glad, thinking the Didi had forgotten her dead little one, and had gone away back to her mate. He went hunting again, for he wanted meat sorely. This day his luck came back to him, and at sunset he returned home glad, carrying a fat *labba* and two *accouries*. He thought how good his wife would make that *labba* taste for supper, and how much better *labba* was than the cassava-cakes which she would perhaps have already baked for supper.

"There were no hot cassava-cakes waiting for him in his *benab*, and no wife, and no quiet little baby. He wondered why she stayed so late at his little cassava-clearing, and he went to fetch her home. Before he reached the cassava-ground he found her. She was lying across the path leading to the *benab*, and she was very much dead, for fierce and strong hands had twisted off her head, as a man twists off the head of a fowl. Her baby was clasped tight to her breast, but its head lay with its mother's a little way apart. My brother's eyes saw everything, and he knew that the Didi had not forgotten her dead little one. He sat down on the ground beside the bodies of his wife and child. He would not have cared just then had the Didi come back and twisted off his head too. After a little time he rose and gathered up the bodies and heads, and carried them back to the *benab*, and laid them in his wife's hammock. He himself sat on the ground beneath the hammock, and the night was very long to him.

"Next day I came back from where I had been on a big hunt up the river for many days with others of my tribe. I went to my brother's *benab* to greet him and his wife. He still sat on the ground beneath his wife's hammock. He did not greet me. He pointed in silence to the hammock above. I looked, and saw what the hammock held. Then my heart was very sore for my brother. There were only we two left of our family, for my wife had been dead many moons, and I had not yet taken another. My brother then told me all that had happened in the matter of the Didi and the killing of his wife and child.

"I said, 'The Didi has killed more of yours than you have killed of hers. Let us go and find her, and exact the blood-atonement. There are two of us.'

"'The Didi is very cunning and very strong,' he said, 'and we are but men. Yet, if we find her I will kill her.'

"For many days we hunted for the Didi—we two alone, for the others of our tribe were afraid, and said, 'Why seek death?' We never found her. She was cunning and kept out of the way, knowing that men who have blood to avenge can sometimes be as strong as Didi. We hunted for the Didi all the time it takes a moon to grow big in the sky and to grow small again. Then we tired because we could not find her, and we hunted for her no more; we went only on the tracks of the deer and the peccary and the other animals of the forest.

"One day, towards sunset, my brother and I were returning through the forest from our hunting. He carried across his shoulders a *wiriebiserie* (a small forest-deer) that he had shot. I had had no luck with my bow and arrow that day, and carried nothing; therefore I walked lightly and drew far ahead of him. From behind me, suddenly, there reached my ears a cry—a cry very bad to hear—the cry of a man who dies in much pain. It was my brother's voice. I turned and ran swiftly back along the forest path. There lay my brother on the ground, and over him stooped a strange hairy creature that worked with its hands about his throat. I knew it was the Didi; and it came into my mind then that she, unseen, had been watching us mockingly from tree-tops and from behind dense undergrowths all the days we had hunted for her, and that she had been waiting for her chance. It had come when my brother, off his guard and burdened with the dead *wiriebiserie*, had passed along the path far behind me.

"All this came into my mind, and, still running forward, I fixed an arrow in my bow and sent it flying on before me. It struck the Didi on the forearm, and, snarling like a dog disturbed at his food, she raised her head and saw me. Instantly she took away her hands from where they had been, and straightening herself up, made the motion of throwing. Something came rushing through the air and struck me on the chest, knocking all the wind out of me. Then it fell on the ground. I looked. It was my brother's head, and it was his blood that was running down my body and staining my 'lap' red.

"My running stopped short, as if my ankles had been firmly seized hold of from behind. I looked at my brother's head and I looked at the Didi. She opened her mouth very wide, showing great tusks like a peccary's, and she laughed in my face. Loud, harsh, yelping laughter it was, human-like yet not human, for no man or woman ever laughed a laugh like hers, with the howl of a beast running through it. It turned the blood in my heart to water, and made my knees weak. I no longer burned to rush forward and avenge my brother. Her laugh had made me a coward. I wanted to get away and hide; but I was afraid to turn my back to her. I was afraid to look away from her. She did not look away from me. Steadily eying me all the while, she plucked my arrow out of her forearm, in which I saw it had stuck but lightly by reason of the thickness of her pelt Then she raised the hairy arm to her lips and began to suck the shallow wound, thus showing herself crafty as an Indian in her knowledge of the *woralli* poison with which we smear our arrowheads.

"Still sucking at her arm, she came forward till she stood within two paces of me. My eyes were fastened on her. She stood on her flat-soled feet no higher than a woman, but she was very broad and very strongly made. She was covered all over with a thick coat of coarse red hair, save where the hair of her head, long, tangled, and black, hung around her face. Her face was as the face of one of the human race, save that it also was covered with hair smooth and close and short as the hair of a terrier dog. Her arms were twice as big as a man's. Her hands, with great talons at the hairy finger-ends, looked fit for what they had done to my brother and his wife and child. Just now blood was dripping from the Didi's hands, but it was not her blood. My arrow had not drawn blood from her.

"With thick, slobbering lips still on the wound, she stood before me, and looked at me over her great arm. Her wild, cruel, red eyes mocked me as they looked into mine from out of their deep sockets. They mocked me with the mocking of an evil spirit. Nevertheless, they told me seriously many things, and as plainly as if the Didi had spoken to me in my own speech. They told me that she knew I feared her with a fear passing the fear of death, and that her heart was glad to know this. They told me that she would kill me as she had killed my brother and his wife and child, because I was the brother of him who had killed her little one; also, because I had struck her with my arrow. They told, moreover, that it was her humour not to kill me then, but that, sooner or later, by her hands my death would come. Her eyes told me all this and much besides. Then she took the great bow from my slack hand, and she bent the hard redwood between her thumb and forefinger, and broke it as if it had been a reed; and as she did that she opened her wide, slobbering mouth, and again she laughed the laugh that had made me a coward. Then she slowly stepped aside, and the forest swallowed her up.

"I stood there on the path alone, and my brother's head was at my feet. I left the head where it was, and my brother's body, and the dead *wiriebiserie* he had been carrying. I left them to the jaguars and the pumas, and, fearful as a woman, ran fast away from the place. I ran to the nearest village of the people of my tribe, and I told all that had happened. They were all much afraid, and said, 'It is an ill thing to quarrel with the hairy wild-people of the forest.'

"That evening I took my woodskin, and I put in it a *cartowerie* (an Indian basket made of canework), in which I had packed my hammock and some cassava bread, and barbecued fish, and plenty arrowheads; and I took with me another bow in place of the one the Didi had broken between her thumb and finger. All night I paddled down the great Cuyuni River. In the morning I came to the village of a tribe friendly to mine, and there I stayed. This I did thinking to outwit the Didi, who would not know where to find me. But that same evening, as I stood alone beneath a clump of papaw-trees close to the village of my new friends, I heard behind me the laugh of the Didi. I turned, and she was there; and again she mocked me with her wild red eyes and slobbering lips, and then was gone.

"Next morning I departed from the village of the friendly tribe, and again went away in my woodskin. This time I paddled two days' journey down the river, and I came to people strangers to my tribe, but good Indians, and they made me welcome at their village; and there I stayed three days, and went on the hunt with them.

"On the third day it happened that I went to the creek alone to see if there were any fish in the snares I had set. As I came back the Didi stood in my path. She put her great heavy arms on my shoulders, so that the sharp claws went deep into my flesh, and you may see the scars there to this day. She looked into my face and laughed the laugh that made me too weak to fight, too weak to flee, and then she was gone again. It came into my mind that the Didi was playing with me, as a jaguar might play with an *accourie* before it killed him. Wherever I should go, there, by her own hidden ways of travel, would she follow until her humour tired, when she would kill me as she had killed my brother.

"Nevertheless, when a party of Indians, in a big woodskin, with hammocks, and arrowroot to trade at the coast, stopped at the village next day, and told us they were going down the river to the coast where live the *parangheries* (sea-people: an Indian name for white people who come from the sea), my heart leapt in my breast, and I asked to go with them. For I had heard tales of the *parangheries*, and I knew that they were a big, wonderful people, with a magic greater than all the magic of all the Indian *peimans* that ever lived; and I said in my mind, 'Surely the Didi will fear to seek me among the *parangheries*.'

"I went many days' journey with the Indians, in the big woodskin, down the great river, which, mingling with another, grew ever greater as we went, until, when we reached the coast, we could not tell where the river ended and the sea began. I found the *parangheries* wonderful and great—though not as wonderful and great as the tales said—and they have been good to me.

"On this plantation have I lived ever since I came to the coast, and never have I seen the Didi since that time she put her hands on my shoulders and made the scars you see there; for the forest is the home of the Didi, even more than it is the home of the Indian, and they will not come out of the forest even to seek revenge. While I live here the Didi, my enemy, cannot harm me; but if I go back to the forest she will kill me as she killed my brother. And the fear is in my heart that some day I shall go back to the forest. Ah, you do not know how the forest draws the Indian home to it again! At first, to live here did not make me feel bad, and I was glad that the Didi came no longer before me, save in my dreams; but, afterwards, every day more and more has the forest tugged at the strings of my heart. There will come a time when I shall die if I do not go back to the forest. It is in my mind that, when that time draws near, my fear of the Didi will grow small, and I will go back to the forest, and breathe the breath and drink the water of my own place again before my enemy kills me as she killed my brother. The mind of the Didi knows that the forest will draw the Indian home again, and she laughs and waits.

"This is all the tale I have to tell. To only one man, since I left the forest, have I spoken of the Didi who is my enemy. You are that man. You know why I stay here as yet, though my heart is sick, sick for the forest."

The foregoing, told in his own mongrel English, was Alfred Jenkins's story. The five tiny, smooth scars which he showed me on each of his shoulders near the base of the neck certainly suggested, in their arrangement and conformation, the imprint of the nails of an exceedingly large human hand; but, of course, I could not accept them as evidence of the existence of the monstrous semi-human creature of his story in the face of my common-sense, which, assured me that such a creature could not exist. The man, however, was so evidently sane, simple, and sincere that I was very much puzzled to make out what could have been the actual phenomena which had assumed such strange and revoltingly tragic shapes in his brain.

I did not repay the confidence he had given me by attempting the impossible task of reasoning him out of his belief in Didi in general, and in his own particular Didi; but I tried to reassure him with the suggestion that his dreaded Didi had likely forgotten all about him by this time, or that she might even be dead. He only shook his head, however, and said that she had not forgotten him, and that she would not die before he did.

The fish began to bite just then, and they kept us too busy for further talk until dusk suddenly fell on the sea, and we turned our boat's-head landward with a fair catch of fish.

Next day my brief stay with Byngham came to an end, and I went back to Georgetown, leaving Alfred Jenkins happy for the nonce with a specially large parting gift of tobacco.

Now for the queer sequel to Alfred Jenkins's story.

Shortly after this, business connected with my office took me to Barbadoes, and kept me there some time, so it was over a year before I saw Byngham again. He looked me up at my quarters in Georgetown after my return; and as we chatted about things on the Victoria Regina, I remembered to ask after my Indian friend Alfred Jenkins.

"Oh, we've lost Alfred Jenkins," said Byngham. "I'm sorry, for the overseers all declare that he worked as well as any negro or coolie in the whole lot. But the Indian's longing for the forest overmastered him at last, even after all those years of plantation-life, and about eight months ago he cut back to his own people."

"He told me he was bound to go sooner or later," I said, taking a couple of thoughtful pulls at my pipe.

"Well, as it happened, it would have been better for the poor chap had he remained on the Victoria," went on Byngham in his languid West Indian drawl. "About a fortnight ago I came across a half-caste who had just come down from somewhere away back, near the headwaters of the Cuyuni River, where Alfred Jenkins's people live, and he told me that poor Alfred Jenkins was killed the week after his return. The odd thing is nobody seemed to know who killed him. He was found lying across an Indian path close to his village, with his head completely severed from his body; not cut off, mind you, so the man said, but *wrenched* off.”

A smothered exclamation escaped my lips.

“Yes, of course, it *is* a little too strong, the statement about its being wrenched off,” went on Byngham, mistaking the cause of my exclamation; “more especially as the half-caste laid much stress on the fact that it couldn’t have been the work of wild beasts, as both head and body were found intact. The fellow talked a lot of rubbish, to which I paid little heed, about the tribe believing that Alfred Jenkins had met his death at the hands of some supernaturally strong and cunning creature, half-brute, half-human, which is supposed to haunt the bush. I suppose, however, that we may take it for a certainty that his death was the outcome of some Indian feud. I often used to say—don’t you remember?—that it was fear of the Indian law of blood-atonement which kept Alfred Jenkins so long away from his beloved forest.”

I was genuinely sorry to hear of the poor Ackawoise’s death, and very much disquieted, I confess, to learn the manner of it. That he should have been killed in exactly the fashion he had predicted seemed to place all the particulars of his strange and gruesome story on the impressive footing of actual facts—at least it seemed to me for the moment to do so. I was conscious of a queer, disagreeable sensation, such as a man may be excused for feeling when he finds himself confronted with apparent evidences of the existence of certain things in nature which lie uncomfortably outside the teaching of his traditions and experiences.

I had never told Alfred Jenkins’s story to any one; but, under the pressure of this queer sensation, I now told it to Byngham. By the time I had finished he was looking rather nonplussed.

“But it’s all rubbish, you know,” he protested after a pause—“utter rubbish! His death and the way of it is just one of those odd coincidences that are always happening. Didi or their like, of course, don’t exist outside the superstitious brain of an Indian.”

I gave but a dubious assent to this confident declaration. I was not prepared to say what, at that particular moment, I believed or did not believe concerning Didi and their like.

"Poor old Alfred Jenkins!" commented Byngham, leisurely sipping his brandy-and-soda, "he was not a bad sort; but who would ever have credited the beggar with an imagination equal to spinning a yarn like that? For, of course, it was imagination. His story was all either lies or delusions," he concluded positively.

"It wasn't lies," I said just as positively; but that was really all I could say positively about the matter.

The Gregosaur of Black Lake

JULIEN JOSEPHSON

Some three years ago when my old friend and former college instructor, Professor Wharton, was appointed by the United States Government to search for the bones of extinct animals in the Black Lake country of Southwestern Oregon, it was my good fortune to accompany him as assistant and private secretary.

This Black Lake country, I should explain, lies in the heart of rugged and forbidding mountains; and, in order to reach it, one is obliged to journey on foot and with pack horses over a trackless wilderness for a distance of nearly one hundred and fifty miles. As neither the professor nor myself had ever been in this region before, our first task was to find a strong, reliable guide. And here we met with great difficulty. For although many skilled hunters and trappers who made their living chiefly by acting as guides offered us their services, they one and all declined to take the position as soon as they found out that we were bound for Black Lake.

Professor Wharton was both vexed and puzzled at this strange conduct. Finally in despair he bluntly asked one of the men, "Why do you all refuse to go with us as soon as you learn that we are going to Black Lake? Surely for trained mountaineers like you the journey is not too hard or too long?" The man, a tanned, gray-haired old hunter, shook his head slowly and smiled in a peculiar manner. "I reckon you're a stranger in these parts," he said, gravely, "or you'd know the reason. Why, sir, you couldn't get a white man to go into the Black Lake country if you offered him a cold thousand dollars!" And with this strange remark he was gone before we could question him further.

Finally, however, after many discouraging failures, we succeeded in finding a man who consented to act as our guide to Black Lake. He was an old Klamath Indian, Poji by name; and he assured us that he knew the Black Lake country thoroughly, as he had often hunted there for the great red elk. Now, as you may suppose, our curiosity had been considerably aroused by the refusal of the white men to go into the Black Lake region; so we asked Poji if he knew the reason of this strange fear.

At the question old Poji smiled until we could see every one of his scattered, yellow front teeth. Then he told us in his broken English that some twenty years ago a party of four men had gone into the region in search of gold and that three of them had never returned. The single survivor, Poji declared, told a strange story about a huge monster that lived in a great cave at the head of the lake; and about how it had killed and eaten his companions. But no one believed his story. Everybody thought that his hardships and sufferings had made him insane, and that he merely imagined that he had seen the monster. "But," Poji concluded, "since that time no white man has ever gone near the borders of Black Lake."

I thought the story an interesting one. Of course, I did not believe it. But somehow nevertheless it made me feel uncomfortable. As for the professor he smiled broadly. "And what sort of a monster was this?" he asked Poji, jokingly.

Poji looked very serious. "The grandfather of my father's father has seen it," he declared solemnly. "And the white man whom they called crazy told the truth. A terrible creature it is—with a head like a snake, a body like that of an immense bull, and a tail like a huge lizzard. 'Ijiwat,' my people of long ago called him— Ijiwat, the devourer of men!"

I had been watching the professor closely to see what effect the story would have upon him. Once I thought that he turned a little pale, but I may have been mistaken. At any rate, when Poji was through speaking the professor simply said: "And do these white men actually believe this foolish story?"

"It is true!" replied Poji, doggedly. "The fathers of my people did not lie!"

"Nonsense!" exclaimed the professor, addressing me in a low tone. "Why, the animal which Poji has described is a gregosaur—a creature that has been extinct for at least five thousand years. His story is probably one that has been handed down from the most ancient times." He paused a moment as if buried in thought. "And yet," he continued, half to himself, "these Indians can not date further back than two thousand years. It's very strange, very strange!"

But, gregosaur or no gregosaur, we at last had a guide; and within two days we had secured our pack horses and begun our long journey to Black Lake. From the very beginning of the trip until the day when we set foot on the shores of Black Lake, we were continually beset with serious difficulties. For the first fifty miles of the distance we were able to travel along roads and paths. But as we penetrated deeper into the mountains, both paths and roads disappeared. We were setting foot in places where, perhaps, no white man had ever set foot before. Many a time we were obliged to take our axes and cut a way through the dense undergrowth in order to enable our pack animals to get through. As we advanced into the heart of the mountains the country became wilder and wilder. Great, towering rocks, almost as high as mountains, rose on every side, hemming us in completely. Through dark forests of oak and pine, through dense thickets of hazel and arrow-wood we slowly and laboriously made our way. Every now and then a deer, startled by the unaccustomed sight of men and horses, would go crashing through the brush. Once we saw a great brown bear which looked at us curiously for a moment and then turned and fled at the top of its speed. At last, on the twentieth evening of our journey, we pitched our tent upon the shores of Black Lake.

Poji and I were feeling tired and somewhat gloomy, but the professor was in high spirits. By the time supper was over the night air was beginning to grow uncomfortably sharp. So we built a small camp-fire near the tent and stretched ourselves comfortably about it. A little later in the evening, at the suggestion of Poji, we cleaned our guns and pistols and loaded them with fresh cartridges.

When we were done the professor turned suddenly to Poji. "Poji," he said good naturedly, "I don't think that you really believe there is such a thing as this monster which you call 'Ijiwat.' If you do believe it, why did you come along and risk your life?"

"Ijiwat is here!" replied the old Indian in such an impressive tone that I glanced involuntarily around. "I came with you because I am old and must die soon, anyway!"

But at any rate the gregosaur did not see fit to terrify us with its presence on that night. Bright and early we arose, ate our breakfast, and under the guidance of Poji set out upon our search for the bones of the gregosaur. We found nothing that morning. But about the middle of the afternoon, while we were exploring the floor of a large cave at the head of the lake, I heard a sudden cry of delight from the professor, who had advanced far into the cave. The next moment I saw him coming toward me, staggering under the weight of an immense bone which he was carrying over his shoulder. "It's a gregosaur!" he shouted. "A gregosaur! The only remains of the gregosaur that has ever been found. Why, this bone alone is worth all our trouble!"

I ran to his assistance and together we carried the immense bone out into the light—Poji watching us with curious, half-frightened eyes. We deposited our precious burden gently upon the sand. Then the professor took out his glass to examine his find. For one moment he gazed at it through the powerful microscope. Then the glass dropped from his hand, he turned white, sprang to his feet and looked wildly about him. "God help us!" he exclaimed hoarsely. "The Indian has told the truth! This bone is not fifty years old. The mate of the dead gregosaur may still be alive and in the cave!"

I shuddered at his words and I could see that Poji was trembling. In a moment, however, the professor had regained his customary coolness, and this had a wonderfully bracing effect upon Poji and myself. We turned instinctively to the professor for advice. "We must get out of this place at once!" he said, speaking in quick, decisive tones. "If the gregosaur is really here, it has failed to discover us only because it is asleep. For when awake it is able to scent its prey at an enormous distance. If our bullets are able to kill it, we are safe. If not—God help us!"

We started to leave the place on the run. But we had scarcely taken a hundred strides when there came from the depths of the cave a terrible, deafening bellow which sounded as if it might have been produced by a throat of brass. "The gregosaur!" panted the professor, glancing back at the cave. "It's useless to run," he continued grimly, "We've got to fight for our lives!"

We halted suddenly and faced about toward the cave, which was only a hundred and fifty yards away. Unslinging our rifles, we loosened our pistols in their holsters and waited for the monster to issue from the cave. A few moments later the Thing came slowly forth, and for a short space gazed at us curiously with its great, blood-red eyes, all the while baring its huge yellow teeth in a horrible manner. Then with long clumsy leaps that carried it over the ground at a tremendous speed, it bore down swiftly upon us.

"Shoot for the head and aim true!" warned the professor, raising his heavy rifle to his shoulder with a hand that was steady as a rock. Then he fired twice in quick succession. Almost at the same instant Poji and myself each sent two well-aimed bullets into the onrushing monster. The gregosaur gave a deafening roar of pain and for a moment stopped short in its tracks. In a flash we realized that in this moment lay our sole hope of escaping with our lives. And so, taking a careful aim at the crouching monster—which was now less than fifty paces distant—we fired again and again. The gregosaur leaped high in the air, with blood spurting from between its immense jaws, and struck the earth with a dull, heavy shock. Then suddenly it sprang to its feet and made swiftly in the direction of the lake. Far out into the water it swam, leaving in its wake a trail of blood. All at once it sank from sight—and that was the last we ever saw of the gregosaur of Black Lake.

Now that the monster was killed, we explored its cave from beginning to end. We found a number of gregosaur bones, but all of these were undoubtedly of very great age. As for our story about the live gregosaur, scientists were at first inclined to discredit and ridicule it. But when we showed them the huge, comparatively fresh bone they quickly changed their opinion. The entire scientific world became intensely excited. An expedition composed of the most noted scientists of this country was sent to search Black Lake in the hope of finding the remains of the gregosaur which we had killed. But although the lake was dragged, and although skillful divers were sent down to examine its bottom, no trace of the animal was ever found. It had probably sunk deep into the soft thick slime at the bottom of Black Lake.

Why the gregosaur should have existed at a time five thousand years later than its proper period is a question which the greatest scientists have been unable to answer. So you are at liberty to draw your own conclusions.

The Death-Trap

George Daulton

A cab had not been to my fancy that night. As I left the club I really had nothing to complain of, for I had not been unsuccessful; but I felt sick with something akin to remorse. The game had been of the right sort, among men who were close friends and all able to pay a good sum for a night's amusement; there had been high stakes, but no ugly action in the bets, though the cards ran snappy and full of surprises; a lounging, friendly game, with no litter of discarded packs on the floor, for we all liked a seasoned deck when the cards began to run naturally into flushes and fulls. My remorse was perhaps a reaction from a surfeit of pleasure, and a longing to turn myself to something more satisfying than killing time. I decided to walk home, though it was two o'clock; I needed the thirty minutes' sharp exercise to pump the fumes of smoke and wine out of me in the invigorating lake air.

But my depression was not relieved, when, having passed the open front of the city's heart, the stately wall of granite buildings stopped, and Michigan Avenue, without electricity, plunged on between grimy wholesale houses in a black sweep dimly defined by a few gaslights.

Hesitating there under the gigantic lamps of the library, the loneliness of the gloomy streets made me think better of a cab. I remembered the hold-ups so common in Chicago during the late fall, and a number of mysterious disappearances that had kept the whole city in dread of the unfrequented business districts at night. There were no cab lamps in sight up Randolph Street, and none nearer down Michigan than those I had passed at the Athletic Club. So I went on into the gloom, not wishing to appear daunted even to myself, though I knew it was not safe at that hour for a man alone and in evening dress to cross the river through that deserted street.

But the black dog was on my shoulder. My sense of folly became a dread and helpless loneliness, at once so great that I greeted the odors of sugar, coffee and tobacco that issued from the black solitudes of the great business houses as pleasant and safe company that stood for the comfortable human affairs of the broad, honest day. The empty chasm of the narrowed street echoed to my nervous footfalls; otherwise it was so silent that the sleepless growl of the surrounding streets made its loneliness all the more pronounced.

I am almost ashamed to tell—even now that I know that I must have experienced one of those strange premonitions of danger that sometimes forewarn us—how I rushed away from my fear more than from that which I feared.

When I had but a block more to go before reaching the Rush Street drawbridge, a small, thick-set man lurched out of Water Street from the direction of Randolph Station. I saw him pass under the corner lamp as plainly as I ever saw anything under similar conditions—I was alert for just such an encounter. The man had fallen into himself and was weaving his way over a good breadth of the pavement, and added to his drunken reel I thought I saw the sailor in the swaying of his shoulders.

We met on the corner, or rather, he stopped before the inlet of the sewer, while I was on the curb above him. I was so close to him I saw a look in his blood-shot eyes challenging the very idea that he was drunk.

I had no time to feel relieved. I *saw* the glance, I *saw* it; but with it on the instant came a black, lightning-like flicker out of the granite pavement on which we stood, as though the tongue of a monstrous serpent gave one devilish, wavering lick that encircled the man and dashed him down the mouth of the sewer—a clot of thin mud spattered my cheek—and the drunken sailor had vanished.

The shock of it made me leap and tremble, and horror struck me cold in the pit of the stomach, while waves of it rolled out over my body like the rings on smitten water—I must have been demented for the moment, else I should have fled my own immediate danger. There had been no sound of breaking bones upon the stony jaws of the sewer; but at that instant some sudden up-starting of night traffic had barked loudly round the corner of a by-street and may have drowned the thud. To the eye it had been as though the man had been blown away by an explosion—one instant there, bestial in his human bulk, the next scuttled, annihilated.

I do not know what I did just after the shock. It seems to me, in recalling my distraught fancies, that I heard the "whimper" of that passing soul and saw it curl upward in a thin mist, like the breath from a foul maw. When I came to I was crouching on the stones looking down the black gullet of the drain. There was nothing to be seen in its capacious mouth; but the brown, greasy sweat of traffic that glistened everywhere upon the paving was plainly wiped from the granite lips of the sewer, and with this as evidence of the reality of what I had seen I awoke to the hideous peril of that death-trap. I sprang up and backed away, then turned and fled up the street.

Coming out of that accursed and forsaken strip of the avenue was like escaping from a den of murderers to the shelter of a friendly home. The great bridge was rumbling on its cogs and sweeping majestically through arc-lit volumes of smoke and steam to let some sluggish freighter of the lakes trail by. I ran over the slippery pavement of the approach and leaped upon the last yard of the bridge as it swung out over the river.

I felt the unspeakable relief of escape, but I did not stop until I had crossed over the two roadways, though the bridge was still moving. How kindly powerful and humanly helpful the huge truss seemed as it widened the gulf between me and the South Side abutment, where I fancied the flickering phantom was licking over the water toward me! How good it was to hear the business-like breath of the tug, the sob of the steam imprisoned in the passing monster! The firm command and sensible response of bells and obedient

feet upon the decks—all the worthiness of the grimy labor of honest men I joyfully greeted with noble comparisons, while the prosy
tug and stupid barge seemed to sweep by me as stately as a classic
chorus.

The bridge was beginning slowly to follow the retreating stern
of the vessel when I became aware that I was not alone on the foot-
way. Perhaps the smoke and steam had at first concealed the man,
or in my excitement I had overlooked him; at any rate he was at
my elbow before I knew it, giving my overwrought nerves such a
shock that my first impulse was to fly at him like a savage dog. But
the changing shadows of the bridge just then allowed the white
light of an arc-lamp to fall upon his face, which was strangely sad
and refined and certainly friendly.

"Sir," said the man, with quaint politeness and solemnity, "I
see you are ill. Will you accept a restorative? A Special Reserve
that I can recommend."

With a grace that at once gave me confidence he proffered a
flask handsome enough for the traveling companion of a king.

"You have had a shock," he observed, as I thanked him, "a shock
that might prostrate any man. I saw you fly panic-stricken out of
the mouth of Michigan Avenue, and caught the change of relief
that came over you as you gained the draw and your white face
was swept away from the glare of the shore lamp. Nevertheless I
believe I knew you from that glance. 'Now here is a man to depend
on,' thought I; 'one to face and fight to the last, when the dread
mystery that has sent him into a panic becomes a reality that may
be reached.' Such was my own case, and—since I am persuaded
that we have been brought together for death or life—you will see
that I shall not flinch when the test comes."

I searched the man's face. Had fate played that night with my
life and reason only to finish me on the bridge with a madman? He
seemed to read my thought, and denied it with a sad smile which
added charm to the grace that had given me confidence.

"Why, you yourself will say to-morrow," he pursued with renewed assurance, "'Is it not passing strange that we two men of all
Chicago should have met?' But I believe there is no chance. What

we call chance only seems so, and I mean no irreverence when I say that the Almighty, playing this great solemn game of solitaire through the ages, intended that we should rid the world of that dreadful thing that flickers out of the pavements at night and makes a death-trap of the sewer."

"That black flicker of death out of the sewer!" I cried, starting up from the bridge rail. "What do you mean, sir—merciful heaven! what do you mean? Have you, too, seen it?"

"I have seen it, too," he returned with intense feeling, and I thought the light of relief that he had made no mistake shone in his eyes. "Now, is it not strange that we should have met? I ran out of that street one night myself, more unmanned with terror, I doubt not, than you; I, too, had seen a human being, a life perhaps more worthy than my own, scooped down the gutter sewer like a truss of hay drawn through a mow door."

The stranger paused and with apologetic courtesy drew my attention to a clot of thin mud staining my shirt front, which to me seemed as gruesome as a gout of blood.

"Chicago streets gleamed underfoot just as they do tonight," he mused. "Down here in these granite gulches nature's sweet dew is befouled by the young giant wallowing in the madness of his toil, and with some of this oily smear of the streets the black deed bespattered my face, too, and my clothing. Since that night I have been fascinated by the incredible horror of what I saw, and I have haunted the streets that I might find it; tempting the fiend, if possible, to an attack and a fight to the death. But now you have seen it—I beg of you, tell me what you saw!"

"I had an unnatural and overpowering sense of depression and foreboding as I came up the avenue," I responded, as if that was an inseparable part of what I had seen. My companion acknowledged it with a nod of understanding, and verified each horrid detail of my story as I told it to him.

"God alone knows how many have gone that way," said the stranger solemnly when I had finished. "Unseen and unfriended, how should they be reported? But the city rang with the one I saw. Water Street, you say? Mine was at Lake, but a block away. They are never far from the river, which at night gives an unfrequented district for the murderer's work."

"Why didn't you report this to the police!" I exclaimed. "We must lose no more time in this way, but do it at once."

"No; by no means," objected my companion, "consider the incredible story we have to tell. Do you want to be listened to with insolent indulgence for a swell that has taken a bit too much? Very likely you would be received with cold doubt, or even suspicion; I have known men to be clapped into the sweat-box who brought their information to the authorities as innocently as you would. Your introduction at the sergeant's desk would be like an arraignment, and perhaps for weeks you would be kept under a mild surveillance. Do you want to be the tool of Pinkerton, when you can be a free lance? Do you want the thousand and one questions and comments of friends, the common notoriety of the papers, the interviews and headlines and pictures, when you can quietly perform this sacred duty as a gentleman and at the same time, even in this most modern city, have an adventure prodigious as those of the sagas?"

"What is the hazard that you have in mind?" I demanded, and, strange to say, I felt my nerves refresh as the world-old thirst of men for the chancing life against great odds in a dangerous mystery, tempted me. "This business is too wild and dangerous for a man of affairs to undertake upon a chance meeting and its premonitions."

The strange man stopped me with his lifted hand.

"My dear sir," he said with quiet decision, "though I did say I thought we had been brought together for a determined purpose, I haven't asked you to go—nor to take any risks."

"But I want to!" I flung out. The words came almost against my will.

"Ah, well, if you want to, that is another thing," responded my companion with satisfaction, and with that his manner changed. He was still quaint and fanciful, but something of reserve power became apparent, his whole being knit itself together and somehow I felt myself included in the effect. The spirit of the hunt took possession of him.

"But what more foolhardy thing could a man do than to go into the sewer after this murderer?—for that is what we shall have to do," I exclaimed, with some irritation at my own determination to do it. "Perhaps that is the reason it lures me; at any rate I am going to follow you, taking your integrity for granted."

"I took you from the first, as you have accepted me," returned my comrade, and, if I may say it, even there, in the gloom of the bridge, I felt the gentlemanliness of the man flow over me, and yet I can mention nothing more of it than the endearing confidence of his smile. Then our hands gripped, and it was done—each knew without saying that the word passed for life or death.

"My family name," he resumed, "is known round the world; but until this business is transacted I hope you will be satisfied to call me 'Hood.' Most men of my station, who wish to be men in spite of their wealth, plunge into money-getting, or enter politics; they explore Africa or the Amazon; they lose themselves in Tibet or the South Seas, or even take to mountain climbing.

"Now I seek to be the exponent of the dark and terrible in human passion, the apologist of the degenerate and gruesome. I pondered one day upon the moral condition of the slaughterer with a knife, as I stood on the Halsted Street bridge and heard the dying screams of the swine, and saw their limp carcasses continuously passing before the upper windows of a packing house. The following week I became a pig-sticker at the Stock Yards, and read my subject to a conclusion. To-night you find me an embalmer."

I am glad to say, unnatural as it may seem, that it was not because the hag-ridden night could add no more of horror that I did not fly from him in fear and loathing; but truly the charm of the man's gentleness seemed heightened by his strange confession, and, more convincing still, he gave me the feeling that he put his soul in my place and in the same fullness admitted mine to the motives of his own, as I have never known any other human being to do. I cleaved to him then, as I have ever since, in the most perfect friendship a man ever had.

"There are some who would say that such gruesome affairs have tempted me to my ruin, as drink or drugs do many men," he mused sadly. "I cannot deny that I have made it too much the book and the lamp in my life; I love it and loathe it as the drunkard does the drink; but while I am in it I am not of it."

He broke off with a sudden start and, gripping my wrist, leaned over the rail, pointing down to the water. Down in the gloomy city-built gully through which the river flows I caught the disappearing dive of some black waving object, then there was a quiet eddy of the water, and further on a series of V-shaped ripples came to the surface and shot toward the South Side wharves; again a long, dark, indefinite thing lifted from the river and waved glistening wet one instant under an arc-lamp and then disappeared, as though it plunged under the stone-walled embankment of the street.

"Merciful heaven!" I cried, "the submerged outlet of a sewer must be there!''

"Yes," said Hood. "It is nearly wide enough to drive through. Now," he said solemnly, "we shall solve this hideous mystery of the sewers and shall do away with it as sure as there is a God in Heaven!"

His tone of suppressed exultation changed to one of solicitude as he saw that horror was again crawling over my back—for neither of us dared compare the hideous surmises that had taken shape in our minds.

"We would better go," he said; "your nerves have had all they should stand. Ten or twelve hours in bed will make you over."

"Did you notice the length and peculiar motion of that arm?" I whispered.

"I did," he answered, laying his hand upon my shoulder; "perhaps before this time to-morrow morning we shall know."

The clock on the old Inter-Ocean Building had just tolled midnight when I turned into a cross-town street and rang the night bell of the undertaking establishment that Hood had given me as his address.

A handsome, ruddy-cheeked youth admitted me with subdued professional concern that changed to a cheery welcome upon his learning my business was a matter of personal friendship with Mr.

Hood. Behind a reception room, I was led through a heavily carpeted and dimly lighted hall, into another room at the foot of which
was a huge bronze sarcophagus in a plate-glass case; from behind
this Hood came forward to greet and conduct me on through a big,
barren workroom, where beneath their sheets lay two rigid and
indistinct forms, so awfully withdrawn from life yet so pathetically
helpless against intrusion.

Into one of three or four stall-like compartments, partitioned
but half-way to the ceiling off this work-room, Hood ushered me,
explaining that they were the bedrooms of the employees who must
be in constant attendance at the establishment.

"I shall not offer you my one chair," said he, as we both glanced
with a smile at the odd and meager furnishings of the room; "it is
high time we were down to business. You may open your hunting
case here on the cot—that's good: a sweater, a duck coat, hip boots
and two 44-caliber sixes—better for our purpose than rifles—a
practical lot of stuff. Now I," he went on, "am going to be rather
unsportsman-like, if I am driven to it. The vampire has put himself beyond mercy; so, like Puckle, who invented a double-barreled
gun, one side firing balls 'for shootinge ye Christians,' and the other
square bullets 'for shootinge ye Turks,' I have a special charge that
I shall fire at the fiend—there is enough acid in this big syringe to
bring an elephant to his knees."

Hood was also armed with a long, keen knife, which, he said,
since his packing-house experience, he trusted more than firearms.
For our light he had provided two new electric clubs, like the
morocco-covered section of a telescope, which on pressing a
button emitted a powerful beam of light through the big lens set in
the end.

"Are you ready now?" asked Hood, laying his hand upon my
shoulder. "The affair that we are undertaking cannot be long in
any case; but on the other hand, are you prepared to risk it should
our return be—"

"Indefinitely extended?" I concluded. "Yes, I am ready. The
thought that at this moment some one, happy and full of life, may
be snatched down to that foul death makes my very soul yearn to

hunt this mystery to the end. The papers gave no report of last night's disappearance, and, as you say, God alone knows how many have gone that way for us to avenge."

Hood led the way through the rear wareroom to the alley, and we cautiously crept between iron-shuttered walls of business houses to the middle of the next block without encountering a watchman. Here he knelt on the paving, and after some groping lifted the lid of a manhole, thrusting his electric truncheon down into the black opening. A glare of white light showed a narrow shaft of masonry eight feet deep, connecting with a conduit scarcely large enough to crawl through. A warm, white, malodorous vapor arose from the glowing opening on the keen outer air. The place looked ratty and so confined that I dreaded sticking fast in it; but Hood motioned me to go in, and I filled my lungs with pure air and dropped down into total darkness.

At the bottom my light showed a drain so narrow that I found it better to back in feet first. I had at once the feeling of crushing suffocation, but I crawled away from the manhole to make room for Hood, and I heard his scuffling descent and the iron cover drop into its place. Lying almost upon my face I had little room for movement, but the fury with which I wormed my way through twenty yards of that drain was marvelous. I think Hood himself found the passage irksome, and when we dropped into a feeder of the trunk sewer we were glad enough to stand ankle-deep in a dark tunnel of sewage and breathe in the freedom of space, if not of purity.

We had gained the underground system that drained the city. A noisome sweat, the dank contamination of humanity, covered the walls; the arch of masonry was mottled with dark stains and straggling patches of a soot-like growth, through which a snow-white vermicular fungus wriggled, fed by the peculiar properties of the seepage above; over the sloping floor the foul flow from the many stories of life in the upper world sneaked away in the darkness with a loathsome gurgle, as though it would invite us that way to seek the murderer of the sewer.

Following the course of the brown streams for a block or two we entered what proved to be the main artery of the sewers, as

spacious as a railway tunnel and as well-built as an ancient wine-
cellar. We did not expect to find the outlaw in this thoroughfare,
for even in the solitudes of the city's vaults he would find some
blind passage more to his purpose; but the trunk sewer was the
natural base of our operations, the beginning and termination of
each long excursion to the right or left with which we traced every
feeder and cross tunnel in the hunt that followed—traced them of
necessity in silence, and as much as possible in darkness, which
encouraged the imagination to shrink all the more from fetid mois-
tures and smells and the touch of vermin that we heard scurrying
and gliding away from our footsteps.

Hood read the gush of every drain as an archeologist reads the
layers of earth that cover a buried city: here was a hotel; there a
wholesale chemist's; this sickening spout of offal, he declared, came
from the night cleansing of a dissecting-room; this was a livery
stable, and that the emptying vats of a dye-house, and there the
drain of a milk depot spouting a river of sour milk. Yet Hood never
forgot the hunt; each flash of the light was first used to search for
traces of the murderer, and at a single glance he saw things that
might have escaped my prolonged quest. I fear I was of little use
save as a companion in the black, lonely labyrinth, and while I kept
myself alert my imagination heard a startled exclamation in every
drip, retreating footfalls as our own echoed along the dark vaulting, and a disturbed snarl in the gurgle of the moving offal.

Without acknowledging it to each other, we had purposely
avoided the fatal locality under Michigan Avenue, each feeling that
it was best to become used to the strange conditions of the hunt
before we risked the attempt on the murderer's most probable lurking place. We must have been in the neighborhood of the Masonic
Temple; I was about to flash my light into a branch sewer, my body
bent against the angle of the wall, my finger ready upon the electric button, when there was a sudden snarl almost in my face and a
hoarse voice whispered:

"Whist! Is it the murderin' devil ye're after at last?"

I leaped back, jostling Hood, and our electric clubs shot un-
steady beams of white glare into the eyes of an enormous figure,
that with a guttural curse cowered and buried his face in his arm.

"Take the light aff me! Take it aff, dom it!"

We poured the intense rays over the man and needed no other weapon to cover him, for he staggered against the wall and turned his back to the light.

"Shut it aff, men, shut it aff!" he wailed; "d'ye want to blind me? I'm Officer Kindelon, on duty, by —, on since Wednesday night, from Harrison Station."

The lights showed a burly shape in brass buttons, the twisted wrack of a mighty man, who leaned forward and sideways in spite of painful effort to straighten up. His face, it seemed, had been florid, but black rings under his eyes made its unnatural pallor all the more noticeable. He was hatless; one arm was bare to the shoulder and bruised black and blue; the remnant of a white glove encircled his wrist in a dirty rag; his coat was ripped up the back, and what had been a smart uniform hung on him in tatters, befouled by the splash of the sewage.

Hood tucked his light under his arm and produced his flask; the big policeman brightened eagerly, but controlled himself like an abused simpleton.

"By the growth on me face it would be three days since I tasted food," grumbled the poor fellow, and gulped the dram Hood poured for him; "three days since I saw the impudent devil himself reach up out of hell, as cool as you please, and drag a poor creature from aff his bones, without by yer leave—bad luck to the size of the sewer-trap that let me follow him, and the devil's own mommickin' up he give me!"

We had half guessed this, but we looked at each other in amazement. Here, then, was a man who had not only seen, but had even dared the death-trap in its hiding-place, and by reason of superhuman strength had brought himself off to tell it.

"Officer Kindelon," said I, with a kindly force that seemed necessary to stir his clouded understanding, "you were a powerful man and you must have met something of tremendous strength to have given you this terrible punishment. We are here to find this demon—where is he and what is he like?"

The man leaped up, and wrestling grotesquely with himself imitated the manner of his defense in the clutch of the death-trap.

"The Old One himself, none less, I tell ye," he answered, drawing us both toward him and looking fearfully down the dark vaulting of the sewer. "He had no science; but he was hell for reach and for strength. D'ye think Kindelon was whipped?—what good is the science of the ring when ye fight the devil in the dark? Come, since ye have lights. I have listened to him wanderin' about and never askin' what's the time of day. I'm domned if I don't show ye the fight of yer life."

The man beckoned us down the passage, and limping, humped and askew, went ahead in the gloom, turning now and then to grimace us to be cautious. He led us into the trunk sewer and for a block or more down its wide vaulting; then turning to the right we knew, without his pantomime, we were nearing the lair of the murderer of the sewers.

At the next turn Kindelon stopped and motioned us to come on without lights. In total darkness we stood grouped and breathless listening to sounds so suggestive of the devil that they did not need the denunciation of Kindelon. They did not seem human, and yet they were, too; as though some human work was being lazily done, a long-drawn, gliding movement ending in a fleshy thud, then a deep breath of satisfaction followed by a sound as of something bone-like moving on the stone floor.

"Och, ye hellion!" muttered the big policeman, and spat in disgust.

I found that inaction and the presence of that awful mystery in the darkness was more than I could stand. I must have it out, even if it had to come to the repellent thing I had dreaded, a hand-to-hand contest with that foul fiend in the filth of the sewer floor. I whispered to Hood that I would try to cut off the retreat of the monster by slipping by him in the dark. He would have detained me, but Kindelon was working himself into a fury, and I glided away in the darkness while he was trying to control the policeman's fever for revenge.

Foot by foot, nearer and nearer, I drew to the death-trap, feeling my way, no longer daintily, but low down and nearly upon all fours, along the wall, that seemed to draw out like elastic as I crept on. The vaulting became a whispering gallery of those hideous sounds, and they hummed in my ears with the blood that was rushing to my brain. As I came opposite them my lungs seemed to fail and then fill to bursting with the fetid breath of the place, and my heart rebelled with furious pounding at every thought I made to quiet it. I was in the midst of my peril when I stumbled over what I took to be a log; but it instantly arose and I leaped on, though not quickly enough, for a glancing blow across the shoulders sent me staggering down the sewer.

I shot my light and Hood's followed on the instant. For a moment we all stood paralyzed by what we saw. Never since man began to kill has he brought to bay such a monster.

Gigantic it was, but its horror partook of no one of the familiar forms of this latter world's creatures; it was not of earth, air or water, though it hideously combined the beast, the reptile and the bird; and yet I felt it was not misbegotten, but was perhaps the last survival of some species from the mesozoic era, a disinherited offspring of Mother Earth that had been overlooked in the ruthless management of her family affairs, bred down through the ages in some deep retreat in the receding lake. The thing reared itself at bay, dazzled by the bright shafts of light we poured over it, and still we gazed, fascinated by its hideous loathsomeness.

Then I noticed that the beam of Hood's light was wavering, and out of the tail of my eye I saw Kindelon creeping toward the monster. Hood tried to restrain him, and at the same time manage his light, while he aimed his charge of acid. The stream of liquid fire shot toward the great creature and for an instant played upon its head. Then the stone vaulting of the sewer was full of the writhing of those agile, squid-like arms and their multiplying shadows. I fired in quick succession three shots and then saw the policeman straighten up to his full height and with a roar charge like a bull upon the writhing knot of tentacles. Hood clutched at him; he might as well have tried to stop a rhinoceros. Kindelon threw himself into the midst of the snaky turmoil, and unmindful of the burning fluid that dripped from it throttled the deathtrap. Any other than a man of his gigantic strength would have been instantly wrung to death in that vortex; but the policeman fastened his great hands on the warty leathern throat and clung to it while the huge beast tore at him cruelly.

Hood and I hovered about the fight, retreating as we were forced to, closing in as we saw opportunity. Twice Hood flashed his long keen knife and buried it in the monster with an accurate thrust. I shot a dozen times, but I doubt if more than three of the bullets were effective. Suddenly the fury of the fight slackened and Hood, seeing his chance, swung the knife. The death-trap reared and tearing Kindelon from his hold threshed the great body of the policeman like a rag between the walls of the sewer—then it began to waver, and sinking, sinking, sinking, it dropped lifeless, with the dead officer still in its grasp, upon the hideous debris of its lair.

Last of the Race

WILLIAM FRYER HARVEY

Little Billy Mungo, who kept the Accommodation House on Jackson's Sound, refused to believe in them. Flinders, who had prospected the whole country for coal, and was besides a naturalist, had seen them himself. He said that they were the footprints of a large apteryx.

But old Macnaughten, whisky sodden and argumentative, still held to his original opinion, that somewhere between Te Anau and the sea there was a new bird—rather a bird so old that with its death the race would become extinct.

And though in Pembroke, where Macnaughten spent his money, the man's story was taken for what it was worth, there was something in it that rang true.

So at least thought Tradescant, as he sat listening to the fellow, watching his reserve thaw beneath the combined influence of the whisky and the naturalist's congenial company.

"I ought to know," said Macnaughten; "I've seen apteryx by the hundred in the North Island, and I've killed them too before the Government made their regulations. I've seen the mud by the lake shore covered with their footprints, and I'll bet my bottom dollar that not a single one was over three inches long. Why, those I saw in the bush that spring were twice as big. And Flinders says it's an apteryx! I measured them myself, and that'll tell you if I lie!"

He took out of his pocket a slip of brown paper with two marks in pencil about eight inches apart. To Tradescant the proof hardly seemed conclusive.

"I'll tell you how I first came across them," he continued. "I was working on my own, trying to find a new route to the West Coast Sounds from this side. It was just at this time of the year, and the weather was cold, and there was rain. I'd been out all day, and when at night I came to the place where I was camping, there were footprints everywhere. The bird had been looking for something to eat. I've seen them every year since, barring last year. This much I'll say. They're not so common as they were. Have you ever seen a feather like that before?" He took out of his leather purse a scrap of newspaper, and a little piece of down lay on the table.

Tradescant took it up, held it in his hand, and after carefully scrutinising it with his lens, handed the feather back to Macnaughten.

"My dear fellow," he said, "I've seen hundreds of feathers like that. Open your pillow case when you go home, and you'll find a few more."

"By God!" exclaimed Macnaughten, "you mean I'm a liar?"

"Hardly that," the other replied. "I mean that I don't believe you. I should be glad to listen to anything more you have to say when I've seen your footprints."

There was silence in the room, silence broken only by the ticking of the cheap alarm clock on the mantelpiece.

Then Macnaughten spoke.

"Look here," he said; "I'm a poor man, but I've got brains, and I know how to use them. When I left England, a thick-headed fool could always earn a shilling a day and his keep by standing outside the barrack doors. Give me what your blasted Tommy gets for a week, and I'll show you them. If I don't, I'll call Flinders a gentleman to his face!"

"Very well," said Tradescant, and he drank to the bargain.

He was standing alone in the heart of the New Zealand bush. Macnaughten had left him three hours ago. He had done what he had promised to do, and it was no business of his, if the conceited English fool lost himself before he reached Mungo's Accommodation House.

As for the bird, Macnaughten had no fears of it ever being discovered by a man who took that feather for goose's down, by a naturalist who called a kea a hawk, and who asked if there had ever been kangaroos in the island.

Macnaughten could have laughed in his face; but then he never saw Tradescant as he knelt in the mud, scanning eagerly that faint impression on its surface, smelling it like a dog. He had only donned for a short week the unpopular but effective disguise of ignorance.

Tradescant had taken stock of his belongings. In his knapsack was food that might at a pinch last for three days. He had his maps and his compass.

"One cigarette," he said, "and then my last little bid for fame."

His whole life was traversed, from the time between the lighting of the match to when, five minutes later, the glowing stump burned his fingers.

His whole life was traversed. Perhaps that was why the cigarette was not so pleasant as it might have been.

He had made so many mistakes.

There was the mistake of ever being born, that all the future honour of his family should have been left to him alone to augment or mar. There was the mistake of his marriage; though perhaps that was not a mistake, but only a tragedy. Then there was that awful failure of his scientific career. It was intolerable that, after spending the ten best years of his life in perfecting his discovery, an American, with all his nation's luck, should have proved and published the identical thing six months before his work was finished. He who should have been first, followed with the rest of the honourably mentioned.

It was a mistake Jack dying as he did at Eton, just the boy any man would have wished for an only son.

Perhaps the least of all his mistakes was this wild goose chase.

For Tradescant had sickened of the laboratory. The vibrations of the ether which had fascinated him of old, had become too intangible. And here he was in the heart of the primeval forest with the old ancestral passion for nature strong upon him.

A Maori carving had first put the idea into his head, and then he had seen a paragraph in an evening paper at Christchurch.

"My boy's dead," he said to himself, as he gazed at the grey cigarette ash, "but I'll hand my name down to posterity somehow, and this bird shall do it. 'Apteryx Tradescantii, Number 999 in the catalogue. Unique.' Yes, little bird, I'm afraid your days are numbered."

He shouldered his knapsack and followed the footprints into the bush.

The evening of the third day found Tradescant wet through, sitting at the foot of a giant totara. He had lit a fire of the driest twigs he could find, and was warming himself before the spluttering flame.

It was a foolish thing to do, for the bird was not far away now; all day the footprints had been fresher, and he knew that the smoke might frighten it.

But he was chilled to the bone, and felt certain of his success.

His face, as he bent over the flame, glowed; he was beginning almost to enjoy the cleansing feel of the three days' rain. And all the time his hand never left the barrel of his gun. He fondled it, stroking the dull metal lovingly.

What days those had been! The mid-day gloom of the forest with its wealth of timber, the rippling of the streams, English streams where English trout would thrive far better than in limpid Hampshire waters or brown North Country becks.

Then the scarlet wonder of a late flowering rata, that giant parasite of the forest; the scramble up the slopes where the tree ferns no longer showed their shabby dressing of faded fronds, and nothing but shrub and thorn found root on the shelving screes.

Was it yesterday or the night before that he had camped high up on the hill, and had seen to the eastward the snow-clad range of the Southern Alps rise cold and ghostly against the blue night with its strange stars?

Then there was the moment when, kneeling to pick a gentian, he had found the feather, and the feelings of love and wonder which the flower had aroused in him, suddenly changed into one of strange lust and hate, as he held the grey little piece of fluff in his palm.

There was the wonder of the rain, too. The torrents that scoured the hillsides, the shrouding mist. And, best of all, three hours ago, when he had come to an impenetrable thicket of some dark-leaved thorny plant, to find more feathers, and, how his heart had exulted, a little patch of blood.

Tradescant was fondling his gun as twenty years before he had fondled his boy.

He arose in the morning stiff and with a fever. There was only half a round of bread in his wallet, and this he kept, breakfasting on the contents of his flask. From his sodden maps he calculated that he could not be more than twenty miles from a civilisation, represented by ten tin roofs and a beer and spirit licence. This was to be the last day's hunt.

The rain had not ceased all night, the streams were rivers, but Tradescant did not heed. He could hear now and then a monotonous piping ahead, and now and then the cracking of twigs.

The bird was leading him into the valley, and by mid-day he had reached the spot where two streams joined, a narrow tongue of land jutting between. Here he stopped, uncertain what course to pursue. Then he felt a sudden throbbing in the arteries of his neck. A tree had fallen across the smaller of the two streams, forming a natural bridge, and in the centre stood his bird. Of this much he could be sure, that no bird like this had ever before been seen by a white man. It was perhaps four feet high, almost wingless, as Tradescant had surmised, and covered with a softly-dappled plumage.

The man waited till the bird had reached a point where its body would fall clear of the water, took steady aim, and fired. The shot rang through the bush sharp and clear; the bird gave a shrill pipe, and half-fluttered to the tongue of land.

"Missed!" said Tradescant, "but I'll kill you yet."

It was no easy thing to cross the river, swollen with the three days' rain. The only way was to follow the bird.

Creeping on hands and knees, clutching the slippery bark with bleeding fingers, he had almost reached the further side when there was a cracking underneath him.

The bridge had broken. A minute's frantic scramble, with the water rushing below his dangling legs, while branches struck him in the face, and he was on firm ground again.

Then a mighty log, carried down in mid-stream, crashed against the broken tree and bore it away.

Of a truth the floods were out.

The spit he was on was low and sandy. There was little to hinder the flight of the bird. Tradescant began to run.

He ran a hundred yards, and then he burst out laughing, for he was on an island. The bird had gone into a death-trap. There it stood by the water side, flapping the useless wings, uttering its monotonous pipe. Tradescant had laughed, now he smiled, his old sarcastic smile, for he realised that if the bird had walked into its death-trap, it was to be his own too. Between the island and the further bank, there was a brown flood three hundred yards across, and he was no swimmer.

"But I've got the bird."

It did not resist. The bird opened its long, thin beak and made a faint hissing sound, as Tradescant, after tying the legs together, swung it over his shoulder. At the end of the island stood the stump of a tree, hollowed, and affording shelter from the rain. The ground around it was higher than elsewhere.

There he sat and waited. After a time he felt in his pocket for a piece of cord. He was no fisherman, and had always been clumsy with his fingers, but he finally succeeded in making a running noose to his liking, and slipped it over the bird's neck.

It was not perhaps the simplest way of killing it, but the body would not be spoiled. He tightened it, and the bird opened its mouth and began to gape, beating its wings.

"Come," said Tradescant, "no fuss, and don't look at me in that pathetic way, as if you'd never deserved this. It's the way of the world! Confound it!" he said, "the bird struggles too much. I shall have to postpone the operation," and he loosened the knots. "Cheer up, bird!" he said, addressing the beast. "I have no wish to put you to unnecessary discomfort. Now no shamming! When my boy carried on as you are doing now, I used to call him Charles Edward, known to history as the Young Pretender. Pluck up courage, Charles Edward, the date of your execution for the time being is postponed."

The south wind was bitterly cold; it might have come straight from the Antarctic icebergs, and the rain was turning to sleet.

Late in the afternoon, Tradescant awoke with a sense of warmth he had not felt all day. The bird had crept within his coat and now lay nestling close.

"A remarkably good idea, Charles Edward," he said. "I appreciate your returning good for evil in this way, and overlook the fact that your ulterior motive was probably selfish. If you'll excuse me one moment I'll ring for tea. I beg pardon, I was forgetting where I was. But I can still offer you refreshment. I have here," he continued, "brandy and bread. The brandy, I am informed, will cause a temporary dilation of the skin capillaries, accompanied by a feeling of warmth, which, however, is shortly followed by slight cardiac and nervous depression. As a stimulant it should only be used under exceptional circumstances and with moderation. I think we may call these circumstances exceptional. The state of the flask forbids excess. You decline the brandy? Let me call your attention to the bread, I believe a large part of its nutritious constituents has been removed in the process of manufacture, but it contains a percentage of carbohydrate varying from 55 per cent. in the best white bread, to 40 per cent. in the coarser varieties. The sample I hold in my hand would be classed among the coarse varieties. As a food, it far exceeds the value of the alcohol. Estimable bird! You choose the bread. It would have been my own choice, but you are my guest."

The bird pecked greedily at the crumbs Tradescant offered it, and showed the whites of its eyes every time it swallowed.

As the brandy reached the brain, the man began to laugh.

"Charles Edward!" he said, "has it ever struck you how grotesque it is, that I, the last of my family, should be sitting talking to you, the last of yours? We came over with the Conqueror. Tell me something about your ancestors!

"My dear bird, if you must yawn in that shockingly rude manner, do put your flapper in front of your mouth. If you have no objection to make, I now intend to go for a short stroll."

He had hardly walked a dozen yards when he came to the edge of the island. While he gazed, he saw the water rising inch by inch. Out in mid-stream the sodden body of a sheep was carried by. It was held for a minute entangled in the branches of a tree; then the eddy swept it clear, and bumping against logs and boulders, the yellow water washed it downwards. Far up the glen Tradescant heard the bleating of a solitary lamb.

After ten minutes, Tradescant walked back to the hollow trunk; the fever was still upon him. He was delirious now.

"There's no sign of the carriage yet," he said, addressing the bird, "so we must shelter here as best we can. You'll have to sit close. I'm afraid your feet will be simply sopping, and you'll catch your death of cold, but if you were such a goose to come out—" Then he broke off laughing.

"Not goose," he said, "I'm forgetting myself, Apteryx. *Apteryx Tradescantii*. That's what I meant.

"And by the way, that reminds me I wanted to ask you about your wings. What's the use of having wings if you can't fly with them? I've often been told that I have wings myself, and my friends tell me that I ought to try and fly, and all I can do is to flop, flop, along the ground just like you. There's something wrong there, you know, Charles Edward."

Tradescant laughed again the high-pitched senseless laugh of delirium. He no longer saw the water rising inch by inch, making the ground at his feet a sponge-like mass. It was of the past he was thinking, of the other Charles Edward, his boy. And amid the rain thresh, his voice drowned by the turbulent cry of the stream, he talked to the phantasms he saw.

The bird crept nearer to its strange companion, it no longer seemed to fear him. And he putting out his hand, drew it towards him, wrapping it in his coat.

"Keep close, and don't gape, Charles Edward. One of us may weather it yet. Half a minute though; I was forgetting there are advantages in the appurtenances of civilisation, even in the bush!"

He searched in his pocket-book and took out a card,

> Mr. Montague Tradescant,
> 9 Ilsley Gardens, W.

On the back, his half-numbed fingers scribbled

> *Apteryx Tradescantii.*

He tied the slip of pasteboard to the cord around the bird's throat.

"It's awfully cold," he said. "I'll tuck you up, and then we'll both go to sleep, and I think I owe you an apology for hustling you so, the last three days. Good-night!"

The Air Serpent
WILL A. PAGE

Gentlemen: The report which I now have the honor to submit to your honorable body is so extraordinary, and deals with facts so difficult to prove—beyond my own mere word and the records of my barograph which indicate the approximate height reached by my machine—that it is with much trepidation that I now appear before you. In presenting to you the results of my recent exploration of the upper ether, and the mysterious disappearance of my late mechanic, John Ald, of which cognizance has already been taken by the police, I realize that I am taxing the limit of credulity; yet before passing final judgment upon the extraordinary narrative I am about to place before you, let me call your attention to the fact that my record hitherto in the annals of aviation has been a story of unquestioned achievements, of daring which has often been characterized as reckless, and of an earnest and constant effort to discover new truths in that wonderful air world which has been opened up to exploration through the recent development of the aëroplane.

I cannot refrain, also, from reminding your learned body that pioneers in all fields of endeavor suffer martyrdom from the unthinking and the unbelieving. Half a century ago, a ribald rhymster mocked at Darius Green and his flying machine; yet within the brief space of half-a-dozen years, the perfect aëroplane expresses of to-day have been evolved before our very eyes. Even last year, when a new world's altitude record of 16,374 feet was established by the lamented Renegal, your sub-committee on altitude adopted a resolution that the limit of attainment in the upper ether had been reached; yet less than two months after, Santuza, the daring Spanish aviator, flying his 200-horse-power Mercadio tri-plane with the improved ailerons, reached the incredible height of 23,760 feet, when the ink in his barograph ran out and refused to register a greater height, although Santuza is of the belief that he climbed almost 1,000 feet higher.

To pause for a moment from the subject nearest our hearts, let me only speak for a moment of the derision and ridicule heaped upon Columbus when he planned his first voyage; of the insults and scorn directed at Galileo; or of the thousands of martyrs in the realm of science, invention and discovery who, at first denounced as fakers and preposterous humbugs, were proven after a lapse of time to have been honest, sincere and truthful in their claims.

Bearing these facts of history in mind, permit me to present herewith a brief, accurate and truthful account of all that happened during my recent ascent when, with the aid of John Ald, my invaluable and greatly mourned mechanic, I established an altitude record which I do not believe will ever be exceeded, if indeed it is reached by other aviators within our time. For not only are the difficulties such that our machines will have to be improved in some miraculous manner to go higher, but there are living, breathing obstacles to further exploration of the upper ether which will make all such experiments extremely hazardous, and probably fatal, to even the most venturesome aviator. For I have the important announcement to make, almost beyond your powers of belief, that I have discovered that the upper ether is inhabited. This astounding discovery was made simultaneously by me and my mechanic, John Ald, for whom the voyage of exploration brought death in an unprecedented and most deplorable manner. Had not the mysterious creature of the air claimed my poor mechanic as its first earthly victim, he would now be standing here beside me upon this platform, to corroborate my unsupported testimony with his own verbal report of the most extraordinary experience that ever befell mortal man.

As your honorable body well knows, I have secured patents
from time to time for improvements in the Gesler engines with
which my aëroplanes have been fitted the past two years. By enlarging the plane surface and fitting four blades to each propeller
instead of two, I have been enabled to increase the speed record to
97.16 miles per hour, this having been officially accomplished at
the July Palm Beach meeting. Having established a new speed
record, which I confidently think will stand for some months, I
determined to try for new altitude records, but in view of the
numerous unfortunate accidents resulting from experiments in the
upper ether, I determined to secure safety at all hazards. I therefore reconstructed my last imported Garnier tri-plane so that the
improved ailerons invented by Santuza could be applied not only
to the main planes, but to the forward controlling and lifting planes
as well. This preserved the lateral balance to such a perfect degree
that it was easily possible to make a turn in eight seconds in a 25-
mile wind, without banking the machine more than 30 degrees. I
found, also, that by fitting the new plane with three propellers,
three Gesler engines, and three gasoline tanks of ample size, I could
feel reasonably certain that my power would not be exhausted without warning, for a single turn of the lever would put any or all of
the three engines in operation, singly or together, and if I wished
to economize on power, I could climb with only one propeller, holding the others in reserve for possible accidents or in case I wished
to combat any of the strong air currents sometimes encountered
above the 12,000 foot level.

It was a clear August day, late in the afternoon, when John and
a couple of hangers-on wheeled the big tri-plane out of the hangar
at Belmont Park, the beautiful Long Island aviation ground where
aërial history has been made in the past two years. Both John and
I were determined that before another sun should rise, we would
bring back as a trophy from the air a record for altitude that would
never be broken. How little we knew at what a price we would succeed, or through what dangers we would pass before I returned to
that dear old hangar where we had chummed together and experimented so much.

I was determined to go after the record at nightfall, because so far above the clouds the sun's rays prove a trifle too glaring. It was undoubtedly the tremendous light from the sun which affected the sight of poor Renegal when his machine fell from a height of 14,800 feet when he tried to exceed his own altitude record at San Francisco. Therefore I determined to do my high flying at night, when the moon was at the quarter and gave just enough light for us to see clearly and distinctly after we had passed from the lower levels.

The gasoline tanks were carefully filled, the engines tested, a supply of light provisions placed in the basket between the two seats, and the oxygen tanks carefully strapped in place on both of us, with the connecting tubes and the helmets under the arms ready to be applied when we had passed the 15,000-foot level into the upper strata where the rarefied air made the oxygen tanks a necessity.

Egerton Brooks, the official secretary of the Montauk Aëro Club, personally adjusted the official barograph of the American Aëronautical Society, and sealed it with his own seal.

"I hope you will get the record above 25,000 feet," he cried, as the mechanics began to start the engines. "It is a new Angiers barograph, adjusted to register up to 50,000 feet, though of course no living thing could attain such an absurd height. You will notice that it is surrounded by cork, so that if you fall into the water, the record will not be injured or lost."

Giving Brooks a hearty hand-shake and a few words of farewell, I gave the signal and Ald started the middle engine, No. 2.

"You may expect me about midnight," I cried in farewell. "Keep the beacons burning until then, and if I don't return you will know I have been blown out of my course."

The great whirring of the propellers drowned further speech. I rang the forward bell, the mechanics let go, and like an eagle the tri-plane sprang aloft.

Forward, upward, over the field, over the grandstand, and ever onward and upward the giant tri-plane mounted. I had tilted the lifting forward planes to 28 degrees, and now started engine No. 1.

The added power sent us upward at nearly twice the speed first employed, and in a few seconds the earth below was but a dull, dark, blurred mass, with now and then a faint twinkling from an electric light far below.

The early twilight faded into darkness when we had reached the 3,000 level and I directed Ald, who was looking after the engines behind me, to turn on the electric search-light. The warning came none too soon, for almost as I spoke there was a little fluttering, crashing sound as the machine plunged headlong into a flock of sea gulls which had not noticed our approach.

"Better look at the compass," shouted Ald. "You are out at sea."

Brushing two of the dead gulls from the plane at my side, and turning on the pocket electric light which was placed at my left over the map and compass, I soon realized that we had indeed been following a straight course across Long Island and were now probably over the Fire Island light. Shifting the vertical planes in the rear a trifle I set them at 18 degrees, which would mean that the tri-plane would describe great circles approximately ten miles in diameter, as it gradually ploughed upward through the atmosphere.

The earth was now entirely out of sight. In daylight, as all experienced aviators know, the earth becomes practically invisible at the 7,000-foot level, even on a clear day. On cloudy days one is lost to the earth after ascending a few hundred feet. Just as the waiting crowds below at an aviation meeting find it impossible to distinguish even a speck on the horizon ten minutes after a swift machine leaves the earth, so the aviator aloft on his speedy career finds himself absolutely alone in a new world.

The sensation is indescribable. One feels that one has opened up a new territory, discovered a new realm, in which he alone is king. Preserving the balance when thus out of sight of the earth is not as difficult as one might imagine, as the laws of gravitation operate through the unseen space, and one has only to watch the delicate mechanism of the anograph to ascertain whether one is losing the equilibrium of the machine.

Slowly the needle moved round and round on the barograph, steadily registering our ascent. Within the first hour, when darkness had completely shut us off from the rest of the universe, we had passed the 10,000-foot level, which for almost a year in the early days of aviation had been a prize goal for the amateur aviators before the business had been placed on the firm footing it now enjoys.

Then came the moon. It rose at 9:02 on the 75th meridian, but as we were nearly three miles above the horizon, we saw it much sooner. It seemed reflected in some faint, misty manner by the water which he knew must be far below us, but as we mounted higher and higher, even the faint reflection disappeared.

At 9:37 P.M. Ald leaned over my shoulder and grunted.

"Fifteen thousand feet," he muttered. "We can do it faster if we use the other engine."

"No," I replied. "Hold engine No. 3 for emergencies."

"Emergencies?" he repeated, with a laugh. "Good Lord, what emergencies can happen now? What? As if the tri-planes are not as safe as an express train or a submarine nowadays."

I did not argue with him. Ald was noted for his fondness for a controversy. I merely signaled to him to get the oxygen helmets ready, for the increased difficulty of breathing showed me that the rarefied air was fast becoming too thin for us to breathe with comfort. I noticed, too, that our speed seemed to diminish slightly, as the planes found the supporting air becoming thinner and thinner. I fondly reflected, however, that the third engine would remedy this when it became necessary to get more speed to keep aloft on the last leg of our upward climb. However, we were soon inside the oxygen helmets, and once more I could take a long, full breath of life-giving ozone.

The helmets of course made further conversation impossible, but long experience in the higher altitudes had perfected a system of signals between my mechanic and myself which enabled us to carry on a conversation fairly well.

John leaned over my shoulder at 10:38 and pointed to the needle of the barograph. It registered 22,380 feet. He nudged me.

I understood that nudge perfectly. It meant that in less than ten minutes more of climbing, we would have passed the best record of Santuza, officially 23,760 feet, and would have the world's altitude record within our grasp.

So absorbed were we in watching the barograph that we both neglected the engines, and it was only a miracle that something did not happen when engine No. 2 developed a hot bearing because of lack of oil. I sharply reprimanded John for not attending to such details, and bade him by signals to attend to his business, while I would watch the needle.

Up, around it moved. First it reached the 23,000 mark, then hundred by hundred, ten by ten, it moved on and on. I turned and gave a silent signal of joy when we passed Santuza's mark. Then I set forward determined to establish a world altitude record that would never be broken. And I succeeded.

It must have been shortly after 11 o'clock when the barograph registered 30,000 feet. This gigantic achievement, nearly six miles away from the earth, higher than the loftiest mountain peak, higher than any balloon had ever floated, should have satisfied us. I deeply regret that we were not content to rest upon these laurels, but with a foolhardiness for which I can never forgive myself, I tried to see how much higher we could go without using the reserve supply of gasoline contained in the tank of engine No. 3—which fortunately, we had not yet started. In fact, I venture the assertion that had it not been for the precaution of providing a third engine neither of us would have been saved from the catastrophe that followed.

Onward, upward, past the 33,000 foot level the sturdy tri-plane, steady as a ship in a calm, continued to forge. When 35,000 was reached I turned and signaled John for his advice. The poor fellow, who didn't realize how near he was to the end of all earthly things, answered to keep on going. So we went up past the 36,000 foot level.

And then we saw *it*.

Never to my dying day, gentlemen, will I forget the horror of that moment. Never will I be able to efface from memory the dread picture of that gigantic monster of the air, lazily floating along on the ether, scarcely moving the great, finnish wings with which a wonderful creator had endowed it. Although the cold was almost unendurable, and I had thought myself as nearly frozen as possible, I felt a sudden stiffness permeate my veins and I shook with terror. I felt John grasp my shoulder, his hand shaking as with the palsy, and though neither of us could speak because of the oxygen helmets, we both felt a grim horror which would no doubt have stricken us dumb under any circumstances.

For there, almost in front of us, a trifle to the right, coming in an opposite direction, and gazing at us with mild curiosity and perhaps astonishment, was a gigantic monster, utterly unlike anything I have ever seen before. The light from the electric searchlight cast a weird reflection upon the great creature, and this light, I believe, was one instrument which proved our salvation temporarily, for it struck the giant monster fairly in the eyes, and seemed to blind him.

The monster—or air serpent, for so I must call it—seemed to be about ninety or a hundred feet in length. Its physical structure seemed a cross between a bat and a snake. There were undulating movements as it slowly drifted, together with flapping of the twenty or thirty batlike wings which projected from its sides. The head was enormous, and it was not the head of a bird. Two great eyes, approximately a foot in diameter each, glared and blinked over a cavernous maw which opened and closed spasmodically as the creature breathed. This much we saw, and then as the swift tri-plane shot by almost under the creature's startled eyes, I felt a sudden blast of hot air which made the tri-plane quiver and tremble for a moment. Then we had passed the creature and had sped forth into the darkness, for the moonlight was very faint.

I felt John grasp me for support. He was trembling. I turned, pointed toward engine No. 3, and at the same time deflected the forward controlling plane to an angle of 20 degrees, determined to make the quickest and yet safest descent on record. I had no desire to get a second look at the monster of the air.

The jarring of the third engine made a terrific noise, but we could not hear it. The stalwart tri-plane shook under the added pressure, and we sprang forward at a speed which I estimated at 80 miles an hour. The needle of the barograph began to settle quickly, as we dropped to the 35,000-foot level.

Suddenly I felt John's convulsive grasp upon my shoulder. I turned, and he pointed off to the left.

"It's there, sir," he cried, as plainly by his signals as though he had spoken out loud.

I looked as he indicated. There, two hundred feet away, following us almost without an effort while we were making 80 miles an hour, was the air serpent.

I shifted the vertical plane sharply to the right and veered off to escape. Almost before I had settled down to a straight course ahead, I felt again that hot, nauseous breath, which I knew came from the giant monster hovering so near us.

John was trembling all over. We were descending fast, for the barograph now registered 33,750, and our course ahead was being made at 80 miles an hour, yet that gigantic, wonderful, monstrous *thing* seemed able to keep up with us without an effort.

I determined to try strategy. Remembering how the eyes had blinked at the electric searchlight, I suddenly turned a trifle to the left, shifted the searchlight, and struck the creature with it squarely in the eyes.

The air serpent backed off instantly, I turned sharply to the right, extinguished the searchlight as I did so and lowered the forward planes to 25 degrees, a dangerous angle for a descent, as all aviators know, but I was determined to escape from the monster if possible.

But it was futile. Before the barograph showed 30,000 feet, I felt the hot breath again, and this time it came from beneath.

With incredible ingenuity, probably realizing from the changing air pressure that its prey was trying to escape into the lower ether, the monster had placed himself under the aëroplane, and I firmly believe that if I had not suddenly shifted the forward lateral planes to the horizontal, we would have struck the creature from above.

I turned to John, mutely asking advice. He was quivering with fear. And I too began to tremble anew when I realized how completely this mysterious monster of the air had us in his power.

I switched on the searchlight again and aimed it below us. There he was, the giant, undulating, fin-like creature, his sixty wings flapping noiselessly, his hulking, soft, snaky body moving forward without an effort, and the great head and the cavernous maw turned upward as if it had not yet determined what manner of bird or beast this was which had invaded the upper realms where this creature alone seemed able to exist.

I turned the plane sharply to the right, and keeping the searchlight pointing downward, shifted the forward planes again for a descent. It was our only chance and we had to take it.

But the enemy was vigilant and ever-watchful. It followed us curiously to the 25,000-foot level. Then it evidently became oppressed by the thickness of the atmosphere, and decided we had gone far enough. With a quick, sudden lashing of the fins, it dived under us, the hot breath again making the planes tremble, and loomed up straight ahead. In another moment we would have struck it had I not tilted the vertical planes sharply to the left. I turned completely around in less than three seconds, the quickest turn on record, I believe, but while the strain on the ailerons was terrific, the tri-plane held on its course.

But we could not escape the enemy. The giant monster merely gave about two jumps, and with incredible speed, repeated the maneuver. Once more I jammed the wheel sharply to the right, and once more the ailerons creaked as the strain of the sudden turn almost tore them loose.

Then came the catastrophe. The next time the monster leaped before us I flashed the searchlight into its great wicked eyes. It blinked and ducked, and in an instant we had passed over it.

I firmly believe that John Ald expected me to execute another sharp turn. Perhaps he leaned too far over in an effort to help maintain the balance. Perhaps fear and the terror took possession of his heart, and he thought the end was near anyhow. Whether he fell or jumped from his seat I know not, but when I turned my head the instant after we had passed the creature, I realized that I was alone.

I swung about instantly, and felt an ominous snap about the ailerons under the terrific strain of the turn, but fortunately all held. Then I directed the searchlight downward, and what I saw by the brilliant flashing rays I shall never forget.

There, three hundred feet below me, I saw the giant monster of the air, his great maw pointing upward. A dark object hurtled through the air, falling like a stone. It passed the startled gaze of the air serpent and fell into space below. Quicker than I can speak the words the monster darted downward after the falling object. Sick with horror, scarcely able to work the controlling levers, I saw by the faint, flickering rays of the searchlight, down below, the monster suddenly pause in its mad dash. It had caught the falling object and swallowed it in its maw.

How I reached the lower levels I know not. My arms worked the planes automatically, the terrific descent was made in thirty minutes, and sometime about midnight I landed on the sandy beach of the south shore of Long Island near Montauk Point. Too weak to remove the oxygen helmet, which fortunately was charged for twelve hours, I lay there in a daze. About five o'clock some fisher-men found me and aided in removing the helmet. The tri-plane, slightly injured by its sudden contact with the beach, was taken apart and shipped back to New York, and I personally brought the barograph, still sealed as I thought, to the rooms of the Montauk Aëro Club. There a cruel disappointment awaited me, for it appears that the shock of landing broke the seal, and the record, while perfectly clear, could not be accepted as official without the official seal showing that it had not been tampered with.

I made a preliminary report on the extraordinary adventure to the newspaper reporters, and notified the police of the accident to my mechanic, but only to meet with such ridicule that I speedily decided to delay my report for careful reflection and consideration. The accepted version of the death of John Ald is that he dropped into the ocean, but gentlemen, I have made here my report, and in view of my hitherto unquestioned word, I believe I have the right to demand that it be accepted as authentic. Some day a venture-some air-man will penetrate to the upper levels, five miles from the earth, and discover new evidence to corroborate my unsupported word. And then, gentlemen, the world will realize that just as in the farthest depths of the sea, there are strange monsters we have never seen, so in the thin upper strata of air there are tenu-ous creatures living in a world of their own, which we have never seen.

The Terror of Blue John Gap

ARTHUR CONAN DOYLE

The following narrative was found among the papers of Dr. James Hardcastle, who died of phthisis on February 4th, 1908, at 36, Upper Coventry Flats, South Kensington. Those who knew him best, while refusing to express an opinion upon this particular statement, are unanimous in asserting that he was a man of a sober and scientific turn of mind, absolutely devoid of imagination, and most unlikely to invent any abnormal series of events. The paper was contained in an envelope, which was docketed, "A Short Account of the Circumstances which occurred near Miss Allerton's Farm in North-West Derbyshire in the Spring of Last Year." The envelope was sealed, and on the other side was written in pencil—

> "Dear Seaton,—
>
> "It may interest, and perhaps pain you, to know that the incredulity with which you met my story has prevented me from ever opening my mouth upon the subject again. I leave this record after my death, and perhaps strangers may be found to have more confidence in me than my friend."

Inquiry has failed to elicit who this Seaton may have been. I may add that the visit of the deceased to Allerton's Farm, and the general nature of the alarm there, apart from his particular explanation, have been absolutely established. With this foreword I append his account exactly as he left it. It is in the form of a diary, some entries in which have been expanded, while a few have been erased.

April 17.—Already I feel the benefit of this wonderful upland air. The farm of the Allertons lies fourteen hundred and twenty feet above sea-level, so it may well be a bracing climate. Beyond the usual morning cough I have very little discomfort, and, what with the fresh milk and the home-grown mutton, I have every chance of putting on weight. I think Saunderson will be pleased.

The two Miss Allertons are charmingly quaint and kind, two dear little hard-working old maids, who are ready to lavish all the heart which might have gone out to husband and to children upon an invalid stranger. Truly, the old maid is a most useful person, one of the reserve forces of the community. They talk of the super-fluous woman, but what would the poor superfluous man do with-out her kindly presence? By the way, in their simplicity they very quickly let out the reason why Saunderson recommended their farm. The Professor rose from the ranks himself, and I believe that in his youth he was not above scaring crows in these very fields.

It is a most lonely spot, and the walks are picturesque in the extreme. The farm consists of grazing land lying at the bottom of an irregular valley. On each side are the fantastic limestone hills, formed of rock so soft that you can break it away with your hands. All this country is hollow. Could you strike it with some gigantic hammer it would boom like a drum, or possibly cave in altogether and expose some huge subterranean sea. A great sea there must surely be, for on all sides the streams run into the mountain itself, never to reappear. There are gaps everywhere amid the rocks, and when you pass through them you find yourself in great caverns, which wind down into the bowels of the earth. I have a small bi-cycle lamp, and it is a perpetual joy to me to carry it into these weird solitudes, and to see the wonderful silver and black effect when I throw its light upon the stalactites which drape the lofty roofs. Shut off the lamp, and you are in the blackest darkness. Turn it on, and it is a scene from the Arabian Nights.

But there is one of these strange openings in the earth which has a special interest, for it is the handiwork, not of nature, but of man. I had never heard of Blue John when I came to these parts. It is the name given to a peculiar mineral of a beautiful purple shade, which is only found at one or two places in the world. It is so rare that an ordinary vase of Blue John would be valued at a great price. The Romans, with that extraordinary instinct of theirs, discovered that it was to be found in this valley, and sank a horizontal shaft deep into the mountain side. The opening of their mine has been called Blue John Gap, a clean-cut arch in the rock, the mouth all overgrown with bushes. It is a goodly passage which the Roman miners have cut, and it intersects some of the great water-worn caves, so that if you enter Blue John Gap you would do well to mark your steps and to have a good store of candles, or you may never make your way back to the daylight again. I have not yet gone deeply into it, but this very day I stood at the mouth of the arched tunnel, and peering down into the black recesses beyond, I vowed that when my health returned I would devote some holiday to exploring those mysterious depths and finding out for myself how far the Roman had penetrated into the Derbyshire hills.

Strange how superstitious these countrymen are! I should have thought better of young Armitage, for he is a man of some education and character, and a very fine fellow for his station in life. I was standing at the Blue John Gap when he came across the field to me.

"Well, doctor," said he, "you're not afraid, anyhow."

"Afraid!" I answered. "Afraid of what?"

"Of it," said he, with a jerk of his thumb towards the black vault, "of the Terror that lives in the Blue John Cave."

How absurdly easy it is for a legend to arise in a lonely countryside! I examined him as to the reasons for his weird belief. It seems that from time to time sheep have been missing from the fields, carried bodily away, according to Armitage. That they could have wandered away of their own accord and disappeared among the mountains was an explanation to which he would not listen. On one occasion a pool of blood had been found, and some tufts of wool. That also, I pointed out, could be explained in a perfectly natural way. Further, the nights upon which sheep disappeared were invariably very dark, cloudy nights with no moon. This I met with the obvious retort that those were the nights which a commonplace sheep-stealer would naturally choose for his work. On one occasion a gap had been made in a wall, and some of the stones scattered for a considerable distance. Human agency again, in my opinion. Finally, Armitage clinched all his arguments by telling me that he had actually heard the Creature—indeed, that anyone could hear it who remained long enough at the Gap. It was a distant roaring of an immense volume. I could not but smile at this, knowing, as I do, the strange reverberations which come out of an underground water system running amid the chasms of a limestone formation. My incredulity annoyed Armitage so that he turned and left me with some abruptness.

And now comes the queer point about the whole business. I was still standing near the mouth of the cave turning over in my mind the various statements of Armitage, and reflecting how readily they could be explained away, when suddenly, from the depth of the tunnel beside me, there issued a most extraordinary sound. How shall I describe it? First of all, it seemed to be a great distance away, far down in the bowels of the earth. Secondly, in spite of this suggestion of distance, it was very loud. Lastly, it was not a boom, nor a crash, such as one would associate with falling water or tumbling rock, but it was a high whine, tremulous and vibrating, almost like the whinnying of a horse. It was certainly a most remarkable experience, and one which for a moment, I must admit, gave a new significance to Armitage's words. I waited by the Blue John Gap for half an hour or more, but there was no return of the sound, so at last I wandered back to the farmhouse, rather mystified by what had occurred. Decidedly I shall explore that cavern when my strength is restored. Of course, Armitage's explanation is too absurd for discussion, and yet that sound was certainly very strange. It still rings in my ears as I write.

April 20.—In the last three days I have made several expeditions to the Blue John Gap, and have even penetrated some short distance, but my bicycle lantern is so small and weak that I dare not trust myself very far. I shall do the thing more systematically. I have heard no sound at all, and could almost believe that I had been the victim of some hallucination suggested, perhaps, by Armitage's conversation. Of course, the whole idea is absurd, and yet I must confess that those bushes at the entrance of the cave do present an appearance as if some heavy creature had forced its way through them. I begin to be keenly interested. I have said nothing to the Miss Allertons, for they are quite superstitious enough already, but I have bought some candles, and mean to investigate for myself.

I observed this morning that among the numerous tufts of sheep's wool which lay among the bushes near the cavern there was one which was smeared with blood. Of course, my reason tells me that if sheep wander into such rocky places they are likely to injure themselves, and yet somehow that splash of crimson gave me a sudden shock, and for a moment I found myself shrinking back in horror from the old Roman arch. A fetid breath seemed to ooze from the black depths into which I peered. Could it indeed be possible that some nameless thing, some dreadful presence, was lurking down yonder? I should have been incapable of such feelings in the days of my strength, but one grows more nervous and fanciful when one's health is shaken.

For the moment I weakened in my resolution, and was ready to leave the secret of the old mine, if one exists, for ever unsolved. But tonight my interest has returned and my nerves grown more steady. Tomorrow I trust that I shall have gone more deeply into this matter.

April 22.—Let me try and set down as accurately as I can my extraordinary experience of yesterday. I started in the afternoon, and made my way to the Blue John Gap. I confess that my misgivings returned as I gazed into its depths, and I wished that I had brought a companion to share my exploration. Finally, with a return of resolution, I lit my candle, pushed my way through the briars, and descended into the rocky shaft.

It went down at an acute angle for some fifty feet, the floor being covered with broken stone. Thence there extended a long, straight passage cut in the solid rock. I am no geologist, but the lining of this corridor was certainly of some harder material than limestone, for there were points where I could actually see the tool-marks which the old miners had left in their excavation, as fresh as if they had been done yesterday. Down this strange, old-world corridor I stumbled, my feeble flame throwing a dim circle of light around me, which made the shadows beyond the more threatening and obscure. Finally, I came to a spot where the Roman tunnel opened into a water-worn cavern—a huge hall, hung with long white icicles of lime deposit. From this central chamber I could dimly perceive that a number of passages worn by the subterranean streams wound away into the depths of the earth. I was standing there wondering whether I had better return, or whether I dare venture farther into this dangerous labyrinth, when my eyes fell upon something at my feet which strongly arrested my attention.

The greater part of the floor of the cavern was covered with boulders of rock or with hard incrustations of lime, but at this particular point there had been a drip from the distant roof, which had left a patch of soft mud. In the very centre of this there was a huge mark—an ill-defined blotch, deep, broad and irregular, as if a great boulder had fallen upon it. No loose stone lay near, however, nor was there anything to account for the impression. It was far too large to be caused by any possible animal, and besides, there was only the one, and the patch of mud was of such a size that no reasonable stride could have covered it. As I rose from the examination of that singular mark and then looked round into the black shadows which hemmed me in, I must confess that I felt for a moment a most unpleasant sinking of my heart, and that, do what I could, the candle trembled in my outstretched hand.

I soon recovered my nerve, however, when I reflected how absurd it was to associate so huge and shapeless a mark with the track of any known animal. Even an elephant could not have produced it. I determined, therefore, that I would not be scared by vague and senseless fears from carrying out my exploration. Before proceeding, I took good note of a curious rock formation in the wall by which I could recognize the entrance of the Roman tunnel. The precaution was very necessary, for the great cave, so far as I could see it, was intersected by passages. Having made sure of my position, and reassured myself by examining my spare candles and my matches, I advanced slowly over the rocky and uneven surface of the cavern.

And now I come to the point where I met with such sudden and desperate disaster. A stream, some twenty feet broad, ran across my path, and I walked for some little distance along the bank to find a spot where I could cross dry-shod. Finally, I came to a place where a single flat boulder lay near the centre, which I could reach in a stride. As it chanced, however, the rock had been cut away and made top-heavy by the rush of the stream, so that it tilted over as I landed on it and shot me into the ice-cold water. My candle went out, and I found myself floundering about in utter and absolute darkness.

I staggered to my feet again, more amused than alarmed by my adventure. The candle had fallen from my hand, and was lost in the stream, but I had two others in my pocket, so that it was of no importance. I got one of them ready, and drew out my box of matches to light it. Only then did I realize my position. The box had been soaked in my fall into the river. It was impossible to strike the matches.

A cold hand seemed to close round my heart as I realized my position. The darkness was opaque and horrible. It was so utter one put one's hand up to one's face as if to press off something solid. I stood still, and by an effort I steadied myself. I tried to reconstruct in my mind a map of the floor of the cavern as I had last seen it. Alas! the bearings which had impressed themselves upon my mind were high on the wall, and not to be found by touch. Still, I remembered in a general way how the sides were situated, and I hoped that by groping my way along them I should at last come to the opening of the Roman tunnel. Moving very slowly, and continually striking against the rocks, I set out on this desperate quest.

But I very soon realized how impossible it was. In that black, velvety darkness one lost all one's bearings in an instant. Before I had made a dozen paces, I was utterly bewildered as to my whereabouts. The rippling of the stream, which was the one sound audible, showed me where it lay, but the moment that I left its bank I was utterly lost. The idea of finding my way back in absolute darkness through that limestone labyrinth was clearly an impossible one.

I sat down upon a boulder and reflected upon my unfortunate plight. I had not told anyone that I proposed to come to the Blue John mine, and it was unlikely that a search party would come after me. Therefore I must trust to my own resources to get clear of the danger. There was only one hope, and that was that the matches might dry. When I fell into the river, only half of me had got thoroughly wet. My left shoulder had remained above the water. I took the box of matches, therefore, and put it into my left armpit. The moist air of the cavern might possibly be counteracted by the heat of my body, but even so, I knew that I could not hope to get a light for many hours. Meanwhile there was nothing for it but to wait.

By good luck I had slipped several biscuits into my pocket before I left the farm-house. These I now devoured, and washed them down with a draught from that wretched stream which had been the cause of all my misfortunes. Then I felt about for a comfortable seat among the rocks, and, having discovered a place where I could get a support for my back, I stretched out my legs and settled myself down to wait. I was wretchedly damp and cold, but I tried to cheer myself with the reflection that modern science prescribed open windows and walks in all weather for my disease. Gradually, lulled by the monotonous gurgle of the stream, and by the absolute darkness, I sank into an uneasy slumber.

How long this lasted I cannot say. It may have been for an hour, it may have been for several. Suddenly I sat up on my rock couch, with every nerve thrilling and every sense acutely on the alert. Beyond all doubt I had heard a sound—some sound very distinct from the gurgling of the waters. It had passed, but the reverberation of it still lingered in my ear. Was it a search party? They would most certainly have shouted, and vague as this sound was which had wakened me, it was very distinct from the human voice. I sat palpitating and hardly daring to breathe. There it was again! And again! Now it had become continuous. It was a tread—yes, surely it was the tread of some living creature. But what a tread it was! It gave one the impression of enormous weight carried upon sponge-like feet, which gave forth a muffled but ear-filling sound. The darkness was as complete as ever, but the tread was regular and decisive. And it was coming beyond all question in my direction.

My skin grew cold, and my hair stood on end as I listened to that steady and ponderous footfall. There was some creature there, and surely by the speed of its advance, it was one which could see in the dark. I crouched low on my rock and tried to blend myself into it. The steps grew nearer still, then stopped, and presently I was aware of a loud lapping and gurgling. The creature was drinking at the stream. Then again there was silence, broken by a succession of long sniffs and snorts of tremendous volume and energy. Had it caught the scent of me? My own nostrils were filled by a low fetid odour, mephitic and abominable. Then I heard the steps again. They were on my side of the stream now. The stones rattled within a few yards of where I lay. Hardly daring to breathe, I crouched upon my rock. Then the steps drew away. I heard the splash as it returned across the river, and the sound died away into the distance in the direction from which it had come.

For a long time I lay upon the rock, too much horrified to move. I thought of the sound which I had heard coming from the depths of the cave, of Armitage's fears, of the strange impression in the mud, and now came this final and absolute proof that there was indeed some inconceivable monster, something utterly unearthly and dreadful, which lurked in the hollow of the mountain. Of its nature or form I could frame no conception, save that it was both light-footed and gigantic. The combat between my reason, which told me that such things could not be, and my senses, which told me that they were, raged within me as I lay. Finally, I was almost ready to persuade myself that this experience had been part of some evil dream, and that my abnormal condition might have conjured up an hallucination. But there remained one final experience which removed the last possibility of doubt from my mind.

I had taken my matches from my armpit and felt them. They seemed perfectly hard and dry. Stooping down into a crevice of the rocks, I tried one of them. To my delight it took fire at once. I lit the candle, and, with a terrified backward glance into the obscure depths of the cavern, I hurried in the direction of the Roman passage. As I did so I passed the patch of mud on which I had seen the huge imprint. Now I stood astonished before it, for there were three similar imprints upon its surface, enormous in size, irregular in outline, of a depth which indicated the ponderous weight which had left them. Then a great terror surged over me. Stooping and shading my candle with my hand, I ran in a frenzy of fear to the rocky archway, hastened up it, and never stopped until, with weary feet and panting lungs, I rushed up the final slope of stones, broke through the tangle of briars, and flung myself exhausted upon the soft grass under the peaceful light of the stars. It was three in the morning when I reached the farm-house, and today I am all unstrung and quivering after my terrific adventure. As yet I have told no one. I must move warily in the matter. What would the poor lonely women, or the uneducated yokels here think of it if I were to tell them my experience? Let me go to someone who can understand and advise.

April 25.—I was laid up in bed for two days after my incredible adventure in the cavern. I use the adjective with a very definite meaning, for I have had an experience since which has shocked me almost as much as the other. I have said that I was looking round for someone who could advise me. There is a Dr. Mark Johnson who practices some few miles away, to whom I had a note of recommendation from Professor Saunderson. To him I drove, when I was strong enough to get about, and I recounted to him my whole strange experience. He listened intently, and then carefully examined me, paying special attention to my reflexes and to the pupils of my eyes. When he had finished, he refused to discuss my adventure, saying that it was entirely beyond him, but he gave me the

card of a Mr. Picton at Castleton, with the advice that I should instantly go to him and tell him the story exactly as I had done to
himself. He was, according to my adviser, the very man who was
pre-eminently suited to help me. I went on to the station, therefore, and made my way to the little town, which is some ten miles
away. Mr. Picton appeared to be a man of importance, as his brass
plate was displayed upon the door of a considerable building on
the outskirts of the town. I was about to ring his bell, when some
misgiving came into my mind, and, crossing to a neighbouring
shop, I asked the man behind the counter if he could tell me anything of Mr. Picton. "Why," said he, "he is the best mad doctor in
Derbyshire, and yonder is his asylum." You can imagine that it was
not long before I had shaken the dust of Castleton from my feet
and returned to the farm, cursing all unimaginative pedants who
cannot conceive that there may be things in creation which have
never yet chanced to come across their mole's vision. After all, now
that I am cooler, I can afford to admit that I have been no more
sympathetic to Armitage than Dr. Johnson has been to me.

April 27.—When I was a student I had the reputation of being
a man of courage and enterprise. I remember that when there was
a ghost-hunt at Coltbridge it was I who sat up in the haunted house.
Is it advancing years (after all, I am only thirty-five), or is it this
physical malady which has caused degeneration? Certainly my
heart quails when I think of that horrible cavern in the hill, and
the certainty that it has some monstrous occupant. What shall I
do? There is not an hour in the day that I do not debate the question. If I say nothing, then the mystery remains unsolved. If I do
say anything, then I have the alternative of mad alarm over the
whole countryside, or of absolute incredulity which may end in
consigning me to an asylum. On the whole, I think that my best
course is to wait, and to prepare for some expedition which shall
be more deliberate and better thought out than the last. As a first
step I have been to Castleton and obtained a few essentials—a large
acetylene lantern for one thing, and a good double-barrelled sport-
ing rifle for another. The latter I have hired, but I have bought a

dozen heavy game cartridges, which would bring down a rhinoceros. Now I am ready for my troglodyte friend. Give me better health and a little spate of energy, and I shall try conclusions with him yet. But who and what is he? Ah! there is the question which stands between me and my sleep. How many theories do I form, only to discard each in turn! It is all so utterly unthinkable. And yet the cry, the footmark, the tread in the cavern—no reasoning can get past these I think of the old-world legends of dragons and of other monsters. Were they, perhaps, not such fairy-tales as we have thought? Can it be that there is some fact which underlies them, and am I, of all mortals, the one who is chosen to expose it?

May 3.—For several days I have been laid up by the vagaries of an English spring, and during those days there have been developments, the true and sinister meaning of which no one can appreciate save myself. I may say that we have had cloudy and moonless nights of late, which according to my information were the seasons upon which sheep disappeared. Well, sheep *have* disappeared. Two of Miss Allerton's, one of old Pearson's of the Cat Walk, and one of Mrs. Moulton's. Four in all during three nights. No trace is left of them at all, and the countryside is buzzing with rumours of gipsies and of sheep-stealers.

But there is something more serious than that. Young Armitage has disappeared also. He left his moorland cottage early on Wednesday night and has never been heard of since. He was an unattached man, so there is less sensation than would otherwise be the case. The popular explanation is that he owes money, and has found a situation in some other part of the country, whence he will presently write for his belongings. But I have grave misgivings. Is it not much more likely that the recent tragedy of the sheep has caused him to take some steps which may have ended in his own destruction? He may, for example, have lain in wait for the creature and been carried off by it into the recesses of the mountains. What an inconceivable fate for a civilized Englishman of the twentieth century! And yet I feel that it is possible and even probable. But in that case, how far am I answerable both for his death

and for any other mishap which may occur? Surely with the knowledge I already possess it must be my duty to see that something is
done, or if necessary to do it myself. It must be the latter, for this
morning I went down to the local police-station and told my story.
The inspector entered it all in a large book and bowed me out with
commendable gravity, but I heard a burst of laughter before I had
got down his garden path. No doubt he was recounting my adventure to his family.

June 10.—I am writing this, propped up in bed, six weeks after
my last entry in this journal. I have gone through a terrible shock
both to mind and body, arising from such an experience as has
seldom befallen a human being before. But I have attained my end.
The danger from the Terror which dwells in the Blue John Gap has
passed never to return. Thus much at least I, a broken invalid, have
done for the common good. Let me now recount what occurred as
clearly as I may.

The night of Friday, May 3rd, was dark and cloudy—the very
night for the monster to walk. About eleven o'clock I went from
the farm-house with my lantern and my rifle, having first left a
note upon the table of my bedroom in which I said that, if I were
missing, search should be made for me in the direction of the Gap.
I made my way to the mouth of the Roman shaft, and, having
perched myself among the rocks close to the opening, I shut off
my lantern and waited patiently with my loaded rifle ready to my
hand.

It was a melancholy vigil. All down the winding valley I could
see the scattered lights of the farm-houses, and the church clock
of Chapel-le-Dale tolling the hours came faintly to my ears. These
tokens of my fellow-men served only to make my own position seem
the more lonely, and to call for a greater effort to overcome the
terror which tempted me continually to get back to the farm, and
abandon for ever this dangerous quest. And yet there lies deep in
every man a rooted self-respect which makes it hard for him to
turn back from that which he has once undertaken. This feeling of
personal pride was my salvation now, and it was that alone which

held me fast when every instinct of my nature was dragging me away. I am glad now that I had the strength. In spite of all that is has cost me, my manhood is at least above reproach.

Twelve o'clock struck in the distant church, then one, then two. It was the darkest hour of the night. The clouds were drifting low, and there was not a star in the sky. An owl was hooting somewhere among the rocks, but no other sound, save the gentle sough of the wind, came to my ears. And then suddenly I heard it! From far away down the tunnel came those muffled steps, so soft and yet so ponderous. I heard also the rattle of stones as they gave way under that giant tread. They drew nearer. They were close upon me. I heard the crashing of the bushes round the entrance, and then dimly through the darkness I was conscious of the loom of some enormous shape, some monstrous inchoate creature, passing swiftly and very silently out from the tunnel. I was paralysed with fear and amazement. Long as I had waited, now that it had actually come I was unprepared for the shock. I lay motionless and breathless, whilst the great dark mass whisked by me and was swallowed up in the night.

But now I nerved myself for its return. No sound came from the sleeping countryside to tell of the horror which was loose. In no way could I judge how far off it was, what it was doing, or when it might be back. But not a second time should my nerve fail me, not a second time should it pass unchallenged. I swore it between my clenched teeth as I laid my cocked rifle across the rock.

And yet it nearly happened. There was no warning of approach now as the creature passed over the grass. Suddenly, like a dark, drifting shadow, the huge bulk loomed up once more before me, making for the entrance of the cave. Again came that paralysis of volition which held my crooked forefinger impotent upon the trigger. But with a desperate effort I shook it off. Even as the brushwood rustled, and the monstrous beast blended with the shadow of the Gap, I fired at the retreating form. In the blaze of the gun I caught a glimpse of a great shaggy mass, something with rough and bristling hair of a withered grey colour, fading away to white in its lower parts, the huge body supported upon short, thick, curving legs. I had just that glance, and then I heard the rattle of the stones as the creature tore down into its burrow. In an instant, with a triumphant revulsion of feeling, I had cast my fears to the wind, and uncovering my powerful lantern, with my rifle in my hand, I sprang down from my rock and rushed after the monster down the old Roman shaft.

My splendid lamp cast a brilliant flood of vivid light in front of me, very different from the yellow glimmer which had aided me down the same passage only twelve days before. As I ran, I saw the great beast lurching along before me, its huge bulk filling up the whole space from wall to wall. Its hair looked like coarse faded oakum, and hung down in long, dense masses which swayed as it moved. It was like an enormous unclipped sheep in its fleece, but in size it was far larger than the largest elephant, and its breadth seemed to be nearly as great as its height. It fills me with amazement now to think that I should have dared to follow such a horror into the bowels of the earth, but when one's blood is up, and when one's quarry seems to be flying, the old primeval hunting-spirit awakes and prudence is cast to the wind. Rifle in hand, I ran at the top of my speed upon the trail of the monster.

I had seen that the creature was swift. Now I was to find out to my cost that it was also very cunning. I had imagined that it was in panic flight, and that I had only to pursue it. The idea that it might turn upon me never entered my excited brain. I have already explained that the passage down which I was racing opened into a great central cave. Into this I rushed, fearful lest I should lose all trace of the beast. But he had turned upon his own traces, and in a moment we were face to face.

That picture, seen in the brilliant white light of the lantern, is etched for ever upon my brain. He had reared up on his hind legs as a bear would do, and stood above me, enormous, menacing—such a creature as no nightmare had ever brought to my imagination. I have said that he reared like a bear, and there was something bear-like—if one could conceive a bear which was ten-fold the bulk of any bear seen upon earth—in his whole pose and attitude, in his great crooked forelegs with their ivory-white claws, in his rugged skin, and in his red, gaping mouth, fringed with monstrous fangs. Only in one point did he differ from the bear, or from any other creature which walks the earth, and even at that supreme moment a shudder of horror passed over me as I observed that the eyes which glistened in the glow of my lantern were huge, projecting bulbs, white and sightless. For a moment his great paws swung over my head. The next he fell forward upon me, I and my broken lantern crashed to the earth, and I remember no more.

When I came to myself I was back in the farm-house of the Allertons. Two days had passed since my terrible adventure in the Blue John Gap. It seems that I had lain all night in the cave insensible from concussion of the brain, with my left arm and two ribs badly fractured. In the morning my note had been found, a search party of a dozen farmers assembled, and I had been tracked down and carried back to my bedroom, where I had lain in high delirium ever since. There was, it seems, no sign of the creature, and no bloodstain which would show that my bullet had found him as he passed. Save for my own plight and the marks upon the mud, there was nothing to prove that what I said was true.

Six weeks have now elapsed, and I am able to sit out once more in the sunshine. Just opposite me is the steep hillside, grey with shaly rock, and yonder on its flank is the dark cleft which marks the opening of the Blue John Gap. But it is no longer a source of terror. Never again through that ill-omened tunnel shall any strange shape flit out into the world of men. The educated and the scientific, the Dr. Johnsons and the like, may smile at my narrative, but the poorer folk of the countryside had never a doubt as to its truth. On the day after my recovering consciousness they assembled in their hundreds round the Blue John Gap. As the *Castleton Courier* said:

"It was useless for our correspondent, or for any of the adventurous gentlemen who had come from Matlock, Buxton, and other parts, to offer to descend, to explore the cave to the end, and to finally test the extraordinary narrative of Dr. James Hardcastle. The country people had taken the matter into their own hands,

and from an early hour of the morning they had worked hard in
stopping up the entrance of the tunnel. There is a sharp slope where
the shaft begins, and great boulders, rolled along by many willing
hands, were thrust down it until the Gap was absolutely sealed. So
ends the episode which has caused such excitement throughout the
country. Local opinion is fiercely divided upon the subject. On the
one hand are those who point to Dr. Hardcastle's impaired health,
and to the possibility of cerebral lesions of tubercular origin
giving rise to strange hallucinations. Some *idée fixe*, according to
these gentlemen, caused the doctor to wander down the tunnel,
and a fall among the rocks was sufficient to account for his injuries. On the other hand, a legend of a strange creature in the Gap
has existed for some months back, and the farmers look upon Dr.
Hardcastle's narrative and his personal injuries as a final corrobo-
ration. So the matter stands, and so the matter will continue to
stand, for no definite solution seems to us to be now possible. It
transcends human wit to give any scientific explanation which
could cover the alleged facts."

Perhaps before the *Courier* published these words they would
have been wise to send their representative to me. I have thought
the matter out, as no one else has occasion to do, and it is possible
that I might have removed some of the more obvious difficulties of
the narrative and brought it one degree nearer to scientific accep-
tance. Let me then write down the only explanation which seems
to me to elucidate what I know to my cost to have been a series of
facts. My theory may seem to be wildly improbable, but at least no
one can venture to say that it is impossible.

My view is—and it was formed, as is shown by my diary, before
my personal adventure—that in this part of England there is a vast
subterranean lake or sea, which is fed by the great number of
streams which pass down through the limestone. Where there is a
large collection of water there must also be some evaporation, mists
or rain, and a possibility of vegetation. This in turn suggests that
there may be animal life, arising, as the vegetable life would also
do, from those seeds and types which had been introduced at an
early period of the world's history, when communication with the

outer air was more easy. This place had then developed a fauna and flora of its own, including such monsters as the one which I had seen, which may well have been the old cave-bear, enormously enlarged and modified by its new environment. For countless aeons the internal and the external creation had kept apart, growing steadily away from each other. Then there had come some rift in the depths of the mountain which had enabled one creature to wander up and, by means of the Roman tunnel, to reach the open air. Like all subterranean life, it had lost the power of sight, but this had no doubt been compensated for by nature in other directions. Certainly it had some means of finding its way about, and of hunting down the sheep upon the hillside. As to its choice of dark nights, it is part of my theory that light was painful to those great white eyeballs, and that it was only a pitch-black world which it could tolerate. Perhaps, indeed, it was the glare of my lantern which saved my life at that awful moment when we were face to face. So I read the riddle. I leave these facts behind me, and if you can explain them, do so; or if you choose to doubt them, do so. Neither your belief nor your incredulity can alter them, nor affect one whose task is nearly over.

So ended the strange narrative of Dr. James Hardcastle.

The Horror of the Heights

Sir Arthur Conan Doyle

The idea that the extraordinary narrative which has been called the Joyce-Armstrong Fragment is an elaborate practical joke evolved by some unknown person, cursed by a perverted and sinister sense of humour, has now been abandoned by all who have examined the matter. The most *macabre* and imaginative of plotters would hesitate before linking his morbid fancies with the unquestioned and tragic facts which reinforce the statement. Though the assertions contained in it are amazing and even monstrous, it is none the less forcing itself upon the general intelligence that they are true, and that we must readjust our ideas to the new situation. This world of ours appears to be separated by a slight and precarious margin of safety from a most singular and unexpected danger. I will endeavour in this narrative, which reproduces the original document in its necessarily somewhat fragmentary form, to lay before the reader the whole of the facts up to date, prefacing my statement by saying that, if there be any who doubt the narrative of Joyce-Armstrong, there can be no question at all as to the facts concerning Lieutenant Myrtle, R. N., and Mr. Hay Connor, who undoubtedly met their end in the manner described.

The Joyce-Armstrong Fragment was found in the field which is called Lower Haycock, lying one mile to the westward of the village of Withyham, upon the Kent and Sussex border. It was on the 15th September last that an agricultural labourer, James Flynn, in the employment of Mathew Dodd, farmer, of the Chauntry Farm, Withyham, perceived a briar pipe lying near the footpath which skirts the hedge in Lower Haycock. A few paces farther on he picked up a pair of broken binocular glasses. Finally, among some nettles in the ditch, he caught sight of a flat, canvas-backed book, which proved to be a note-book with detachable leaves, some of which had come loose and were fluttering along the base of the hedge. These he collected, but some, including the first, were never recovered, and leave a deplorable hiatus in this all-important statement. The note-book was taken by the labourer to his master, who in turn showed it to Dr. J. H. Atherton, of Hartfield. This gentleman at once recognized the need for an expert examination, and the manuscript was forwarded to the Aero Club in London, where it now lies.

The first two pages of the manuscript are missing. There is also one torn away at the end of the narrative, though none of these affect the general coherence of the story. It is conjectured that the missing opening is concerned with the record of Mr. Joyce-Armstrong's qualifications as an aeronaut, which can be gathered from other sources and are admitted to be unsurpassed among the air-pilots of England. For many years he has been looked upon as among the most daring and the most intellectual of flying men, a combination which has enabled him to both invent and test several new devices, including the common gyroscopic attachment which is known by his name. The main body of the manuscript is written neatly in ink, but the last few lines are in pencil and are so ragged as to be hardly legible—exactly, in fact, as they might be expected to appear if they were scribbled off hurriedly from the seat of a moving aeroplane. There are, it may be added, several stains, both on the last page and on the outside cover which have been pronounced by the Home Office experts to be blood—probably human and certainly mammalian. The fact that something closely resembling the organism of malaria was discovered in this blood, and that Joyce-Armstrong is known to have suffered from intermittent fever, is a remarkable example of the new weapons which modern science has placed in the hands of our detectives.

And now a word as to the personality of the author of this epoch-making statement. Joyce-Armstrong, according to the few

friends who really knew something of the man, was a poet and a
dreamer, as well as a mechanic and an inventor. He was a man of
considerable wealth, much of which he had spent in the pursuit of
his aeronautical hobby. He had four private aeroplanes in his
hangars near Devizes, and is said to have made no fewer than one
hundred and seventy ascents in the course of last year. He was a
retiring man with dark moods, in which he would avoid the society of his fellows. Captain Dangerfield, who knew him better than
anyone, says that there were times when his eccentricity threatened to develop into something more serious. His habit of carrying a shot-gun with him in his aeroplane was one manifestation of
it.

Another was the morbid effect which the fall of Lieutenant
Myrtle had upon his mind. Myrtle, who was attempting the height
record, fell from an altitude of something over thirty thousand feet.
Horrible to narrate, his head was entirely obliterated, though his
body and limbs preserved their configuration. At every gathering
of airmen, Joyce-Armstrong, according to Dangerfield, would ask,
with an enigmatic smile: "And where, pray, is Myrtle's head?"

On another occasion after dinner, at the mess of the Flying
School on Salisbury Plain, he started a debate as to what will be
the most permanent danger which airmen will have to encounter.
Having listened to successive opinions as to air-pockets, faulty
construction, and over-banking, he ended by shrugging his shoulders and refusing to put forward his own views, though he gave
the impression that they differed from any advanced by his companions.

It is worth remarking that after his own complete disappearance it was found that his private affairs were arranged with a pre-
cision which may show that he had a strong premonition of disaster. With these essential explanations I will now give the narrative
exactly as it stands, beginning at page three of the blood-soaked
note-book:—

"Nevertheless, when I dined at Rheims with Coselli and Gustav
Raymond I found that neither of them was aware of any particular

danger in the higher layers of the atmosphere. I did not actually say what was in my thoughts, but I got so near to it that if they had any corresponding idea they could not have failed to express it. But then they are two empty, vainglorious fellows with no thought beyond seeing their silly names in the newspaper. It is interesting to note that neither of them had ever been much beyond the twenty-thousand-foot level. Of course, men have been higher than this both in balloons and in the ascent of mountains. It must be well above that point that the aeroplane enters the danger zone—always presuming that my premonitions are correct.

"Aeroplaning has been with us now for more than twenty years, and one might well ask: Why should this peril be only revealing itself in our day? The answer is obvious. In the old days of weak engines, when a hundred horse-power Gnome or Green was considered ample for every need, the flights were very restricted. Now that three hundred horse-power is the rule rather than the exception, visits to the upper layers have become easier and more common. Some of us can remember how, in our youth, Garros made a world-wide reputation by attaining nineteen thousand feet, and it was considered a remarkable achievement to fly over the Alps. Our standard now has been immeasurably raised, and there are twenty high flights for one in former years. Many of them have been undertaken with impunity. The thirty-thousand-foot level has been reached time after time with no discomfort beyond cold and asthma. What does this prove? A visitor might descend upon this planet a thousand times and never see a tiger. Yet tigers exist, and if he chanced to come down into a jungle he might be devoured. There are jungles of the upper air, and there are worse things than tigers which inhabit them. I believe in time they will map these jungles accurately out. Even at the present moment I could name two of them. One of them lies over the Pau-Biarritz district of France. Another is just over my head as I write here in my house in Wiltshire. I rather think there is a third in the Homburg-Wiesbaden district.

"It was the disappearance of the airmen that first set me thinking. Of course, everyone said that they had fallen into the sea, but that did not satisfy me at all. First, there was Verrier in France; his machine was found near Bayonne, but they never got his body. There was the case of Baxter also, who vanished, though his engine and some of the iron fixings were found in a wood in Leicestershire. In that case, Dr. Middleton, of Amesbury, who was watching the flight with a telescope, declares that just before the clouds obscured the view he saw the machine, which was at an enormous height, suddenly rise perpendicularly upwards in a succession of jerks in a manner that he would have thought to be impossible. That was the last seen of Baxter. There was a correspondence in the papers, but it never led to anything. There were several other similar cases, and then there was the death of Hay Connor. What a cackle there was about an unsolved mystery of the air, and what columns in the halfpenny papers, and yet how little was ever done to get to the bottom of the business! He came down in a tremendous vol-plané from an unknown height. He never got off his machine and died in his pilot's seat. Died of what? 'Heart disease,' said the doctors. Rubbish! Hay Connor's heart was as sound as mine is. What did Venables say? Venables was the only man who was at his side when he died. He said that he was shivering and looked like a man who had been badly scared. 'Died of fright,' said Venables, but could not imagine what he was frightened about. Only said one word to Venables, which sounded like 'Monstrous.' They could make nothing of that at the inquest. But I could make something of it. Monsters! That was the last word of poor Harry Hay Connor. And he *did* die of fright, just as Venables thought.

"And then there was Myrtle's head. Do you really believe—does anybody really believe—that a man's head could be driven clean into his body by the force of a fall? Well, perhaps it may be possible, but I, for one, have never believed that it was so with Myrtle. And the grease upon his clothes— 'all slimy with grease,' said somebody at the inquest. Queer that nobody got thinking after that! I did—but, then, I had been thinking for a good long time. I've made three ascents—how Dangerfield used to chaff me about my shotgun—but I've never been high enough. Now, with this new, light

Paul Veroner machine and its one hundred and seventy-five Robur, I should easily touch the thirty thousand tomorrow. I'll have a shot at the record. Maybe I shall have a shot at something else as well. Of course, it's dangerous. If a fellow wants to avoid danger he had best keep out of flying altogether and subside finally into flannel slippers and a dressing-gown. But I'll visit the air-jungle tomorrow—and if there's anything there I shall know it. If I return, I'll find myself a bit of a celebrity. If I don't this note-book may explain what I am trying to do, and how I lost my life in doing it. But no drivel about accidents or mysteries, if you please.

"I chose my Paul Veroner monoplane for the job. There's nothing like a monoplane when real work is to be done. Beaumont found that out in very early days. For one thing it doesn't mind damp, and the weather looks as if we should be in the clouds all the time. It's a bonny little model and answers my hand like a tender-mouthed horse. The engine is a ten-cylinder rotary Robur working up to one hundred and seventy-five. It has all the modern improvements—enclosed fuselage, high-curved landing skids, brakes, gyroscopic steadiers, and three speeds, worked by an alteration of the angle of the planes upon the Venetian-blind principle. I took a shot-gun with me and a dozen cartridges filled with buck-shot. You should have seen the face of Perkins, my old mechanic, when I directed him to put them in. I was dressed like an Arctic explorer, with two jerseys under my overalls, thick socks inside my padded boots, a storm-cap with flaps, and my talc goggles. It was stifling outside the hangars, but I was going for the summit of the Himalayas, and had to dress for the part. Perkins knew there was something on and implored me to take him with me. Perhaps I should if I were using the biplane, but a monoplane is a one-man show—if you want to get the last foot of life out of it. Of course, I took an oxygen bag; the man who goes for the altitude record without one will either be frozen or smothered—or both.

"I had a good look at the planes, the rudder-bar, and the elevating lever before I got in. Everything was in order so far as I could see. Then I switched on my engine and found that she was running sweetly. When they let her go she rose almost at once upon the lowest speed. I circled my home field once or twice just to warm her up, and then with a wave to Perkins and the others, I flattened out my planes and put her on her highest. She skimmed like a swallow down wind for eight or ten miles until I turned her nose up a little and she began to climb in a great spiral for the cloud-bank above me. It's all-important to rise slowly and adapt yourself to the pressure as you go.

"It was a close, warm day for an English September, and there was the hush and heaviness of impending rain. Now and then there came sudden puffs of wind from the south-west—one of them so gusty and unexpected that it caught me napping and turned me half-round for an instant. I remember the time when gusts and whirls and air-pockets used to be things of danger—before we learned to put an overmastering power into our engines. Just as I reached the cloud-banks, with the altimeter marking three thousand, down came the rain. My word, how it poured! It drummed upon my wings and lashed against my face, blurring my glasses so that I could hardly see. I got down on to a low speed, for it was painful to travel against it. As I got higher it became hail, and I had to turn tail to it. One of my cylinders was out of action—a dirty plug, I should imagine, but still I was rising steadily with plenty of power. After a bit the trouble passed, whatever it was, and I heard the full, deep-throated purr—the ten singing as one. That's where the beauty of our modern silencers comes in. We can at last control our engines by ear. How they squeal and squeak and sob when they are in trouble! All those cries for help were wasted in the old days, when every sound was swallowed up by the monstrous racket of the machine. If only the early aviators could come back to see the beauty and perfection of the mechanism which have been bought at the cost of their lives!

"About nine-thirty I was nearing the clouds. Down below me, all blurred and shadowed with rain, lay the vast expanse of Salisbury Plain. Half a dozen flying machines were doing hackwork at the thousand-foot level, looking like little black swallows against the green background. I dare say they were wondering what I was doing up in cloud-land. Suddenly a grey curtain drew across beneath me and the wet folds of vapours were swirling round my face. It was clammily cold and miserable. But I was above the hail-storm, and that was something gained. The cloud was as dark and thick as a London fog. In my anxiety to get clear, I cocked her nose up until the automatic alarm-bell rang, and I actually began to slide backwards. My sopped and dripping wings had made me heavier than I thought, but presently I was in lighter cloud, and soon had cleared the first layer. There was a second—opal-coloured and fleecy—at a great height above my head, a white, unbroken ceiling above, and a dark, unbroken floor below, with the monoplane labouring upwards upon a vast spiral between them. It is deadly lonely in these cloud-spaces. Once a great flight of some small water-birds went past me, flying very fast to the westwards. The quick whir of their wings and their musical cry were cheery to my ear. I fancy that they were teal, but I am a wretched zoologist. Now that we humans have become birds we must really learn to know our brethren by sight.

"The wind down beneath me whirled and swayed the broad cloud-pain. Once a great eddy formed in it, a whirlpool of vapour, and through it, as down a funnel, I caught sight of the distant world. A large white biplane was passing at a vast depth beneath me. I fancy it was the morning mail service betwixt Bristol and London. Then the drift swirled inwards again and the great solitude was unbroken.

"Just after ten I touched the lower edge of the upper cloud-stratum. It consisted of fine diaphanous vapour drifting swiftly from the westwards. The wind had been steadily rising all this time and it was now blowing a sharp breeze—twenty-eight an hour by my gauge. Already it was very cold, though my altimeter only marked nine thousand. The engines were working beautifully, and we went droning steadily upwards. The cloud-bank was thicker than I had expected, but at last it thinned out into a golden mist before me, and then in an instant I had shot out from it, and there was an unclouded sky and a brilliant sun above my head—all blue and gold above, all shining silver below, one vast, glimmering plain as far as my eyes could reach. It was a quarter past ten o'clock, and the barograph needle pointed to twelve thousand eight hundred. Up I went and up, my ears concentrated upon the deep purring of my motor, my eyes busy always with the watch, the revolution indicator, the petrol lever, and the oil pump. No wonder aviators are said to be a fearless race. With so many things to think of there is no time to trouble about oneself. About this time I noted how unreliable is the compass when above a certain height from earth. At fifteen thousand feet mine was pointing east and a point south. The sun and the wind gave me my true bearings.

"I had hoped to reach an eternal stillness in these high altitudes, but with every thousand feet of ascent the gale grew stronger. My machine groaned and trembled in every joint and rivet as she faced it, and swept away like a sheet of paper when I banked her on the turn, skimming down wind at a greater pace, perhaps, than ever mortal man has moved. Yet I had always to turn again and tack up in the wind's eye, for it was not merely a height record that I was after. By all my calculations it was above little Wiltshire that my air-jungle lay, and all my labour might be lost if I struck the outer layers at some farther point.

"When I reached the nineteen-thousand-foot level, which was about midday, the wind was so severe that I looked with some anxiety to the stays of my wings, expecting momentarily to see them snap or slacken. I even cast loose the parachute behind me, and fastened its hook into the ring of my leathern belt, so as to be ready for the worst. Now was the time when a bit of scamped work by the mechanic is paid for by the life of the aeronaut. But she held together bravely. Every cord and strut was humming and vibrating like so many harp-strings, but it was glorious to see how, for all the beating and the buffeting, she was still the conqueror of Nature and the mistress of the sky. There is surely something divine in man himself that he should rise so superior to the limitations which Creation seemed to impose—rise, too, by such unselfish, heroic devotion as this air-conquest has shown. Talk of human degeneration! When has such a story as this been written in the annals of our race?

"These were the thoughts in my head as I climbed that monstrous, inclined plane with the wind sometimes beating in my face and sometimes whistling behind my ears, while the cloud-land beneath me fell away to such a distance that the folds and hummocks of silver had all smoothed out into one flat, shining plain. But suddenly I had a horrible and unprecedented experience. I have known before what it is to be in what our neighbours have called a *tourbillon*, but never on such a scale as this. That huge, sweeping river of wind of which I have spoken had, as it appears, whirlpools within it which were as monstrous as itself. Without a moment's warning I was dragged suddenly into the heart of one. I spun round for a minute or two with such velocity that I almost lost my senses, and then fell suddenly, left wing foremost, down the vacuum funnel in the centre. I dropped like a stone, and lost nearly a thousand feet. It was only my belt that kept me in my seat, and the shock and breathlessness left me hanging half- insensible over the side of the fuselage. But I am always capable of a supreme effort—it is my one great merit as an aviator. I was conscious that the descent was slower. The whirlpool was a cone rather than a funnel, and I had come to the apex. With a terrific wrench, throwing my weight all to one side, I levelled my planes and brought her head away from the wind. In an instant I had shot out of the eddies and was skimming down the sky. Then, shaken but victorious, I turned her nose up and began once more my steady grind on the upward spiral. I took a large sweep to avoid the danger-spot of the whirlpool, and soon I was safely above it. Just after one o'clock I was twenty-one thousand feet above the sea-level. To my great joy I had topped the gale, and with every hundred feet of ascent the air grew stiller. On the other hand, it was very cold, and I was conscious of that peculiar nausea which goes with rarefaction of the air. For the first time I unscrewed the mouth of my oxygen bag and took an occasional whiff of the glorious gas. I could feel it running like a cordial through my veins, and I was exhilarated almost to the point of drunkenness. I shouted and sang as I soared upwards into the cold, still outer world.

"It is very clear to me that the insensibility which came upon Glaisher, and in a lesser degree upon Coxwell, when, in 1862, they ascended in a balloon to the height of thirty thousand feet, was due to the extreme speed with which a perpendicular ascent is made. Doing it at an easy gradient and accustoming oneself to the lessened barometric pressure by slow degrees, there are no such dreadful symptoms. At the same great height I found that even without my oxygen inhaler I could breathe without undue distress. It was bitterly cold, however, and my thermometer was at zero, Fahrenheit. At one-thirty I was nearly seven miles above the surface of the earth, and still ascending steadily. I found, however, that the rarefied air was giving markedly less support to my planes, and that my angle of ascent had to be considerably lowered in consequence. It was already clear that even with my light weight and strong engine-power there was a point in front of me where I should be held. To make matters worse, one of my sparking-plugs was in trouble again and there was intermittent misfiring in the engine. My heart was heavy with the fear of failure.

"It was about that time that I had a most extraordinary experience. Something whizzed past me in a trail of smoke and exploded with a loud, hissing sound, sending forth a cloud of steam. For the instant I could not imagine what had happened. Then I remembered that the earth is for ever being bombarded by meteor stones, and would be hardly inhabitable were they not in nearly every case turned to vapour in the outer layers of the atmosphere. Here is a new danger for the high-altitude man, for two others passed me when I was nearing the forty-thousand-foot mark. I cannot doubt that at the edge of the earth's envelope the risk would be a very real one.

"My barograph needle marked forty-one thousand three hundred when I became aware that I could go no farther. Physically, the strain was not as yet greater than I could bear but my machine had reached its limit. The attenuated air gave no firm support to the wings, and the least tilt developed into side-slip, while she seemed sluggish on her controls. Possibly, had the engine been at its best, another thousand feet might have been within our capacity, but it was still misfiring, and two out of the ten cylinders appeared to be out of action. If I had not already reached the zone for which I was searching then I should never see it upon this journey. But was it not possible that I had attained it? Soaring in circles like a monstrous hawk upon the forty-thousand-foot level I let the monoplane guide herself, and with my Mannheim glass I made a careful observation of my surroundings. The heavens were perfectly clear; there was no indication of those dangers which I had imagined.

"I have said that I was soaring in circles. It struck me suddenly that I would do well to take a wider sweep and open up a new airtract. If the hunter entered an earth-jungle he would drive through it if he wished to find his game. My reasoning had led me to believe that the air-jungle which I had imagined lay somewhere over Wiltshire. This should be to the south and west of me. I took my bearings from the sun, for the compass was hopeless and no trace of earth was to be seen—nothing but the distant, silver cloud-plain. However, I got my direction as best I might and kept her head straight to the mark. I reckoned that my petrol supply would not last for more than another hour or so, but I could afford to use it to the last drop, since a single magnificent vol-plané could at any time take me to the earth.

"Suddenly I was aware of something new. The air in front of me had lost its crystal clearness. It was full of long, ragged wisps of something which I can only compare to very fine cigarette smoke. It hung about in wreaths and coils, turning and twisting slowly in the sunlight. As the monoplane shot through it, I was aware of a faint taste of oil upon my lips, and there was a greasy scum upon the woodwork of the machine. Some infinitely fine organic matter appeared to be suspended in the atmosphere. There was no life there. It was inchoate and diffuse, extending for many square acres and then fringing off into the void. No, it was not life. But might it not be the remains of life? Above all, might it not be the food of life, of monstrous life, even as the humble grease of the ocean is the food for the mighty whale? The thought was in my mind when my eyes looked upwards and I saw the most wonderful vision that ever man has seen. Can I hope to convey it to you even as I saw it myself last Thursday?

"Conceive a jelly-fish such as sails in our summer seas, bell-shaped and of enormous size—far larger, I should judge, than the dome of St. Paul's. It was of a light pink colour veined with a delicate green, but the whole huge fabric so tenuous that it was but a fairy outline against the dark blue sky. It pulsated with a delicate and regular rhythm. From it there depended two long, drooping, green tentacles, which swayed slowly backwards and forwards. This gorgeous vision passed gently with noiseless dignity over my head, as light and fragile as a soap-bubble, and drifted upon its stately way.

"I had half-turned my monoplane, that I might look after this beautiful creature, when, in a moment, I found myself amidst a perfect fleet of them, of all sizes, but none so large as the first. Some were quite small, but the majority about as big as an average balloon, and with much the same curvature at the top. There was in them a delicacy of texture and colouring which reminded me of the finest Venetian glass. Pale shades of pink and green were the prevailing tints, but all had a lovely iridescence where the sun shimmered through their dainty forms. Some hundreds of them drifted past me, a wonderful fairy squadron of strange unknown argosies of the sky—creatures whose forms and substance were so attuned to these pure heights that one could not conceive anything so delicate within actual sight or sound of earth.

"But soon my attention was drawn to a new phenomenon—the serpents of the outer air. These were long, thin, fantastic coils of vapour-like material, which turned and twisted with great speed, flying round and round at such a pace that the eyes could hardly follow them. Some of these ghost-like creatures were twenty or thirty feet long, but it was difficult to tell their girth, for their outline was so hazy that it seemed to fade away into the air around them. These air-snakes were of a very light grey or smoke colour, with some darker lines within, which gave the impression of a definite organism. One of them whisked past my very face, and I was conscious of a cold, clammy contact, but their composition was so unsubstantial that I could not connect them with any thought of physical danger, any more than the beautiful bell-like creatures which had preceded them. There was no more solidity in their frames than in the floating spume from a broken wave.

"But a more terrible experience was in store for me. Floating downwards from a great height there came a purplish patch of vapour, small as I saw it first, but rapidly enlarging as it approached me, until it appeared to be hundreds of square feet in size. Though fashioned of some transparent, jelly-like substance, it was none the less of much more definite outline and solid consistence than anything which I had seen before. There were more traces, too, of a physical organization, especially two vast, shadowy, circular plates upon either side, which may have been eyes, and a perfectly solid white projection between them which was as curved and cruel as the beak of a vulture.

"The whole aspect of this monster was formidable and threatening, and it kept changing its colour from a very light mauve to a dark, angry purple so thick that it cast a shadow as it drifted between my monoplane and the sun. On the upper curve of its huge body there were three great projections which I can only describe as enormous bubbles, and I was convinced as I looked at them that they were charged with some extremely light gas which served to buoy up the misshapen and semi-solid mass in the rarefied air. The creature moved swiftly along, keeping pace easily with the monoplane, and for twenty miles or more it formed my horrible escort, hovering over me like a bird of prey which is waiting to pounce. Its method of progression—done so swiftly that it was not easy to follow—was to throw out a long, glutinous streamer in front of it, which in turn seemed to draw forward the rest of the writhing body. So elastic and gelatinous was it that never for two successive minutes was it the same shape, and yet each change made it more threatening and loathsome than the last.

"I knew that it meant mischief. Every purple flush of its hideous body told me so. The vague, goggling eyes which were turned always upon me were cold and merciless in their viscid hatred. I dipped the nose of my monoplane downwards to escape it. As I did so, as quick as a flash there shot out a long tentacle from this mass of floating blubber, and it fell as light and sinuous as a whip-lash

across the front of my machine. There was a loud hiss as it lay for
a moment across the hot engine, and it whisked itself into the air
again, while the huge, flat body drew itself together as if in sudden
pain. I dipped to a vol-piqué, but again a tentacle fell over the
monoplane and was shorn off by the propeller as easily as it might
have cut through a smoke wreath. A long, gliding, sticky, serpent-
like coil came from behind and caught me round the waist, dragging me out of the fuselage. I tore at it, my fingers sinking into the
smooth, glue-like surface, and for an instant I disengaged myself,
but only to be caught round the boot by another coil, which gave
me a jerk that tilted me almost on to my back.

"As I fell over I blazed off both barrels of my gun, though, indeed, it was like attacking an elephant with a pea-shooter to
imagine that any human weapon could cripple that mighty bulk.
And yet I aimed better than I knew, for, with a loud report, one of
the great blisters upon the creature's back exploded with the
puncture of the buck-shot. It was very clear that my conjecture
was right, and that these vast, clear bladders were distended with
some lifting gas, for in an instant the huge, cloud-like body turned
sideways, writhing desperately to find its balance, while the white
beak snapped and gaped in horrible fury. But already I had shot
away on the steepest glide that I dared to attempt, my engine still
full on, the flying propeller and the force of gravity shooting me
downwards like an aerolite. Far behind me I saw a dull, purplish
smudge growing swiftly smaller and merging into the blue sky
behind it. I was safe out of the deadly jungle of the outer air.

"Once out of danger I throttled my engine, for nothing tears a
machine to pieces quicker than running on full power from a height.
It was a glorious, spiral vol-plané from nearly eight miles of altitude—first, to the level of the silver cloud-bank, then to that of the
storm-cloud beneath it, and finally, in beating rain, to the surface
of the earth. I saw the Bristol Channel beneath me as I broke from
the clouds, but, having still some petrol in my tank, I got twenty
miles inland before I found myself stranded in a field half a mile
from the village of Ashcombe. There I got three tins of petrol from
a passing motor-car, and at ten minutes past six that evening I

alighted gently in my own home meadow at Devizes, after such a journey as no mortal upon earth has ever yet taken and lived to tell the tale. I have seen the beauty and I have seen the horror of the heights—and greater beauty or greater horror than that is not within the ken of man.

"And now it is my plan to go once again before I give my results to the world. My reason for this is that I must surely have something to show by way of proof before I lay such a tale before my fellow-men. It is true that others will soon follow and will confirm what I have said, and yet I should wish to carry conviction from the first. Those lovely iridescent bubbles of the air should not be hard to capture. They drift slowly upon their way, and the swift monoplane could intercept their leisurely course. It is likely enough that they would dissolve in the heavier layers of the atmosphere, and that some small heap of amorphous jelly might be all that I should bring to earth with me. And yet something there would surely be by which I could substantiate my story. Yes, I will go, even if I run a risk by doing so. These purple horrors would not seem to be numerous. It is probable that I shall not see one. If I do I shall dive at once. At the worst there is always the shot-gun and my knowledge of..."

Here a page of the manuscript is unfortunately missing. On the next page is written, in large, straggling writing:

"Forty-three thousand feet. I shall never see earth again. They are beneath me, three of them. God help me; it is a dreadful death to die!"

Such in its entirety is the Joyce-Armstrong Statement. Of the man nothing has since been seen. Pieces of his shattered monoplane have been picked up in the preserves of Mr. Budd-Lushington upon the borders of Kent and Sussex, within a few miles of the spot where the note-book was discovered. If the unfortunate aviator's theory is correct that this air-jungle, as he called it, existed only over the south-west of England, then it would seem that he had fled from it at the full speed of his monoplane, but had been overtaken and devoured by these horrible creatures at some spot in the outer atmosphere above the place where the grim relics were found. The picture of that monoplane skimming down the sky, with the nameless terrors flying as swiftly beneath it and cutting it off always from the earth while they gradually closed in upon their victim, is one upon which a man who valued his sanity would prefer not to dwell. There are many, as I am aware, who still jeer at the facts which I have here set down, but even they must admit that Joyce-Armstrong has disappeared, and I would commend to them his own words: "This note-book may explain what I am trying to do, and how I lost my life in doing it. But no drivel about accidents or mysteries, if *you* please."

The Humming Bats

WILDER ANTHONY

Doctor Morgaridge ducked suddenly and threw up his arm in a posture of defense. The movement was so quick, so unexpected, coming while we were seated in front of Rodney's, sipping our juleps and enjoying the faint breeze that came out of the canyon, that it startled us all. It was uncalled for, too, so far as we could see. There was nothing unusual in sight, and save for the loud buzz of a great black hornet, which passed over us like a rifle bullet, not a sound had broken the stillness for several minutes.

With the half-apologetic smile of one caught in something foolish, the doctor settled himself in his chair again. No one said anything. There was nothing to say. Men—even strong men like our friend—sometimes possess nerves, and all of us assembled there that day had seen enough of the other side of life to know it.

A long pull at his julep—such a julep as Rodney alone can build—steadied Morgaridge somewhat. The color came back into his lean cheeks, and he lit a fresh cigar.

"Your pardon, gentlemen," he begged, in his deep, soft voice, "I forgot myself. That hornet's buzzing pricked an unhealed wound. One sometimes has memories, you know. This was one of them."

He paused and fussed with his glass as though nothing further could be said; but Werner would not let it drop.

"Why not spin the yarn, Doc?" he asked, in the freedom of a long friendship. "We all know there is a yarn, when a man like you dodges a buzzing insect. It must be interesting, and we have nothing at all to do but talk. Tell us about it, like a good chap, unless, of course, the subject is too unpleasant."

219

The explorer and orchid hunter smiled—one of those slow, rippling smiles, that made him friends in all corners of the world.

"The subject," he said quietly, "is unpleasant—very; but it might do me good to speak of it to some one who would believe as I think you might. You all knew him once, and it may be that you can credit what even I, although I saw it, often look back upon as a horrible dream. You remember Billy Prentiss?"

We all nodded. Until about two years before, Prentiss had been one of us. A homeless wandering adventurer, now here, now there, always in search of excitement and whatever else might lie at the end of a trail.

Then he had disappeared, and none of us had heard of him in months.

"My story," Doctor Morgaridge went on, "has to do with him and his last great adventure. It is the last word from a brave man whose greatest weakness was the *wanderlust*. The tale will sound incredible to you who have not seen; but it is true—absolutely. I can see it all now even more clearly, perhaps, than I could at the time it happened.

"Three years ago, Billy Prentiss and I joined forces in an orchid hunt that took us far into the interior of Borneo. We were after the Maxler Orchid—you've heard of it, maybe, that exceedingly rare and beautiful plant in the discovery of which Sir James Maxler gave up his life. Only two perfect specimens of it have ever been brought to civilization, although more than one good man lost his life in the effort.

"Maxler's discovery was made somewhere in the vicinity of Kini-Balu, and early in October of the year nineteen hundred and nine, we—Prentiss and I—entered this region. Like a great part of Borneo, it is a wild, desolate, unhealthy country, peopled by head-hunters and cannibals, and fairly overrun by snakes and other poisonous vermin.

"For six weeks we met with little success. Orchids grew every-where, but the one we sought was not among them. We had a good outfit. Three gobangs—the canoe of the Dyaks—with six men in each as a crew. They were Coast Dyaks from near Taban, brown-skinned and small, but mighty well-built and resolute. Like all of their race, they went practically naked, clad only in loin-cloth and all kinds of grotesque ornaments, most of which were suspended from the ears or nose. They were deadly enemies of the head-hunters, who inhabited the country through which we were travel-ling.

"One day, owing to a slight leak in Prentiss's canoe, we decided to go ashore early and camp. It was mid-afternoon and half dark, as it always is in the jungle, when we struck a sort of clearing on the bank of the slow-moving, muddy stream we traveled. Swishing and snapping through the rank lush-grass and ferns that fringed the river, we finally reached the bank and disembarked, much to the anger and fear of a large band of monkeys, which began a chat-tering flight through the treetops at our approach. At one side of the little park there was a huge flat rock—a fine place for a bed in that country, where, as a rule, the ground is nothing more than a putrid mass of rotten vegetation, and Prentiss and I took immedi-ate possession of it.

"The gobang had been repaired, and we were enjoying a smoke while our men cooked supper, when we were startled by a commo-tion in the jungle behind us. There was a snapping of dry vines and a swaying of the tall grass; and then something rolled or bounded into the comparative open of our clearing. By this time, we were both on our feet, weapons in hand, for in that region one cannot afford to take chances, when Prentiss let out a shout.

"'My God!' he cried in amazement. 'It's a man.'

"He was right. The rolling, misshapen thing on the ground, which, at first, we had taken for some unknown kind of beast, was a white man, although I hope it may never again be my fortune to look upon such a face as the creature turned towards us. It was ghastly—it wasn't human—it was... Well, it made me sick at my stomach when I saw it, and I'm not naturally a squeamish man.

"The man's lips, nose, and ears were gone—eaten out by the roots, you might say, with nothing left in their places but raw meat. His face, by reason of his teeth being constantly exposed, seemed set in a perpetual and indescribably horrible grin, and his entire head was covered with dried blood and flies! It was awful, I tell you.

"For a few seconds, Billy and I gazed at this apparition in dumb horror, while our Dyaks—superstitious little beggars, in spite of their courage—huddled around our rock and jabbered at each other like monkeys. Then, coming to ourselves with a jerk, we sprang to the stranger's assistance. Between us—the Dyaks wouldn't touch him at first—we got him into the tent and on to some blankets, where he collapsed like a pricked bubble.

"At first we thought he had gone for good, but a liberal dose of brandy revived him, and by the time we had finished a hurried dressing of his horrible wounds he was able to sit up. From the beginning, however, we knew that the man had not long to live. Indeed, it was wonderful that he had kept alive so long in his terribly mutilated state. It was only by an almost superhuman drain on his extraordinary vitality that he kept alive long enough to tell his story.

"His name, he said, was Conroy—Walter Conroy; he was English, and he had not been outside Borneo for ten years. Two months before, while on an ivory hunt, he had been captured by head-hunters and subjected to tortures too horrible to relate. These tortures culminated in the most fiendish act mortal man ever heard of—it was a masterstroke in cruelty even for the head-hunters, which is making it pretty strong.

"About ten days before we found him, as nearly as he could judge,—the poor devil had lost all sense of reckoning,—Conroy had been shut up in a cave in the side of the mountain, which, he thought, could not be more than four days' travel from our camp. It was a sacrificial temple of the head-hunters; one wing of it was given over to the priests and their horrible orgies, and the other occupied by the heads of their victims and—

"This last, gentlemen, is almost beyond my power to tell; it is too awful to contemplate; that poor devil, already racked by torture of the most terrible kind, thrust into that evil-smelling hole with—but I'll try to give you the rest of the story as nearly as possible in his own words. The mental picture of that night will always be with me. The dark, stinking swamp, filled with its myriads of reptilian life that surrounded us, the solemn Dyaks sitting motionless as images around our rock, the little tent with its open flaps, lighted by a single torch, and that awful wreck of a thing, once a man, lying on a pile of blankets in its center. Prentiss and I crouched on either side of him, listening to his jerky, feverish words, and keeping up the faint spark of life inside of him by every means at our command.

"'They thrust me into the cave,' he gasped, the words coming horribly from his mutilated lips, 'a big cave—God knows how big—filled with drying heads, stinking terribly, and guarded by those black monkey-devils—the priests. At first, after they turned me loose, I was too weak to look around much; I fell in the nasty filth that was at the bottom of the hole, and lay still. Then—I don't know how much later—I sat up and looked around. It was dark—dark as hell; but I was used to darkness by that time, and my eyes made out a part of the big chamber that held me.

"'It was mostly solid rock—walls and roof—with a narrow opening at one side that led into the priests' room; I could see 'em moving about their fire. A terrible stench filled the place, which, I soon discovered, came from hundreds of partly decomposed heads and bodies that festooned the cave on all sides. It was a fearful sight—those skulls grinning at me every way I turned—and to escape them and the smell, I went further back into the chamber. Here it was higher and dry, and pretty soon I came to a pile of what I thought at first was stones.

"'It wasn't, though. That pile was made of human skulls and bones—hundreds of 'em—and then I saw it: gold, gentlemen, gold! piles of it, pure virgin metal, red as the blood it had probably been drenched with, and half-covered with skulls. For a little, weak as I was, the sight staggered me. I forgot everything—the savages, the priests, my own danger—all but the fact that I was gazing at a king's fortune—God knows where it came from; but it's there—heaps and heaps and piles of it!'

"The dying man stopped here, and for a moment we thought he was gone, but the brandy worked once more, and after a little, he revived. Half delirious, Conroy was going off into a wild ramble about hairy creatures with yellow eyes that were chasing him, when Prentiss seized him by the arm.

"'The treasure, man!' he hissed, voicing the thought uppermost in both our minds. 'The treasure—the gold—where is it?'

"'In the cave,' Conroy gurgled, 'the cave with the ladder entrance in the big rock. It's there—piles of it; but the bats, man,—the bats! My God, the humming bats! In my face—they buzz—they bite—they... My God, they're eating...'

"At last his voice rose to a terrible scream. He struggled convulsively a few seconds, choked, and fell back dead.

"Prentiss and I looked at each other across the body. Neither of us spoke then, I think. We just looked, reading each other's thoughts like a printed page; then Billy pulled his pipe from his pocket and stepped out of the tent. I followed him.

"Outside it was dark, black as the pit, a typical jungle night. The air, laden with dew, felt like a wet blanket against our faces as we stood there smoking. Save for the occasional splash of a crocodile in the river, there wasn't a sound of any kind.

"'Morgaridge,' Prentiss said quietly, at length, 'I'm going after it. Are you game?'

"I did not reply at once. Even then I had misgivings, the raving of a dying man and all that, but the lure of the gold proved too strong in the end, just as Billy knew it would.

"'Yes,' I answered.

"At daylight, the next morning, we buried what was left of Conroy as decently as we could, packed the canoes and pushed out onto the river. Prentiss had been in that country before; he knew it better than I, and he thought that he could find the cave. Like all places of the kind, we reasoned that it would be removed at some little distance from the headhunters' village, and we felt that we could surprise the priests—there wouldn't be more than half a dozen at most—and walk off with part of the treasure before the tribe discovered us. It was risky, of course; we might find ourselves in a fight with savages at any minute; but we were used to that; we were well-armed and our Dyaks were faithful At the time, we practically forgot the Englishman's ravings about the bats.

"We did not go far that day. Coming to a good landing place, we beached and hid the canoes, and set out through the jungle in the direction of the mountain that Conroy had mentioned. Silent and determined, we left the gobangs beneath their screen of ferns and lianas, and started up a game trail scoured by the rains and feet of ages. We were in the jungle and the jungle-gloom was on us all.

"It was here that the real hardship and trouble began. Plodding in single file through ankle-deep mud, brushed shoulder high by rank weeds and grass, fighting poisonous insects and sweating like stokers, we made our way from the river to a little plateau where we pitched camp.

"In response to an order from Prentiss, one of our Dyaks began to climb a tall tree in an attempt to locate the head-hunters' village. The little brown man had gone about half way up when a thing like a green spear—a great rock snake—suddenly shot out from its lair behind some vines and struck him on the hip. He screamed in terror and fell headlong to the ground. After writhing in agony for a few minutes, he died.

"Next morning, when we gave orders to break camp, our Dyaks balked. They were afraid, they said; the mountain was taboo, the home of an evil spirit. Although we stormed and swore, and finally fell, to pleading, they refused to accompany us farther. They promised to wait, however, until we returned, so with this assurance we loaded ourselves with duffle and set forth alone.

"By this time, I think, we were both treasure mad. We dwelt in that cursed jungle so long that we'd lost the power to reason as sane men should, and we pushed on in grim determination to find the gold or perish. We did not forget to be cautious, however. Certain signs in the runway we traveled told us that we were nearing a village; at any moment we might meet a band of hunters or feel the sting of a poisoned dart in our ribs and we stole through the shadows, rifles at trail, like a pair of Apache warriors. The deep, stinking mud helped us to be quiet, although it impeded progress terribly.

"Mid-afternoon found us on somewhat higher and firmer ground. We were stealing through a clump of till ferns, when Prentiss, who was ahead, raised his hand warningly. I crept forward and peered over his shoulder.

"Fifteen yards ahead, in a cleared space, crouched on his hams, sat a naked savage behind a small fire. His long black hair was matted and whitened with ashes, and he was scowling like an imp from Hades. His body was streaked and ornamented with wood juices and charcoal, and his long sumpitan, or blow-gun, lay by his side.

"For a little, we stared in silence; then Prentiss began to whisper.

"'It's a Kapoeas,' he said. 'He's on a lone war-trail after his wedding head, I think. The young men among 'em can't marry, you know, till they've presented the bride-elect with the head of an enemy. We need a guide—let's get him alive.'

"We separated, and crawling on our stomachs in the tall growth, moved around the little clearing in opposite directions. We wanted to get at hand-grips with our quarry before he had a chance to use his deadly weapon. One prick of those bari-tipped darts is sure death, you know. Keen as were the head-hunter's ears, he did not hear us until too late; before he could use his blow-gun, we had him pinned helpless. Then we tied him securely and stepped back, while Prentiss began to volley questions in the fellow's own jargon.

"At first, he was sullen and wouldn't answer. Merely stared at us in amazed fright. Finally, however, he opened up and he and Billy talked for some time. Just what they said, I don't know—I never learned more than a smattering of Dyak; but the upshot of it was that the Kapoeas agreed to guide us to the temple

"Somewhat against my will, Prentiss freed our prisoner's feet and let him stand up. Then he fastened a stout withe to his pinioned arms and motioned him ahead of us. Without a murmur, the head-hunter walked off and we followed him up the rotting trail.

"It grew steeper and steeper. Many times we were forced to rest, although our guide seemed tireless. About an hour after the steamy night had fallen, we arrived at the bottom of a great cliff, which reached up out of sight into the darkness. Here, Prentiss and the Dyak had a long powwow, while I busied myself in winding rags about my feet, which were cut and bleeding from contact with the razor-edged grass.

"Prentiss finally turned to me.

"'We're there, Morgaridge,' he began abruptly. 'At least, so the nigger says, and I don't think he lies. Around the corner of this cliff we'll find a ladder that will lead us to the cave. There's only four priests and we can handle 'em all right if we surprise 'em. I'm going to truss our nigger up to a tree; then we'll tackle it.'

"I nodded assent, for in spite of my hurt feet, I was as keen and eager as he to view the gold. Our falling in with the Kapoeas had saved us a lot of time, and if we could surprise the priests without being ourselves surprised by a horde of savages, the thing looked fairly simple. We tied up the guide and started for the ladder, which we found easily enough.

"It was a long, narrow, flimsy contraption of poles, slippery with dew and set nearly perpendicular against the rock. After an instant's hesitation, we started to climb, Prentiss leading, I close at his heels.

"It was an eerie job. All the way up—it seemed miles, although I don't suppose we ascended over a hundred feet—I kept wondering what would happen if our prisoner got loose and warned his friends, or if the priests heard us and met us at the top. Cramped as we were on that narrow ladder with its slimy rungs and treacherous handholds, a child might have sent us into eternity with a single shove. Luck seemed with us, however. Without mishap we reached a kind of shelf in the cliff and pulled ourselves over its edge, where we lay at full length, panting and regaining our strength.

"Here we talked a little in whispers, and decided that if we should overpower the priests and find the treasure, we would drop as much of it as we could over the ledge. Afterwards, we could descend and pack it away to a place of safety. As I've already told you, I think that we were both temporarily insane; the plan looked good to us then, although I could pick flaws in it now.

"After we had rested awhile, we explored the ledge. It was about twenty feet long by six wide, level and dry—owing to a projection above—as a floor. In one corner, a mass of vines half covered a hole in the cliff, which was curtained from within by skins. A faint light filtered around these, and we finally managed to move them enough to permit ourselves a glimpse of the interior

"At the end of a narrow tunnel, a dozen feet or so from the entrance, the cave widened into a large chamber, which was lighted by a rude lamp, set high up on the wall, and a charcoal fire. Hunched over this fire and staring squarely at us, was the ugliest man I ever saw. At first, thinking he must see us, we drew back instinctively; but the outer darkness sheltered us, and as soon as we realized this, we settled down to watch.

"He was a little, gnome-like creature, this fire-tender. Blacker than most Dyaks and misshapen as a toad. His bestial face, sunk deep between heavy shoulders, was daubed with white, his eyes were round and puff-lidded, like a snake's, and he crooned to himself in a strange, weird gibberish as he stirred the fire with a long bone. Apparently, he was alone, for, look as hard as we could, we saw no other sign of life in the cavern.

"In whispers, we decided to wait until his back was turned; then to creep inside and spring upon him in much the same way that we had captured the Kapoeas in the jungle. It was the only way that we could see, and we had gone too far by that time to turn back empty-handed. Before many minutes, our chance came.

"The priest ceased his chanting and stood up. Waddling on his shrunken legs, he moved away from the fire, and stooped over a bag that lay nearby. Before he could straighten up or turn, we were in the tunnel, but his quick ears caught the sound of our entrance and he whirled around on his haunches like a huge ape.

"In one panther-like jump, Prentiss landed in front of him and shoved the muzzle of an automatic pistol against his head.

"'No noise!' he hissed.

"Although he could not have understood the order, the priest made none. He was literally scared speechless. He could only glare and gurgle like a stranded carp at our menacing pistols. He was a very old man, but the chances are that never in his life had he received such a fright.

"Prentiss tried to question him in Dyak, but after several attempts, gave up in disgust. We had no time to waste in that fashion. Herding the priest in front of us, we made a circuit of the cave, looking for the other chamber Conroy had spoken of. The entrance to it was cleverly concealed, but we finally found it and forced our prisoner into it ahead of us, for we had no intention of giving him a chance to spread an alarm.

"This chamber was hollowed out of solid rock to the size of a large room. The roof and walls were hung with metal ornaments and long rows of grinning skulls. In the center was a cleared space where stood a lamp made from a long bamboo tube. Beyond this was a shadowy heap of bones and skulls, just as Conroy had described, and the whole place, full of smoke as it was, stunk fearfully. Prentiss bent over the pile and picked up something that made my heart pound madly and my senses reel.

"It was a nugget—a lump of virgin gold as big as a goose egg, and beneath that covering of bones there were thousands more just like it. Conroy had not lied—one glance told us that. There in that charcoal house of the head-hunters, was a king's ransom. The very thought of the thing fairly took my breath away. I was like a drunken man as I staggered through the haze to the treasure and ran my hands into it

"I was instantly sobered by a loud cry from Prentiss.

"'The Dyak!' he shouted. 'My God, Morgaridge, the priest, man! Where is he?'

"He was right. For an instant, fascinated by the sight of the treasure we had come so far to get, we had forgotten our prisoner, and he had seized the opportunity to escape. Even as we stood there, sweating copiously and glaring wildly into the darkness in a hopeless attempt to discover him, we heard a loud crash, which told us that the news of our presence had gone forth.

"Together we dashed for the outer chamber; gained it, and found it empty, and quiet as a tomb. Not a sound broke the stillness of that awful place—not a sound. What was that? From somewhere in the room we had just quitted, came an ominous hum—a vibrant, tremulous buzzing, like the hum of a gas engine, but many, many times louder and more terrible. Suddenly, Conroy's words flashed into my mind: 'The bats—the bats—the humming bats!' Instinctively, I dodged, and at the same instant, Billy Prentiss gave a scream of agony.

"One look at him was enough. From somewhere in the darkness, a blow-gun had launched its deadly missle—the dart that now stood quivering in my companion's cheek. No mortal hand could save him, I knew that well; but for a second, I hesitated. Something struck me a sharp blow on the forehead. I looked up. The air was full of bats, great hairy bats, dull brown in color, with long, crooked talons, and horrible, blazing yellow eyes. As they flew around my head, the nasty things gave out a strange humming sound that nearly deafened me. Then the power to move came back to my shaking limbs.

"Seizing Prentiss by the collar, and swinging my free arm like a flail, I dashed through the cloud of bats for the tunnel exit. We made it; but on the ledge, my companion fell for the last time. The poison in his blood, and the bats which clung upon him and tore at his flesh, had done their work—he was stone dead. I left him there and sprang to the ladder.

"Somehow, still alive and whole,—the bats did not follow me after Prentiss fell—I reached the bottom of the cliff just as a horde of head-hunters, captained by their ugly priest, swept upon me. Eight times my automatic spat death into their midst—some small atonement for the brave life lost in that awful charnel pit—and then I dodged into the jungle.

"Two days later, more dead than alive, I reached my own men and comparative safety, and a month later, I quit the jungle for good."

The Devil's Fish

FREDERICK SIMPICH

"But Meyer," Lutz complained, "I tell you this is something new—startling—and I want it. As the official naturalist with this expedition, I protest against discarding this unique specimen just because a fool Indian fears it may 'hoodoo' him!"

And he shook the odd, wriggling fish-like thing from its net into a camp pail and poured water on it to keep it alive.

During which the old Chief Wubi, plainly a much frightened Indian, continued his excited protests. For the thing Lutz had caught was not a fish at all, Wubi declared, but an Avenging Devil in fish's form and known to the Indians of the Isthmus as the "Keechi-Ro." For ages, he said, these sinister creatures had lived in their forbidden haunt—the deep green pool beside the river Mombra-bo.

In vain did Meyer, the head of our party, seek to pacify the old Chief. Nothing short of the immediate liberation of the Devil's Fish would satisfy the frightened Indian. By the creed of his tribe, he warned us, any man is doomed who harms the Keechi-Ro; should he consent to our keeping the Devil's agent as a prisoner, some grave disaster must surely befall his tribe. He was astonished that Lutz, a learned white man, should thus dare defy the Evil Spirit.

"I think you'd better turn the fish loose, Lutz," admonished Meyer.

But Lutz was new to the Isthmus, with its swamps and superstitions. From books he knew much of the tropics, and back at the Varsity he had taken many prizes with his clever papers on wild

231

animals. But he lacked experience with wild men! Wherefore he argued with wise old Meyer, who had studied savage peoples from the Congo to the Caribbean, insisting that the creature he had caught was but an odd young fish, and that the Chief's dire prediction was all rot.

"Of course Wubi's talk is rot," assented Meyer quietly, patiently. "But our expedition was sent here from Washington to cultivate the friendship of these Indians and to secure certain information from them; and if they dread this Keechi-Ro, and object to having us bring it near the village, the wise course for us is to put it back in the pool.

"Besides," he went on, after a moment, "that's not an unknown fish, Lutz. Your bureau at Washington knows of this hybrid, half sturgeon, half shark. And I'll tell you something else you don't know, even if you are the official naturalist: that creature grows to prodigious size and is found nowhere on earth except in that green pool where you caught your specimen. It is one of those occasional stray creatures, remnants of prehistoric days, perhaps, stuck off in the nooks of the world, like the reputed hairy elephant of Alaska, which it would be risky to say too much about. You might be discredited!"

It was a hideous creature, this thing that Lutz had caught in his net—an unspeakably ugly object, with a clumsy head, tooth-lined jaws, lidless eyes and a tapering, placoid-covered body. And, fish or devil, it was only natural that old Chief Wubi, an untutored Indian of the Isthmian jungles, should fear it, even if it was "only a little young one," as Lutz insisted.

"Well, Meyer, you're the head of the expedition," growled Lutz, at last, "and since you're so squeamish about the feelings of your savage friend, I'll throw the fish back in the water." And he picked up the pail, wherein the odd creature still floundered, and walked out of our camp and down the river bank to the green pool—a deep basin hollowed from the low stone cliffs beside the Mombra-bo.

Wubi's fears subsided quickly, when he saw that the dreaded Keechi-Ro was really to be liberated. Finding the old man willing to talk now of tribal superstitions and folk-lore, themes of peculiar

interest to Meyer in his ethnological researches, we listened
intently to his strange recital. Squatting on the ground, native
fashion, Wubi told us how in the old days of the Spanish invasion,
his tribe had taken all prisoners and thrown them into the green
pool, where a giant Keechi-Ro appeared and swallowed them
bodily.

And he told us, too, that now, when a man broke faith with a
maid of his tribe, the girl would be set adrift in a canoe to make
her way down stream to the trading posts—an outcast; but that
her male relatives would hunt down the man who had wronged
her, and bind the wretch, and take him and cast him into the green
pool to be eaten by its evil denizens. This human sacrifice, he said,
seemed to appease the Evil Spirit, for after such a ceremony it was
always a long, long, time before another maid would be cast adrift.
He had seen the singular executions at the green pool on but two
occasions in his life of three score wet seasons. And it had been no
pleasant spectacle! With graphic gestures he showed us how the
victims went down the monster's throat, headfirst, kicking their
feet vigorously till the fish's tooth-lined jaws shut them in.

Evening fell as we sat talking with Wubi, and the women of the
tribe began to come in from their work in the fields. Our camp was
pitched on the bank of the Mombra-bo, a short distance below the
Indian village of Eupac. Opposite us, low, steep cliffs faced the
river, and in the fields back of these cliffs/the Indians grew their
yams and yucca. In our weeks among the tribe, we had observed
that drones were unknown—that even the Chief's family worked
in the fields. And as old Wubi finished his recital, his family, con-
sisting of his wife and five daughters, appeared on the crest of the
cliffs across the stream from us.

Stacking their crude hoes, the day's work done, they climbed
gracefully down the steep bank to a jutting rock, at a point some
thirty feet above the river. Save for their short grass girdles, all
were naked.

Poising a moment, the mother, a vigorous woman of perhaps
thirty-five, raised her shapely arms above her head and dived, swift
and straight as a kingfisher, headfirst, in the Mombra-bo. In an

instant she reappeared, shaking the water from her round head, and swam towards us with strong, easy strokes.

Then, one after another, the daughters, ranging from ten to sixteen years of age, supple, bronzed and beautiful, followed their mother into the stream, diving from the rock and swimming towards us.

It was a splendid scene, primitive, startling, as it must have been in the beginning. Dignified, natural, wholly unmindful of our gaze, the wild mother and her girls crawled from the stream onto the mossy bank before our camp, shaking the water from their glistening brown bodies and long, thick black hair.

"Ichi!" called Chief Wubi, and the tallest of the five girls, a perfect specimen of the Chocosee Indian, sprang lightly up the bank and stood respectfully before her father. As the old Chief was making some inquiry as to their work in the yam patches, Lutz came suddenly around our tent, returning from his errand to the green pool.

To our amazement, Ichi and Lutz exchanged some friendly words of greeting, the Indian girl smiling on our big, handsome companion with ill-concealed admiration. Now, by an unwritten law, it was understood among us that, no matter in what regions our expedition might find itself, or no matter how hospitable the natives, we were to hold ourselves absolutely aloof from the home life of the wild people—to get our needed information from the men and to ignore all others.

All of us, including Lutz, had worked for weeks to gain a necessary knowledge of the Chocosee dialect, but till this moment, we had not suspected that Lutz had been practising conversation with the Chief's daughter.

"I don't think much of their superstitions," growled Lutz, his mind still on the coveted rare fish, "but there certainly is class to their women folks!" and he beamed admiringly on Ichi.

Though Wubi knew no English, he saw the look of admiration that Lutz had bestowed on Ichi.

"Is she not beautiful?" asked the old man, proudly. "My enemies call me 'Chief-with-no-sons'; but soon my daughters will marry and I shall have sons in plenty."

Lutz turned abruptly, whistling tunelessly, and entered our mess tent.

Bidding Meyer and me good night, Chief Wubi followed his daughter into the path leading up to the village and the two were lost to our view in the swiftly darkening night.

We had planned to break camp next day. Meyer and I, with our boatmen and packers, were to drop down stream to the point where the Mombra-bo flows into the Itrata, on its way to the Gulf of Darien. We had research work to do in that region and would establish our next camp at the junction of the two streams.

It had been agreed that Lutz should remain at Eupac, completing some photography and mounting his specimens. This task would occupy him for ten days, he had told us. At the end of that time he, too, was to come down stream and join us at the new camp.

When Wubi and his daughter had left us, Meyer sat silent and we entered the mess tent. I could tell by Meyer's troubled face that he was worried. He spoke scarcely a word during the meal, but Lutz chattered incessantly of his plans for the coming week. Suddenly it came to me that Meyer was unwilling to leave Lutz alone among the Indians. In some vague way, he seemed to feel that danger threatened.

While I was busy packing late that night, I heard Meyer outside the tent, talking earnestly to Lutz, in a low, kindly voice. The latter was plainly vexed at something Meyer had said. "I hope you don't think I'm fool enough to make *that* mistake!" he spluttered.

"It's for your own good, Lutz," Meyer answered. "I've worked among wild tribes for thirty years, now; and I tell you a white man's only safe bet, in any savage land, is to stick close to his duty, as prescribed by the *Bureau*. You must make friends of the men, of course, but don't play any favorites among the opposite sex; they must be ignored, absolutely."

At sunrise, we embarked in our loaded canoes for the voyage down stream. The natives were astir, as usual, long before sunrise, but practically the whole village left its daily work and flocked down to our camp to see us off. Chief Wubi came, rubbing his nose on the backs of our hands, after the manner of salutation among his tribe, and wished us a safe trip. His women folk came, too, bringing fruit and a jar of native wine, as a good-will offering from Chief Wubi.

As we floated out into the current, Lutz waved us a farewell from before his tent. Wubi and his family had taken their place beside the lone white man. "The Bureau should send only old, ugly men to the tropics," grumbled Meyer, enigmatically, as we gathered speed with the stream.

The crowd remained on the bank, shouting after us, till we reached the big bend below Eupac and were lost to their sight. Passing the green pool, we turned into the jungle-lined stream below and settled down to make ourselves comfortable for the long trip.

It is an unmapped region, this northern wilderness of Colombia. Few geographers know that in the rainy seasons an Indian can paddle from the Atlantic to the Pacific without porterage! Swamps, lagoons, creeks, are everywhere. Here, and there rise ridges of high land, with scattered Indian villages, but for the most part swamps, shaded with moss-hung trees, trailing vines, and rank, tough grasses and reeds.

It was through such dismal regions that we made our way, after leaving the hill country about Eupac. Sleeping in our canoes by night, using our head-nets for protection against the swarms of angry mosquitoes, and paddling and floating by day, we came at last to the river Itrata and made camp. Here was a better country, with many Indians, and many cultivated fields.

In the tropics, where man works or idles, time flies swiftly, for one day is like another. Almost before we realized it, ten days had passed, and we began to talk of Lutz and his coming. By then his work in Eupac should have been finished and in four days more he should be with us.

On that day, therefore, we stayed in camp, waiting to meet Lutz. But he did not come. So we waited another day, and still another; still Lutz did not come.

"We'd better go upstream," said Meyer, thoughtfully. So we packed a long canoe that same night and took three strong boatmen, our rifles and some food, and started at dawn.

"Lutz must be ill," commented Meyer at the end of our first day's ride upstream, "and we should hurry." So we slept and got an early start.

To rest the men, Meyer and I took a hand at the paddles. Paddling thus, in relays, we kept the canoe going rapidly ahead throughout the night. At sunrise, a breeze sprang up, blowing stiffly upstream, so we rigged a rude sail from a piece of canvas off one of our packs and increased our speed. We had made such good time, that by evening of the third day we were nearing Eupac, but still there had been no sign of Lutz.

By this time, Meyer and I were both alarmed. We had made a grave mistake, we now feared, in allowing Lutz to remain alone with the Indians.

Suddenly, from around the bend—the first big bend below the green pool—a canoe appeared, with someone in it. But no one paddled the craft; it swung and turned with the current, around and around slowly.

Meyer got out his glasses and for a full moment surveyed the approaching boat in silence.

"It's Ichi!" he exclaimed, in a strained voice, lowering his binoculars.

And it was. The canoe was nearing us now and we could see the girl, crouched motionless in the bottom of the boat, her stoic face set and expressionless, heedless of us, of everything.

We steered towards her boat and Meyer hailed her. But there was no reply. We could see into her canoe now; it held clay jars of native wine, quantities of fruit and yams, and a straw mat to sleep on. It was provisioned for a long voyage.

As our canoe bumped the derelict, Meyer reached out and grasped the edge of the swinging craft. "What is it, Ichi?" he asked, in the Chocosee dialect.

But the girl made no answer. Not once did she so much as even glance in our direction.

After a moment, Meyer gently pushed off the runaway canoe and it drifted back again with the current—bearing its silent, stricken passenger. There were tears in old Meyer's eyes, as he looked sadly at the retreating figure of the unhappy girl.

"This is bad business, I'm afraid," he muttered.

Without further words, we reached with one accord for our rifles, and quickly threw cartridges into their chambers. And up to the Mombra-bo we raced, the men bending their backs and fairly lifting the narrow canoe along.

We were almost abreast of the green pool when Meyer's keen eye caught a movement in the edge of the jungle and he gave a quick order to the men to run the boat ashore.

Wubi, with a number of Chocosees, all carrying long blow guns and darts, emerged suddenly from the jungle above us and hurried away from the region of the pool.

We took cover quickly, prepared to stand off any attack.

But the Indians showed no sign of hostility; on the contrary, they hastened away from us, running up the river bank towards their village.

Suddenly Meyer, who was slightly in advance of me and near the edge of the green pool, beckoned to me excitedly. I ran up, gripping my rifle, trembling with some vague, nameless fear. The reeds and moss about the stagnant pool were trampled and crushed, showing unmistakable signs of some recent, violent struggle. The green waters of the deep hole were strangely agitated, as if some large body had lately stirred them.

"My God!" cried Meyer, his voice breaking, "look! look over there!" And he pointed with shaking finger, and across the green pool, beneath overhanging vines, appeared slowly the dorsal fin and prodigious head, and the gray, lidless eyes of a monster—a giant Keechi-Ro!

Slowly the great bulk emerged from the green-scummed pool, rolling sluggishly, like a water-soaked log. And there, between its huge jaws, we saw a man's foot—*with a shoe on it!*

An Alaskan Monster

CHARLES E. HOWARD

We had been up into New Mexico on a scout after cow-thieves, and were on our way back to camp.

Owing to a heavy drought we had found water scarce and the grass bad everywhere.

Our horses and pack animals were pretty well fagged out when we reached Toyah Station, on the Texas Pacific Railway.

There is a hotel here for the accommodation of the traveling public, and we were very glad to lay by at the canal and give our jaded stock a chance to recuperate.

The corral master placed at our disposal a comfortable frame house, and, as there was plenty of grain and fodder, and the horses were improving rapidly, we halted at the station two days.

Trains going both ways stop here for meals, and, as the lay-over is quite a long one, we had plenty of visitors to our camp, most of whom were impelled by motives of curiosity, as one man put it, "to see how Rangers live and just what they are like."

The second night the eastern-bound express was nearly two hours late, and when it finally steamed up to the station we learned that the delay had been caused by an accident to the locomotive.

Shortly after leaving Sierra Blanco some part of the machinery had given way, and at the first telegraph office a message had been dispatched for a new engine.

Pending its arrival the disabled train was ordered to remain at Toyah and allow the Western express to pass.

239

The train happened to be a full one, and our camp was soon crowded with visitors.

The men were all busy answering the questions that a chronic curiosity-seeker is sure to propound, and we were becoming, to put it colloquially, "very uneasy," when a man pushed his way through the crowd that surrounded our camp, scanned the faces of the men sharply, and then sprang forward and grasped my hand.

"George, old companiero," he cried, in a hearty, ringing voice, "I am mighty glad to see you."

"What!" I ejaculated, as he wrung my hand, "Is it possible that this is my old bunkey and messmate, Charlie Trenham?"

"The same old 'Reckless Charlie!'" he answered, with a laugh. "I haven't seen you for six years, and thought you had quit the service long ago."

He had many questions to ask about old friends—we had been brother Rangers in the days when ranging in Texas was no child's play—and I answered his questions to the best of my ability.

"But you must come up to the station and be introduced to my wife," he said, finally. "She has heard so much about you from me that it will be like meeting an old friend."

"Your wife!" I cried. "Are you married?"

"Yes, indeed; and I've got one of the dearest, sweetest women in the world. I've made money since I quit ranging, and now I'm on my way East, where I expect to settle down and go into active business."

I protested, when he urged me, that my attire was hardly presentable; but he insisted that Mrs. Trenham would overlook any deficiency, and I was soon chatting with her and as much at home as though we had been friends for a lifetime.

Finally I tore myself away from her very agreeable companionship, and Charlie and I took a stroll up and down the station platform while he "spun his yarn."

After leaving the Ranger service, he had drifted up into California, and in San Francisco had met Professor James Watson, a scientist, well known as an extensive traveler and an indefatigable and intrepid collector.

He was then on the eve of departure for Alaska, to make an exploration and scientific examination of the White and Yukon River Valleys.

A half-hour's acquaintance sufficed to make the professor Charlie's firm friend, and he invited the ex-Ranger to accompany him into the frozen North.

Charlie was nothing loth, but it was not until he found himself on board one of the Oregon Steamship Company's boats that he learned that the professor's daughter, Annie, was to be one of the explorers.

She was eighteen years of age, and had been her father's traveling companion almost since babyhood, when her mother had died.

It seemed to Charlie almost akin to crime to drag this refined and beautiful girl into such a wild, unknown country. But he was not long in discovering that Miss Watson liked the excitement of such a life, and was able to stand fatigue and hardship as well as the male members of the party.

The professor was acting as the agent of a wealthy company which had obtained from the government some valuable grants and concessions in the "Frozen Territory," and in order to thoroughly investigate the resources of the section of country which was controlled by his employers he had organized as well-equipped a corps of scientists as could be ordinarily got together.

Supplies were purchased at Napusiak, and the little party pushed across the country, finally striking a Big Stick Indian village on the White River.

A small army of retainers and baggage carriers was enlisted in the Indian village, and one morning the expedition started toward the Chigmit Mountains, in the rocky foothills of which the White River has its source.

For several weeks they proceeded slowly, and the scientists added many specimens of fauna and flora to their collection, and increased their store of knowledge concerning the strange country.

Forty-two days after leaving the Stick village they reached a considerable fall and a long stretch of dangerous rapids.

The explorers had now reached a section of country never before visited by white men.

Even the Indians were ignorant of its real physical features, and many of them were timid about proceeding further.

It was part of Charlie's duties to keep these Indians under control, and, when one after another of the principal men of the tribe objected to pushing forward, he called a consultation.

He had learned enough of the Stick dialect to make himself understood, and he demanded of them why they were averse to fulfilling their contract.

His speech was quite a long one, and, when he finished, the eyes of the warriors were turned toward Tall Pine, the oldest man and principal chief.

He was a fine specimen of the red man, six feet tall, well-formed, and, despite his seventy years, as straight as an arrow.

When the silence that had followed Charlie's speech had become impressive, Tall Pine arose slowly, and, throwing back his blanket, thus delivered himself:

"Rushing Stream" (that is the name they had given Charlie) "speaks boldly and without fear, but it is because he knows nothing of the dangers that lurk in the great woods that stretch yonder many days' journey to the great salt lake. Many moons ago, when I was young and bold like Rushing Stream, I went into the unknown country. None of the Sticks had ever been so far, and the wise men of the tribe bade me stay back. I would not, and I came up the river and camped a day's journey beyond here. I was in a new land, full of great, hairy monsters, with teeth longer than a young tree. They are the bad spirits of that country, and were angry with Tall Pine for daring to come among them. All night they filled the air with strange noises, and I was afraid. When day came I saw them looking at me with eyes of fire among the trees. Then I saw that the wise men were right, and I came away. Rushing Stream may go on, but Tall Pine will go back to his people."

He finished, and every brave who followed echoed the sentiments of their chieftain.

In vain Charlie stormed and raved, alternately pleading and threatening.

The Indians were immovable. Finally he became angry, and declared that if they did not go on he would take away their arms and provisions and leave them to starve.

This threat seemed to have the desired effect, for, after a short consultation among the principal men, Tall Pine said that his men were still afraid, but rather than lose their arms they would go on.

"I thought you'd come to your senses," Charlie said, and he gave the matter no further concern.

That night the Indians stole away from the camp one by one, taking with them everything they could lay their hands on.

At this duplicity Charlie's anger was fearfully aroused.

"I'll teach the rascals a lesson," he declared.

And, calling for volunteers, he took up the trail of the renegades, followed by all the white men except Professor Watson and Antoine, the cook, who were left behind to guard the camp and protect the scientist's daughter.

Unfortunately for the success of the expedition, Charlie had a thorough contempt for the Sticks, and, when he came upon their camp, he attacked them boldly.

The Indians outnumbered the white men, ten to one, and a fierce battle ensued.

Dozens of the Indians were slain, but Charlie's little army kept dropping off one by one, and he finally discovered, to his dismay, that he was the sole survivor of the gallant band.

He was wounded himself, and, as the Indians were still in considerable force, he came to the conclusion that his only hope of salvation lay in flight.

Night coming on aided his escape, and he was soon a safe distance from the battle-ground, where the Indians, maddened over their losses, were revenging themselves by mutilating the bodies of the slain.

Taking great care to destroy his trail, the wounded man hurried back to the spot where he had left the professor, Annie and Antoine.

He traveled all night, and day was just breaking when he reached the camp.

In a few words he told the story of disaster.

The professor, though ordinarily a brave man, was completely disheartened at the dread intelligence, and Antoine was frightened into idiocy.

Annie alone retained her courage and presence of mind.

"After what has happened," she said, "we must not allow ourselves to fall into the hands of those red miscreants. You are skilled in woodcraft. What shall we do to save ourselves?"

"We must push on!" cried Charlie. "The Indians may return this far in search of us, but they will not dare go further for fear of the mythical monsters that lying old rascal, Tall Pine, declares live up near the head-waters of the river."

"Yes, we must push on," agreed the courageous girl.

And she and Charlie set themselves to the task of reviving the professor's hope and allaying Antoine's fears.

In order to travel with all speed, and thus outstrip the Indians, in case rage over their heavy losses should overcome their superstitious fears, everything except necessary articles of camp furniture and a supply of provisions was abandoned.

It brought tears to Professor Watson's eyes to be obliged to leave behind their splendid scientific collection, and, while the others were getting ready to pack, Charlie cached the more valuable specimens and marked the spot so that it could be found.

Finally everything was ready, and the little band took up the march into the country of the hairy monsters.

For three days they proceeded without particular incident, and then Professor Watson fell sick.

Charlie constructed a litter, and, in addition to their other burdens, he and Antoine carried the invalid.

They had no medicine to give him and he grew worse.

Five days after being taken down, he died, and they buried him on the river bank, marking his grave with a rudely-heaped cairn of stones.

The blow was a bitter one to Annie, but she sustained herself bravely, and, with a last fond look at her father's grave, gave the signal to continue the march.

That afternoon, as they were making their way along, Antoine uttered an exclamation of amazement, and pointed to a long, white object that projected from the sand and driftwood in a little cove.

Charlie walked forward to examine the object, and discovered that it was a gigantic ivory tusk, larger around than his body, yellowish in color, and about fifteen feet in length.

Near it were bones of monstrous size. He remembered Tall Pine's story of the hairy monsters and an awesome feeling came over him.

Antoine began to blubber and wanted to turn back.

He threw down his pack and declared in broken English that he would sooner go back and be killed by the Indians than push on to meet a monster like the one whose skeleton lay in the cove.

Charlie was obliged to point a rifle at him and threaten him with death before he could be prevailed upon to continue the march and then he kept to the rear and started with fright at every sound.

As they proceeded they found more tusks and bones, and it was evident that the gigantic creatures to whom these belonged had not been dead more than four or five years, judging from the well-preserved condition of the skeletons.

It was the evening of the second day after the professor's death, and they were looking for a favorable place to camp, when, in crossing a bit of beach, Charlie saw deeply indented in the yielding sand the gigantic footprints of one of the monsters.

It was larger around than a barrel, and the shape of every toe and the peculiar conformation of the ball of the great foot were plainly imprinted.

The trail was quite fresh, and the monster had evidently passed along that day.

He knew that the sight would drive Antoine to frenzy, and he turned sharply in another direction.

Finding a bubbling spring a little distance from the river, he threw down his pack and they camped there that night.

The next day the march was resumed.

For the following three days it would be tedious to detail their adventures.

Even Antoine knew that they were in the country of the hairy monsters, and at any unusual sound he shook as with an ague.

Charlie said but little; his face was grave. Another and to him greater danger than could be apprehended from the great animals stared them in the face.

Their provisions were nearly exhausted, and no small game had been seen since the day when Antoine discovered the big tusks on the bank of the river.

They were in danger of starvation!

Food had been dealt out sparingly, but barely enough remained to last them another day.

In this emergency Charlie shouldered his rifle one morning, and bidding Antoine remain in camp to protect Annie, he started out in search of game.

He crossed many tracks of the monsters, but he was not anxious to meet any of the immense beasts.

Discouraged at last and without having seen so much as a bird, Charlie turned back toward camp.

He had nearly reached it and had halted for a moment on a slight elevation to look around him when he heard a shrill noise like the discordant blare of a bugle, followed by a woman's frantic scream and a man's cries of terror.

"Great heavens!" he cried, "one of the monsters has attacked them!"

The rifle that he carried was of large caliber, throwing a steel-pointed ball; seeing that a cartridge was in the chamber, he rushed toward the camp.

As he approached, Annie, with disheveled hair and screaming with terror, crashed through the underbrush and ran toward him.

Behind her was a gigantic animal, whose heavy footfalls made the ground tremble.

"Get in there!" urged Charlie, pointing to a cave-like opening in a nearby ledge of rock, and he pushed the terrorized girl toward the place.

There was a wild scream of agony borne to his ears, followed by a hoarse bellow of triumph.

Turning quickly, he witnessed a horrible sight.

Antoine had been overtaken by the monster, and the creature had thrust the poor fellow's body through and through with one of its long, curved tusks, and halting for a moment, was brandishing the victim in mid-air!

"It was a horrible creature," said Charlie, "at least twenty feet in height and thirty feet in length. In general shape it was not unlike an elephant, but its ears were smaller, its eyes bigger, and its trunk longer and more slender. Its yellow tusks, of which it had six, were the most awful sight I have ever looked upon. Four of these tusks were placed like the fangs of a boar, one on either side in each jaw, they were about four feet long, and came to a sharp point. The other two tusks were at least fifteen feet long, and curved inward. Its body was covered with long, coarse hair of a reddish dun color. As I stood gazing in paralyzed amazement, it raised poor Antoine's body on high, then uttering a terrible roar, threw him a distance of fifty feet."

At the same instant the beast discovered Charlie, and made a rush toward him, with its big eyes leering horribly, its trunk upraised, and its great mouth wide open.

"I knew I must do or die," said Charlie, "and dropping on one knee, I took quick aim at the red, cavernous mouth, and pulled the trigger."

The monster stopped, and, whether frightened by the unusual noise or dismayed by the pain, wheeled suddenly and crushed off through the timber.

It had attacked Annie and Antoine without warning, as they were sitting around the camp-fire, and the cook had not been nimble enough to escape.

Badly frightened, but thankful for their deliverance from the monster, Charlie and Annie gathered together a few of their scattered camp utensils, and continued their eastward march.

They saw no more of the monsters, and the next day Charlie was fortunate enough to kill a deer.

A week later they came upon a camp of Indians, and the promise of one of the fire-tubes (guns) and a supply of ammunition was sufficient inducement to get guides to Fort Kalmukoff.

After a weary march through the forests, they reached the fort, and, quickly communicating with Professor Watson's employer, apprised them of the disasters which had befallen the expedition.

"They wanted me to go back into that awful country," said Charlie, in conclusion, "but one experience was enough; and besides, Annie had promised to become my wife, and she made me promise to give up my wild life."

The Last Egg of the Great Auk

BERNARD SEXTON

Leger St. John, veteran explorer and traveler in the far North, drew his two younger comrades aside into a doorway of the church in Battle Harbor. His eyes sparkled with characteristic enthusiasm. "Listen to me, fellows. I've just hit on a juicy bit of news. Want to share it?"

"Do we?" responded the older of the two boys he addressed. "You bet we want your news. We're as hungry for news as an Eskimo is for blubber. Fork it over!"

The other lad grinned delightedly, as if he exactly shared the sentiment of his "pal."

"Listen, then. You know how long we've been waiting for Oleson's ship that was to take us to Greenland on the year's exploring trip. Well, I've just received a message that the old man has canceled the trip for the year because of inability to raise the funds he needs. It was half an hour ago when I got the letter and I was mighty downhearted, when who should I run into but an old friend of mine, Cap'n Slocum you know, the old grizzled sailor-chap."

"You mean the old fellow with a very red face?" said the older of the boys.

"The same," answered St. John. "When he spotted me he sings out, 'Well! Look what the dogs drug in!' and gave my right hand a grip that made me realize what a soft thing I was after all. And when he asked me what I was doing, I told him that I was a has-been and that my hopes for a scientific survey of the birds of

Greenland had gone to smash. The old rascal winked at me then and said slyly, 'I can put ye next to a leetle bit of knowledge that'll warm that cold scientific heart of yours!' I asked him what it was, and he said, 'Have ye e'er heerd of a bird called the great hauk?'

"'Have I heard of the great auk!' said I. 'The great auk! Haven't you ever heard of my essay, "The Final Distribution of the Great Auk?"'

"'I have not,' said the old man, unblushingly; 'but by some remarks ye let drop when last I saw ye, I inferred that ye were slightly interested in the subject.'

"I told him that 'slightly' was a feeble word to use concerning my interest in the great auk.

"'Well,' said he, winking at space, 'what would you say if I offered to take ye to where there is a living great hauk?'

"'There's no such thing, worse luck!' said I; 'the last great auk was seen in 1844. Then the race became extinct.'

"'Don't ye know, me b'y,' said the old man, 'that there's many a bird and beastie reported gone from the world when, as a fact, it's not gone from the world, but seeking refuge from the savagery of man. I've *seed* the great hauk, so I know it's not out of fashion yet. And what's more, me lad, if ye'll jine me in a little trip I'll take ye to the spot where I saw it.'

"'Where was that?' I asked.

"'T was on a wild, remote little shore down north—one of the group of islands around American Tickle. I sees a pair of the hauks on the beach near a little cave. I can take ye there on the chance of seein' 'em again, or perhaps finding their eggs.'"

"Well, what did you say?" asked the older boy, breathlessly.

"I said I'd go, and I asked if you fellows could go too; and the old man said he'd be glad of your help in manning the schooner."

"Good for you!" cried the older boy, excitedly, wringing the hand of St. John. "Isn't that fine, Jack?" he cried.

The other fellow grinned, "Sure it's fine, Whitey," said he.

"We sail to-morrow morning with the turn of the tide," went on St. John. "So long, then, till supper-time to-night. Amuse yourselves as best you can."

"All right. Trust us for that!" called Whitey, as the explorer strode off; "hey, Jack, old boy?"

And Jack grinned his assent.

From the deck of the snug little schooner they watched the coast of Labrador slipping by. As the sun went down, Cape Spear loomed up ahead.

The weather roughened a bit during the night, but the crew handled the boat with that skill which is the inheritance of the Labrador fisherman. The breeze held, and they were past Boulter's Rock and Venison Tickle by breakfast-time. Jack would hardly look at the shore, he was so fascinated with the stately icebergs which they saw all day. Some loomed up out of the water on thin stems— these the captain called "mushrooms"; others had perfect natural bridges; a few soared up "like the Woolworth tower," Whitey said.

In the middle of the afternoon a heavy sea was running. The water heaved up curling green mountains; and into the liquid valleys between them, the schooner ran like a swift, live thing. "I guess I'll put into Snug Harbor for the night," remarked the captain to St. John, who stood by him at the wheel.

They covered the half of Frenchman's Run in a wild smother of foam. Tall green seas fell thundering on the deck. Jack and Whitey, in oilskins, held on to anything within reach, and watched with deep interest, for they had not known such seas before. Once in a while they could see the black, wicked-looking coast, with its succession of naked cliffs, conveying to the mind the quality that has made the name Labrador stand for all that is grim and forbidding.

How smooth and quiet were the waters of Snug Harbor after the storm and scurry outside! Sunset emerged in splendor out of the end of the wild day, and as they sat at supper in the little cabin, with late sunlight streaming in through the portholes, Whitey stretched himself luxuriously.

"Say, Labrador's a dandy place!" he exclaimed; a sentiment in which Jack fully agreed.

It was long after sunrise when the boys woke—and yet by Whitey's time-piece it was only five o'clock. After breakfast they went up on deck. There, half hidden, each behind a huge boulder, they saw the half-dozen houses of the settlement. The harbor was almost perfectly round, a snug, tight little bowl of sea-water hidden in that forbidding coast. On the low cliffs near the village they could see innumerable huskies, each dog with his nose up in the air, dolefully howling. As the schooner worked out of the harbor, that was the last sight they saw, the last sound they heard.

Whitey and Jack leaned over the rail together. They had discovered that the work they were supposed to do lay entirely in the imagination of the jovial captain. "Have a good time, b'ys," he would say; "ye'll have lots to look at. I'll tell ye when I needs ye." The wind had fallen, and they were only spinning off four or five knots an hour. "Gee! Look at that sea!" said Whitey, pointing. "Did you ever see anything like that?"

"No I didn't, ever," answered Jack.

Although the wind had gone down, the seas were still heaving skyward in huge, green, sloping hills. Far as the eye could reach, extended the wide and moving waste. Now and then a wave higher than the others slapped the side of the little craft and came aboard, burying the deck in a foot of water. The boys stood there, gripped by the feeling that has sent millions of boys to sea since that time long ago when the first hollowed log hoisted sail and launched out on green, tossing waters.

St. John was standing behind them. "It gets you, doesn't it?" he said. "I never come up along this coast that I don't get hit with the tremendous fascination of this icy, savage sea. Everything up here is reduced to the simplest lines. Life and nature are stripped of ornament. Men are primitive as they can be without becoming savage."

"Yes, there's something in it I can't explain," said Whitey. "I've often wondered why these people stay here when there's rich land and an easy living to be made in lots of places farther south. But I s'pose it gets them the way it gets us."

About noon they made a group of islands a little way out from the coast. The captain pointed. "It's on one of these that I saw the auks. We'll have to go through American Tickle, as it's called, and anchor inside."

"Why do they call 'em tickles?" asked Jack.

"It's the Labrador man's name for a narrow run between two islands," answered St. John; "in other words, a place so narrow that you tickle the sides of your craft going through."

All hands, except the steersman, now turned to and ate a hasty lunch. The captain took the wheel himself, for the operation of getting into the tickle was one that required the most skilled seamanship. The matter was complicated by three vicious-looking black needles of rock that stuck up out of the water just outside the inlet of the tickle.

At just the right distance from the entrance, the captain called out the order that let fall the sails. Everybody's labor was welcome in this emergency, and the boys had a real pride in helping handle the boat. Slowly then they drifted toward the black needles. With slight movements of the rudder the captain made allowance for tide and even for the pressure of the wind against the sides of his ship. They passed the nearest of the needles only six inches away, and a second later the high, precipitous black rocks on both sides of the tickle loomed up. Whitey was leaning over the rail on the port side, and Jack hung over the starboard.

"This rock is scraping my nose!" called Whitey. "How is it on your side, Jack?"

"I've had to lean backward," called Jack. "If I hadn't, it'd have taken my face clean off."

Shut off from the sunlight by the high walls of this watery canon, they felt the sudden increase of cold. Ghostly, silent, the schooner glided through the narrow way. The tickle made a sharp turn, and the captain looked anxious as he came to it. Slowly the vessel made the movement, obeying the rudder with exquisite exactness; but even so, the bowsprit slightly scraped the black rock as she swung about. A few yards farther on, and the tickle began to widen. Everybody breathed easy once more.

They dropped anchor in a narrow harbor completely shut in by high black walls. Both ends of the harbor were open to the sea, but in each case it was only through a narrow tickle that the waters came and went. The unceasing roar of the ocean could be heard

from outside, but in the tickle there was an intense, calm loneliness that was all the more impressive for the furor of the encir-
cling seas. "Not much chance of seeing the birds, I'm afraid," said
St. John, as he got into the skiff with the two boys and the captain,
"but we'll have a hunt for possible eggs. They'll be more likely to
be laid in a hidden ledge of the rock than anywhere else."

They found a tiny beach half-way up toward the north exit of
the harbor, and there they beached the boat. The two boys agreed
that they would keep together, while St. John and the captain
searched in another direction.

"Say! This island is full of cracks in the rocks!" called Jack, who
was first up the slippery side of the cliffs that surrounded the beach.

"Yes, we'll have to look out not to fall down one," answered
Whitey. "Gee, this is a mysterious-looking island! Why, it's full of
caves. Here, look at this, will you?"

He had turned a little to the left on an irregular ledge that he
had found half-way up the face of the rock, and, entering a dark
opening, had found himself in a sizable cave. It had a hole in the
roof, very small, through which the blue sky was visible. "Say, this
is a peach of a cave!" cried Whitey. "Why, there's a chimney to take
away the smoke and everything!"

"So it is," answered Jack. "Say!" he cried, excited by a big idea,
"do you suppose Mr. St. John would let us camp in this cave tonight?"

"We can ask him. Guess he will. I sure would like to do it," said
Whitey, enthusiastically.

They went out of the cave and explored further. They were
astonished at the complexity of the island. It was filled with min-
iature mountains, having stony valleys between. There were many
high cliffs, almost unscalable except with the help of ropes, and
dozens of caves.

"It will certainly take us some time to explore this island,"
grunted Whitey. "You'd never think it was anything like this just
from seeing it on the outside, would you, Jack?"

"No, you wouldn't," answered Jack. "And I tell you, it's very
dangerous, too. You have to be careful, walking over these slippery rocks."

"That's so," agreed Whitey. "If one of us fell into one of these cracks, there's not enough rope on the schooner to get us out."

They found the further exploration of the island no easy task. It was a mass of caves and labyrinths, accessible only by crawling and climbing. The boys had never been on such an island before, and they became completely absorbed in the search. It was not till the ship's bell gave the signal for supper that they remembered time, and even then it took them half an hour to get back to the beach where St. John and the captain were waiting.

Whitey immediately broached the subject of camping out on the island. "Certainly!" exclaimed St. John. "I'd go with you myself, only I have to develop some negatives."

After supper the sun still shone into the little harbor, and the boys packed their duffle in the tiny skiff. As they pulled ashore, the captain called:

"Don't eat the egg, b'ys, if you finds it!"

They landed on the tiny beach, which was still in sunlight, being on the eastern island. On the previous visit they had been much excited by the discovery of the wreckage of a rowboat scattered on another little beach by the northern end of the island. Immediately on going ashore they walked and crawled to the northern beach and by making several trips, gathered enough of the broken boat to keep their fire going.

When it was ready to light and the sleeping-bags in place, they found that two hours had gone by. The sun had not yet gone down.

"Let's go up to the ridge and have a look around before turning in," suggested Whitey.

They climbed to the central ridge of the island and looked out to sea. There were white and green icebergs floating majestically in the offshore waters, and one which they had not noticed before had slowly drifted down until it was now only a hundred yards from the island.

"Golly!" exclaimed Jack, "if she touches, let's get on and explore! I've never been on an iceberg."

"I'm game for that!" cried Whitey, with enthusiasm; "she'll be in by to-morrow, maybe."

They clambered down to the cave again and lit the fire. The oak made a warm, steady blaze and gave plenty of light. White started to explore their cave. It was roughly semicircular, about fifteen feet in diameter—not too large to be kept warm, nor too small to move about in.

"Say, Jack! here's another opening," called Whitey. "Come and look."

He had found, in a fold of the wall, a narrow crack which seemed to lead somewhere.

"That's great!" cried Jack. "Couldn't we squeeze in and explore it?"

"You try it," suggested Whitey; "you're small."

Jack squeezed through the opening without any trouble. "Come on through, it's easy!" he called. He switched on his glow-light and showed Whitey the other side.

Whitey applied his more bulky form to the crack and tried to wriggle through. At the end of five minutes he had got himself wedged in the crack so that he couldn't move one way or the other.

"Gee!" he cried, "I guess we're done for! I'm stuck here, and that makes you a prisoner. Looks as if we got to stay here all night."

"Yes," answered Jack, "and if a polar bear or something comes sniffin' around, he'll get you, sure."

This thought seemed to give Whitey new strength. He made himself as small as possible, wriggled furiously, and, after a couple of minutes, he struggled through.

"Now," he gasped, "how'll I ever get back? That's what I want to know!"

"That's easy," answered Jack. "Just stay here a couple of days till you get thin."

The prospect thus held forth did not seem alluring to Whiter. "I'll bet there's another way out, 'n I'm goin' to find it. What do you say, Jack?"

"I think you're right," replied Jack. "It's kind of dark in here, but I'm game to explore. Say, you don't suppose it's something's den, do you?"

"Course not!" scoffed Whitey. "No animals, except small ones like foxes, have dens down this coast. I mean, in summer. And I wouldn't mind catching a silver fox worth about a thousand dollars, would you, Jack?"

"I guess not! Come on, then. Let's go on. It's getting a little darker outside. The sun'll be down soon." Jack, the leader now by virtue of his smaller size, led the way along a tortuous passageway. Never had they known a place that offered so many twistings and turnings. They came to a larger cave, where the passageway they were on was crossed by three other corridors, and, after some hesitation, they took the one that they thought led toward the surface of the island. But after they had gone fifty yards, it plunged down again and they knew they must be going deeper than before. They turned back, but, to their dismay, could not find the three corridors from which they had started five minutes before.

"We must have gone down another crack without noticing," said Whitey.

The boys were by this time a little scared. They were buried in the heart of the island, completely lost. Whichever path they took, it seemed to lead nowhere. Fortunately, Whitey had on his wrist a little scout-compass, and as he knew that the island was less than a quarter of a mile wide from east to west, there was a chance that one of the passageways might lead them to an opening on the ocean side if they could only keep working toward the east.

Following this principle, they began to plan out a scheme of direction. Every crack that led toward the east, they took. Many times they found the cracks ended in a blank wall of rock, or else they narrowed down to nothing. The work was frightfully exhausting, and down there in the depths of the rocks the great cold and the dampness began to affect them. They had an awful feeling of being buried alive in their gloomy prison, yet with help within easy reach.

Jack was the first to give in. "Say, Whitey," he called faintly, "I'm feeling kind o' weak and queer inside. Let's just stop a minute, will you?"

"Sure, Jack!" answered Whitey. "You're a little tired, that's all. Say!" he exclaimed, looking at his watch, "d' you know what time it is? Twelve o'clock! We've been down here three hours!"

Jack said nothing. He was staring at the glow-light, and there was a queer look on his face. "What is it, Jack?" asked Whitey; "what are you staring at the light for?"

Jack turned to his friend a horror-stricken face. "It's going out, that's what!" he cried hoarsely.

Whitey looked at the yellowing light. "Why, I brought mine!" he said, feeling in his pockets, one after the other. "No, I'm wrong!" he cried. "Now I remember I left it on top of my bed in the cave. Jack, we've got to save up the light. Every second counts. Shut it off while you're resting."

Jack shut off the light, and the boys leaned against the wall. The silence and coldness of the labyrinth closed around them. In the darkness, Whitey realized how tired he was. For three hours they had been going without a pause. Utter weariness fell on him. For the time being his spirit sank to zero, and he saw only the worst. Starving and frozen, they would meet a horrible doom in the cold and gloom of the labyrinth. They were in a great stone tomb. Even if the captain and St. John could squeeze through the crack, and he knew they couldn't, the chances were a hundred to one against a meeting.

Presently, Jack turned on the light and sighed wearily. "I'm ready," he said.

The battery having been given a little rest, the light was not as yellow as before. Jack added the precaution of switching it off when they found themselves on a fairly straight stretch. After going on for about a hundred yards, they felt their way around a corner. Jack switched on the light. There, ahead, was another clear run, so he turned it off again.

They rested, leaning against the damp walls. "Do you see anything?" asked Jack, suddenly.

"No. Why?"

"Look again! Look straight ahead. I seem to see a queer sort of something. Maybe it's just imagination."

Whitey stared ahead, and it seemed to him that it *was* a little different. The darkness seemed to be pervaded with a weird, greenish glow. "Don't switch on the light, Jack," he whispered. "Let's move along and see what it is."

Even as he spoke, a childish terror clutched his heart and he half wished he had not spoken. What could it be that was that cause of the mysterious and terrifying phosphorescence?

Silent as Indians, they stole along. The green effect turned to grey—and then it burst upon them that the thing they saw was not some dreadful and deadly vapor or an equally awe-compelling apparition, but—*light!*

They both yelled and hurled themselves forward regardless of bruises and collisions. A few seconds later, Jack violently halted. "Back!" he shouted. Whitey cannoned into him, almost knocking him over.

They had come out on a high and perilous ledge—a cliff, black and forbidding above; down far below, the sea. It was night, but the whole northern sky was aflame with the splendor of the aurora. It was the reflection of this on a great green iceberg, floating close in, that had thrown the weird light into their rock tomb.

"The iceberg!" yelled Whitey, "the one we were going to explore!"

"Yes!" answered Jack. "It's almost close enough to jump to it. At sun-up, it'll be touching."

They looked around their ledge. It jutted out half-way down the face of the black, wet cliff. It was absolutely cut off from access on any side. There was no path, no crack, no hand-hold of any kind.

"We're almost as badly off as before," said Whitey, in dismay. "They'll have to search for us and get us away with ropes."

"Look, Whitey!" cried Jack, pointing. "For the love of Pete, what's that?"

Whitey stared. At one end of the ledge a white object gleamed. A brighter flashing of the aurora had brought it to Jack's eye. Whitey shrunk back. "A bear or something!" he whispered.

"How can it be a polar bear?" questioned Jack, rather shakily. "They can't curl up as small as that?"

"Yes, it is small—no bigger than a dog," admitted Whitey.

"Why, it isn't even the size of a dog!" exclaimed Jack, in disgust; "it isn't bigger than a cat!"

"Maybe it's a fox or a ptarmigan!" whispered Whitey; "they're about that size."

"Gee! we've lost our nerve being in the cave," jeered Jack "I'll bet it's only a white stone."

"Maybe you're right," whispered Whitey, with a feeling of relief. "Let's go up and see."

They crept along the ledge in silence. Within a foot of the motionless, white object they paused and stared at it.

"It's a stone," whispered Whitey.

"So it is," agreed Jack. He put out a tentative finger and touched the thing. "Gee! How smooth it is!" he went on.

Whitey touched it with his hand. "It's egg-shaped," he said. "Why, it is an egg!" he exclaimed. "It's a bird's egg, Jack. An *auk's egg!* By Jupiter! we've found the *auk's egg!*" he shouted. "Don't you see, Jack, there's no other egg in the world like that. St. John told me all about it. Oh, Jack! We've discovered the nest of the auk!"

"Why, I guess you're right!" cried Jack, excitedly. "I can hardly wait till daylight. Won't we yell for help, though!"

They examined the egg with infinite care. It seemed to be about four and a half inches long and a little less than three inches across. The color was a pale olive-buff, marked with brown and black.

"What's become of the mother and father auk?" asked Jack, in wonder.

"I don't know. Auks can't fly, so they must have had an entrance from this ledge to the upper surface of the island. I guess the mother auk laid the egg here and then maybe they were both frightened away, or even killed by some wandering polar bear."

"That sounds reasonable," answered Jack. "This island, with all its caves and runways, must have been about their last refuge."

Whitey yawned. "Auk or no auk," he said, "I feel awfully sleepy. Say, Jack, I'm almost dead. Aren't you?"

Jack admitted he was. Now that the excitement of discovery was over, both the boys realized how tired they were. They placed the egg in a small, sheltered recess in the rock at the other end of the ledge, and, finding a safe level spot some distance away, lay down close together. Neither the great cold of the Labrador night nor the hardness of their bed had any power to keep them awake. Five minutes later they were both dead asleep.

Whitey dreamed that some one had given him the job of grinding up tons of ice in a stone-crusher to make a giant feast of ice-cream. It was cold, freezing work, and he was longing intensely to get away from it. Then the grinding machine fell over and dumped the whole mass of ice on him. He struggled to free himself from it by shaking his limbs and slowly drawing himself out—and suddenly he was awake and sitting up! But the terrific noise of the ice-grinding went on. Whitey stared wildly around. It was broad daylight, but the sun was entirely shut off from them by the green, towering mass of the iceberg which had at last made contact with the shore and was slowly grinding its way along the rocks. That was the noise that had given him the foundation for his dream. His limbs were so cold and numb that he could hardly move.

A sudden alarm came into his mind. The auk's egg! Was it injured by the small lumps of ice which were flying in all directions?

Slowly and stiffly, Whitey turned his half-frozen body and directed his eyes to the other end of the shelf where they had left the egg. It was gone! But there was that in its place which instantly sent his blood leaping through his veins in such absolute terror as he had never known before. An enormous polar bear was licking up the last fragments of the precious egg. He had climbed over the iceberg, where he must have been floating for days, and had easily leaped on the ledge when he spied the shining egg.

Instantly, Whitey lost all sense of personal fear. His mind was filled with a feeling of infinite outrage that the bear should destroy their precious egg. With a sort of unthinking passion, hoping that even yet he might save some fragments of shell, he shouted at the bear! "G'wan! Get out!" and staggering to his feet, he waved numb ineffectual hands.

The big white monster turned. In its eagerness for the egg, it had paid no heed to the two silent forms lying on the rock. Whitey, still fearless with rage, approached a little closer and shook his fist at the beast "G'wan!" he yelled, as if ordering a dog out of the house. Perhaps it was that half crazy boldness which saved the boy. The great brute turned and stared at him. Then suddenly he reached out a lightning paw and, with a gentle tap of it, struck Whitey out of his way.

One tremendous leap, and the big bear was back on the iceberg again. He flashed around a corner and disappeared. Whitey went spinning down into the deep, narrow, green strip of water between the island and the berg.

At Whitey's shouts, Jack had waked up, and he witnessed with stupefied senses the extraordinary scene between Whitey and the bear. Then he saw the white monster brush Whitey aside, and, with sudden terror, saw his pal spinning over the verge of the cliff. He jumped up, took two steps, and leaped after him. Down, down he went, until, with a shock of ferocious arctic cold, he hit the salt, freezing water. Whitey came up close by as he went down, and he grabbed the unconscious form and held it.

It was not till a week later that the two boys were able to compare notes. They were lying side by side in Dr. Grenfell's hospital in Battle Harbor. The case-card at the head of Jack's bed read, "Freezing"; and over Whitey's head was a card reading, "Freezing and contusions of the head." No one had been allowed to talk to them till they were out of danger. Then, on this bright, sparkling, sunny Labrador day, St. John had come in and was sitting between the two beds, helping them to piece out the thrilling story of their last hour on the island. "We went to the cave, when you fellows didn't turn up for breakfast, and found you gone. So we got a scare and started to row around the island, knowing that would be the best way to see you, wherever you were. We'd got as far as the outer side of the berg, when we heard Whitey's yell, and then, a second later, an enormous polar bear bounded by us on the berg, plunged into the water and started across to the other islands. Well, you can imagine what we thought might have happened. We rowed like men possessed, and a few moments later we found Jack, half frozen himself, dragging you out of the water. He was delirious with cold and shock, but he was right on the job, every ounce of him. We got you back on the ship, gave you both what treatment we could, and put back to Battle Harbor. I've been wondering ever since how in the world you got around to that side of the island and what you were doing."

Whitey sat up with shining eyes. "Hasn't any one told you?" he cried. "Why of course not! How could they? Just listen!" And he went on to tell St. John the tale of their night's adventures. When he came to the story of their discovery of the auk's egg, St. John was on his feet, his face glowing with excitement.

"Where was the egg?" he cried; "on a big black ledge half-way up the cliff?"

"Yes," answered Whitey, eagerly, "and I saw that beastly polar bear eat up the last scrap of it—egg, shell, and all! I was never so mad!"

St. John gripped both their hands. "That polar bear saved your lives!" he cried.

"You're joking!" cried Whitey.

"We saw the ledge," went on St. John, "and as we were rowing away, the captain pointed to it and said, 'Look yonder!' I looked. An upper mass on the iceberg had become loosened, and, even as we looked, it fell crashing down upon the ledge. Had you been there, you would have been crushed under a thousand tons of ice!

The boys looked at each other.

"Whew!" exclaimed Whitey, slowly; "I'll never kill a polar bear as long as I live."

"Same here!" cried Jack. "Whitey, I move we adopt the polar bear as our Totem."

"Shake on it," answered Whitey, thrusting out his hand.

Solemnly the pals gripped hands.

The Shame Of Gold

CHARLES J. FINGER

L'Intransigeant recently printed a short account of the failure of the Franco-Brazilian ornithological expedition. Reading, you may have caught a hint of tragedy in it; but it may have escaped you, because our papers barely noticed the matter. I was specially interested because of a conversation I had had with a stranger who knew Brazil in a peculiar way.

Knowing Columbus, Ohio, you can not fail to remember the place where the C. D. & M. Traction crosses the main business street. It is crowded at the corner, for a newspaper office is there, and bulletins of the world happenings are posted every hour or so. On the day that I have in mind, Hall and I paused there for a moment. A new bulletin was being put up, which read:

Franco-Brazilian expedition formed to explore upper Amazon territory.

Hall made a remark laughingly as to new markets to exploit, and hurried on his way to Broad Street to meet his investment broker; but I, gazing upward, unaware of his disappearance, said:

"Yes, there are still spots on this little world untrodden by the foot of man."

Turning, I discovered his absence, while from another man who stood where he had been came the words, very decidedly:

"I doubt it."

"But why?" I asked, mildly interested.

"Good reason," he replied, with a little shrug of his shoulders. There was a moment of hesitation, then, simultaneously, we both started off in the same direction, and for half a block walked almost side by side. At a word it transpired that we were both bound for the depot, for the Cincinnati train.

Later, on the train, he resumed the subject. "I know Brazil a little," he said, "and far out of the beaten track, but I know it superficially. Others have been there—many others, and their lines are crossed and crisscrossed."

"White men?" I asked.

"Certainly, white men. That's how I was surprised into the remark I made there at the bulletin-board. Men poke everywhere about the world." The man sketched out roughly on the palm of his hand, and with his pipe-stem, an imaginary map. "You recall the outline of South America," he went on, "nearly pear-shaped, an elongated pear. Now, here is Peru, a little above the base of the thumb. Over here, under the little finger, is Cape St. Roque. I have been here. Cut across like this." He drew a bold stroke entirely across, his hand. "That means Callao, into the Andes, and so north. North to strike the head-waters of the Amazon, and then trouble, fever and hunger. Wealth, too, in a way."

"Love of adventure?" I hazarded.

He regarded me intently for a moment. I noticed his iron-gray hair and queerly wrinkled face. He was not yet middle-aged.

"No. I never tried to analyze. I don't know. I'm not really adventurous. I like to be alone. Also, I drift, perhaps. When in a crowd, nothing seems to be worth while, and one is an ant in a hurrying mass. Alone, thoughts come with force. They strike one as bluntly as seen things impress themselves. I can't explain."

I was unwilling to press him with questions. He was not the kind of man that could be drawn out. When he spoke again there was a note of quiet, pleasant excitement.

"By the way, in Prescott's 'Peru' there is a passage somewhere telling of one party of Spaniards crossing the Andes and discovering silver. Then, being unable to get back, they built a boat and floated down the Amazon, and presently turned up in Cuba again. It's there somewhere. Or in Irving. In Prescott, I think."

I told him that I had a faint recollection of something like that.

"Well," he continued, paying little heed, "that was, roughly, four hundred years ago. No modern things to use, no chart, no map, no compass, no tools, or camp paraphernalia; just plain, dogged go-at-it and keep on. Keep in one direction, and you get somewhere. That's how Magellan felt his way, and Columbus his. Then the old Norsemen in open boats. It excites me thinking of that. It was always that way, one man pushing on."

Again he lapsed into one of his ruminating moods.

"But about Prescott—Once I was nearly all in. Over the Andes I'd gone, and if I didn't hit the trail of the Pizarro men, I'm crazy. I never saw a helmet in my life until then, and I came across one under an overhanging rock. A mighty thing it was,—the rock I mean,—a kind of excavation under it that formed a cave.

"The helmet was there, and a few pieces of steel—short pieces; a broken sword, perhaps. I took the helmet and carried it for days, then threw it away. A man can't be burdened with plunder like that.

"You see, I'd been on the trail for more than three months that time. Now and then I caught sight of an Indian, and once I got an arrow through my left shoulder. There were days and weeks in which I saw no sign of human life, but, by George! there was plenty of good company. Insects, you know, great glorious things. Butterflies, too—butterflies that run and make a little noise like a rattle when they fly away. It's laughable. Living things are great fun to watch. And then the concerts at evening at sunset, crickets and things. I don't know their names. Magnify insects, and I reckon you'd have a fantastic world.

"When I did see a human face again, it gave me a start. I'd found a good spot in the jungle to rest in. The stream ran clear there, this stream I'd been following, and the bottom of it was sandy. One does not often find a place like that. Thinking of an ideal spot, you imagine a stream in the shade of a tree, with grass all about. But when you get your stream, there is often mud, and where there is shade there is no grass. Here there was everything; a pleasant kind of spot, and I didn't move all day. I just rested and smoked and bathed my feet and watched the insects. It was quiet, too, still as midnight, and the sun never pierced the leafy roof. It was just a great, green arch like a cathedral, with smooth, lofty tree-trunks, chamber after chamber of green, and, what was specially fine, the place was clear of lianas. So I rested there and read an old newspaper I had picked up in Callao and brought along. I'd read it before, dozens of times. Then my eyes would tire of the print, and I'd doze off. I did that dozens of times. The peace of the place was too much for me—too much both ways. The perfectness of it overcame me, and drove me to the little thing, the silly newspaper.

"Once I woke with the notion that someone was watching me. What I saw gave me a shiver. There was a big flowering bush not ten yards away. They were great red flowers, meat color, like raw beef, and right between two of the flowers, as if it was stuck in a cleft, was a man's face, snag-toothed, red-bearded, shock-haired. It might have been a great ape. The eyes stared straight at me. Remember, I'd seen no natives for a long while, nor was there a settlement near, and it was a region as big as the State of Illinois, and no white man, I thought, had ever set foot there. Yet here was a face, and it was not the face of a native. I knew enough to keep still, and only peered through the narrowest slits I could make with my eyelids, so I judged that the face in the flower would think I slept. Believe me, I watched closely.

"It moved my way, but cautiously as a snake, and I saw a hairy chest, a hairy human being, and stark. He came on hands and toes, and I knew that he was a fellow used to the jungle and no native. Noiselessly he came, not stirring leaf or blade, hardly. The smell of his body assailed me unpleasantly, for there were sweetly smelling spice-trees, and the human smell was rank as poison.

"I sat up suddenly when the fellow was not more than five yards away. He stopped, rigid, expectant. Fear was in his eyes. Perhaps he saw it in mine. In such cases men hate each other. Each resents the presence of the other where white man should not be. Then he rose to his feet, turned without a word, his feet making no sound, and made for the flowering bush again. I knew in a moment, somehow, that he was ashamed of his nakedness in the presence of another of his race. So I hailed him. At that he stood, regarding me with doubt.

"Well, he was one of these queer fish found everywhere. He told me his tale that night. Of months and of years he had long lost count, and he wanted to know of things strange to me. Queer things he had been interested in, it seemed—a Londoner I guess, with the peculiar sharpness of interest in political things that they have. It must have been meat and drink to him, his interest in public affairs. He talked of Gladstone and wanted to know whether some fellow named O'Donnell who had killed some informer was hanged or not. From such things we located the date when he left his own country as about 1883. So he had been there nearly thirty-five years. Think of it!

"But as to the unbelief of people who are credulous on some things—tell people that for that length of time a white man, an Englishman, had lived with savages, and every single one would jump to the conclusion that he was chief among them. Naturally. On the general principle, I suppose, that it is better to reign in hell than to serve in heaven. But was he king? Boss? Chief? Not by a long chalk. And naturally, the man from civilization was the servitor. The savages were the superiors. Such things as he once knew were useless in the wilds. Mind you, in civilization machinery is master, and man the servant of the machine. Take him away from the mechanical things and cast him on his own resources, and ninety-nine cases out of a hundred he starves. He can't make a fire, catch his food, build his shelter. He is afraid to test things as to their edibility. He cannot run, fight, or climb. Among animals he is a weakling. Face to face with nature he despairs. His education he finds to be ignorance. His overpowering fear is that he may be hurt. You see, in civilization man is protected; he does not have to struggle. All that he needs to do is to sell himself, his time, his life, for the best price he can command. So he becomes soft. He is unfit for liberty. Turn him loose, and he is as useless as a canary-bird or a common hen turned adrift. So was it with this fellow, Elfner. The savages were his superiors, and he was the servitor. He had ceased to concern himself about anything more than the needs of the body; and his brain had gone. Once, I gathered, he had told them tales of the city life, but the things he tried to picture they could not conceive; so he was lowered still further in their estimation and set down as a liar.

"From this Elfner I learned of the Chiqua tribe. He warned me against them as a vicious people that had no dealings with other tribes, and indicated their valley as farther east. That I was not to be led to his tribe was made very clear. Obviously, he was ashamed of his degradation. But really it was not degradation in one way of looking at it. There are almost no men who would not rapidly find their level in a savage tribe, and that level would be below its general average, because of the new valuations that the man from civilization cannot compass.

"There was a stranger tale he began to tell me—a tale of a swamp-land to the south-east and of monstrous, yellow earth creatures that heaved themselves out of the mire. Then I was sure he was crazed. I knew of the giant armadillos and great sloths, but it was none of these. He was loath to continue, and parried my questions. He wanted to know of things in the world that he would never again see. He wanted to talk about John L. Sullivan and Jake Kilrain, and of sordid crimes that had interested him. Above all he wanted to talk of eating, of ham and eggs, of bread and cheese and beer. Once, for instance, when he had begun to tell me something of the Chiquas, he broke off quite unexpectedly, and apropos of nothing went into a little rhapsody. 'Say,' he said, 'this 'ere is a dull place. I often think of colors, and there's a bird all colors, and I always think of how it looks when you hold a glass of whisky up to the light. Lord! Lord!' At that he fell into a reverie and sat hunched, his chin on clenched fist. Then he grew melancholy. 'These 'ere fellers in my tribe they got me goin', they 'ave. It's work, work, work. An' if I don't, it's punishment tied up to a ant's nest.'

"His talk was jumbled, disjointed, and I had much ado to get something from him relative to the country. Very little I got, after all. We had talked for perhaps a couple of hours when an ululation filled the air. 'It's them blacks callin' me,' he said, leaping to his feet. Now, while I was not anxious for his company, I felt an urge to invite him to go with me; but, to my relief, he refused on the ground that his masters would follow, capture, and kill him. When the ululation was again heard, he seemed panic-stricken, stood a moment irresolute, then turned and fled into the bush as a dog would on hearing an insistent call."

The man stopped, and I hazarded the remark that it was strange to meet a white man thus, because the chances against an encounter were so numerous.

"That's so," he said.

"And the reference to those strange earth creatures. Didn't you learn anything further?"

He looked at me and shook his head, doubtfully, and a little puzzled frown appeared and disappeared.

"No. But I may have seen one, too. I don't know."

"May I hear?" I asked.

"There's nothing to tell, because I'm not sure. And yet—" He passed his hand over his brow. "I may have been mistaken. It was after I had left the gentle people, and I was not myself then. I was worried, grieved, half starved. It is all muddled.

"You see, after Elfner left I decided to find the valley he had told me of, and I did find it without any particular difficulty. It was a bird that attracted me, a quetzal. If I had not gone toward it, I might have missed the place. But I never could resist watching a quetzal, for it is the most wonderful thing that God has made, the most exquisite thing in creation. To see it, a living thing of metallic green—gold-green and scarlet-breasted, with tail feathers of jet and ivory, is an experience. You watch it and lose yourself in admiration. Nothing else is so gorgeous. I have watched as the light struck them, and have seen them change from violet to steel-blue, but colors that live. Then the bird moves slightly, and the blue is blue-green, then again gold-green, and there are crimson flashes and purple. And there was the valley, and it was the valley of quetzals and butterflies, and in it lived the gentle people. I stayed there many months, peaceful months, only to leave in sorrow. A gentle people, indeed! Never did I hear a harsh word or see an ungentle thing. I do not think that they knew of war or of violence. To live was sweet in that valley of flowers and birds. There were sounds of living things as sweet as the musical ripples of a little brook, and the breeze was soft and laden with perfume. So I came to love the gentle people and their land.

"It may seem odd to tell you this, but I have told you much, and the mood is on me, and the place in which I tell it to you is odd, here where there is the noise of people and of the moving train and where there is glaring light or sooty smoke, and where every one is burdened with the stern anxiety of duty. And yet it all comes to me as the memory of a summer day may come to some poor fellow in prison—the memory of that spot where existence is facile and where trifles give joy and where people live as birds live. While there I knew a fresh vigor of soul. I always seemed to be on the point of grasping and understanding things, and the thought lived in me always that I should never do a thing to bring the sorrow of the outside world among this people. The memory is strong upon me now, and it came to me as a dull blow when I read the bulletin up-town. I felt as I imagine a prisoner might feel when the judge spoke the death-sentence. It seemed to mean that, you know."

The man paused, and relit his pipe. He gave a puff or two and laid it aside again. Then he leaned back in his seat, folded his arms, and dropped his chin on his chest.

"All this noise about us must make what I tell you seem unreal. I appreciate that fully. Sometimes I think that out there I lost something well worth the losing, and found instead a precious thing. Looking back, I seemed to have touched the supernatural. I wonder if you understand. What I lost enriched me, and I seemed to have left forever my own people and the sins of avarice and anger and pettiness. It was no illusion. There was the valley of peace. There is the valley of peace. But I fear the ravening hand now stretched out. I fear the men of my own race and what must come in the search for new world-markets.

"There was a child there, a thing of beauty, who led me about at times after I had been accepted as a visitor. Endol was her name, and she was a dancing creature, who weaved circlets of flowers, and often brought to me, laughingly, water to drink, bearing it in a flattish shell which held only a taste. I see her now, a bright fairy, dancing and chasing the cloud shadows on the green, playing with the birds, clapping her hands as she ran after butterflies, but never trying to catch them. Do you know, at such times the memory of my own land was as a dark and fearful dream. I remembered slum children. The memory of the things that clatter about us in houses and in cities, and the fret and the evil and the filth and the sickness—these things bore upon me and oppressed my spirit. Now, sitting here, remembering that valley of joy, it is as if I were in hell, and it is from that hell that I am trying to escape, for all has been dark and ugly since I left.

"One day Endol brought me a golden-colored flower, a new one to me. I saw that she bore a shell in her left hand. When I made a motion to take it, she prevented me. Playfully, I held her, and as I did so, she chanced to tip the shell, and a yellowish sand poured forth and lay lightly on a large leaf. Looking, I saw that it was gold-dust. At that Endol laughed, stooped, scattered the gold, and, gathering the grains that lay on the leaf, threw them afar.

"That naturally set me to wondering as well as wandering, for thus far I had confined my walks to the upper end of the valley. As it fell out, the next day I came upon a flat rock at the foot of a vine-hung tree, and there in plain view was a shell, much larger than that which Endol had held. It held gold-dust, and a few nuggets, the best of them not larger than a small pea. The shell had apparently been set there and forgotten with the carelessness of a child tired of a plaything. The gold was not free from iron dust, but I saw at a glance that the vein from which it had been taken must have been extraordinarily rich. So it came to me to think that this people knew nothing of the value of gold and perhaps used it as a plaything. I suppose I should have left it there, but I did not. Few men living as you and I have lived in a workaday world could resist the temptation to bear it away. So I took it to the bower in which I slept.

"Now, Endol and another child met me on the way and, chattering and laughing, reached for the shell. I handed it to them. Their actions astonished me. They drew slightly aside, their merriment fell from them, and they held a rapid, whispered conference. Endol's friend, the older of the two, seemed the most urgent, and her counsel apparently prevailed, for they set off running down the valley with the gold. They seemed possessed of a new fear, one that I could not understand.

"Soon after they returned with others, men and women, and I could see that there was consternation. I was reminded of a crowd I once saw running to the pit-mouth when the news of trouble came.

"Sima, a handsome youth with a splendid head ornament of quetzal feathers, addressed me. He was gentle, almost persuasive. At first I could not understand what he was driving at. There were evidently references to a people and the setting sun, and in the midst of his discourse others came up and now and again tried to aid him in making me understand, as people will do all over the world when a foreigner is dense. Presently Sima ceased, and another, an older man, took up the parable. He grew excited in the telling of the tale and, as I gathered, was eager to impress upon me that there was an evil time when hate and murder and greed, until then unknown, had come into the land. But it was not until he roughly fashioned a cross with a couple of sticks and broke it to pieces that a light dawned on me. Then when he told me of white men from the north, it dawned upon me with clearness that here was a tribal memory of the coming of Pizarro into the land of the Incas. Understanding that, I could piece things together, the ancient wrong done to a gentle people in the name of the cross, the white man's greed for gold, which had been a specific cause of strife and disorder, the hopeless resistance of an unarmed people, and the cruel acts of retaliation. From another point of view I saw what the lust of empire meant, and I saw how those who preached civilization, philanthropy, and religion came burning, shooting, destroying, and subjugating the weak, the simple, the harmless. The forefathers of this people had escaped. What wonder, then, that to them gold stood as an evil, something to hide and thrust away as unclean lest its glitter again attract these who bear death in their hands?

"I saw all that in a flash, and I understood the vague sense of imminent chaos that must have possessed the simple, happy folk when they pondered on what might happen if gold-mad white men again came ravening. The wonder was that they did not slay me when first I came.

"The gold-bearing sand was exceptionally rich in the little river. Grubbing about, I found pockets in the bed-rock full of gold. I even amused myself for a time extracting some of it and piling it in little heaps here and there on stones, and once I dammed up a section of the stream, turning the current so as to expose the river-bed, thus laying bare a new and unexpected vein. But it meant nothing to me then, for I still enjoyed the sighing of the wind through the silky grass, the sweetness of the day, and the fullness of the earth. The water that dripped sparkling from my finger-tips was finer to me than the sifting gold.

"One day I found the cave. I had not found it before simply because I had not sought it. There was no attempt on the part of the folk to conceal its location, nor was there displayed any desire to keep me from it.

"It was an opening in a hillside almost six feet long and four high, a square, natural gap, and the chamber within was at least thirty by thirty. The rays of the western sun flooded the place. For over three hundred years, perhaps, the people had hidden their gold there. From that you may have some idea how things were. The stuff lay scattered over the floor of the cave. I worked my fingers through the gold near the opening, and it was knuckle-deep before I touched the rock. In the farther corner was a sloping heap of the stuff, and it had been there so long that the iron dust had blown away. It shone dully as the sun touched it. Here and there were small nuggets, some as large as a cherry. Leaving the cave, I found a pile of them, oddly shaped, laid along a large, flat rock. They were evidently the playthings of children. I remember noticing one, flattish and almost heart-shaped. It had a hole through it, and I strung it and hung it round my neck. Look at this."

As he spoke he fumbled at his soft shirt-collar and pulled up a little nugget, which he handed to me.

"It's all I have to show," he said as he returned it to its place. "That night I did not sleep. Strangely enough, my mind took a twist. The life I was living fell behind me, as it were, and I was filled with a new desire. It was not really a desire for wealth, but rather a desire for power. That was it, a desire for power. That old newspaper I told you of came to my mind, with all that it stood for. I began to dream of walking into my native town, into Hillsboro, and showing off. Crazy, isn't it? But it was so. They were daydreams that might have pleased a boy, and it is almost too banal to tell, the rapid succumbing to temptation. I had a vision of becoming the local 'big man,' of buying out the banker, of building a fine house, of owning a splendid automobile, of servants, and all that kind of thing. Things! things! things! The pageantry of wealth! So dreaming, the quiet of the valley and the peace of it became a hateful thing, and I longed for the sound of a thousand footsteps and a thousand wheels, for the noise of streets, and the haste and the clatter and the excitement. Gradually the idea took possession of me that the gold was mine and that it was a weak sentimentality which would prevent a capable white race from using that which a brown-skinned folk knew not how to use. I planned and dreamed, planned and dreamed. The poison was at work.

"Weeks and weeks it took me to carry the gold to the hidden canoe. I thought at the time that I was unwatched, but I do not think so now. Some of the stuff I loaded direct from the river sand, but by far the greater part I bore from the cave. Of course there were days when I hesitated, half repenting. But, on the whole, greed had me.

"One day I saw Sima and Capaca, standing side by side, looking at me, and I was suddenly overcome with shame. Then fell away from me my desire to leave. The glamour faded. It was as if I had been discovered handling filth by those whose good opinion I valued, and the hot blood rushed tingling to my cheeks. I wanted to make my peace with the people again, but knew that to do so was hopeless now. So I stood irresolutely by my canoe, and I hated myself for my insincerity.

"Sima came down to me. He said no word, but, with a look of half-pity, half-contempt, handed me his spear, and with a gesture dismissed me and turned his back. For a moment I wished that he had thrust the spear through me.

"So it was that I came to leave the valley where I had known peace, and from then time was for me little but physical weariness. There were days when I lay half dead in the canoe on my bed of gold, tortured by flies and things that bit and stung— days and days of misery when I wished myself dead. Once, it seemed ages, a hovering cloud of insects followed me, sometimes settling on me so thickly that my arms were black. My bodily suffering was great, but greater still the suffering within.

"I think that day after day in that jungle drove me mad, and there were times when I was aware of nothing in the world but the rank smell of decaying vegetation and a black strip of water winding, winding, winding through a canon of dark-brown earth through which great roots thrust themselves like snakes. Days of impenetrable gloom there were, and there were days when all about me there seemed to be hushings, then hissing whisperings and pointing fingers and peering eyes. Again there was a sensation that music was about me, and I seemed to hear at a distance the opening chords of a brass band. I knew then that I was fever-stricken.

"Once I dared to land at a place where the virgin forest seemed to end. There was a great green, open space, a mighty clearing, and a fringe of trees between that and the river. I was the victim of a strange hallucination, and it was as if the whole world were moving swiftly to the right, swiftly, horribly swiftly, and I alone stood still. I fought against it, fought myself. Do you understand? It changed to a sensation of rushing backward. So dizzy I became that I was constrained to squat at the foot of a tree, pushing against it hard with my back, and press my temples until I felt the pain of it. Then I heard a sound, and looked up. I saw, or thought I saw, something. The earth seemed to tremble and heave. Out from it came swiftly a hideous thing, clay-colored and huge, a mighty mass of living flesh. The mud fell from it to right and left. I was breathless and unable to stir. The thing pushed upward and forward with clumsy, lumbering movements, side to side, extricating itself, growing huger each moment. Then I realized that what I saw was only the head and shoulders. The head turned slightly, so that I saw the upper part of it, blunt and triangular beyond the shoulder. The heavy-lidded eyes I saw. Then I noticed the mud dripping heavily, and part of the fore leg coming from the slime. My God! send that there are no such things on earth and that I was really mad!

"I remember rolling down the steep bank and falling into the river, so shaded and still, and then there was an awe-inspiring roar, dreadful to hear. I swam. I do not know. I cannot talk of it."

The man sighed deeply. It was almost a stifled sob. He was ashen-faced. When he spoke again, his voice was perceptibly huskier.

"There is no more to tell," he said. "There were weeks and weeks of misery in that jungle, and wanderings that I forget—wanderings in the swamp lands, and most wonderfully I came to Mannos and, in time, to Para, where the consul was good to me."

He ceased suddenly and fell to smoking. It was a long time before I cared to speak, but I said at last:

"And you purpose to return?"

"I want to get back to the people, to where the superstition of gold is absent," he said. "Only there is the world sane. Only there do people enjoy their days and love the earth and know the beauty of life. Gold blinds all others. So I must go to the gentle people again. That is, if they will have me. Then there's this expedition."

His voice was tense now.

"Suppose. You see, once I might have been a traitor to them. I dreamed of something of the sort, a betrayal to my own people. If this expedition is a success— Well, where white people go and where there is gold, sorrow and disease and death follow. The consul at Para knew something of my story. Would it not be a good thing to save a race, a gentle people, from destruction?"

The man's story stayed with me. And, as I said, since learning of the failure of the expedition, I have wondered much.

An Undiscovered "Isle in the Far Sea"

CHARLES LORING JACKSON

Natural history has always been my hobby, so, when my friend, Captain Shaw, invited me to join him in one of his voyages to the Southern Pacific, I was only too glad to accept his invitation, and, although it seemed impossible that my wild expectations could be fulfilled, as a matter of fact the reality even surpassed them. The islands teemed with interest, and the long voyages between were never tedious, since they barely gave me time for the preparation and study of my collections.

At first, however, the trip did not come up to my hopes in one respect, as it was entirely without adventure until a fortnight or so after we had left New Zealand, but then we sighted a small boat in mid-ocean, which was flying, as a signal of distress, a shirt tied by its sleeves to an oar. In it we found three men at the last gasp from thirst and hunger, who told us that nearly a week before their schooner had gone to the bottom, leaving them time to save nothing but their lives.

I was much interested in them, as they seemed to be genuine beach-combers, and fresh from my South Sea novels I set them down as labor-traders, pearl smugglers, or some such picturesque desperadoes. It is possible, of course, that they may have been mere respectable sailors, as they claimed, but in that case their looks certainly belied them.

Soon after this we ran into a fierce storm. I believe we were in no great danger, although it seemed fearful enough to my landsman's eyes, but certainly it was no trifle, as we were obliged to run before it three days; and then after a slight lull it began again even more furiously, so that we could do nothing but lie to for another three. When on the seventh day the sun broke through long enough for an observation, Captain Shaw found that we must have drifted rapidly the whole time that we had been lying to, as we were far out of our course, and in one of the least frequented parts of the South Sea.

Just as he was pointing out to me our position on the chart, before he gave the order to steer for our proper course again, we were startled by a hail from the look out,

"Land dead ahead."

"What!" shouted the Captain, "the damn lubber! Look at that!"

And he swept his finger in a wide circle around our position on the chart. There were no islands within hundreds of miles of us— and yet, when we tumbled up on deck, there right over the bow a faint blue peak was lifting itself on the horizon. I clutched the captain's arm,

"We must find out what it is!"

"Well! Rather!" said he, and reached for his spyglass.

After this we took turns at the telescope, until we were near enough for my field glasses, and then I kept them glued to my eyes. It turned out to be a large island wooded to the top of its central mountain, and unknown—utterly and completely unknown!

I wish I could give you some idea of the thrill—the rapture of such a discovery, but it is no use. It can be realized only by those who have felt it.

We held on until the spouting reefs warned us to come no farther, and then sailed around the island keeping as near to the coast as we dared. It seemed to be the earthly paradise, and even now, after the glamour of the discovery has worn off, and, when I am not sick for land after a long voyage, it lives in my memory as the most delightful spot I have ever seen.

The sharp peak, towering from the middle of the island, sloped at its base into a wide plain, falling gently toward the sea. Like the central mountain, much of it was clothed with lofty woods, but elsewhere it spread into rich savannahs, or smiling valleys carried their little brooks to the ocean. The heavy surf rolled in on long beaches of the whitest sand, or, foamed and roared against abrupt rocky promontories, except on the southwest where it raged at the base of frowning precipitous cliffs.

The blue sea, the white sand, the intense green of the trees against the glory of a tropical sky! What a picture!

Among the trees I made out with my glasses cocoanut palms, orange and breadfruit trees, and many others of species entirely unknown to me. At this I could contain myself no longer.

"We must land, Captain!" I shouted. "We must land! We must!"

But he was not moved in the least. He pointed to the broken line of reefs, which guarded the coast, among which the sea was boiling, throwing up great columns of spray against the rocks, while huge combers betrayed the still more deadly sunken reefs, as they careered over them.

"Too dangerous!" said he. "Do you want me to throw away the ship? I have already taken more risks than I ought."

"Then," I begged, "land me alone! If you won't, I shall swim ashore!"

"Land you alone!"

"Yes! Why not? You can pick me up when you come back. It will not take you much out of your course to touch here, and a fortnight will be little enough for the exploration of the island."

At first he would not hear of it, urging the danger from hostile natives, although, as I pointed out, we had seen no signs of them, or of any other animals, but I was so insistent that at last I wrung from him a reluctant consent, provided I took with me five well-armed sailors.

By this time we had reached our starting point, and, after giving the island a wide enough berth for safety, Captain Shaw called for volunteers, and the whole ship's company came forward. So, as the choice was left to him, he selected five men, three of whom were the superfluous beach-combers.

Now all was bustle. Arms were served out to the men, one of the spare boats got ready and hastily loaded with a tent, provisions, and such other stores as we might need for our fortnight on the island; and in less time than I should have thought possible we were rowing for the land.

A little cove offered some protection from the heavy surf, and here we made a landing, steered through the rollers by one of the beach-combers with a skill born of long experience. As soon as this was accomplished, the Captain dipped his colors in salute, and put the ship about to regain her course.

I leaped ashore, almost before we touched land, and, even while the sailors were pulling up the boat, my attention was caught by some very curious marks in the sand. They looked as if they had been made by thrusting a small tripod into it, and followed each other in such a way that, if they were the tracks of an animal, it was a quadruped, and one with a very long stride.

After the boat had been made snug, the first business was to find a good place for our camp, and we were lucky enough to hit upon a spot about two hundred yards from the beach, which might have been made for our purpose. It was a small plateau, looking toward the sea, bordered on one side by a little stream of delicious water, which afterward flowed noisily down to the ocean.

I ordered the men to pitch the tent here, and, bring up the stores from the boat; and then started with one of them on a preliminary exploration of the country, as I could not restrain my eagerness any longer.

We promised to bring back plenty of fruit for the others, and so were glad to find almost in sight of the camp a grove of trees loaded with unusually large and fine oranges. My first glance at them convinced me they belonged to an entirely new species, because the flowers, instead of having a few stamens as at home, were crammed with them in circle above circle to the number of fifty or more, and, as, too, they had no fragrance, I inferred they relied on the winds for spreading their pollen, and that there were no insects on the island, which later was proved to be the case by a careful search of the whole country.

My study of the flowers was broken off by a furious spluttering and spitting, and turning I saw that the sailor was trying to get rid of a mouthful of dry yellow powder. As soon as he could speak, he poured forth a terrific string of oaths, and after this relief told me that he had bitten into one of the oranges, and it was full of this repulsive yellow powder, as dry as a limekiln and as bitter as gall. We broke open a great many others and in every one of them the pulp and juice had completely given place to this bilious abomination. They were real apples of Sodom.

This was a bitter disappointment in more senses than one, but we were able to bring back a good supply of breadfruit and cocoanuts, and as our mouths were watering for fruit after our long voyage we all set to work opening the cocoanuts. This, however, proved not so easy, for they resisted all our attacks. Even when one was thrown against a rock, it bounced off unhurt, as if made of solid *lignum-vitæ*; and at last, when after a great deal of trouble we succeeded in cutting one in halves with our axe, we found the shell at least two inches thick and the small cavity filled with a green viscid mass, which had such a disgusting putrid smell that no one had the courage to taste it.

There still remained the breadfruit, which we had put on to cook immediately after we got home; but this turned out no better, for it was as tough as sole-leather. We could not get our teeth into it, even after it had broiled the whole afternoon, and, in fact, we found later that no amount of cooking would soften it.

These disappointments threw the men into a very sulky humor. I was not surprised, as all of us had been looking forward to the fruits of the island as the greatest of treats, but they might have taken them a little more cheerfully, and I must confess it made me dread the prospect, if we were to meet with real hardships.

The next morning the beautiful weather and the island laughing in the sun drove away these clouds, which had dimmed our first evening; and after a hearty breakfast we all started off on our first real exploration. Such an excursion after their long confinement on shipboard drove the sailors wild with delight, and I was even wilder, for every step yielded some wonderful discovery.

This is not the place for a detailed account of my observations, which will soon appear in my "Flora and Fauna of the Island." It is enough to say that, although animal life was very scarce, the plants, of which there was a marvellous variety, showed the curious and interesting modifications to be expected in such an isolated habitat.

When, after a most exciting morning, we reached our tent, the first of the men to enter it broke out into such a shout of astonishment that it brought us all up on the run, and there we saw two of the strangest of creatures. The sailor had already levelled his gun at one of them, but I knocked it up and ordered him not to fire for, as they seemed to be entirely fearless, I hoped I might be able to study them alive.

Their bodies of a flattened egg shape about two feet long, one thick and eighteen inches high, were slung from four long thin legs hard and bony like those of a crane or stork. I speak of them as slung, because they were suspended below the knees by the short muscular thighs, which sloped downward at a very sharp angle. This made their knees the tallest parts of the creatures, rising even a few inches above the ridges of their backs, and standing quite five feet above the ground. The body of a mosquito hangs below its knees in much the same fashion.

At eight inches from the ground each leg divided into three still more slender feet, also hard and bony, and ending in a single long massive toe or talon, so that it was evidently the tracks of these animals, which I had observed in the sand on the beach.

Apart from this similarity in general structure the two beasts had little in common. The body of one was covered with a thick glossy black hair, like horse-hair, except that it was coarser, and its head, clothed with the same hair was like that of a huge bird, with a large triangular beak, massive and powerful at its base but tapering to an exceedingly sharp point—apparently a formidable weapon. Its frontal development was uncommonly great and its eyes, which were very large and beautiful, faced to the front instead of being set on the sides of the head as in a bird. Its neck, about two feet long, was thick and flexible, and covered with a black wool. It was usually carried bent, bringing the head against the body so closely that at first I thought the two were attached without any neck. All parts of the beast not clothed with hair were shining black.

The other was much less attractive. Most of its body was bare and of a dirty brownish flesh color; there were, however, a few large shapeless brown blotches irregularly scattered over it, and on these grew a sparse crop of whitish bristles. The head seemed to be a degraded form of the bird-like type appearing in the other. The beak was no longer horny, but soft and flexible, the upper mandible looking like a broad-based pointed nose, while the lower had retreated into a rudimentary chin and a short fleshy jaw armed with two large tusks. The eyes were small and red, the forehead retreating, and, as the back of the head was covered with one of the brown sparsely bristled spots, the whole looked much like the head of a degenerate vicious old man. Its neck, less than a foot long, was bare and not flexible.

The black animal, who had been examining our belongings with great interest, at once turned his attention to us, and looked each one of us over from head to foot with the greatest and most minute care. From time to time he gave out a curious cry— "Ravenole!" which changed to "Graverole!" whenever he looked at the other beast, who, for his part, stood half asleep in a corner of the tent, and seemed as stolid as the other was inquisitive.

We christened the black one Ravenole, and the other Graverole, and to my great satisfaction both of them, instead of being afraid, passed the whole afternoon with us, Ravenole watching everything we did with the greatest interest. He grew especially excited over our dinner and my work in preserving my specimens, and before long had made friends with all of us. Graverole, on the other hand, remained stupid and sulky, or, if much disturbed, uttered a low hiss, except for which he seemed entirely dumb.

When it grew dark, they slipped away, and I spent the evening in making plans for capturing them, if they came back in the morning; but these proved unnecessary, as then they attached themselves to our party, and after that passed every day with us.

Our great excitement on the second day was the exploration of another part of the island, which brought many interesting discoveries, but none striking enough to be described here. I was impressed once more with the extreme paucity of the fauna. The only mammal we observed was a little rodent something between a squirrel and a rat, which lived upon the oranges. We succeeded in shooting one of them, but found its flesh so impregnated with bitterness from its food, that it was entirely inedible.

The effect of the shooting on our two companions was most characteristic. At the report Ravenole started running with almost incredible speed, but pulled up after some ten steps; came back and examined the gun and the dead arboreal rat with his usual curiosity. Graverole only backed into a tree and hissed.

The day's exploration convinced me that we could find nothing to eat upon the island, and this was such a serious matter that the instant I reached home I made an examination of our stores; and found with the greatest alarm they could hold out only nine days, even if we used rigid economy, while Captain Shaw's return was not to be expected in less than fourteen.

I knew that the expedition had been somewhat meagerly provisioned, because we had planned to live in great measure on the fruits of the island, but there was so little food, that I felt certain one or more of the boxes had been left behind in the hurry of leaving the ship.

It was easier to account for our plight than to find a remedy for it, but there was still one hope left. As we landed, I had noticed quantities of a large mollusc at a little distance from the beach, so I called the sailors together, and after impressing upon them the alarming scarcity of our provisions, told them about the shell-fish, and proposed we should collect some of them and see if they were good to eat.

When we reached the shore, one of the men waded into the sea after the shellfish, while the rest busied themselves in launching the boat to get a larger supply of them; but I had no eyes for anything except a most curious network, which covered the whole of the sand left bare by the tide. It was apparently some kind of a jelly-fish, as it was formed of a pinkish-white, semitransparent cord half an inch in diameter, making meshes a little more than an inch across. To examine it more closely I lifted one of the meshes, and thought I must have injured the animal, as it turned deep red on each side of my thumb and finger.

I had just observed this, when a piercing scream from the man in the water brought his messmates to the rescue, but, although they rowed as hard as they could, they reached him only in time to catch him by his shoulders, just as he was sinking. When they pulled him out, I saw, as his legs came above the water, that below the knees they were dangling like a pair of empty stockings. There was nothing left of them but the loose skin. All the solid muscle and bone had disappeared. At first the men were so overwhelmed by this dreadful sight that they could hardly lift the body into the boat, and, as soon as they recovered, they made for the shore at the top of their speed.

I was not less shaken than they, but even this horror was driven out of my mind by the intolerable pain, which now attacked the soles of my feet and my right thumb and forefinger. I staggered to the dry sand, and slumping down there saw that large and deep blisters covered those parts of my hand. Tearing off my boots, whose pressure drove me nearly frantic, I found a similar state of things on my feet. The whole skin of each sole was hanging loose, and a later examination showed that the flesh had been removed from all of these surfaces to the depth of nearly an eighth of an inch.

The position of my injuries seemed to prove that they were caused by the net-shaped jelly-fish I had been examining, and in that case the red stain meant, not that I had injured the animal, but that it had absorbed portions of my solid tissues, after liquefying them, perhaps by the action of some very energetic ferment, which it secreted. If this was true, the beast was also responsible for the fearful death of the sailor, whose bare feet were especially open to its attack. I did not work out this explanation until some days later, for at the time the pain was too intense to allow coherent thought.

The sailors were thrown into a panic by the horrible death of their shipmate, and, as beside two of them had been slightly touched by the beast, nothing would induce them to run the risk of another encounter with it. In fact, it was only by a stern exercise of my authority that I could make them carry me from the beach to the tent, instead of at once putting the greatest possible distance between themselves and the slimy-bottom-beast, as they called this terrible monster, and this they did, as soon as they had laid me on my pallet in the tent. There I passed all that afternoon and night in great agony, so that I was not even able to attend the burial of my fellow victim.

By the next day the pain, although still intense, had subsided enough for me to review our situation, and I realized at once that nothing but the greatest economy could save us from absolute want, as, with the shell-fish cut off, we must depend entirely on our stores, and even on half rations these would barely last till Captain Shaw's return. I explained this to the sailors, and urged in the strongest terms the necessity of using less food, but I might as well have held my tongue, as, so far from coming to half rations, they still went on cooking twice as much as was needed, and throwing away what thy could not eat.

On the second day after my accident, when the sailors were away on a long aimless ramble, and I, worn out by two restless nights, had fallen asleep, I was rudely awakened by a heavy blow on the chest, and looking up saw Graverole straddling across me. Before I had time to take in the situation, he threw out his legs sideways, and once more let his body drop with crushing weight upon my chest. A few more such blows would break it in, and now fully alive to my danger, I grasped him by the throat, before he could scramble to his feet again. The pain in my wounded hand was excruciating, but in spite of it I clung to him, as we rolled over and over, his long legs rattling on the hard earth like drum-sticks.

I soon mastered him, but, as I held him down under me, my chances seemed desperate, for what could my bare hands do against his formidable tusks and powerful legs armed with their three stout sharp talons? And it was a fight to the death, as I could see by the malignant fury, which glared from his little eyes, the maddened gnashing of his jaws, and his fierce hissing—all the more sinister, because of the weakness of the sound which carried such venomous hatred.

But, as the struggle went on, I took heart, for I began to see that I was well inside of his long clumsy legs, so that he could not reach me with his sharp toes, and my clutch on his throat prevented him from hurting me with his teeth. Indeed, my principal danger was that the pain in my injured hand would disable me, before I could strangle him. More than once I felt I could bear it no longer, but if I slackened my grasp in the least, he renewed the attack with such insane fury that I was forced to hold on until the end.

When at last I pushed his dead body away from me, I was so exhausted that I could hardly crawl back to my pallet; and must have lain there an hour before I had even partially recovered my balance.

While I was still far from calm, Ravenole came into the tent, but catching sight of Graverole's body he turned, and began to scuttle out again. He was an engaging beast, most unlike the malignant Graverole, and I did not want to lose him, so I called him back in the gentlest tones I could, and, when he paused, told him the full story of Graverole's attack upon me, for, although he could not understand the words, I hoped my expression and voice might reassure him, as he was very intelligent. In this I succeeded beyond my hopes. At first he stood doubtfully in the opening of the tent, but, as I went on he came nearer and nearer, until squatting down beside me, he fixed his large beautiful eyes on my face with the utmost attention. When I had finished, he poured out a perfect volley of ravenoles with an occasional graverole among them, all with an air of great satisfaction; and at last stroked my hand with his beak, which I took to be a declaration of friendship.

After Ravenole had gone, I grew calm enough to realize that I had gained a priceless specimen, and determined as soon as the sailors came back to set them to work preserving Graverole's body. With this in mind I looked gloatingly over to where it lay in the middle of the tent, and was struck with the change in its appearance. The outlines had bulged out of their original flowing curves, and in the neighborhood of the stomach the tissues seemed to be turning into a gelatinous mass. This change, once started, went on so rapidly that after two hours the whole body had become converted into a formless lump of stiff gelatine, like that at one time used for the rollers in printing-presses. Only the legs sticking out of it in all directions remained solid, and they were already sagging, as they lost their stiffness. By the next morning they had grown as thoroughly gelatinous as the rest, and had been absorbed into the shapeless mass. It was a crushing disappointment.

The first day after I was disabled the sailors collected a few specimens for me, but on the second they entirely disregarded my orders, and brought back nothing from their long rambles in the woods; and as time went on, and I was still tied to my pallet by the frightful pain from my injuries, they got more and more out of hand. My helplessness was, I am sure, the principal reason for this, but I doubt if I could have enforced discipline in any case, as the death of our comrade had left only one of Captain Shaw's sailors, on whom we had counted to keep the untrustworthy beachcombers in check, and he had become thoroughly corrupted by them.

It was hard to lie still, and watch their indifference changing into sullen hostility, as the rapid dwindling of our stores forced itself on their notice, although even that did not in the least check their reckless waste.

In time their surliness became so menacing that I began to fear for my life, and I was entirely at their mercy, for, although I kept my revolver strapped about my waist day and night, it was doubtful, if I could use it efficiently with my injured right hand, and at best what chance should I have against four determined ruffians armed with guns and knives? For that matter, if, as I feared, they had made up their minds to get rid of me, they could easily despatch me in my sleep without danger of any resistance from me.

On the seventh day after our landing, while the sailors were as usual wandering about the country, until at noon dinner called them home, I was lying in the tent full of these gloomy thoughts. Whichever way I looked there was no comfort in sight, and I wondered drearily whether I should see another day, and even be allowed the poor consolation of selling my life dearly. Then Ravenole came stalking into the tent, squatted down before me, opened his great beak, and, after a torrent of oaths, said in English—positively in English:

"The sailor-men will kill you."

I was struck dumb with astonishment, and before I could collect myself enough to answer, he swore again profusely, and broke out with:

"Ravenole's the boy! You trust Ravenole! — you! Ravenole will pull you through!"*

What did it mean? Ravenole talking English! It was too incredible! But at this instant we heard the sailors coming back, and springing to his feet he whispered,

"— your soul! You trust Ravenole."

And left the tent.

His confirmation of my fears was fully borne out by the surly fierceness of the men's behavior. They set about preparing dinner, and the last of our stores went into the frying pan without any protest from me, as I saw it would do no good.

As I lay there braced for the attack with my hand close to my revolver, it was some little consolation to feel I had an ally, even if it was only this helpless awkward beast, who, apparently half asleep, was squatting in front of the tent near the rock, against which the men had left their guns.

At last the food was ready, and the sailors were sitting down to it with no sign of bringing any to me, so, as I thought it safer to keep up appearances, I ordered them sharply to give me my dinner. One of them muttered something, that sounded like:

"Don't waste good food."

But another gave him a warning kick, and my share was brought me.

As I ate I kept my eyes fixed on Ravenole and, when the sailors were busy with their meal, I saw him rise cautiously, and begin to

---

* I represent the oaths by blanks to make his talk a little less lurid.

pick up their guns from the rock, until he had all four of them stowed across his beak. That was his plan then, and an astonishingly intelligent one for him, but really how childish and futile! As, supposing he could get away with the guns, the men could easily despatch me with their knives. And he was not able to carry through even this simple plan, for suddenly I heard:

"Ravenole!"

The cry was indistinct and muffled, as he was carrying four guns in his beak, but it was loud enough to reach the ears of the sailors, one of whom shouted:

"If that straddle-beast isn't running off with our guns!" and, with a volley of oaths and yells, they sprang to their feet, and started after him at the top of their speed.

Even yet, however, I did not despair, as Ravenole's clumsy run was surprisingly fast, and he might get away in spite of the weight of the guns, but here he lost his head completely, for, instead of running toward the hills, he turned to the beach, where the sea cut off his escape. On he ran, the sailors whooping behind, and hemming him in, so that they drove him into the water. Farther and farther he waded out and they rushed in after him. At last, just as they were upon him, one of them threw up his arms and screamed.

The slimy-bottom-beast had them.

In a flash it was all over, and the bubbles were rising, where they had sunk.

Then Ravenole opened his great beak, sending an avalanche of guns into the sea, and crying exultantly:

"What did I tell you! — you! Ravenole is the boy!" waded ashore in triumph.

When he joined me in the tent we had a long talk, and I found, with the greatest surprise that the human intelligence is but a poor thing beside that of the ravenole. In the six days he had passed with us, he had not only learned to talk English fluently and even too idiomatically, but he had gained an idea of the nature of that entirely strange animal—man, and of his modes of thought and action, which was astonishingly full and accurate, considering his restricted chances for observation. This was shown by everything he said about us, as well as by the ingenious plan he had contrived to get rid of the sailors.

Among other things he told me that he had found out the deadly nature of a gun, when the arboreal rat was shot, and then realized I had saved his life at our first meeting, when I prevented the sailor from firing at him. So, as he learned English, and discovered the men's plot against me, he had hidden his knowledge of the language, that he might protect me the better.

After I had thanked him for this most heartily, and we had congratulated ourselves on the success of his plan, I could not restrain my curiosity any longer, and begged him to tell me about the ravenoles. He was quite ready to do so, and I learned that there were over five hundred of them on the island, but they had withdrawn into the secret recesses of the hills, as they felt a great contempt for these strange animals, which had appeared on their shores. He had distinctly lost caste, because he would associate with us; although he was sure the more advanced among them, if the truth were told, envied him this fascinating study.

The graveroles, he told me, were dying out. At that time there were only seventeen left, and he thought a few years would see the last of them, and, as they were both stupid and vicious, no one would regret their extinction. They were a subject race, but entirely useless; in fact, they could not even feed themselves.

"Why do they become gelatinous after death? I don't know. All I can say is they do always."*

---

* After much thought I have worked out the following hypothesis to explain this strange phenomenon, but I propose it with all possible reserve. May it not be caused by a ferment similar to the one I have assumed in the slimy bottom beast? Although its action must be less intense, as it stops at gelatinization, instead of extending to liquefaction. If there were such a secretion in the body of the graverole, it is fair to suppose that his living tissues would resist it, and, therefore, its effects would appear only after death.

He, naturally, was as curious about mankind, as I about ravenoles, and we became so much interested in our talk, that the long shadows thrown by the setting sun came as a surprise to both of us. Ravenole, when he noticed them, sprang to his feet, bade me good night, and waddled away.

Left alone at first I could think of nothing but my great deliverance from the sailors, and I was filled with joyful thankfulness and wonder at the cleverness of Ravenole; but this jubilant mood vanished, as soon as the question of food occurred to me. With great pain and difficulty I crawled across the tent to our stores, and found that the few crumbs left in the boxes and the remains of the men's dinner made barely enough for one scanty meal, so even, if I could spread this out over two days, there would be nothing left to keep me till Captain Shaw's return, at the best, five days later.

This threw me into the deepest depression, and in this mood I began to doubt Ravenole. Might he not conceal the malignant nature of a graverole under a mask of friendliness? Certainly in the affair of the sailors he had shown himself an adept in concealing his feelings, and contriving an elaborate plot. Or, even supposing he meant well, what reason had I for believing he would be willing to take trouble enough to befriend me? What did I know about ravenoles anyway?

These dreary thoughts were broken off by the appearance of Ravenole himself, who stalked solemnly into the tent, opened his great beak, and poured forth a cataract of shell-fish, one of which he opened with astonishing skill, and put it into my hand. It was delicious, and the food problem was solved.

After this the time passed almost too rapidly. In Ravenole I had the most intelligent and enthusiastic of collectors, and he showed himself wonderfully expert, too, in preparing and preserving the specimens under my direction, his beak and toes soon becoming more skillful than my rather clumsy left hand.

The intervals of collecting were filled with engrossing talks, for Ravenole was never tired of hearing about our civilization. Often he took in the new ideas with surprising quickness. For instance, he understood the complex doctrine of evolution the instant I explained it to him, and told me there was a tradition that centuries ago the ravenoles had lived upon fruits, and from this he reasoned out at once the gradual extinction of edible fruits on the island, and the development of the peculiar structure of the ravenoles by their struggle for existence against the slimy-bottom-beast.

On the other hand, I found it necessary to begin at the very bottom in explaining to him many things, which seem absolutely simple to us. Thus, it took me many hours to make him understand the nature and uses of writing; and still longer, to prove that it had any advantage over the phenomenal ravenole memory. I did not succeed in doing this, until I had impressed on him the fact that the millions of mankind could be reached only by a device like writing (and printing), while with only five hundred ravenoles there was need of nothing more than the word of mouth.

In return he explained to me the strange sciences originated by the ravenoles, especially their philosophy, so different from ours, but in no way inferior to it in penetration or grasp. This is not the place to give even an idea of it, but when my book on ravenole philosophy comes out, it will introduce to mankind the most startling progress ever made in that branch of study.

Perhaps the strangest thing he described to me was the ravenole language. It consists of but two words "graverole," which means only a graverole and "ravenole," which means everything else, the different meanings being expressed by variations in accent and cadence, but—and this seems almost incredible—in spite of this handicap it is a full rich language capable of expressing as varied and subtle ideas as English. I tried in vain to learn it. Some of the "ravenoles" were distinctly unlike one another, but in other cases my ear was not delicate enough to perceive any difference whatever. For instance, "ravenole," when it meant "shell-fish," and when it meant "evolution through the struggle for existence," sounded exactly alike to me, although Ravenole insisted that the two expressions were as unlike in his language as in English.

While I am talking of language, I may say that, when I had grown intimate enough with him, I called Ravenole's attention to the fact that gentlemen did not swear. He was terribly mortified. Should have noticed that I did not swear, and from that moment I never heard an oath drop from his beak.

When one morning Ravenole brought word that the ship was on the horizon, I found it hard to realize that more than a week had passed. I managed to crawl out of the tent, and together we watched her as she grew larger and larger, until at last she dropped anchor about a gunshot from the shore.

When the boat put off, Ravenole went down to the beach to meet it, but by my advice hid behind a rock, and did not show himself, until he had explained the situation to the landing party, as I could not bear to run the least risk of his being taken for a wild animal, and receiving a bullet.

It was not long before he brought Captain Shaw and his party to the tent. What a delight it was to see them! And with what wonder they listened open-mouthed to my story, although even the most exciting part of it could not draw their eyes away from Ravenole!

When I had satisfied their first curiosity, Ravenole took them for a walk to see the wonders of the island, and then came dinner, when the ship food tasted like real ambrosia after my long diet of shell-fish.

During the meal Captain Shaw and I urged Ravenole to come to America with us, promising him, in addition to the marvels of our civilization, an unheard of triumph in society. We were very eloquent, but he disposed of our arguments by the single question:

"What! To eat salt beef?"

This was out of the question, as the sailors once had persuaded him to try that and ship-bread with disastrous results, and as, of course, it was impossible to take enough fresh shell-fish to last him through the voyage, that plan had to be dropped.

He accepted with delight, however, Captain Shaw's invitation to visit the ship, although first he took the precaution of making the captain promise to return him to the island in safety. I wish I could have gone with him to see his wild enthusiasm, as he poked his beak into everything above and below deck, and astonished all by his interest and intelligent questions.

The next day I was to embark, and at daybreak Ravenole turned up carrying a large bundle wrapped in leaves.

"Here," said he, "is my farewell present. What I know you would like better than anything else—the bones of one of my ancestors. But I hope the other ravenoles will never find out that I have given them to you."

He was right. There was nothing I wanted more; and my present to him—an English dictionary—seemed to please him quite as much.

Then came the parting, and I could hardly bear to say goodbye to this tried friend. As the boat rowed away to the ship, he waved a fore-leg to me from a rock, and shouted:

"Come back in three years, and you will find me the head of a colony of English-speaking ravenoles."

As I lay in the stern of the boat, I kept my eyes fixed upon him, and afterward watched him from the deck of the ship, until he was lost in the distance. Then sadly I allowed the men to carry me to my stateroom. My only consolation was that I should see him again in three years; but I have not been able to go back, as the injuries to my hand and feet have never healed, and the use of them still causes me such violent pain, that my life is passed between my bed and a wheeled chair. I am sorry to say, too, that the trouble in my right hand has delayed very seriously the publication of my great work— "The Flora and Fauna of Ravenole Island."

Coachwhip Publications

CoachwhipBooks.com

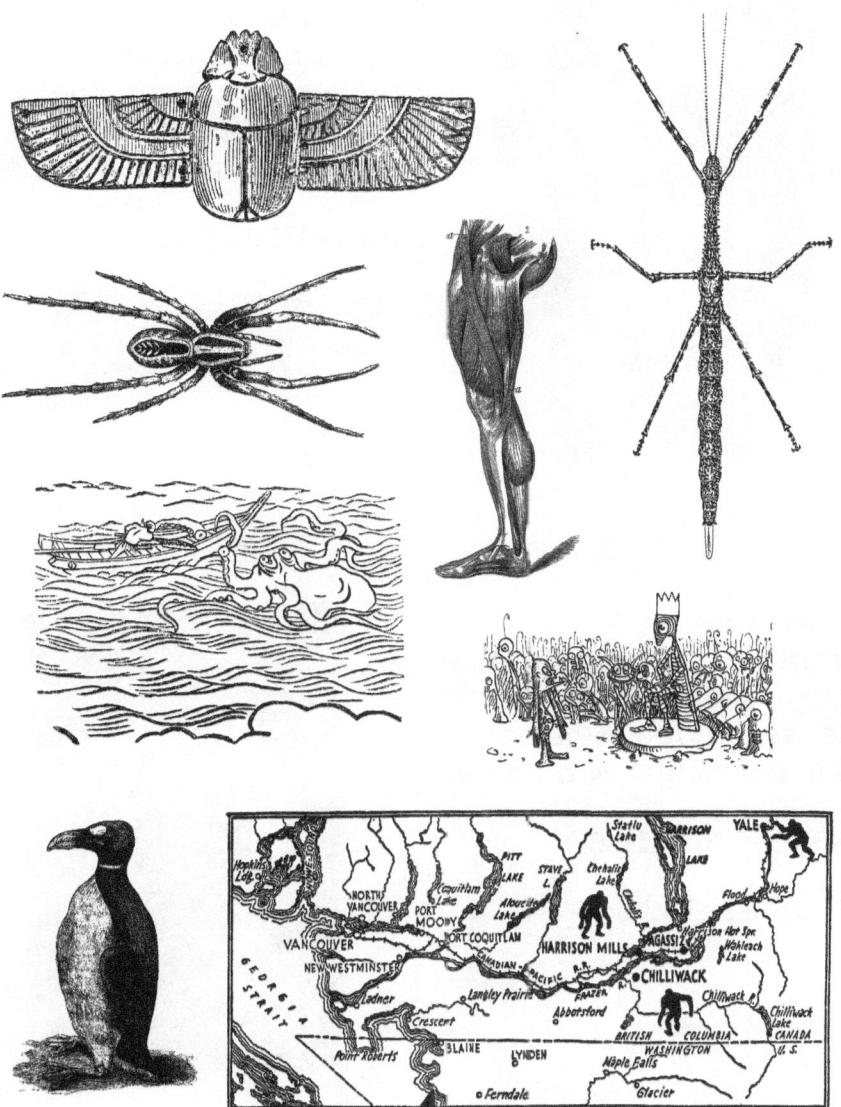

COACHWHIP PUBLICATIONS

COACHWHIPBOOKS.COM

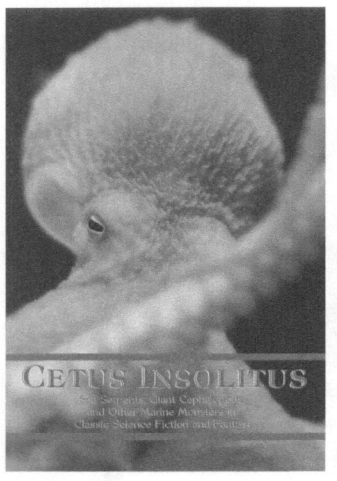

CETUS INSOLITUS:
Sea Serpents, Giant
Cephalopods, and Other
Marine Monsters in Classic
Science Fiction and Fantasy

ISBN 1-930585-66-7

26 stories, 391 pp.

FLORA CURIOSA:
Cryptobotany, Mysterious
Fungi, Sentient Trees, and
Deadly Plants in Classic
Science Fiction and Fantasy

ISBN 1-930585-56-X

20 stories, 337 pp.

COACHWHIP PUBLICATIONS

COACHWHIPBOOKS.COM

SAURIA MONSTRA: Dinosaurs, Pterosaurs, and Other Fossil Saurians in Classic Science Fiction and Fantasy

ISBN 1-930585-77-2

14 stories, 1 novel, 413 pp.

INVERTEBRATA ENIGMATICA: Giant Spiders, Dangerous Insects, and Other Strange Invertebrates in Classic Science Fiction and Fantasy

ISBN 1-930585-65-9

30 stories, 396 pp.

COACHWHIP PUBLICATIONS

COACHWHIPBOOKS.COM

ANTHROPOLOGICA INCOGNITA:
Wild Men, Strange Apes, and Fantastic Races
in Classic Science Fiction and Fantasy

ISBN 1-61646-000-8

COACHWHIP PUBLICATIONS
COACHWHIPBOOKS.COM

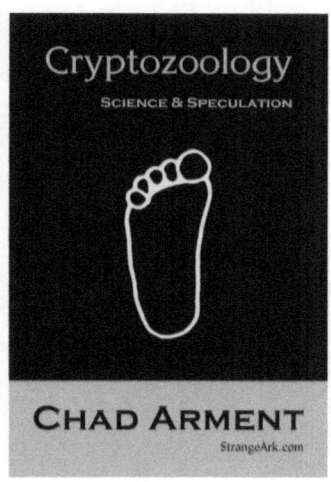

CRYPTOZOOLOGY: SCIENCE & SPECULATION

ISBN 1-930585-15-2

The methodology of cryptozoology, and the rational investigation of mystery animals. Also includes chapters on various alleged or suspected unknown species.

THE HISTORICAL BIGFOOT

ISBN 1-930585-30-6

Stories of "gorillas," wild men, and strange apelike creatures from North America before the term Bigfoot was ever coined.